In the Time of Green Blimps

Henry Melton

In the Time of Green Blimps

Henry Melton

Wire Rim Books
Hutto, Texas

WRB

In the Time of Green Blimps © 2013 by Henry Melton
All Rights Reserved

Printing History
First Edition: August 2013
ISBN 978-1-935236-51-1

ePub ISBN 978-1-935236-52-8
Kindle ISBN 978-1-935236-53-5

Website of Henry Melton
www.HenryMelton.com

Character images © 2013 by Djamila Knopf
http://shilesque.deviantart.com/

Printed in the United States of America

Wire Rim Books
www.wirerimbooks.com

For their help getting this book from manuscript to a finished book, I want to thank some long-suffering volunteers who've given me ideas, suggestions, and a much better grasp of grammar than I started with: Jonathan and Debra Andrews, Jim Dunn, Linda Elliott, Mike Lynch, Alan McConnell, Mary Ann Melton, Jim Reader, Mary Solomon, and Tom Stock.

In addition I want to thank the people of the Commemorative Air Force Airpower Museum in Midland, Texas for their help letting me get a good first hand look at the setting of much of this book.

For Joy Rook, my aunt, and my inpiration for women everywhere who demand to put their own mark on the world.

Contents

Blimp Cross Section

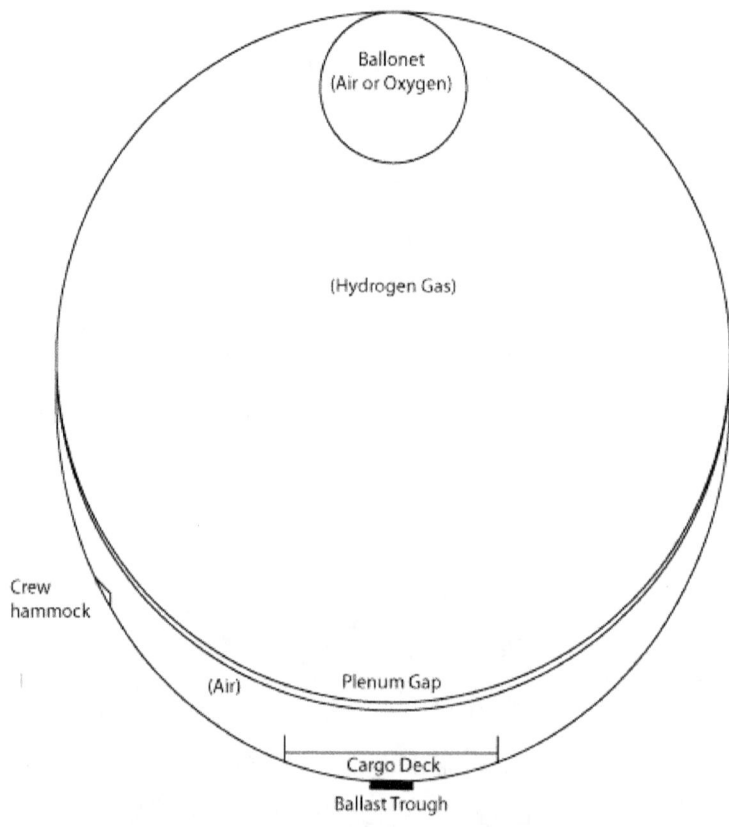

Ballonet
(Air or Oxygen)

(Hydrogen Gas)

Crew
hammock

(Air)

Plenum Gap

Cargo Deck

Ballast Trough

Going Down

Caleb Race jerked awake when he heard her voice echoing in the vast cargo deck. "Rig for water. We're going down!" The captain's alert sounded like his mother's last call before things got physical. He was the new guy—the teenage kid. No excuses tolerated.

Clipped to the black drape that gave his hammock some pretense of privacy and blocked out the sun off-shifts, his timer only showed fifty minutes since he'd collapsed into the canvas. With a groan, he stretched one time and flexed his bare toes. The green hull below was angled steeply, so he kept one hand on a strap as he dug through his duffel and slipped on some stained white socks and headed down slope.

The interior of the airship curved up into the distance, with the belly of the hydrogen gas bag obscuring his view of the port side. Only two of the crew of twelve were visible, heading to their duty stations. Caleb bounced gently as he walked, trying to stay close to the veins where the outer skin of the *Lance* was a couple of millimeters thicker. He resisted the urge to break into a run moving downslope. It would not be healthy to punch through the semi-transparent membrane and go for a swim in the Pacific. Waves sparkling from the afternoon sun were still a few of thousand feet below.

His cattle were stirring on the wooden platform, and it was his job to see that they stayed calm. Some of them recognized him and began walking his way.

"No, girls," he shouted, "Behave yourselves. Now is not feeding time."

The corral was a long, boarded platform stretching nearly five hundred feet long and forty feet wide, riding directly above the ballast trough. He'd rigged temporary divider lines to keep the herd separated into four groups—it wouldn't do to have all their weight collect at one end of the ship.

Even as he reached the decking, he could feel the *Lance* nose down a couple of degrees as outside air was pumped into the bow trim ballonet. He grabbed the line and heaved himself up on the wooden deck, keeping a lookout for stray cow patties. He hated the feel of fresh or drying goop in his socks.

The freshwater troughs were aligned along the edges, to keep a wandering bovine from falling through the lines and discovering for herself the ocean below. The hull would grow back over time, but it would have to be patched and bandaged until it did. It had to hurt the blimp, Caleb believed, although giving the craft that much awareness wasn't a popular opinion. Clouds were moving in the sky, visible through the semi-transparent layers of the green gas-hull, bulging just a few feet overhead. *Isolated cumulus. We should have plenty of sun when we lift back off.*

Caleb grabbed lines and began dashing through the herd, dividing the big corral into a checkerboard of small pens, with only two to four beasties in each.

He patted the green hides. "Be calm. You've been through this before. Just stay put and have a good chew."

He stepped into an unseen patch of poop and tried to ignore it.

"Caleb! Is the cargo secure?" Up above and forward from the command deck, the captain looked down at him. For a thirty-some year old brunette who looked as stunning to him in her uniform as any girl on a dance floor, she had a voice that couldn't be ignored.

He yelled back, "Two minutes!"

"Touchdown in three!"

...

Two miles to the west a cruise ship plowed its iron bulk through the waves. A deck steward in a stiff white coat with gold buttons left a trio of passengers with fresh lemonade. Samuel Bolls looked out over the water as his deck chair neighbor, Emily Pommer, tipped the brim of her straw hat and pointed, "Is that airship going down?"

Samuel at twenty-three was by far the youngest of the three, but while his ticket had included most amenities, he frequently found the company of these two grandmotherly ladies more pleasant than those his own age in the lounge.

The next group over on the port side of the Queen Helen also looked in the same direction. A dozen green airships were riding a favorable wind toward the coast of California. One of then was nosed down and approaching the water.

A distinguished looking man, mustached and dressed more for the dining room than the deck, stood nearby. He looked perfectly at home on the deck, face a little tanned and weathered, but comfortable, as if he'd seen the world, and everything in it. He nodded, his hands crossed behind him. "Yes, it's going down for water. It's in no danger of crashing."

"It needs water?" Mrs. Pommer asked.

A parasol twirled in the hands of the third member of Samuel's group as it shaded a striking looking, much older Polynesian woman. She spoke to her neighbor, in a slightly clipped accent. "Yes, Mrs. Pommer. The blimps were born in the sea, and they have to settle back down from time to time."

Samuel reached into his pocket and clicked his pocketbook-sized handset to record audio. Years of interviews made it a habit. The ladies often had interesting things to say. He prompted, "Mrs. Taylor, it sounds like you have some experience with the blimps."

"Mmm. Yes. A long time ago."

"Well, you know me and my questions. Would you care to tell your story? I'd love to hear it."

"Yes, Kai, please do," added Mrs. Pommer.

"Oh, it was a long time ago."

"All the better. The blimps used to be rare, and now they're everywhere. It sounds like you know more about them than most people."

She twirled her parasol again. "I guess I do." She glanced at Samuel. "You may not believe it, but I was once a young girl."

"Bora Bora was blessed during the Star Time. As you youngsters may not realize, many of the islands of the Pacific were wiped out by the radiation. There was no place to hide from it. Not so on the island of my birth. My family and their neighbors were able to shelter from the star shine on the sides of a tall volcano, Mt. Onemanu.

"For many years after that, we were an isolated people, much like our ancestors. With, of course, the advantage of living in the abandoned hotels instead of grass huts."

Samuel chuckled. Everyone had abandoned buildings.

She smiled. "By the time I was born, we were getting some visits in the lagoon. There were people from the other islands, of course, but soon ships arrived from Australia. At first, all they wanted was fresh water and supplies, and occasional protection from the storms.

"But when I was twelve, a company came and made an agreement with the Governor to rent the island of Tupai, just a short sail north of us. At the time, no one lived there. It was a simple, lovely lagoon, a band of coconut palms surrounding a protected pool a couple of miles wide."

...

"Kai!"

"Yes, Daddy?" She swam up beside the dock.

"I'll be inside talking to the company men for a little while. Keep quiet and stay out of trouble."

She smiled sweetly. "Of course."

As soon as he was out of sight, she snatched her net from where she'd hidden it under her towel and ducked back into the water.

It had taken her a week to talk Daddy into letting her come along on the trip to resupply the company's kitchen. While he was carrying hams and pineapples into their building, she could swim the lagoon.

Tupai's lagoon was much different from the waters just a few paces from her bedroom in the little town of Faanui on Bora Bora. The company had put up barriers in the gaps that separated the lagoon from the ocean waters. Fine underwater nets were strung all over the place, making pens where numals were being raised. There were all kinds of numals—new animals. Many were green, since the company was in the habit of splicing chlorophyl into its products. From the rumors at home, some of these fish tasted like beef or pork. Supposedly there was something like a squid with extremely long tentacles that could be harvested for fibers.

And there were more than fish. Growing like a shelf above an old coral reef was something that looked more like metal than rock. It was like swimming through a zoo, seeing the strange and wonderful beasts confined to their pens.

An experienced diver, she only needed to pop up to the surface every minute or so to get a breath of air, before diving back down among the exotic fish. She fancied the coin-shaped, sparkling ones.

Tupai had become a laboratory, where numals that had survived the aquarium tanks were tested in the ocean waters. It was a protected place, where the researchers didn't have to worry too much about the outside waters. Their gates and the surrounding atoll kept the numals in, and the sharks and other predators out.

The water abruptly went dark. If there were clouds coming in, she'd have to turn back. *But not yet.* There was still too much to see. And maybe, just maybe, she could snag one of those coin fish to add to her tank back at home.

Daddy would double her chores if he found out, but she needed something to prove that she'd been here. The rumors back among her friends were freaky and fantastic, and no one had been allowed past the company dock.

She kicked for the surface, and was shocked to see just how dark it was above her. *This isn't the air!* Something large and green was laying on the surface.

Monsters! It was one of the rumors—something large and fierce had been the tale.

As she pushed her hand up, she felt a slick skin. She was trapped!

She had to find the air, no matter what kind of monster it was. Her lungs were protesting.

She ducked down a few feet and looked all around her.

Back the way she'd come there was nothing but dark green skin as far as she could see. It must have moved in quickly.

If I can't find air, I'll drown.

She went deeper and looked up again. *There. That looks like air.*

But there were ridges all around the dark, circular patch, like teeth on a mouth. No help for it, she had to breathe.

Why didn't I bring my knife? At worst, she could have irritated it, made it move.

Sticking her head in an unknown mouth was terrifying, but she did, and she broke the surface into a dark cavity. She gasped. It was air, and she could breathe it. The scent was overpowering, like deep in the forest. But the air was good, and her panting stopped quickly.

5

The space was like a dome over her head, five feet or more around. From the dim green light that leaked through its skin, she could see pores, many thousands of them. Some of them were bubbling from the gas that was coming out.

I've got to get back.

She ducked down and swam quickly to the coral sands below. *That way.* She rose back up into the gas pocket and pumped her lungs a few times, before swimming hard and fast toward the edge of the dark patch.

Blue sunny sky above made her cry with joy as she broke the surface, free of the monster. It was still close, but she almost didn't understand what she was seeing. She sculled in the water, drifting closer.

It's a leaf. At the edge, it was thin. But if it was a leaf, then it was the largest leaf she had ever seen.

There were shouts from the other direction. Someone on the dock had seen her. Maybe they'd heard her. A couple of men were jumping into her dad's boat, coming for her.

...

The elderly Kai twirled her parasol, her face lost in old memories.

"The company man wasn't too concerned with my safety. He was worried that I'd damaged his numal. Daddy almost lost his contract and I was in trouble for oh... a long time after. No more swimming at Tupai.

"But I found out more about my leaf. It was a proper numal... more plant than animal. It was like a giant lily pad. There was even a large tap root when it was young. But as it grew, it split the water into hydrogen and oxygen. The hydrogen filled a large internal bladder and the oxygen was excreted out the pores on the bottom. Over time, it changed from a flat, floating leaf into the long, round, streamlined things you see there." She pointed off at the blimps.

"They can stay floating forever if they get enough rainwater and sunlight, but sometimes a blimp has to settle down on the water to re-inflate itself."

The elderly man with a mustache nodded. "Very nice tale, Mrs. Taylor. I had heard that the prototypes originated in French Polynesia, but I was never able to identify which islands. May I say that we are all glad you were able to swim free."

Samuel nodded in agreement.

She smiled, "Thank you. I'm afraid I've never quite gotten over it. I still shiver whenever one of them drops its shadow over me."

Samuel asked the man, "So, you have been researching the blimps?"

He nodded, with an amused look in his eye. "Is that what you've been doing... on your pocket recorder?"

Mrs. Taylor raised an eyebrow.

He sighed, pulling out the little device. "I hope you don't mind. I'm a screencrafter and I'm always collecting human interest stories. Someday, bits and pieces might make their way into something I write. I don't trust my own memory. I'm Samuel Bolls, on my way to California."

She chuckled. "Well, if you write about me, change my name. I was a silly little girl back then."

He nodded in a slight bow, "An exemplary model of an adventuresome spirit."

She smiled and twirled her parasol.

The man asked, "Bolls? Son of Jason Bolls?"

"My uncle. I've never met him."

"I would think you should, if you're in the screencrafting business. He's one of the top names in the field."

Samuel smiled, "It's on my agenda, if I can make an appointment."

He nodded. "Make it happen. It always helps to have a relative give you an edge."

Samuel held out his hand, "And you are?"

He shook it. "Jenner. Daniel Jenner. Let me know when one of your works hits the Net."

"I'll do that. Thank you."

As he walked away, Samuel fumbled with his recorder and whispered a few notes.

No wonder he was interested in the blimps. Baron Jenner has probably lost half his fortune to them.

The fleet of green blimps, carrying cargo that used to be the domain of Jenner's Europa-flagged transports could not be a welcome sight to his eyes.

Beautiful People

The airships overhead were a call for dozens of the ship passengers to head indoors. The word was spreading fast. The indoor theater and the computer rooms were packed as the Net bandwidth quickly jumped. Most of the trip, the short-wave relays could do little more than pass text messages. For a few minutes at least, the video floodgates would be open.

Samuel headed for the computers. He was sorry for Baron Jenner. While financial news didn't catch his interest often, he had seen the story that detailed how his fleet expansion had happened just as the blimp traffic had nearly doubled, leaving him with idle ships in a collapsing market for intercontinental shipping. It was a fresh blow to the northern economy.

The new rich were all showing up with Australian accents these days as biotech blossomed.

He caught a just-vacated chair and sat down in front of a computer screen. He tapped in his Net ID and his windows popped up quickly. He sighed. It had been days since the Net was this fast. He had to take advantage of it before the blimp fleet with their on-board Net relays drifted out of range. His pocket recorder noticed the same account on the ship's computer and transferred all his recent notes and screen captures over onto the better-connected hardware.

Maybe I'd better check up on my uncle. He queried Jason Bolls and downloaded all the latest news and gossip into his handset. His interview, if it happened, was only a week or so away, and he needed to be up-to-date on his famous relative's latest projects.

The previews of the latest fiction screen by Jason Bolls showed up on the display and he reached to tap it—but then she walked in.

Her golden hair was like a halo, and seemed to shine with its own light. The pale blue deck dress floated around her. Clear blue eyes scanned the room, and when she saw Samuel, she smiled and began walking his way. He could hear a few sighs from the others.

"Hello, are you Samuel?" she asked. Her voice was rich and sweet, like chocolate.

"Um. Yes, I am."

"The screencrafter?"

He straightened up in his chair. "Attempting to become one, at any rate."

She held out her hand, "I'm Rachael Nue. I wish I had discovered you earlier on the voyage. We could have spent more time together."

He stood and took her hand. It made him tingle from head to foot. He cleared his throat. "Are you interested in screencrafting?"

She purred, moving her head a little closer to talk more intimately. "I'm interested in everything having to do with screens. I want to be Diana Jameson."

He smiled and nodded. The actress was a legend, dominating the screens just when the Net started handling the distribution and computers started having displays big and detailed enough to show them. She had acted, written and crafted—building a massive fortune doing so.

"In my dreams, I want to be Uncle Jason."

"Jason Bolls? I'd heard you were his nephew. Did he get you into the business?"

"No, actually. I've lived in Hawaii all my life. He inspired me, though. When I was able to afford a camera, I started composing my own stories."

"Anything that I might have seen?"

"No. Not unless you subscribe to the PopVid feed."

She frowned, "So you're not producing anything?"

He chuckled, "Oh, I'm always working on something. I have several stories in various stages, but the only things I've done professionally other than news captures were Tourist Bureau features."

"Lots of beautiful girls in leis?" She swayed back and forth.

He grinned. "Some of that. I took some interesting volcano video as well. The Big Island is still almost deserted, except for Hilo." He nodded toward the center of the ship. "The liners want more people to come visit. So I captured the dramatic stuff—volcanos, wild cattle herds and deep dark jungles with the threat of unnamed beasts."

She shivered. "I would come for the beaches. But... show me some of your screens." She nodded toward the computer.

He was happy to oblige. The bandwidth was still good, so he trotted out some of his tourist features. She asked some questions—real ones, about lighting and how the captures were made. As she breathed over his shoulder, he rattled on, telling her everything.

"You are going to meet up with your uncle, aren't you? These are certainly good enough to get you into the big budget features even without the connection."

He nodded. "It's my hope. I have a story in mind that I really can't do with my limited resources."

"Oh? Any openings for an up and coming actress?"

"Certainly! It's about a blimp pilot—the girl, and an airplane inventor."

"The metal kind?"

"Yes! You see... oops." He turned to the computer display. "Looks like the bandwidth is fading. I was going to show you some of my short features, but it would take too long."

"That's okay." Rachael looked at the wall clock. "I'm afraid I have to run." She smiled and shrugged. "Previous appointment."

"Maybe we can meet up again later."

She nodded. "I'd like that."

He almost followed her out the door, but then remembered to go back and disconnect his account. He put his handset back in his pocket. He took a deep breath, still humming from the pleasant experience.

He was barely out the door when Baron Jenner strode up, deep lines around his eyes.

"Bolls. I should have expected this."

"Sir?"

The man took his wrist. "Come with me." Leading him like an errant child, he walked Samuel to his large suite. Normally, he'd pull away, but Bolls was peerage, not a citizen. He didn't know what the rules were.

"Sit there." Jenner pointed to a comfortable chair that was angled to view the horizon out the wide windows.

Samuel reached for his handset, tempted to capture a sweep of the interior of this luxurious cabin, but he refrained. *What's going on? I'd better not try without permission.*

The baron came back in holding a small item.

"Did she touch you?"

"What? Who? Oh, you mean Rachael?" He smiled. Even the memory of her was enough to mellow out this frightening interview.

"Yes. Rachael. Did she touch you?"

Samuel nodded.

Jenner's lips compressed into an unpleasant line. "Take this pill."

He handed it over, and poured a glass of water.

"What is it?"

"Just take it. I'll explain in a minute."

If he weren't a baron, perhaps Samuel would have demanded the explanation first, but he was still intimidated by the man. He took the little white pill and then looked up expectantly.

Jenner nodded. "Good. We've probably inoculated you soon enough."

"Inoculated? Against what?"

He tapped his fingers on his table, one bearing a large gold ring with a figure too intricate for Samuel to make out from where he sat. "Samuel, Miss Nue is one of the Beautiful People."

His ignorance must have shown clearly. The baron sighed. "She is one of a handful of people who have had extensive gene modification to give themselves the ability to seduce anyone, anywhere. Not only does she have perfect hair, perfect eyes, a perfect body in many ways, but her voice is tuned to resonate with your nervous system. She can breathe pheromones and her touch can saturate your skin with a compound that can force your impressions of her down into the instinctive level.

"In other words, she can seduce you where you stand and then make you love her forever, just by shaking hands."

He couldn't believe it. Rachael wouldn't do something like that. She was too good for that kind of a....

He shivered a little.

"There may be a slight reaction, as her drug is counteracted. Chills, sweating. It will protect you against future contacts for two or three days. I'd advise you to take precautions for the rest of this trip. I have a limited supply, and it's not something you can get from the ship's doctor, unfortunately."

"She can't be the kind of monster you're describing." Samuel shook his head, trying to reconcile the image he could see in his mind—the smiling, brilliant image of the beautiful girl who was interested in his work—with the manipulative, heartless, and almost mythical predator the older man described.

The baron poured himself a drink. "You still have your handset? Search for 'Beautiful People' and 'Aphrodite Laboratory, Sydney Australia'. Get a product offering."

"Um. My handset doesn't have the range...."

"This is my cabin, on my ship. You'll connect."

Samuel blinked, and then nodded. He tapped out the query—his little mid-range device didn't do voice commands. There was a pause, and then text began appearing on the tiny screen.

The advertising pitch was worded much smoother than the baron's description, but much of it was there. For the terribly wealthy—rich enough to buy companies as casually as he bought lunch—Aphrodite Labs could drop an ordinary man or woman into a vat for six months and rebuild them down to the cellular level. When they came out, they could walk the world like gods and ordinary people would obey with a smile.

"I knew Rachael when she was Daddy's rich little brat. I must say the process has done wonders for her hair and complexion. She's also a better actress than before, but I hardly think that's the new genetics."

Samuel was having a hard time believing it all. "How many are there?"

"BP's? Oh, probably under thirty. It's a very expensive process."

"And you think Rachael was feigning interest in me... because I'm a screencrafter?"

"Because you're Jason Boll's nephew. Men like him are already protected. She's probably looking for a way to become a screen actress."

"So... you are inoculated too?"

He laughed and shook his head sadly. "I had to fund the lab that built that pill—after I gave a wonderful girl a luxury liner as a Christmas gift." He stared up at the ceiling. "Intellectually, I know what she did to me, but I still have to take elaborate precautions to prevent her from seeing me in person. The drug came too late to overcome the imprint she left on me."

"Sounds like an expensive lesson."

"Oh, at the time. But of course, I'm not the only man with money to lose, so I sold my pills to the people who could afford them. Men like your uncle. There are emergency pills like the one I gave you, and another drug that short-circuits the imprinting process altogether. It's expensive, but worth it for a certain clientele."

"Umm. How much did that pill I took cost?"

He dismissed it with a wave of his hand, a frown on his face. "Rachael could have afforded to fly back home. Her father's company has a jet, if you can imagine. Instead she decided to take a leisurely cruise on *my* ship and seduce *my* customers, just so she could try out her new toys. Maybe I can't stop all her mischief, but I certainly couldn't let her imprint the nephew of Jason Bolls. At worst, getting herself installed into the screen actors elite would make her much too dangerous. At *best*, she would have damaged your career. Imprinted people make poor decisions. Believe me, I know!"

"Well then, I thank you."

He nodded. "Just take precautions. You're sure to run into her again. Take these." He tossed a small packet to Samuel. "Pheromone filters. Jam them up your nose. You'll get used to them in an hour or so. And *don't* let her touch you again!"

The Pass

"Washing your socks?" asked Saul Carson, looking down at Caleb, sitting half way into the ballast trough.

He gave a wry smile. "Yeah. It's my best chance before we lift off. We're replacing the ballast water in a minute or so."

"Step in the cow patties again?"

"Hard to avoid it."

Saul chuckled. "Get some real air boots. It'll save you in the long run."

"Ha. Ha," he muttered as Saul moved off to his station at the fuel cells. The engineer had been the one who'd urged him on, betting his boots on the roll of the dice. With shipmates like that, he'd be lucky to have clothes by the time they got back to home base in Brisbane. An airman without his boots was a joke and the whole crew was ready to remind him of it. He was the youngster, and the favorite target of their pranks.

A blimp was a curious creature, with people running around on the inside of its 'stomach' all the time. Walkways were waste-mass. It was all about lifting the most and staying aloft the longest. The *Lance*'s skin was strong enough to bear a man's weight, but rough boots, or horrors, cleats or high-heeled shoes, were tempting fate. Air men wore boots with rounded surfaces and a slip-free surface, so that they could walk up the slope to where the air-filled cargo bay met the hydrogen-filled lift bag.

"Caleb! Caleb Race! Are you down in ballast?" The captain walked to the edge and looked down at him. "Get up here immediately."

He slipped on his wet socks and scrambled up to the platform. "Sorry Captain."

She looked him over with a stern glare. "Socks? You haven't retrieved your boots?"

"No money, Captain."

"Your toenails clipped short?"

He looked down at the deck. "Um. That's why I'm wearing socks."

She sighed. "Stay and mind the cargo until we lift off. Then report to me for clipping."

As she left, Saul off in the stern, grinned and gave him a double thumbs up. All the men had attempted at one time or another to get some personal attention from the captain. Getting his toenails clipped was hardly a win in Caleb's mind.

...

The ballast, a long trough at the very bottom of the hull, running nearly the whole length of the *Lance*, was filling with fresh sea water as the dregs were being flushed out. Hair-like tendrils lined the trough, just like on the external hull—forming the root system. They wanted to lift off with maximum ballast, which meant full lift capacity. The *Lance*, sunning herself in the bright Pacific daylight, used the sunshine to split water into hydrogen which went into the great bag that filled the bulk of her interior. In the air, she would extract the fresh water from the ballast and it would get increasingly salty, which was why they took the opportunity to replace the old ballast with new sea water.

A little later Caleb felt the tilt, and so did the cattle, as they began to lift. He walked the decks, talking to the fat, green girls. Caleb had been told that they were extra vitamin enriched, and quite tasty, not that these were destined for the butchers. They were all female, and all pregnant with female calves. Thus far, not a single bull had been exported. If the dairy farmer in Central Mississippi wanted to pay, frozen sperm could be obtained for an extra fee.

Personally, he didn't think the monopoly could last. Eventually, someone would smuggle out the necessary genes. It's possible the northerners could even engineer the necessary chromosome themselves, although the Australian labs were a couple of decades ahead of everyone else in the world.

We deserve at least a few years to catch up with the northerners economically. And the blimp fleets were finally making it possible. For far too long, the shipping monopolies had taken an outsized chunk of their profits.

16

He rubbed the sweat off his forehead. *I'll be glad when we're back up in the sky. The humidity is terrible down here at the surface.*

...

Sixteen hundred miles to the east, Bill Melear sweated as well, but the breeze in the Tucson airplane graveyard was as dry as the ancient Techno age metal planes that sat parked in rows.

"There are fewer now," explained Jess Daniel, the caretaker. Bill smiled. It was refreshing to have somebody around that looked older than he was. Daniel pulled up to a parked F-111 and they got out of the cart. "I get a half-dozen people like you every year, looking for an old air-frame for some project or another."

Bill tapped the white cockpit. "Why is it painted?" Some flaked off on his fingers.

"Oh, from what I've been told, when the Techno's parked these, they painted a reflective coating to protect the electronics in the planes from baking in the sun. Of course, the Star took care of that."

Bill nodded. He'd built many working airplanes, usually starting with airplane frames left idle since the supernova flare. Unfortunately, derelict airplanes, even ones that hadn't crashed when the world's electronics were fried, were often converted into storage bins, or bedrooms, or even buried under ages of trash.

He looked over the plane, marveling at its shape. Over a century it had been sitting, baking in the sun, but it still looked like a powerful beast, ready to take to the skies. That was an illusion, of course. So much technology had been lost. Inside were electronics—fried electronics—that current companies could not duplicate. And he knew from long personal experience that the metals used to build those turbines were still decades away from being re-invented.

Modern aircraft, the kind he built, were one of a kind. He'd reuse a recovered airframe, gutting out all the electronics, and then install a rebuilt engine. Several of the ones he'd successfully flown had much larger wings than this one. His best effort had just barely cracked the sound barrier and this bird had done twice that when it was alive.

He walked around and checked what he could. So much was obviously defective, from the scraps of the tires to the signs of corrosion in places. The movable sweep wings were a worry. He checked the under-wing mounts.

Daniel said, "These were war planes. Those were for missiles or bombs."

Bill chuckled and shook his head. Most of the world had been free of wars for a couple of decades, and none of the national armies had developed an air force, if you didn't count Australia's blimp shipping fleet. The Techno era mindset was a little incomprehensible. Maybe when the population got up into the billions like it had been before the Star, maybe then they would need air forces. Not now. That kind of war was long gone.

He confided to Daniel, "I've had a couple of governments buy planes from me, but they were more interested in putting cameras in them than guns."

"Oh, what have you built?"

"Passenger planes mainly. Three refurbished DC-10s, built from old 'Fed-Ex' planes—some kind of cargo craft from the Techno days. An assortment of smaller craft, ten-passenger jets and the like."

Daniel looked at the two-seater F-111. "You'll not carry any passengers in these."

"I'm not planning to refurbish it. The tech is beyond me. I don't need a war plane. I just need the airframe. Can you sell me three of them?"

...

A few hundred miles to the west, Carlos set his bat down and pointed across the sunny California valley. "Hey, look at how low that blimp is!"

Terry looked up from the ball and checked the pass in the mountains where the blimps tended to make their crossing. There had been three in the sky today, but this one looked like it was barely clearing the road to Pala.

"Do you think it'll land?"

"That'd be cool. Do you think they need to make a delivery here?"

Terry shrugged. "I don't know. Do you think they need water? Billings in biology class said they needed sunlight and water to make their lifting gas."

"You think they're out of gas?"

"Who knows? Where could they get water here in Temecula?"

"Vail Lake?"

"Hey, that's up in the mountains. If they don't have enough gas to clear the pass properly, then they'd never make it up to the lake." Terry glanced over at the school. "You know, there's water in the swimming pool."

Carlos asked, "Do you think they even know about the pool?"

Terry turned with a great big grin. "If they're in trouble, and we helped them out, maybe they'd let us take a ride!"

"Hey! Yeah! My truck!" They made a dash across the field and spun out of the parking lot.

Carlos raced up Pala Road, passing over the dry riverbed.

Terry shook his head. "They are in trouble! They're steering all over the place."

Carlos flipped the switch on his truck's booster batteries and sped up.

The great green cucumber-looking craft was coming in at an angle, bucking winds from the north. The guys had never seen one this close before. It was huge.

Propellers in the back spun down, and then spun up again as they threatened to get too close to the mountainside. Terry yelled, "They're using the hydrogen to run their engines! They can't steer without losing altitude. They're not going to make it."

"Are you sure? Is there anything we can do?"

"I don't know. Can you get close?"

Carlos eyed the distances. The blimp was almost blocking the pass, like a big dark cloud. They were close enough to see men through the skin, watching their clearances in the tight space and yelling at each other.

"If we could get a rope to them...." He didn't complete the thought.

Toward the rear, the craft drifted sideways and scraped a rock outcropping. The bag tore. The skin rippled, as the gas pressure dropped and the blimp sagged down onto the road and surrounding trees.

There was a spark.

"Back up! Back up!" Terry screamed.

It wasn't an explosion, more an expanding wave of flame, but it flared hot and wide, consuming ship, crew and the countryside. The whole sky was ablaze.

Both boys screamed as the heat of the flames blistered their skin. The truck swerved and rolled. Trees all around burst into flame from the radiated heat.

A tower of flame could be seen by everyone in Temecula. The other blimps in the sky steered wide.

The explosion of the truck's fuel-cells wasn't even noticed.

Wave-off

Caleb was on the command deck of the *Lance*, doing extra cleaning chores as part of his deal with Captain Kelly. A pay advance let him get his boots back.

"Captain!" Ray Nells called her over to the comm. She walked over and read the screen. The gasp of dismay caught everyone's attention.

Caleb only paid attention to rank and protocol when it helped keep him out of trouble. "What is it Captain?"

When she turned to face him, he wished he hadn't said anything. From the look on her face, something bad, very bad, had happened.

"Call the crew."

He blinked. She had a louder voice than he did. Regardless, he scurried down the rope ladder to the cargo deck.

Running down the length of the ship, he yelled, "All hands! All hands! Captain announcement!"

The deck shifted slightly—the pilot making allowances for all the crew collecting at the bow end of the ship.

People started arriving. "What's up?"

"I don't know yet." He tried to keep a poker face. He really didn't know anything, but it was likely bad and he could think of a lot of bad things.

Captain came down the rope ladder, stopping a head taller than every one else.

"We just received a fleet-wide alert a moment ago. The *Southern Star* went down at the Temecula Pass, with all hands lost."

There was a common gasp as they all absorbed the news. The *Southern Star* had been at Brisbane when they were preparing for their departure. One by one, eyes turned on their captain. There had been rumors. She had dined with Captain Murphy of the *Southern Star* a few times.

Her face was drained. She said, "Reports are that the *Star* burned. There is a forest fire at the pass. Messages are stacking up. The Californians are making impossible demands. We may be faced with course changes."

She straightened her back. "Anyone who has been slacking off—catch up. We may need to be on our very best game. No one knows anything just yet, so get back to work. Do your job. Dismissed."

...

Samuel was walking the deck when he overheard one steward whispering to another, "...California is burning! Blimp exploded."

He hurried to the ship's computer room and elbowed his way to one of the chairs. The computers were only connected via short wave but bandwidth seemed to be okay as he hit the news vendors.

This was the first blimp to go down in flames in a populated area, and everyone was waking up to the idea that all those blimps in the sky were filled with flammable hydrogen gas. The town had lost dozens of buildings and the mountainside had a wide-spread blaze. Isolated homes and even the historical Palomar observatory were at risk.

There was a text message from Tad Como back in Hawaii.

Hey, Sammy. Are you in place to run me some vid captures of the California fires? I need news and archive video.

The price was good, but he wasn't in place.

He spoke into the handset. "Sorry, Tad. I'm still on the ocean, enjoying the scenery." He added a one-second clip of Rachael that he'd taken a few days earlier before he knew who she was. He was curious how Tad would react. He might even recognize her.

People were waiting, so he made sure his handset had synced up all his regular updates and disconnected his account.

"Samuel! Samuel Bolls!" It was Rachael, and she'd waved at him the instant he came out on deck. He'd managed to avoid her since Jenner had warned him, but he didn't feel like running today. She approached, still beautiful enough to stop him in his tracks even though he was wearing the nose filters. Cautiously, he slipped his hands in his pockets.

"Rachael." He nodded.

She looked worried. "Is it true they'll divert us to Los Angeles? Because of the fires?"

He shook his head. "You'd better check with the captain about that, but from what I hear, the fire is up in the mountains, well away from the coast. It shouldn't make any difference in where we dock."

She sighed. "Well, that's a relief. I've got people waiting for me in San Diego. LA is a nice place, but I've got contacts to make in the screen industry, like you, right?" She slipped her arm around his, and they sauntered down the deck.

It was very hard to hide his fears. *I can't be prey.* He was a screencrafter, after all. She was a story. He slipped his arm free and pointed to a table. "Let's have a seat. Come tell me about your plans?"

He had gotten interviews with dozens of people. He knew the questions to ask. He pulled out his handset and showed it to her.

"Do you mind if I capture this? My memory isn't the best in the world and I can imagine your life is destined to wind up on the screen eventually."

She hesitated, her eyes checking his face. He put on his timid but honest newcomer face and met her gaze.

...

It was late afternoon when the *Avocado* settled down in the middle of Lake Nacimiento. Captain Conroe yelled orders to his crew and they began filling the ballast tank with the fresh water.

"Captain." His navigator pointed off toward the docks. A motorboat was heading their way.

"Be on alert."

"Yes, sir."

He stepped down the ladder and slipped through a couple of membranes to reach the water level. He picked up a flashlight and unsealed the external door. He leaned out and flashed his light toward the rapidly approaching boat.

They saw him, slowing down and easing up closer. They stopped at shouting distance.

"You can't stay here!"

"This is the *Avocado*. We're on our way to deliver our cargo at Fresno. We need to refill our water tanks. We've done it here before. No problems."

The boater shook his head. "I called the sheriff. The word is that blimps are dangerous. We can't have you stay here. You'd better leave now."

The captain sighed. *Idiots.* There was nothing safer than a blimp taking on water, protected from the wind by a ring of hills like there were here.

"Hey, we're not going to blow up or anything like that! I've lived on this ship for ten years. We're safe. I know the *Southern Star* ruptured, but that's not going to happen to us. That was special circumstances."

The local frowned. "We can't take chances. If you went up, you could start a forest fire here too."

"Chum, can't you just give us until the morning? We need sunlight to fill our gas bag."

The Californian looked back at his marina, and gunned the boat for an instant to drift a little closer.

"It hurts my business too. I've brought meals out to dozens of your blimps, but the sheriff was talking about poking holes in the next one of you that showed up. I don't want an explosion, but I don't want a dead blimp in my lake either. Just go. Please. Before he gets here."

The captain nodded and sealed the door.

"Halbert! Can we make it to Fresno on the water we've got?"

The navigator scratched his beard. "We may not make it out of this basin without dumping some of the ballast." He thought a moment, doing the math. "I recommend we drift close to the ground, maybe at five hundred feet until dawn. We need more sunlight to be at the three thousand foot level we need to get over the ridge line. We can make it. But we'll need more ballast before we leave Fresno."

"Then get us in the air, dump as little ballast water as we can."

The navigator went over to chat with the pilot.

The captain sat down at the comm station. *I need to report this to fleet. And I need to contact Fresno—add a safe landing and water resupply to the contract or they won't get their seedlings.*

A second boat cut its engines as the blimp lifted off the lake's surface, dribbling a long string of water as it rose. The propellers began spinning slowly and it steered to the left. When it passed over the dam, heading downstream, the boats turned back to the dock.

...

On the other side of the world, near Brisbane Harbor, Fleet Admiral Dale watched the glowing dots, each with an associated, barely visible, listing of its course, tonnage, and captain. Along one wall of the large darkened operations room a world map spread out over fifty individual displays, five high and ten wide. It was a custom job the Gnomes had supplied to provide real-time tracking of the entire blimp fleet.

Everyone in the room knew better than to call him 'admiral'. He didn't like his fleet rank any better than his inherited title of Earl of Coonabarabran. He'd explained loudly that nobody controlled the collection of several hundred independent blimp captains. But someone had to do the job.

"Sir!" called out one of the comm operators. "We've got another wave-off. Some little lake in California."

He nodded. "Mark it. Request full details." Reports were coming in fast. Unless something changed, the fleet would run out of watering holes in North America, Europa, and the southern stretches of Africa. There had been a Letter of Concern from the Emperor of Northern China, but thus far, there had been no wave-offs in Asia.

He picked up the headset and called Royal House. The fleet wasn't officially part of the government, but they had common interests. He didn't like calling in favors, but he was running out of options.

The connection came through quickly. The Court switchboard had gotten its nose bruised enough yesterday after trying to give King Thomas his privacy.

After twenty seconds of formality, Dale got to the point.

"If the political situation doesn't stabilize very soon, we'll lose a number of the fleet. Nearly fifty blimps over the Americas and thirty in Europa are being denied water and transit passage. Every little town constable is making new rules and threatening free access. I won't be surprised when someone starts shooting."

The king grumbled. "Are we sure they haven't already? What about that report that the *Southern Star* was approached by a vehicle right before it ignited? Could it have been attacked?"

"Unknown, Your Majesty. It was clear the ship was in trouble—low on gas—before approaching the pass. There had been no prior threat."

"Maybe not by those Californians. But the Northern Countries have been squealing like pigs since the fleet began undercutting their shipping monopoly. They were just looking for an excuse."

Dale spoke respectfully, "Perhaps if the Crown were to intervene and get all these little panicky towns to stand down, we could get back to our business. As it is, no blimp captain will be able to make deliveries. Fleet has already gotten a few requests to dump cargo and return home."

"The Crown is working, Lord Coonabarabran. And getting very little rest, I might add."

"Is there any word I might pass on to the fleet?"

"Not as yet. But keep them flying. Keep them safe."

"Yes, Your Majesty."

...

King Thomas pinched the bridge of his nose. He had known this day would come. Any optimism had faded over the years as the kingdom had expanded, finally, to include the western cities of Australia, and then to extend protectorate status to New Zealand and Tasmania. Half of Micronesia had his face on their money as well.

The lands in easy reach had all opted into the trading partnership, once it was clear how well they could eat once they adopted the Australian numals.

But Berlin ruled the seas, and they had made sure no upstart biotechs would make any dent in that. For years, he'd tried to get someone interested in reactivating the shipbuilding yards, but limited ironworks and pre-Star facilities that were better for aluminum than steel discouraged anyone who took at look at the problem.

Relying on their strengths—designing the blimps—had been a wonderful way to grow their way out of the iron box. And the iron nations had been a hungry market for their superior crops and livestock, once Australia could guarantee delivery.

But the Melbourne and Brisbane harbors were still filled with iron ships containing hard goods, steel beams and trucks. No one was allowed to ship certain goods via blimp, even though the latest generation had certainly grown large enough to handle the more massive items.

In Europa, blimps had been banned from the rail yards, prevented from making easy connections to the rails and the trucking fleets. The Fleet had reacted by developing ways to unload their goods anywhere.

It was a constant battle. The iron technology countries would put up a barrier and the fleet would work around it. The growing blimp fleet had been his best weapon yet. But they weren't enough.

The king shook his head. *It's time. I hoped it would never come to this.*

He pulled out a small handset and tapped a code.

Choices

Rachael was quiet for a moment, sipping her tea. Then she looked at him solemnly.

"The old man got to you, didn't he?"

Samuel thought a moment. Neither of them had mentioned Baron Jenner before. But there was only one person she could have meant.

"He told me a story. I'm not sure I believe it all."

"How I'm a monster, turning people into mindless slaves?"

He chuckled. "Not in those words, exactly. He did mention something about avoiding your touch."

She sighed, staring down at the table, looking at her fingernails. "It's not as bad as he makes it out to be."

"So there *is* some chemical that affects my mind?"

"It's not that, exactly. You know how you really only have one chance to make a good first impression? I still have to do all that! I have to pull out all the stops and wow people with my smile, my cheerfulness, all that. The touch is just to help keep that from fading. It's like your business card."

In spite of the nose plug, and the warnings, he could sympathize with her plea. It was very hard to make a good impression. He dreaded all the networking he'd be doing when they arrived at San Diego.

"I wish I had something like that."

She smiled timidly. "Well, you may say that, but you're doing okay as it is. My situation isn't as great as it seems. If someone knows you've gotten the A-Labs treatment, they steer clear of you. If they don't, and find out later, they never trust their own feelings about you.

"I can't win, even if I don't do anything!"

He nodded. "I believe you. I'm... testing myself, as I talk to you. But then, maybe I always second guess myself when I'm talking to a pretty girl."

She smiled. "You don't need to."

...

The twin propellers that had pushed the *Lance* across the Pacific were still, and although they normally weren't very loud, once the craft had gone quiet, the cattle began moving around uncertainly, mooing.

Captain Kelly gathered the crew in a circle in a little paddock Caleb had emptied of the animals and scraped free of the droppings. No other place on the ship was large enough for everybody.

"The latest reports from Fleet HQ aren't good. We're only an hour or so out from California, but the place has changed. Our original plan had been to land in Oceanside's protected harbor to top up our ballast, and give you men a shore leave before heading into the continent.

"Oceanside, as well as practically every other protected harbor, as well as all the inland watering holes we have marked on our chart, have all begun to wave off incoming blimps."

The men began to grumble. Saul said, "Bloomin' idiots. Are they afraid that we'll all blow up or something?"

She shook her head, "I'm getting conflicting reports over the captain's channel. At first it sounded like a few hot-headed small town officials, but then, as more reports came in, it appears that the stories show suspiciously identical features. Fleet warns that this could be organized—taking advantage of the fire to drum up public distrust of the blimps."

Caleb asked, "Does that make sense? These northerners are paying money for our cows. More expensive shipping means they pay more. I don't get it."

She nodded. "A lot of this doesn't make sense. It probably won't until it's all twenty years gone. Still, we have to make decisions today—in the next few minutes. I'm bringing you all in on this because we have to decide quickly, and it affects us all.

"Choice one: unload the cattle into the ocean, or maybe a sand spit somewhere, and then go back home."

There was an unnerving moo from the cows next to them, and some of the men laughed—not that the cows understood any of this, no matter how much tinkering had been done to their genes.

"Do we get paid if we do that?"

"No. And I get a lawsuit when we dock. I contacted the office in Brisbane and they expect a best effort at delivery."

Before the grumbling got too loud, she continued.

"Choice two: change course to a more southerly route, avoiding California altogether. Perhaps cross over near Veracruz and make the final run up the Mississippi River."

Caleb shook his head. "We don't have cattle feed for that long. And it's already hurricane season. Isn't that why we came north so fast in the first place—to get above the tropics?"

She nodded. "And it's not just California that's waving off blimps. There's some of that in Central Mississippi as well, but at least I've got a guarantee that if we make it there, we will have an open field to land in, with piped-in water for ballast resupply. Our farmer wants his cattle."

She looked around at them, and then took a deep breath.

"Choice three: refill ballast right where we are, and head east at maximum altitude. Make best use of the winds to minimize hydrogen for the props. Actively seek out rainfall, and if we have to, drop down with siphon hoses in the middle of the night to raid water from off-limits lakes or rivers.

"The biggest risk is that we could lose the *Lance*—either from some nutter shooting at us, or capture and confiscation if the northerners get serious about this."

Wizzer, the engine mechanic, asked, "When you say lose the *Lance*, do you mean like the *Southern Star*?"

She nodded. "It's a possibility. Especially if they get crazy and start shooting. There's big risk here, and not just to the *Lance*."

No one had a better option for a fourth choice. They argued for a few minutes. No one wanted to go home broke, but no one wanted to burn to death either. Caleb had to argue long and hard against the southern route. He was the only one who had been trained in the care and feeding of the cattle.

"Look at them now. Agitated and testing the lines. And that's just because we're stopped and they were used to the engine noise. A day without food and they'll be unmanageable. Two days without, and they'll stampede right off the platform and likely rip a huge hole in *Lance*'s skin. Don't let their green hide fool you. They need less food than normal, but they can't do without it."

Danny Lane, the ship's healer, the one who patched blimp's scrapes and attended to its general health, asked, "Couldn't we get more food?"

"If they won't allow us to land, how are we going to get more hay? Drop and grab it from some unsuspecting farmer? Then they really would start shooting at us."

"And we can't do it now, we need to stay light."

"Can't do it later, we'll be over the Gulf of Mexico."

"I say we go high. Can the cattle handle that?"

Captain Kelly watched the arguments shift back and forth, saying nothing unless she was asked for details. It was important that the crew be behind their decision, no matter what it was. She waited until the objections and gripes wound down a bit.

"So, are we agreed?" She didn't have to spell it out.

She got a nod from everyone. Some were more reluctant than others, but everyone was on the same page.

"Okay, batten down for an open-surf refill. Danny, see if you can remove the identification banners while we're down. I've got to go check the weather reports."

···

Bill Melear ran his hands over the seam in the smooth metal hull. The conversion of the first F-111 was on target, the one that had been here at the aircraft museum in Texas since the beginning, but so much could go wrong. The original twin jet engines had been removed and the new engine had slipped into their place. The wing actuators were going much slower. The three new airframes were arriving from Arizona, disassembled there and shipped by rail. They were bought mainly for replacement parts.

His crew of five mechanics were all at work, and everyone knew that this job was unlike anything they had tackled before. The payoff would be huge if they could pull it off.

He opened the gull-wing cockpit window and slipped into the left seat. Most of the controls and instruments were gone, fried long ago. The new ones were on the work bench in his office. Even if the old electronics had been functional, most were useless. The navigation systems required satellites or fixed beacons that had been gone for more than a century. Comm systems—they called them by a number of different codes—didn't work off a modern Net connection. They had all used direct radio broadcasts.

There were the safety systems too. He didn't even want to think about those. This craft had been designed to blast the whole cockpit out of the plane and then land it as a unit with parachutes. He wouldn't trust those old rockets on a bet. They were one of the first sub-systems that had been removed.

I'm going to fly this thing and land it on my own. A production version might have some kind of bail-out system, but this was a prototype, and he didn't have the budget or time for that kind of engineering.

But can we get the sweep wings working properly in time?

Standard flight controls—flaps, ailerons, rudder, etc. were more critical, but they were a known issue. This was a very high performance military aircraft and they were having to simplify much of it. He wasn't about to try any barrel rolls at treetop level in this thing.

He got out and walked out on the wing. For a two-seater, it was a huge plane. They'd rebuilt ten-passenger jets that were smaller than this one. But all the figures had pointed to this airframe for the project.

He really should have turned this over to a younger pilot, someone with better reflexes, but he couldn't even risk taking a copilot along in the navigator seat. Nobody had the experience for something like this, but he was closest. *And I won't turn down this chance for anything!*

He climbed down and headed for the custom trainer the Gnomes had shipped in just yesterday. He needed at least another hundred hours simulated practice flying the radical new engine before he ever dared taxi the real thing on the runway.

I just hope all our calculations were correct. The Gnomes can come up with some great gadgets, but you have to specify them correctly.

There was never going to be any chance to refine the simulator until after he returned from that first flight. Still, the Gnomes had built the engine controller subsystem. If anyone knew how to do it right, they should.

So much new, so much strange. Am I getting too old for this?

Round-up

Samuel sat at a comfortable seat inside, where he could watch the San Diego skyline approach out the windows without jostling elbows with the others out on the deck. Some of these passengers had been onboard since Australia and were eager to get on shore.

It was his first ocean crossing, if you didn't count the little ferries that shuttled between the islands. As much as he was looking forward to meeting his uncle, and seeing California, he was going to miss the big ship and all the interesting people he'd met.

He scrolled through his handset, looking at his captures and notes. Surely some of it would be useful down the line.

Uncle Jason will ask me what I am working on.

He opened up his list of projects, things he planned to do when he got the chance. There were nearly fifty items in all, plus another handful that were barely scraps of ideas.

A smile crept over his face as he reflected on some of them. He'd been building the list since long before he'd gotten the handset.

Adam and Eve story—sole survivors on an island after the Star.

Screencrafter's school project uncovers murder mystery—his teacher is guilty.

Discover the Gnomes—first person interview.

Girl blimp pilot fights with aircraft designer—love story.

A lot of them were typical first-time writer fantasies—things that had been done a million times, and always badly. A couple—he took the opportunity to erase them—were merely a boy's excuse to think about sex.

It was time to grow up and treat these as commercial projects—ones that could be built on a budget and that would attract enough Net traffic to pay for them.

When he glanced up, the scene outside had changed. He looked around. The ship had veered to the north. He tapped up a map on the handset's little screen—they were close enough to shore that there was bandwidth he could pick up.

Ah. San Diego's harbor was through a protected channel. The ship had to thread its way inside before it reached the docks.

Giving into tourist instincts, he went outside with the others—looking at the mountain beside the entrance to the harbor.

There was even a blimp at pretty high altitude, heading south parallel to the coastline, but he quickly lost sight of it as it moved into a cloud layer.

...

The shipping manual for the cattle mentioned a resistance to "brisket disease" caused by high altitudes, but also included a list of possible symptoms. Caleb walked through the herd, checking each of them for the signs of this high-blood-pressure affliction. It wasn't likely to be a problem, even if it took several days at eight thousand feet to get to their destination.

But the captain said everyone needed to be at the top of their game. So he kept at it, patting their sides and talking low. Thus far, none of the girls seemed distressed by the altitude.

I still have to pop my ears with a yawn when we climb. What do cattle do?

Satisfied, he took the opportunity to climb up to the captain's deck to report.

He paused at the top of the ladder. Outside was a featureless cloud bank.

"Turn to port, make it due east for now." She had her eyes closed, as if she were sensing something. "Make it twenty knots air speed until the clouds begin to clear, then notify me."

She looked over at Caleb. "Problem?"

"No, ma'am. No signs of distress in the cattle. The temperature is cooling a bit."

"You're right. Grant, cut flow-through vents to minimum." The cargo deck had vents fore and aft to allow the outside air to flow through the space where the men worked. The *Lance*'s skin was, not surprisingly, air-tight. Not that they were in any danger of suffocating. As part of the surgery that converted a free-flying wild blimp into a cargo ship, oxygen pores were routed to the cargo bay. People had reported long trips with the flow-through vents entirely closed off.

Of course, they weren't carrying a cargo of cattle at the time.

"Caleb, give Danny a hand storing the ship ID banners."

He took the hint and headed back down.

In normal times, the three transparent cloth banners that held the *Lance*'s numeric code in big black letters were tied together and arranged, one on the top and the other two at thirds positions on the lower sides. Any other blimp, or an observer from the ground could tap that code into a comm unit and chat with the captain. But more than half of the sixteen-hundred mile direct route to their destination was over the desert lands of North America, where they couldn't count on cloud banks to keep their presence secret.

If they couldn't hide, then at least they could try to be unidentifiable.

"What's up?"

Danny scowled at the sheets. "When I took them off, I had to pull these two through the sea water. They're drying out, but they'll be salt-encrusted. I'd hate to slap them back on *Lance*'s sides like that. The salt crystals rubbing against the skin might be irritating."

"So we rinse them in fresh water first."

"Yeah. Assuming we'll be allowed in a fresh-water lake any time soon."

"Captain said to help you stow them."

He nodded. "Good enough. Help me roll them all together. Put the clean one on the outside."

A few minutes later they had the roll strapped to one of the internal supports that held the cattle deck. They headed to the break room and snagged some pouches from the cooler.

"It took me a week before I could eat without feeling queasy," Caleb admitted.

Danny nibbled from his pouch, "Oh, why?"

Caleb gestured to the semitransparent floor.

"Fear of falling?"

"Maybe. It was just a little disorienting at first."

Danny chuckled. "Well then, don't volunteer to join a round-up."

"What's that?"

"A round-up?" He shook his head, remembering. "I got my training at Cleveland Bay, off Townsville. That's where they took the new blimps while they grew to their full size."

"They move them. Why and how?"

"Yeah, they need the shallow atolls for the germination stages, but once they start inflating, a motorboat can just attach a rope and tow them to a deeper harbor. Cleveland Bay is where they brought the little ones—no more than a hundred feet long. They'd roll and slosh in the bay, soaking up the sun and getting bigger.

"Eventually, they'd reach the point where their gas bag had enough volume to lift them free of the water. We had to be on guard and get a restraining net over them before that happened. Unfortunately, sometimes one would get away."

"I've heard of wild blimps. I've never seen one."

"Aren't many of them. Expensive to raise. While I was there, we lost two. One came down just a few miles inland, trapped in a gorge. Tore itself on the rocks. It was already stinking by the time we found it. Blimps are creatures of the air and sea. They don't do well on the ground.

"The other got away. I thought we'd never see it again. But one day, we got a call that a wild blimp had been spotted half way to Port Moresby in the Coral Sea. We were the closest blimp station, so a bunch of us volunteered for a round-up."

He shook his head. "Here's where you lose your fear of heights, or gain one.

"We took our rigging and nets on the station's utility blimp and went hunting. After a day, we found it drifting at about three thousand feet, next to a few fluffy clouds.

"The plan was simple. We'd move into position above, and drop a weighted net over it. Unfortunately, it sensed us approaching and moved into the clouds."

Caleb waved his hand. "Just a minute there. This was a wild blimp? You're saying it could see you? And moved on its own? Don't tell me it had grown its own propellers, or I'll know you're spinning a tall one."

Danny grinned, "It's not as crazy as you make it out. Of course blimps can see, in a crude sort of way. They've got chloroplasts all over their skin. There's not much of a brain, more a network of little ones, but if a shadow falls over part of its skin, the blimp will know it.

"And moving, well it's got options. Making more gas, or dumping some ballast, or venting the ballonets. All that is part of a blimp's built-in systems. But what happened to us was a little more amazing. I'd never seen it before.

"You know the siphon hose that's attached to the rear of the ballast channel, near where we've mounted the propellers?" Caleb nodded. "Well, that's part of the tap root that breaks off when a baby blimp starts making gas. Before we trim it back it has sort of a fin attached to it, like a feathery ridge running along the hose. The same muscles that let any blimp raise and lower the siphon hose can also move side to side."

Caleb was trying to visualize it.

"So, that wild blimp began to wave its fin, like a fish waves its tail. It couldn't move fast, but it did move. We didn't realize what was going on until it was already nosing into the cloud.

"A buddy of mine yelled for help with the net. I hadn't planned on getting outside at all, but the two riggers who were handling the net were lashed to our blimp with bungees. They weren't quite in position to get the net centered over the wild one. Like an idiot, I grabbed up the corner of the net still draped in the hatchway and leaned out. They chose that moment to drop it. It pulled me out as it fell down across the rogue's back."

Danny chuckled and shook his head. "I was hanging on for dear life, screaming my head off as I bounced across the big gas bag. I could see my mates up above, their mouths hanging open. But with the weight of the net, and mine added to it, we began dropping out of the cloud and I quickly lost sight of the utility blimp.

"The net had not fallen properly. It wasn't draped evenly. I was praying hard that it wouldn't slip off. Any second, I was sure, Bessie would start to rock back and forth to shake it free, but I guess she just wasn't that smart.

"I climbed the net like a ladder, trying to get closer to the top. We were dropping at, oh, fifty feet per minute, so it seemed like forever. At least I had time to let my heart stop pounding. Moving carefully, I tugged at the net and got it spread out more evenly and centered over her back."

Danny leaned back in his chair and stared through the hull. "That day could have ruined me as a blimp wrangler, but it didn't. Riding alone on Bessie's back with hardly anything to see but the clouds, the sky, and the ocean below—I loved it!"

He shrugged. "But eventually the utility blimp vented enough gas to come down and get close. They lowered a small knife on a rope and one of the old timers coached me on how to punch a vent hole into the hydrogen bag. It was an hour or so before we got her down to the water. We patched the hole and got a better leash around her and towed her back to base. We all got prize money, and I got a yelling for being stupid, but praise for keeping my head."

Danny smiled. "And that's my round-up story. Think you'd like to try my cure for fear of heights?"

Caleb laughed. "Not likely! I'm over it now. But I kind of like the idea of being inside the blimp, rather than riding her back."

He nodded in agreement, but Caleb wondered. Danny's job was blimp healer—including repairing any holes in *Lance*'s skin. Had he gotten that job so that he could ride a blimp's back again—bare to the sky and the clouds?

Getting a Taste

As the tugs moved the Queen Helen into position in the San Diego docks, Samuel was finishing his last-minute packing, getting all his gear back onto the cart. It was a harder job than he'd planned for. Certainly he hadn't bought any new clothes on the ship. But by the time he wheeled it out and took the elevator to the main deck, he was well behind the crowd. He managed to say goodbye to Mrs. Taylor, but among all the faces, she was the only person he knew.

Walking down the gangway, he saw Rachael already on shore. She slipped into a long car and it drove off. It was interesting to see how many people, mostly men, were watching her leave. He was sorry he hadn't taken the opportunity to talk to her again. If she could keep from getting herself in trouble with the enhancements, she was well on her way to becoming famous.

His handset felt curiously warm to the touch. He dug it out of the pocket where he'd shoved it. There were messages.

When did I turn off the chirps? He didn't remember.

There was nothing to do but pause on the sidewalk and get out of the way of the other departing passengers.

Message from Jason Bolls: Sammy! I've been trying to contact you all morning. Look for a gray Bremer I sent to pick you up. Cancel your hotel reservation as soon as you can. You're staying with me.

There were indeed a number of queued messages. Some were from Uncle Jason, some from his company, and one other:

Message from Rachael: Sorry I couldn't get in touch with you for breakfast. Hoped to say goodbye before we left.

Well, I missed that chance.

He looked around. There was a luxury German car with a muscular driver in uniform standing beside it, scanning the crowd. When Samuel started pulling his cart in that direction, the driver's eyes locked onto him and he walked to meet him.

"Samuel Bolls? I'll take your luggage."

He hesitated and then turned the task over to him. "You were sent by my uncle?"

"Yes, sir."

"What is your name?"

The question caught him slightly off guard. "Tate. Sam Tate, sir."

Samuel chuckled. "Then I'd better call you Mr. Tate then. Just to avoid confusion."

"Yes, sir."

Tate's subservient reactions told him a lot. San Diego was the largest city on the North American west coast. Not only was it the center of the glossy and high profile screen industry, but it was the largest shipping center as well. California was hardly the most powerful nation—Europa had that claim by a large margin—but it was making its presence felt.

Out the window as they drove, he could see signs pointing to the Royal Castle in Balboa Park. Drivers like Tate had to know their social position and stick to it to serve the California peerage. Important men like Jason Bolls could aspire to one of the titles, if he chose to go that route.

Not that I'd want something like that. I want to be free to follow my instincts and not be bound to some court. Certainly not the one back on Hawaii. He had the wrong skin color for the Polynesian court.

They drove past a little lake and up into the hills behind it. It was a large house, surrounded by trees in all directions. As soon as he had stepped out, other servants appeared and his luggage disappeared into the house.

"Greetings Mr. Bolls. I'm Mrs. Selena Sanchez, Manager of the House. I've taken the liberty of choosing a room for you on the second floor with a view of Lake Sweetwater."

She looked like some general's grandmother. She smiled a lot, but her eyes were in constant motion, checking the house and her staff.

Uncle Jason was tied up in meetings, he was told, but would be home shortly. A lunch was offered, and he took some fruit. Once he got a moment alone, he checked his handset. Bandwidth was spectacular.

Don't get carried away, Samuel chided himself. *Just because I can view any screen instantly doesn't mean I won't have to pay for it.*

His Net account, which had seemed so fat when he left Hawaii, now seemed rather sparse. He wondered if he would be able to get any captures for Tad's news agency.

He tapped up a map that showed the status of the Temecula fire. It was still burning, and only fifty miles away, up to the north.

I could probably rent a car. But would it be worth it? If he'd gotten the captures when the story was new and everyone wanted to see it, then the tiny fractional credits people paid as they viewed would have added up. Now it wasn't as topical and not only would there be fewer views, likely other screen independents like him had already gotten the most dramatic captures.

He checked his banking account as well. There was a block reserved for his return passage, and another that had to keep him fed and housed for as long as he could. Uncle Jason's hospitality was helping there, but he had no idea how long that would last.

I wonder of I could edit any of the shipboard stuff and put it out there on PopVid. Those didn't make much in terms of Net credits, but anything to keep his account growing. There was always the option of converting cash to credits, or if he got popular, the other way around, but he wanted to keep his Net usage down to what his captures could pay for.

Someday, my stuff will be so popular, I'll be able to live off of converted Net credits.

His glow of optimism wavered just slightly, but munching on strawberries from an ornate silver dish in a room designed for royalty let him hold on the the feeling.

His handset burst forth with the chirps of the iiwi bird. It was too loud for the room, and he fumbled to answer.

"Hello?"

"Samuel, there you are." It was Rachael.

"Hi. I'm sorry I didn't catch your earlier message. My handset got turned off."

"Oh, it happens. I'm just glad you weren't trying to avoid me. Now that we're ashore, the options really open up. How about meeting me this evening?"

He glanced at the clock. When was Uncle Jason going to get back?

He sighed. "I really wish I could join you, but I've got to meet with my uncle soon, and I have no idea when I'll be free."

He could hear her pout. "Oh, so you really are trying to get rid of me."

"No, it's not that! I've just got to be ready when he gets free."

"Don't panic. I got stood up by relatives, too."

They chatted for a few minutes. She described some of the must-see events coming up in San Diego. But the best he could commit to was to note them on his calendar.

Then an incoming call notice scrolled across the display.

"Oops. Sorry. I've got to take this."

"Oh..." she was cut off.

"Please hold for Jason Bolls," said the new woman's voice.

"Yes." What else could he say?

There was a faint click. "Sammy! You made it. Are you at the house?"

"Uh, yes... Uncle Jason."

"Just Jason is fine. 'Uncle' makes me feel old. I'll be by the house in twenty minutes. Would you like to take a run by the docks?"

"That would be fine."

"Good. It would help my schedule if you were waiting out front. Are you still using that handset for video capture?"

"Yes. I've done a lot of work with it."

"Glass lenses?"

"Yes."

"Then would you mind trying out a different unit? Ask Serena for the handset on my office desk. See you." And the call dropped. Rachael was gone too.

But something was up. He hurried down the sweeping curved staircase, looking for the house manager.

She was ahead of him, walking out of a corridor holding a new handset. "Mr. Bolls. I believe your uncle wanted you to carry this."

"Thank you, Mrs. Sanchez."

He barely had a minute to look at it as he waited by the curb. The device was sleek and smooth, like an eroded river rock, in contrast to the square-edged unit he'd used for three years. The display was roughly the same pocketable size, but where he expected to see the camera's lens was a larger patch nearly half the width of the unit.

The gray Bremer pulled up. Sam Tate exited.

"Sir, your uncle has requested we take this car." He opened the door for him.

He was barely seated when a tiny red car zipped up and parked behind them. It was Jason Bolls. Samuel recognized him from entertainment news. He slid in and tapped the front seat. "Hit it."

The Bremer pulled out, moving much faster than it had when he'd been picked up from the Queen Helen.

"So, Samuel...or is it Sammy, Sam?" He held out his hand. They shook.

"Oh, I'm using Samuel as my byline, but anything you're comfortable with."

"Sammy then. How was the trip?"

"It was nice. Nothing at all like the island ferries. And I wanted to thank you for letting me stay at your place. I certainly appreciate it."

Jason was watching him carefully. "I've seen your work. Jumping into the screencrafter game with both feet I see."

"Well, I had an example in the family. And my father told me you had sent money that had helped pay for my handset. It's been most useful getting to capture professional-quality video."

He dismissed the gift. "Fortunately or unfortunately, the public's capacity for consumption is always growing. Would you be willing to experiment with this new handset? It's got a negative lens."

"Hmm. I've heard of that." He pulled it out and looked at the capture side. The patch didn't look at all like glass—not transparent, more like milky marble. From what he'd read, the lens had elements with a negative index of refraction, when enabled it to do things that could never be accomplished with glass. "I'd love to give it a try. Where did you get it?"

"The Gnomes, of course. This is a pre-production unit and I'm supposed to give them an evaluation in a month or so. Unfortunately, I do very little capture myself these days. Too much management and detail work. So if you could help me with that...."

Samuel had already turned it on. It was ready to accept an account ID. "I can enter my code?"

"Yes. Go ahead."

He entered his code. His data and customized layout took over the look of the screen. A couple of quick-taps confirmed that all of his stuff was there. All the controls worked as normal, except that the video had some extras. He tapped the motion dampening and zoomed in on his uncle's face.

"Wow." The zoom kept going, until he could fill the display with details of the iris of his uncle's eye. And the motion dampening was excellent as well, for a hand-held unit.

"Don't break it. No one needs a capture of my wrinkles. But I do have a task for you."

He set it down. "Sure. What do you want?"

"How much experience have you had at event reporting? Crimes, disasters, things like that?"

"A little. When Mauna Loa erupted last year, I did quite a few captures when a lava flow headed toward Hilo. Not too much crime work."

"Good. I'm not sure what we're facing. When we get there, follow your instincts and capture everything you think might be interesting. I'll try to get us closer access."

"Sure—but what are we going to see?"

"The Queen Helen. The liner that you arrived on. There was an explosion and it's sinking at the dock as we speak."

News Report

The docks were blocked off by a large semi-circle of police cars and firetrucks. Light tan uniforms were everywhere. Tate pulled the Bremer up as close to a large police truck as he was allowed. There was a policeman who must have been looking for them, because he waved them into a parking spot inside the barricades.

The Queen Helen was tilted, leaning against the docks as if tired. There was a stream of smoke coming from several of the aft staterooms. Samuel began taking captures as soon as he stood on the pavement.

Their escort waved then into a tent hastily set up in the middle of the street.

"Inspector Coab, this is the man I told you about, my nephew Samuel Bolls. He arrived on the ship just today."

Samuel took the introduction as if he knew what was going on. "Happy to meet you, Inspector. How can I help?"

The man wasn't having a good day. "In one way, we're fortunate that the ship was nearly empty. No fatalities. But with all the passengers dispersed, and many of the crew either on shore leave or tied up fighting the fire and the flooding, I'm still in the dark as to what happened."

Samuel nodded. "Do you have information on where the explosion happened? I could see fire toward the aft."

There was a detailed drawing of the ship, currently marked with where the fire crews were working.

The engine rooms were flooded and currently sealed off to keep the water from spreading. Samuel pointed out what he knew of the ship—where the luggage was stowed, where the galley and activity rooms were.

"Just above the engines, I think those were crew quarters, and above that, some of the staterooms. This one was Baron Jenner's cabin."

He was asked about the trip. Any ill will among passengers? Any suspicious characters joining the ship in Hawaii?

"It was a relatively peaceful journey. There was some grumbling against passengers who had gotten genetic work done, but no more than usual."

He really didn't want to spill Baron Jenner's distaste, or Rachael's part in it, but the policeman barely paid attention to the anti-genie sentiment, as if he'd heard it all before.

Another policeman came into the tent and spoke quietly to the inspector. He nodded.

"Mr. Bolls, thank you for your assistance, but the divers' reports seem to indicate the explosion happened on the outside of the hull. It looks like our pool of suspects has just widened. Thank you for coming down."

Samuel knew he'd be cut out of the action if he didn't make his move. Uncle Jason said to follow his instincts, didn't he?

"Sir, as long as I'm here, this would be a perfect opportunity to take some video captures of the ship in distress. I know you have other requests for access, but I'm familiar with the ship."

The inspector glanced at Jason, who had been standing quietly out of the way, watching everything. "Okay, but only if you stay with a safety officer. Hancock, you're babysitter. Let him take his captures."

Samuel smiled. He'd never turned the new handset off, trusting that there was enough internal memory, or that Net bandwidth was good enough to keep it spooled off to safety.

Hancock walked him around the docks. Samuel he took pictures of the ship, and the divers, then a bit later, other ships moving into position to assist. As soon as the fires were out, there was a plan to move the QH to dry dock. If this had happened at sea, the ship might have been lost, but here, just a stone's throw from one of the largest shipworks in the world, repairs could begin almost immediately.

Samuel played all his cards, including being the nephew of one of the most powerful men in town, and was escorted aboard the listing ship. He toured all the decks and rooms he'd seen before, recording the furniture piled up against the starboard side as if a giant had thrown a tantrum. He even captured a view into Baron Jenner's cabin. There was smoke damage, but the blast and flames had not gotten to that area.

Sunset came too quickly. He didn't have adequate lighting, but the negative lenses did surprisingly well, picking up enough light to give him the mood of the event.

Exhausted, he made his way back the car. His uncle was working away om a portable terminal.

"Did you get your material?"

Samuel smiled. "Yes. Now if I can just get it into shape to put out on the Net."

"I'll trade you license to use it later on my projects for access to my editing station."

"Deal!"

"Great." He nodded to Tate, "Sam, to the office."

...

The special news feature of the Queen Helen burning in San Diego Harbor hit the Net at about seven in the evening, Sydney time. King Thomas was one of the first people to watch the news screen all the way through. He missed nothing, not the position of the explosion, not the name of the young reporter, nor the smoky view of the luxury cabin.

He spoke to no one in particular, but there was an assistant waiting to note down what he said. "Find out what happened to Baron Jenner. If he was injured, prepare a sympathy note for my signature." He turned back to the image he'd frozen on the display, showing the ship burning and listing in the water.

When he flipped back to the updated blimp fleet status forwarded to him, he frowned at the number of dots building up along the coastlines of nearly all of the northern continents. A few were moving on to their destinations, but too many were not.

"It's morning in Berlin. Open a video to the Ambassador." He needed to get the bloated bureaucracy of the European Court moving. They were all too contented with the status quo. He'd to put some pressure on them. Word from on high that blimp traffic could come through would alieve the problem. If he could get Berlin to take a stance, then it would be much easier to get the other nations to follow.

I hate waiting for daylight all the time. I've given up sleep, and I've got no patience for those that waste half their lives like that.

...

When the ornate envelope arrived, Jenner coughed and took a deep breath from the oxygen mask next to his bed before opening it.

From some court or another. Nobody else bothers with paper anymore.

Then he saw the embossed shield on the envelope. It was from King Thomas. He looked the envelope over cautiously, then tore the hard wax seal open.

The words inside were simple and innocuous. A sympathy card, with a pantograph rendition of the king's distinctive signature—it had to have been printed at the local Australian Embassy.

The baron frowned. It was well known that the king didn't sleep, so maybe that explained how quickly the card had arrived. And the southerner was known to be persistent in making his presence known on the world stage. It would be like him to send a casual note to a peer.

Maybe. But somebody set off that bomb. The people with motive are few and far between.

Did King Thomas want to apologize? Or let me know he could have killed me?

...

Aboard the *Lance*, the air-filled ballonets were shrinking. Caleb hadn't ever seen them get quite so small before. He patted the closest heifer and then decided to go check to see if the captain's deck needed any more cleanup. He silently reached the top of the rope ladder. She was giving orders.

"Change course two degrees north. Open the starboard hydration veins by ten percent. Reduce prop rotation to one third until we reach eight thousand feet."

She turned to him. "Caleb. What are you doing here?"

"Um. Ma'am. I was just wondering if the deck needed sweeping."

She shook her head. "What's the real reason?"

The navigator and Grant, her lieutenant both looked his way and grinned.

"Well," he looked out at the clear blue, sunny sky, only lightly tinted green by the *Lance*'s skin. "I was just wondering about the altitude." He stepped up on the deck and tried to look down at the ground. "I'm not used to it."

She frowned. "Are you feeling faint?"

He waved his hand. "No. No. It's nothing like that. I'm just not used to being so high. This is only my second voyage. I saw the ballonets shrink. Sorry."

She nodded. "It's okay. We're at seventy-five hundred feet, and on our course we'll have to get nearly a thousand feet higher to get over the continental divide without scraping the ground. As far as the ballonets go, I'm sure you can get one of the other crewmen to explain it to you. But right now, the hydrogen is expanding, both because of the low pressure at this altitude and the sunshine. As the hydrogen expands, the ballonets must shrink to keep the same pressure on *Lance*'s skin."

He nodded. "I was just wondering. The radiation and all."

She chuckled. "That's just a myth. The high altitude radiation problems are long gone. The atmosphere is healed. Yes, people don't live in the mountains any more, but that will change over time. We certainly can't go so high that it would be a problem. Blimps just can't do it."

He looked outside again. "I can see the ground."

"Right. Ground level is about six thousand. But it's coming up, so we have to do the same." She nodded at the chart on the display. "We're in the deserted lands right now. Old Arizona. But we'll be in old New Mexico before too long."

He grinned at the old-new. "Does that mean we could land on a lake, I mean if there's no one to wave us off?"

She sighed. "Yes, we could, if there were any lakes that had water in them. This is dry country. We've still got a long way to go before we can re-fill. We've got to make the hydrogen last."

She looked up at the sky. "Grant. We've got a tail wind. Cut the props down to minimum—just enough to keep us pointed in the right direction."

"Yes, Ma'am."

She explained, "Conserving hydrogen." She glanced around at the deck. It was clean. "But you can sweep again if you want."

"Thanks."

...

The iiwi bird chirps made him think, just for a moment, that he was back in Hawaii, but then he blinked his eyes awake and fumbled for the new handset.

"Um. Hello?"

Rachael's voice woke him all the way up. "Wow, you've made a splash your first day here! I saw your news item on the ship. What a crazy thing to happen! I'm glad I was early to get ashore."

"Yes. Crazy." He sat up and fumbled for a shirt to pull on. The call was blinking for video. He brushed his fingers through his hair and turned on the camera. Her image appeared, smiling and perfect.

"Oh. I woke you up, didn't I?"

"How can you tell? Sorry. I was up late last night, getting the editing done and feeding the screen to the Queue. So it's out then?"

"Oh, yes. Everybody's seen it. And thanks for the nice captures you included of me. I didn't even know you'd had your camera on."

He doubted that. Rachael was probably aware of every camera that was in range of her.

"I didn't expect to be using all the background captures I made on the voyage so soon, but I was glad I had them. It made a nice contrast, showing the pleasant passage over with the smoke and the fire of the disaster."

She nodded, and then frowned. "Your report said it was an explosion? Did the police say what caused it?"

He chuckled. "Afraid of bad reviews already?"

"Hardly that. I was just puzzled."

"Everyone is puzzled. It was an attack on the ship, not an accident. That's all they're sure of."

On the edge of the display, there was a list of messages that had arrived in the night.

"Oh, Rachael, I see that the police, among others, are sending me messages. It looks like it's going to be a very busy day."

"So no time for lunch?"

He checked the time. It was getting late in the morning. "No. Probably not. It's probably all about the screen. But it's an opportunity."

"Take it. Squeeze it dry." She smiled with the glint of a predator in her eyes. "That's what I'd do."

And he knew she would.

A Friendly Chat

Jason Bolls tapped the display and invited him in.

"Thanks for your time Uncle Jason... Jason."

"No problem, Sammy. I was just about to see if you were awake myself. Have you checked your ratings yet?"

Samuel blinked. "Um, no. Not yet."

"Take a peek. You're on the Big List."

He fumbled for the handset.

"Use the big one." Jason pointed at the computer display next to Samuel's chair.

He logged in and pulled up the impressions list. The news report was two orders of magnitude more popular than anything he'd done before, and the numbers kept churning as he watched. He did a little math. He might actually be making some significant money.

Jason pointed. "Take a look at how much is being re-used."

Last night, as he had prepared to release his news special on the Public Queue, his uncle had coached him on the terms of use to apply. Everyone could pull it up and view it for cheap. He'd added only a little rider above the transport charges. But under Jason's advice he'd added a much more expensive re-use option.

"That's paying off for you. The explosion is still a mystery. Every news organization and every government, for that matter, is paying for the re-use rights for their own analysis and coverage. It should keep paying for as long as this mystery lasts."

Samuel chuckled. "I was going to beg use of one of your cars, but I guess I have enough money to rent my own for now... all thanks to you."

"With luck, you'll be able to buy your own. But this can all dry up in a flash. What are you planning to do next?"

"As a screencrafter?"

Jason smiled. "That is why you're here, isn't it?"

So this is the interview. He'd been expecting it since before he left Hawai'i. He'd practiced it several times. The events of the last twenty-four hours had wiped it out of his head.

He gave an embarrassed smile. "I have a list. Some fiction. Some documentaries. I have to say, I hadn't planned on event coverage, but Tad Como from the agency back in Honolulu had wanted me to capture some of the forest fires started by that blimp explosion—but that's all probably out of date by now. If I had a car, I was thinking of capturing some of the burn, just for background use."

Jason nodded. "Yes, unless the observatory starts burning, the juice is out of that news." He smiled. "As you're aware, it's best to be first on the scene."

Samuel nodded.

"So what else is on your list?"

He hesitated, not wanting to look it up, even though his mind was blank. "Well, I thought of a love story where a female blimp pilot got angry with an airplane designer..."

Jason waved his hand. "It's been done. Twice now, and badly. What else?"

"I've got a lot of archive capture of the lava flows on the Big Island. I thought maybe I could do a murder mystery where a body is discovered..."

"Captured with your old handset?"

He fumbled, forgetting the rest of the idea. "Ah, yes."

Jason frowned. "You saw the difference in the capture quality between the stuff last night and the scenes taken on your trip over, didn't you?"

He had. It had been shocking. He had been in the habit of thinking that everything he had captured over the past few years had been professional quality screens. He'd certainly sold some of them as professional.

But the new stuff with the negative lens camera was shockingly better. It hadn't been obvious on the handset screen, but once he started editing back and forth between captures from the two different cameras, his previous stuff looked flat, colorless, and *old.*

Jason could see it on his face. He nodded. "I'm facing the same problem. It's great to get archive captures of historical events, but they always look old. The Gnomes are coming out with better technology every year. I have to spend a fortune buying the new and expensive cameras. Your volcano mystery would look choppy, switching back and forth from action scene captures with new cameras and your historical archives. People would notice and think the whole production was cheap, even if you had a great story and great acting.

"And you can't shoot it all with old cameras unless you're trying to promote the whole piece as historical fiction.

"What else do you have on your list?"

Samuel was having a hard time, with all his best ideas being shot down so fast. "I had hoped, in a blue-sky sort of way, to write a documentary on the Gnomes."

Jason had a funny look on his face. "The Gnomes, eh? Have you discovered a new insight on the worlds' best kept secret?"

"Well, no. But I've been living off in Hawaii and I had hoped that being here on the mainland would allow me to do more research. I thought I could follow the shipping trail. People buy Net relays, computers, handsets, and all the best high tech devices from the Gnomes and they arrive in a packing crate. Somebody has to ship those crates. I'd track the inventory back to the factories."

"And probably that factory just gets the designs and specs from an untraceable message over the Net. You aren't the first to try to find them. Since the Star, the Net has been totally unhackable. I can't read your messages and you can't read mine. The Gnomes aren't the only anonymous organization out there either. You can follow the computers and handsets back to the factories, even back to the raw ores they are made from, but once you hit the Net, nothing is trackable."

Samuel nodded. "I know all that. But the Gnomes still need cash. They can't live on information credits. Some exchange somewhere has to do the swap, and once there's a money trail, it can be followed."

Jason was quiet for a moment. "I've done this as fiction, a couple of times."

"I know. Santa's elves and the one with the alien spacecraft in orbit."

Jason saw the smile Samuel couldn't quite suppress. "Don't laugh. Both of those made money." He sighed. "But I understand your interest. More than you know."

"What do you mean?"

His uncle blinked and looked out the window. "Oh. It's a long story, and one I've been careful to keep to myself." He looked back and smiled. "Let me think about this for a bit. You can certainly do a documentary on your own, but I can bring some resources to the table. Why don't you flag this one as active for now? But that will take a lot of time. What else is on your list?"

He succumbed to the temptation and pulled up the list. Jason shot down nearly all of them. The most common judgement was, "It's been done."

He drummed his fingers on the table. "You have a lot of fiction ideas, but all your professional work has been documentary and news."

Samuel sighed. "Some of my advertising work has been fiction—but you're right. It's easy to get a lava flow to look photogenic on cue. Not so easy to get friends and co-workers to volunteer as actors."

Jason raised his eyebrows and shook his head. "If I can remember that far back, pitching a story to potential actors without a script just leads to a lot of confusion. When actors get a hold of an idea, they immediately put their own thoughts into the mix. Correct them and you lose their enthusiasm. Handing them a script does a better job of making the project clear.

"Do you have any of the scripts that you have used?"

Samuel immediately thought of several documents that he had in his account, but really didn't want to show them to his uncle.

"Nothing good, I'm afraid."

Jason spread his hands. "That's okay. You have many of the necessary skills already. Creating a script is a skill like many of the tasks that you already do. I certainly don't write all of my scripts. There are a number of really good professionals who do that, and it's not a personal failure to let them do their job."

Samuel nodded, embarrassed.

Jason continued, "Once you have a good script, based on your own work or written by someone else, you'll be able to get a number of actors ready to work on your project."

"I guess so. There was a girl on the voyage over who was interested in working on my projects."

Jason asked, "Rachael Nue?"

Samuel winced. "So you've been told?"

He shrugged. "I wouldn't take it personally. You will find that there are many actresses and actors who are interested in making 'friends' with any screencrafter that they can get close to—whether they are augmented, or not."

Samuel hesitated, trying to think of a way to ask. "So do you believe these things the baron told me?"

"About the Beautiful People, unfortunately yes. About Rachael in particular, I have no way of knowing."

He smiled at his nephew. "I recommend that you spend all your waking time on developing your craft, for now. You will certainly be more attractive to people like Rachael with a few successes under your belt."

Samuel nodded and sighed.

"So what do you think about working with them... the augmented?"

Jason shrugged. "Half of my top-drawing actors have had work done in some form or fashion. It's the nature of this industry, unfortunately."

Then he frowned. "But don't let that get out. There is a growing antagonism against people with genetic alterations—genie hatred."

Samuel nodded. He was getting a new view of it. He'd grown up as the outsider—the white kid of an old Navy family and a tourist on an island where almost everyone else was family. He'd adapted, but being the one always left out had been part of his motivation to go see the world. Now everything was upside down. He didn't know what to think of it all.

But he would have to be careful. It would be nice to get to know Rachael better, but he'd just had his first taste of Net success, and he was well aware that none of it would have happened without his uncle's connections and help. If Jason said, tactfully, to keep his distance, then that's what he should do.

Jason looked up at the wall, where a lighting fixture had faded from white to blue. "It appears I have a call."

Samuel glanced down at the handset, sitting next to him. "I've got several I need to answer as well. I guess I need to give this demo unit back to you. It was great."

He stood, and so did Samuel. "Keep it for now—and we'll continue this talk later."

He snatched it up before his uncle changed his mind. "Later then, and thanks!"

...

The handset had bubbled Rachael's latest call to the top of the list. In the snippet, the software had boiled her latest message down to "I have tickets for the water show tonight."

Fresh off his second warning to stay clear of her, he quick-tapped it, sending it down to the list to be answered later.

He also qt'ed three interview offers from the local news organizations—he'd need Uncle Jason's advice before diving into that shark tank.

A deep breath and he slow-tapped the San Diego police.

"This is Inspector Coab. We spoke briefly at dockside before you went to take your captures."

Samuel recognized the voice. He was the serious man in business attire who ordered the uniformed officers around.

"It would be helpful to my investigation if I could speak with you again, either at my office, or if you prefer, at Bolls House. Please contact this number when your schedule allows."

I've never heard a policeman that polite before. He sighed, this was another one he'd need Uncle Jason's approval for. But he didn't think it was a good idea to keep him waiting either.

He flipped through his numbers, paused over Jason's direct number and moved on to the House number.

"The House of Jason Bolls. How may I help you Samuel?" It was the unnamed woman with the lovely voice he'd heard before.

"Uh, I've gotten a call from the San Diego Police asking to talk to me. I would either need to arrange transportation to their office, or permission to allow them to come here."

Her voice shifted, more businesslike, "I'm Anna, the amanuensis for Bolls House, and you did right calling me. There are protocols between the local police and anyone connected to Jason Bolls. First, do you have any objection to talking to the police?"

"Oh, no. I'm comfortable working with the police. I've done it several times back home."

"And Bolls House makes a point of co-operating with the police, but you may find certain members of the San Diego force less pleasant than others. Would you please forward me the call you received, and I'll make the arrangements for them to come here."

"Thank you." Rich people had the luxury of helpers to make their arrangements. It would be nice to be rich. He tapped and swiped.

"Inspector Coab, I see," she said, and he got an unpleasant feeling from the way she spoke his name. "Leave everything to me."

Lightning

The lower cloud whipped by, giving Caleb a quick glance at a dark streak on the ground. "That's not water, is it?"

Danny looked down through the floor. "No, probably an old lava flow. There's a bunch of—" The great blimp shifted, shoved sideways by a strong gust of thunderstorm winds. "—bunch of old volcanos in this part of the Americas. Extinct volcanos. Nothing to worry about."

"Yeah, unless these winds blow us up against one."

Danny looked thoughtful. "Maybe I'd better get back to my duty station."

Cattle were complaining about the shifting underfoot. "Yeah, me too."

The engines were running at full speed, pushing the *Lance* away from the core of the storm cell. The captain had moved into a gentle rain to wet down the skin and reduce the drain on the water reserves, but instability in the air had triggered the formation of a thunderstorm more quickly than anyone could have guessed.

Lighting flashed, and everyone flinched.

Caleb pulled himself up onto the platform as the thunder shook the cows into fresh distress. "Calm down there." He patted the flank of one of the green beasts. Her eyes were wide and she wheezed in the thin air, wondering which way to run.

He strung extra cross-ropes and hand fed a few of the most anxious to get their minds off the rumbles in the rear. By the time he was done, he was panting himself.

He was a little grateful for the work. Getting struck by lightning while inside a hydrogen-filled blimp was not something he wanted to think about.

When sunlight hit and everything turned bright green, someone in the back yelled, "Aussie, Aussie, Aussie, Oi Oi Oi!" and several joined in.

"Moo!"

"There, there." He patted her neck. "It's over now."

He leaned back against the ropes and sighed.

Looking through the hull, he could see the land below, and they were much closer to the ground. Shrubs and rocks were zipping past. The engines were settling down to a purr, so he didn't worry about it. If they were in danger of touching down, Grant would have tilted nose up and kept the propellers spinning.

He saw someone sitting on the boards, half obscured by the cattle.

"Hey, watch it there."

He moved closer and saw Captain Kelly looking back at him with an amused smile.

"Oh, sorry, Captain. I didn't know it was you. I was just worried. Sitting here will leave your pants marked green, if you're not careful."

She shrugged. "Hardly the most important thing on my mind right now. How are the cattle holding up?"

"They're okay. Didn't like the thunder much."

She nodded. "Pretty much a fiasco all the way around. The moisture we gained from the rains was likely burned up in the engines."

He nodded, glancing down through the skin of the *Lance*. "We're still pretty low."

"We cooled, and the gas contracted. Add to that the weight of the rain on the *Lance*'s skin, and we dropped too fast for my comfort. I really didn't want to have to dump ballast water."

She nodded toward the water swirling in the trough below her feet. The fins that grew inward into the tank kept the water from sloshing too fast for the pilot to compensate whenever they tilted, making it act like a thousand little tanks rather than one big long one.

He nodded. Sunlight and water kept them going, and while the sun was beating down on them now, they were in dry country. He asked, "Are there any pools left by the rains?"

"Probably some. We've been watching for any signs of the old reservoirs marked on the charts. Nobody much lives here in the high, dry parts of America, so anything we can find is free game. Still, the winds are too high this close to the weather cell to attempt to settle down and siphon the water."

Caleb tried to understand all the problems. He'd been lucky to get a posting to the Brisbane Fleet School, with his marginal grades and no family. He couldn't afford the upper levels. His training had been limited to how to handle himself inside a blimp and how to manage his cargo—not how to keep one flying.

"So... stay clear of the storms?"

She shook her head. "No. We need to take advantage of them. We're heading east, so if we see a storm cell, we need to steer to the south of it, to catch the Coriolis winds to increase our speed."

He frowned. "I didn't like the lightning."

"No one does. It's dangerous to let a storm catch you in an updraft. As we climb, and the bags expand, the *Lance* would eventually vent some of the hydrogen into electrically-charged air. Not a good idea. Pure hydrogen doesn't burn. Neither does the air. But mix them, and it's an explosive combination."

She sighed. "But I'd better get back to the deck." She pulled herself up.

Caleb glanced at her rear.

"See anything interesting?"

He flushed. "Uh. No. Just... brush it."

She did and smiled. "Don't get any ideas."

"No, Captain."

But when she walked over to the rope ladder and climbed up, he watched. Sure, she was twice as old he was, but she did make him feel warm inside.

...

Jason Bolls relaxed, leaning back in his comfortable chair, staring at the big display. "It's been too long, Bill. Still building airplanes for the rich and famous?"

Bill Melear's hair had gone prematurely gray and made him look much older. Jason made a mental note to get his own hair re-tinted.

Bill nodded. "Oh, some of that. Are you sure you aren't ready to join the owner's club? From the news, it sounds like you've got money to burn from your Junior King series."

"Hey, you know fads. Here today, despised tomorrow. Besides you know how my financing works. I'm paying off a lot of old debt."

"Don't I know it! My latest project is a black-hole money pit."

"Oh? No investors willing to supply up-front money? I thought that's what you'd decided to stick with."

"Hey, when did we last talk? Fifteen years ago. But it's still how I'm handling most of my planes. I've got real customers, not just wishful thinking like with your entertainment projects."

"But I'm the one with money to burn, right?"

Bill chuckled. "I know. But this latest project is something special. I'm doing it for me. Sure, it'll pay off in the long run, but I don't have investors. I'm not looking for investors."

"Not even an old friend who went to summer camp with you as a kid?"

"No. Not even you, Mr. San Diego Moneybags. I've got it covered, as far as the money goes. I'm just rattling your cage in the hopes that you'll come out and see what I've got cooking."

"Go out to Middle-of-Nowhere, Texas? You know I only travel by sea and land."

"Hey, we've got a wonderful rail line that goes through Midland. The TransAmerican passes through regularly. I'd even fly over to San Diego to pick you up, if I thought I could talk you into it. You don't do nearly enough screen capture in Greater Texas."

"Oh? You've got something to capture? We've got deserts here."

Bill Melear was silent on the other end of the connection. Then he said, "Jason, I'd like you here because you're my oldest friend. But I *need* your cameras."

...

Samuel went over the advice Anna had given him as he walked downstairs to the Presentation Room. The legal advisor had shown up just moments before the police car, and Mr. Winestock barely had time to introduce himself and ask a few simple questions before it was time to go down.

"Inspector," said the legal advisor.

The policeman nodded. "Winestock."

Samuel would have been content to let the two familiar adversaries do all the talking, but the Inspector turned his attention his way.

"Mr. Bolls, thank you for this opportunity to talk."

His voice was so flat and emotionless, Samuel was sure it was a standard greeting.

"Sure."

Winestock gestured toward the table. "Let's all have a seat."

They sat. Samuel felt a little disoriented. "Is there any...?"

His advisor held up his hand. "As young Mr. Bolls has just arrived from Northern Polynesia and is unfamiliar with San Diego legal proceedings, I would ask that all questions come through me."

Inspector Coab showed a glimmer of emotion then—a tightening of his lips, but he didn't object. If Samuel had to guess, he wasn't allowed to object.

The questioning started slow, just repeating a few known facts. He was Jason Bolls nephew, and this was his first visit to California. Samuel was seated where he could look to see a nod or shake of Winestock's head before answering. It didn't take too long before the questions took a more distinct flavor.

"When did you become aware that Rachael of the Rhineberg Family was a genie?"

Winestock began to object, but paused.

Samuel frowned. The question was provocative. He felt his way.

"I've heard the term before. Back in Hawai'i it's derogatory slang for a genetically altered human. Is it the same here?"

Winestock muttered, "Yes. Not usually used in polite conversation."

Samuel nodded, "So. When did I realize Rachael was altered? It was on the last leg of the journey, just a couple of days out. I had not had any contact with her before then."

"So you did have contact with her at that time?"

He frowned. What did the Inspector want? "Um. Yes. She found out I was a screencrafter and she had an interest in the industry."

"And did you know she was altered then?"

"Um, no. Not immediately."

"Someone told you?"

Winestock shifted in his chair. Samuel felt his tension.

"Well. Yes, a little later."

"Who was it?"

Winestock was poised to object, but he was waiting for his moment.

"Um. It was a man I had met earlier on deck."

"What was his name?"

Samuel was looking at Winestock. "I hesitate to say. Is this related to the explosion?"

Winestock cleared his throat. "Mr. Bolls rightly is respectful of the privacy issues that occur when peers mix with citizens in such circumstances."

Inspector Coab frowned down at the table. "Okay, I won't push it. I know it was Baron Jenner who warned you off. I also know he's publicly opposed to the *altered*. Let's talk about you. What are your feelings about genetically altered people?"

Samuel didn't pay any attention to Winestock's subtle shake of the head.

"Up until recently, I hadn't given it much thought. And I still don't know why you ask, but I guess I have some mixed feelings.

"For a couple of years now, I've worked with a man in Hawai'i named Tad Como. He's a news agent, handing out screen capture assignments to people like me. Tad has a daughter about four now. She was born with Down's syndrome. Shortly after I met her, Tad sold his house and arranged for a genetic patch to deactivate some chromosome or another—I never paid any attention to the details.

"Over the next year, the changes were visible, plainly around her eyes, and most certainly in her curiosity. I know Tad was relieved and happy with her improvement.

"I haven't been faced with that kind of problem. I've been lucky. Lucky with my choice of parents. Lucky that I've been given opportunities other people haven't.

"But if I had a daughter whose life could be improved with some gene tinkering, I hope I would make the sacrifices necessary to come up with the cash and get it done. I certainly don't fault Tad for doing it. And I certainly don't think any less of little Clarissa for being a bright little girl."

The Inspector asked, "And what do you think about Rachael Nue? Is she a bright little girl too?"

Samuel shook his head. "Maybe a little too bright for her own good. To be honest, this is my first encounter with genetic alteration as a boost above normal, rather than as just a fancy medical remedy. I guess I have some reservations about the idea."

"Will you be keeping in... contact with her?"

He didn't like the way that was phrased.

Samuel said, "I have had several people suggest that I should keep my distance from her."

The questions spread out a little after that. Samuel talked about his work on the Island, and in spite of Winestock's objections, his relationship with his uncle.

Eventually, the Inspector folded up his notebook, gave a formal thanks for the opportunity and left.

"What was that all about?"

Winestock looked out the window, watching the policeman depart.

"From what I've heard, Coab is under pressure to solve the explosion, and he has no leads. All he has is the fact that the only person hurt was Baron Jenner."

"I hadn't heard. What happened?"

"Oh, just smoke inhalation. And of course, the damage to his vessel. I take that back—there was a crewman who broke his arm while evacuating the ship. But really, it was an attack on the ship when the passengers and most of the crew were already gone. If there had been an explosion at sea, then there would have been many fatalities. The only person hurt was the baron and his finances, and his most likely enemies would be the genetically altered."

Samuel thought about it. "So he's checking that angle."

Winestock nodded, "Without being able to question the baron, or any of the other peers on the ship. If you had refused to co-operate, Bolls House is important enough to keep you away from him as well."

And since the explosion was external, and none of us on the ship are real suspects, he must be grasping at straws.

Police Action

Jason Bolls clicked off the monitor. He was sorry he hadn't followed up on Anna's notice quickly enough. At least the interview had been recorded for him.

Sammy isn't used to the politics around here.

Jason had always been too busy for a family of his own, and to be honest, he rarely thought about his brother Keith, who had gone off to Polynesia a year after he'd followed his own muse to the growing screen capitol of the world, San Diego.

He'd sent little Sammy money for a handset on a whim, back when he had been flush with cash from a big hit, and it tickled his fancy that the boy had emulated him. When he heard that Sammy wanted to come visit, he took the time to see what he had been up to.

His nephew had talent, and it gave him real pleasure to see S. Bolls listed in the credits. But that girl was going to scuttle his career if he didn't watch out. Maybe the inspector had put a scare into him. Maybe not.

He tapped the screen. "Anna, I need you to make some arrangements for me."

"Yes, sir."

...

The grounds of the Bolls House included a shaded and fragrant fountain, populated by so many birds that Samuel suspected a groundskeeper was kept busy by keeping the ornate metalwork benches cleaned of droppings. But it was clean now, so he sat in the shade. It made a big difference in the heat.

After watching a hummingbird methodically visit a row of trumpet-looking red blossoms, he pulled out the handset.

Maybe they won't like me doing this.

But unless someone was watching with binoculars from the house, no one would know. He slow-tapped Rachael's number.

The instant the call opened, the hummingbird zipped off out of sight.

"Please wait. I'll answer soon, really I will." Her nicely posed profile image froze in a smile.

He wasn't used to video calls. He'd never had the bandwidth where he had lived. The recording brought a smile. He was willing to give her a minute or so.

He'd seen a number of the old pre-Star "movies" when he was toying with the idea of making a fiction screen of his own. The Techno-era crime ones were fascinating. It was a given in those tales that police could always find out what people did with their "cell phones". It was incomprehensible. Inspector Coab might want to know if he were going to call Rachael, but he had no way of knowing—not without sneaking up in the bushes and watching him. What he did with his account was his alone. Even if he had to give this gadget back to Uncle Jason, once the account was closed and another entered, there was no history of what had happened before.

The image of her pushing her hair back appeared on the handset's screen. "Samuel! I'm so glad you called. Did you take a look at the information about the water show in the harbor?"

"Hi, Rachael. No, sorry. It's been very busy here, and I'm not sure whether I'll be able to attend."

"Oh," she pouted. "I was planning a dinner at the Green on Shelter Island. You'd love it."

He chuckled. "Probably, but I've been distracted. The police came here."

"Oh." He could see her thinking. She breathed out. "They were asking about me, weren't they?"

"Among other things. I think they're just tugging at all the strings and seeing what moves."

"And they wondered if you'd call to warn me."

He considered it. "Maybe. But I still can't see why they're even interested in you."

"Oh that's pretty clear. It was the baron's ship. The baron hates people like me. That makes me one of the puzzle pieces. The police called here too, but Daddy's man sent them away. I bet I'm not the only one. I know a dozen people on the ship who were returning from having work done on them." She was staring off-camera, distracted by unpleasant thoughts.

He was tempted to ignore the police and just take up her invitation in spite of all the people looking out for him.

"Tell me about this water show."

She turned her intense smile back on him. "Oh, that's out of the question now! Sorry. It was just a whim. We can't be playing into the police paranoia. Besides, Daddy was talking about getting me out of the public until this all blows over. I thought he was crazy, but I guess I'd better take him up on it." She looked sad.

He felt his chest tighten a little. If he had kept quiet....

"Samuel, I want you to stay out of the police's eye as well. I watched your coverage of the ship explosion three times. It was good. You and I will meet up again. We're both in this business for the long term. Bye for now. Stay safe."

When the image faded, he sighed and put the handset back in his pocket and watched the hummingbird return to its rounds.

...

"Coonabarabran," the king nodded over the image. "You don't look pleased."

"I'm not. The *Whistler* is down."

"Details."

The admiral glanced at another display. "Captain Foss had successfully delivered a full medical bay to the University Hospital of Geneva when the ban happened. They were immediately ordered to leave the city, not even given time to refill their water stores. Although they are in an area with several lakes, they were waved off several times. Captain Foss reported to fleet that without water, they weren't going to make it off the continent. They elected to take advantage of a low cloud bank to touch down on Lake Annecy with the plan to cross the Alps to the Mediterranean.

"Unfortunately, local hotheads put a couple of dozen bullet holes in the *Whistler*. The last report from the captain was that they were settling down close to the shore while they could still move.

"News reports from March District agents report that the Australians are being held captive. No lives lost, but the *Whistler* is sagging noticeably and my judgement is that in those waters, it won't heal itself."

The king clenched his jaw and nodded. "They take our goods and then shoot at us. Feed any updates to my system. I'm going to have a face to face with Berlin if I have to fly there myself."

Dale would have liked to watch—from a distance—when that happened. King Thomas was a typhoon at times, but King George and his father before him had made Europa into the strongest power on the planet, and he did not have a reputation for backing down. Thus far, Australia's efforts to get a response from the European Court had been shuttled off into endless bureaucratic dead ends.

It was as if Thomas had been reading his mind. The king grimaced. "They want this chaos to continue. The longer they can scare the populace into fearing the blimps, the more likely they can wipe them from their skies. At least that's what they're hoping for."

"What can we do?"

Thomas glared at him. "Do? We keep flying! You find and map every safe watering hole on the planet. If China still wants our goods, then make them a good deal. Reward our friends and punish our enemies. We certainly don't come running back home and wait for fair weather!

"You're Admiral of the Fleet. Make it happen."

"Yes, Your Grace."

...

The report from Europa was being auto-translated, so the reporter's mouth didn't match his words, but Baron Jenner wasn't paying too much attention to the words anyway. The deflating blimp on the shore of the beautiful Alpine lake was ugly, like a giant jellyfish washed up on a beach. The French reporter was trying to spin the story as a crime committed by the Australians blimp crew, but even he was facing the reality that the attack on the airmen had turned into a huge ecological disaster for the scenic community. Everyone was staying well clear of the dying beast. Right now fear of the hydrogen was rampant. It only needed a spark.

They ought to ignite it deliberately. The more of the numal that they can burn up the better. It will be horrendous when it begins to rot.

Jenner had given a lot of thought to the problems caused by dead blimps. In his dreams they all met similar ends.

But it would be best if they died over the ocean. I'd send ships to rescue the crewmen, if it came to that.

But this sudden turn in the fortunes of the blimp fleet wasn't his doing. Just like any other news spectator, all he could do was watch.

...

Jason found his nephew in the theater room, watching the report from Europa.

"It hasn't ignited yet, I see."

Samuel looked up. "No. Not as spectacular as a forest fire, but I wonder how they're going to dispose of it, once the hydrogen is gone."

"I hear the skin is really thin, so maybe it'll just dry and they can roll it up."

Samuel shook his head. "They shouldn't have shot at it."

"Probably not. But still, if you really wanted to stop one of those things, how could you, other than punching holes in it?"

"They might have hit the crew."

"Yes. I wonder if they deliberately shot at the upper gas bag—or if they were just lucky?"

"And what will happen to the airmen?"

Jason sat in the next chair over and helped himself to a handful of corn chips. "They probably violated some local rule or another. If I were their lawyer, I'd argue necessity. We've all seen what happens when one of those comes down on a hillside. That's a forested area, isn't it? Coming down on the water was the least destructive course of action."

The new announcer paused, and then said, "We have a report..."

The image switched, and King Thomas of Australia appeared. Crawl-text said he was at Graythwaite Castle in Sydney.

"Citizens of the World. We are beginning to see a climate of lawlessness descend across portions of this planet as certain governments goad their people into violating long-standing agreements on free passage and honest commerce. Contracts are being broken, Australian blimps are being destroyed, and innocent airmen are being detained and killed by reckless actions, all designed to cut Australian goods out of European and American markets."

Samuel whispered, "Did he say airmen killed? Does he imply the California crash was an attack?"

"Shhh. Listen."

The king looked stern. "Australia has made extreme efforts to open talks with the courts of Europa, Greater Texas, California, Mexico, Central Mississippi, Carolina, East America, Olympia, and Louisiana in an effort to bring order to this chaos and fear mongering. All have put up barricades to clear communication. Australia has to believe that this is a deliberate policy to harm the blimp fleet and Australian interests. These courts are playing with fire, and the lives of my people."

He took a deep breath. "Unless this changes, Australia will have no choice except to take direct action to protect the lives and wellbeing of both our airmen and the innocent bystanders being caught in this calculated economic ploy."

The speech lasted for twenty minutes more. There was a chart of the safety record of the blimps, highlighted by the two recent crashes—both blamed on a conspiracy of northern governments to hold onto their shipping monopoly. There was a display of his attempts to make contact with the other courts.

"I can't allow this to continue." He held up a finger. "One more attack on a blimp and I will take action."

Jason muted the sound as the news commentators popped up on the display. "Well I guess that answers your question. King Thomas as much as said that he considers the *Southern Cross* crash a deliberate attack."

"Does he know something we don't? I thought it was just an accident."

Jason shrugged. "It doesn't really matter. If he believes it, it's enough."

Samuel spread his hands, "And what kind of action? Cut off the affected governments? Would that do anything?"

"I don't know. I've heard that some fields of agriculture are becoming dependent on augmented crops—productive grains that can't be used as seeds unless treated with pollen imported regularly from Australia. That kind of thing. And then there's the medical applications. Maybe it's not important to you, but to someone with a disease that has to be cured by gene tinkering, it's vital."

Samuel sighed, "It's going to be messy."

"It could be bloody. Sammy, I have an assignment for you. I was going to go with you, but now I think I need to stay close to home base. Could I send you to capture an event in Texas?"

Samuel had expected something like this, a trip to keep him away from Rachael. But now, it sounded good.

"Sure. What is it?"

Strategy

In a secluded mansion on the north shore of Long Island, they talked.

"No matter how he phrased it, it's war he's talking about."

The gray-haired man across the table rubbed his forehead. "We have no more than five hundred troops, and they're scattered all over East America. Since the Berlin Accords, we haven't even thought about maintaining a standing army."

The third man at the table shook his head. "A navy. Australia is halfway around the world. Sure we could collect the ships, but our battle craft are out of date. We don't have the deck guns and torpedoes we'd need for that kind of show of force."

"Are we talking defense, or an attack on Australia? Do we even want that kind of long-distance conflict?"

The king's Minister of Public Affairs shrugged. "He just said 'direct action'. We don't know what that means. Maybe he'll drop bombs from those blimps."

"He'd lose more blimps that way. We have aircraft. It wouldn't take too much effort to toss a few flares out the window. Those gas bags are vulnerable."

Baron Hancock shook his head. "Bombing with blimps makes no sense at all. It would take weeks at best to load a bomb on board, and then deliver it. Unless this has all been planned months in advance, he can't be talking about bombs."

Prince Jeffries asked, "Is he really serious? Could it just be an effort to put Australia on the World Court? I know the second blimp was the result of trigger-happy Frenchmen, but that first one... I thought that was an accident."

"King Franco made a public statement that California had nothing to do with the first crash."

"And privately?"

"He's saying the same thing on the private links. It was an accident, no matter what Thomas is saying."

The Prince sighed. They were getting nowhere.

Around the world, in every targeted nation, identical private meetings struggled over the same issues, but that was no comfort. His king would need a public response soon enough, and it was up to him to prepare it.

...

Baron Jenner frowned at the message, stamped with the Berlin Court's emblem, as if the sending address wasn't enough. They wanted his assessment, in terms of military readiness, of his fleet of ships.

Oh, well. When they gave me the title, I knew there were strings attached.

He forwarded a flash of the message, under his sign, to his staff, with a top priority. That would raise a few eyebrows, and some blood-pressure readings. The message was vague enough that no quick answer would likely be correct.

King Thomas has certainly stirred up the hornet's nest. Does he know what he's getting into?

Probably a dozen nations were formulating plans to take down the blimp fleet. Jenner knew from his own research that Australia would never be stupid enough to formulate a classic Techno-era military attack using its blimps. If it came to direct confrontation, the fleet would scatter high and wide, and nobody had the means to track them all down.

From his own painful experience, he knew that Australia could grow new blimps relatively quickly. Their technology wasn't dependent on mining ores and skilled workers at shipyards. If they had to, they could seed hundreds or thousands of the baby blimps, let them grow wild and just capture the ones they needed. King Thomas might have already begun that process.

Any Northern nation who planned to knock them all down would be faced with too many targets, and little idea of which ones were vessels, and which ones were dumb beasts in the wild.

Is it the time to use it?

He settled back in his chair and let the possibilities play through his head. A few times, he tapped on the screen to bring up current information on the status of his merchant fleet and the blimp fleet. Surely, Australia had better details on their air fleet than he did, but from what he could see, there were dozens out of their habitual shipping lanes, where they followed the prevailing winds across their regular market zones.

Aborted shipments. That has to sting.

But there were still many more, making their way across the Americas and across Europa that were in danger of being shot down like that one at Annecy. While King Thomas might be playing for publicity in his announcement, he wasn't one to make idle threats. The next blimp to come down would be followed by some kind of counter-attack.

Until then, people were just guessing.

I could put my solution into play. I don't have to pull the trigger, but it might take too long to get it into position if Thomas has some real threat waiting.

He nodded to himself, then tapped a command. An anonymous message zipped across the Net requesting a blimp shipment of a cargo container from an isolated shelter near Sailor's Hat crater on the Hawaiian island of Kahoolawe, to a similar isolated facility near the volcanic Tarso Toussid in North Central Africa.

If I don't have to use it, I can have it shipped back later.

He smiled. It was one thing to plan an action for several years. It was another to set things in motion. No one but him would ever know about it, but it was satisfying to see the solution one step closer.

...

King Thomas sat in his quiet study, where no one was allowed to enter, and examined the statement from the Duchy of Louisiana word by word.

"...historic center of international trade..."

We realize siding with the blockade makes us look stupid.

"...deliberation of safety concerns..."

We weren't snubbing you, honest!

"...free and open use of the following waters..."

He frowned at the list. No Lake Pontchartrain. No Lake Borgne. He tapped up a detailed map.

Clever. We can land individual blimps in the area, but no places for convoys or a fleet. They're telling their neighbors that they're still holding the line against the evil Aussies, yet appearing to be a neutral port.

Should he call them on it, or not?

We could always land in the Gulf waters, but calm, protected landing zones and fresh water is nothing to be disdained.

He tapped a text message to the Fleet Admiral. Notify the blimp captains that the listed waters were safe to use, and don't try to push the boundaries.

I can negotiate an expansion once the current tensions ease. This is a political limitation, not a practical one.

He would take a day or so to phrase a proper diplomatic response. Give them time to worry about his silence.

Louisiana was just one little piece of this puzzle. While he could hope that the others would find ways to accommodate the fleet, he wouldn't bet that way. There were already too many little people that had been encouraged to load their guns. They would be resistant to change their minds.

Someone will pull the trigger, and I have to be ready with a careful, proportionate response. They need to realize that I am already acting with restraint.

He pulled up his Black Projects list. *They can't close the sky to me, without risking the loss of the sea.*

...

Travel by rail was different than an ocean voyage. Samuel stared out the window at the rapidly-passing countryside.

I think I like the ocean better.

The broad expanse of water and the seemingly unchanging course and speed of the large ship gave a peacefulness to sitting on the deck chair. You had days to travel, so there was incentive to get to know your neighbors. The deck was wide enough for walking, or running, if you felt energetic, with a variety of indoor entertainments to pull your attention if you were bored.

Outside the train, it was hot, dry desert, with an occasional ghost town flashing by too quickly to let you get more than a taste.

At least they have one thing in common. The bandwidth is horrible.

He played with his handset and discovered that it was a different beast out here where bits tricked in from the slow-speed radio bands. He had taken a few sample captures from the observation car. Samuel had frowned as a memory-use chart appeared, showing how much of the handset's internal storage was used. With the current bandwidth, it would take too long to transfer it to his real account storage. It was discouraging, and he resigned himself to taking fewer background captures and preserving his handset's memory for newsworthy items.

I hope Midland is close enough to Dallas to have a wired Net connection, otherwise it'll be difficult to feed my screens to the Queue.

He had a heavy satchel in his stateroom that Uncle Jason had handed him as they had rushed off to catch the evening departure of the TransAmerica. Supposedly it had more storage and a foldout display for better editing capabilities.

He could tell it was going to be an odd assignment.

"I don't know what Bill Melear has in store. He wouldn't tell me, not over the Net—and that's pretty paranoid, if you ask me. But Bill is the top aircraft designer in the world, and he's not crazy, so if he wants his new project captured, then it's likely something important." Jason scratched his temple, swaying as the car moved through San Diego traffic.

"But there's one other thing. Several times, Bill mentioned an event that happened to us when we were kids. It's been a secret, just between us, for all these years and it's not public knowledge.

"I'll tell Bill that it's alright with me if he shares it with you. I suspect that it just might give you some necessary background to his latest project."

Samuel didn't know what to make of that. Still, an assignment was an assignment, and he had learned to jump in with both feet. Whether it was lava flows or burning ships, it had generally paid off.

Thinking of the ship explosion, he tapped for news. All that was available at this bandwidth was crawling text headlines. Various countries were claiming innocence in the California blimp crash. Other commentators were searching for ways to add their own spin to the events. Many were giving historical summaries of Australia or King Thomas. Others were analyzing the blimp disasters. One even had located pre-Star records of airships and struggled to compare their safety records with the modern numal blimps.

One commentator caught his attention. He was showing Samuel's own coverage of the Queen Helen explosion and was making the effort to fit the still unexplained disaster into the current political news. It was hilarious, reading the text-only commentary, which was probably auto-generated from the commentators voice-over, on top of his own script. He could just imagine the video, and try to make sense of the text as it mangled together his words with the newsman's. He flagged it to watch sometime when he had real bandwidth.

He gave it up as an exercise in frustration and watched the desert again. His mind drifted back to his first trip to the main island of Hawai'i. The interior had some dry landscapes, although not as barren as what was passing by outside the window. It was no wonder that large stretches of the American interior were vacant. After the Star, there had been widespread fear that the atmosphere was permanently damaged. High altitudes were equated with skin cancer. The mountainous backbone of North America, added to the desert landscape, had kept this land empty. There were a few isolated way stations on major highways, but trains had captured the bulk of the travel from coast to coast.

He looked at his fellow passengers in the observation car. Little kids were racing down the narrow aisle, catching glares from a businessman working on his portable. Why the businessman was up on the observation car, he didn't know. He certainly wasn't enjoying the scenery. About half the seats were occupied, and many, like him, just gave momentary attention to the outside.

I guess I don't really have a good excuse to be up here either.

But it wasn't crowded, and it was more restful than sitting in the tiny little sleeping compartment that Uncle Jason had booked for him. It was a day-and-a-half trip, and he was grateful he didn't have to sleep in the seats.

Maybe I should explore the rest of the train. Supposedly there was an entertainment car where kids could play games, and he'd need to visit the dining car before too long. But exploring a long string of nearly identical rail cars didn't appeal to him much. Most were likely just people sitting in their chairs, watching him walk down the aisle.

But food—I could do that.

He was even on an expense account.

He got to his feet and was halfway down the steps to the base level when his handset vibrated. A message must have made its way through the restricted Net.

He paused to lean against the wall before he pulled it out.

Rachael's face appeared almost instantly over the text announcement of her attempt to contact.

"Samuel, I'm sorry, but I've had to leave town, and Daddy was insistent that I contact no one until he had me smuggled away in the middle of the night."

He noted the image quality and wondered just how long ago she had sent it, for it to have made its way through the Net's slow store-and-forward system.

"Daddy's spies even saw the police watching the airplane—like I was some kind of criminal escaping justice! I don't think I like the San Diego police."

There was a *clunk* noise as the train passed over a joint in the rails, and an instant later, he heard a muffled version of the same thing over the handset.

"So Daddy put me on this train and I'm supposed to..."

"Rachael."

She looked puzzled, and then focused on her handset. "Samuel?"

"Yes. I'm on the TransAmerica."

The bandwidth between devices within the train was fast enough to show her quick uptake. "You're here?"

"I guess so."

"I'm restricted to my cabin."

"What number?"

She grinned. "Hang on..." the image motion-blurred then settled back onto her face. "...car 3B8, stateroom 2."

Edits

Her room was right next to the observation car. He knocked on her door a moment later. She opened it up, a brush in her hand and dressed in rumpled khakis.

"You're too early!"

"No matter." He slipped in, and closed the door. Her room was twice the size of his, but it still looked small. He sat on the bench seat and smiled as she made a few token passes with the brush.

"I'm sorry for the mess. I was resigned to spending the whole trip to the Carolinas cooped up in here."

"You're fine."

She smiled, and it was the most timid expression he'd ever seen from her.

She whispered, "I shouldn't have let you in here. Daddy is strict about security. I'm going to be in so much trouble."

He shrugged, "No one has to know."

She looked worried, "No. Daddy always knows. I think his spies follow me around, but I haven't been able to put a face on them this time."

"Well, let's just put that aside for now. I'm happy you're here. I was wondering how I was going to spend then next twenty hours."

She frowned, "Only twenty?"

He nodded. "I'm on assignment. I get off the train in Midland, Greater Texas."

"Oh. I'm here all the way to the coast."

"Then let's quit wasting time! Have you eaten lunch yet? I was on the way to the dining car when I got your call."

"No, but I have to get my food delivered here."

He smiled, "My cabin is close. I'll order something as well on my account and sneak it over."

···

Captain Thorpe eased the *Croc* out of the cloud bank he'd been following. The ban had caught him in the center of the American continent, but he'd managed to reach the wide open Great Lakes, for a safe passage most of the rest of the way east. He rode high over Syracuse and followed the clouds as they eased through the gap between the Appalachians and the Adirondacks. There was a lake below, but he didn't need the water. All he had to do was to stay out of trouble and reach his confirmed landing zone on Long Island.

All was clear. The stars were out, but the moon wasn't up yet. There were moisture droplets all over the *Croc's* skin, but he could see the way—clear and downstream, toward the Hudson River in the distance.

"Shapcott, how is the cargo?"

Down below, among the bundled trees, came a voice. "They ain't complaining."

The captain shook his head. He'd never thought a cargo of thirteen-hundred fruit trees would be so much trouble. With the detours, and the unplanned elevation changes, there'd been a scare when they started dropping leaves. Shapcott seemed to have it under control with a nutrient change and more water. He'd be glad when they had them unloaded.

"Captain! There's a light below."

He moved close to the front. Parker was pointing, but it was bright—probably a searchlight aimed right at them. "Take us up, under power."

Back in the rear, the slow murmur of the propellers rose to a complaining roar. The floor underfoot shifted as they pitched up. Voices of the crew called out below.

The captain called to his Comm officer, "Jerry, let fleet know our position and tell them this lake appears hostile."

"Yes, sir."

"Another light."

As he looked, his pilot gasped. "Rocket."

"Dump ballast. Turn to starboard."

···

The Earl of Coonabarabran dashed down to the big board, his fork still in his hand. "Report!"

"Admiral. The *Croc*, out of Dunedin, reported a rocket launched at them as they were passing high over Ashokan Reservoir, north of New York in East America. They were not attempting a landing. But then their message stream dropped away."

"Tracking beacon?"

"Gone as well."

He closed his eyes. "Log them as missing. I'll be in my office."

"Yes, Admiral."

...

King Thomas took the news matter-of-factly. "Keep me informed."

He retired to his room and pulled up a list. The *Croc* was mid-sized, with a crew of nine. He pulled up another list—the Royal Cargo Vessel Real-Time Registry.

He found a candidate. The *Blue Whale*, leased under the East American flag, carrying shipping containers from New York to Belem on the Brazilian Coast.

It had a crew of nine.

Another list, from his Black Projects, gave him an ID number. He entered the code, and with a solemn face, pulled the trigger.

...

They had her stateroom drapes open wide. With the lobster and steak shared around, the landscape passing by outside didn't look so barren.

"Tell me about your assignment."

He cracked a claw, and picked the white meat out with a tiny fork. "I don't have much to tell. A friend of my uncle wants captures of his latest project, some kind of aircraft. An airplane. I suspect part of it was to get me out of town."

"Away from me?"

He nodded, "And the police." He took a moment to savor the butter-dipped treat. "But I didn't have anyone following me—at least no one I've noticed."

She looked outside. "I think we're already out of California. If the police wanted to stop us, they would have made their move before now."

He smiled, nodding.

"You're enjoying this, aren't you?" she asked.

"A little. One of these days I need to write a script, and I need to know what it feels like to evade the police and escape to another country."

"You'll need to interview a real criminal then, not just be a person the police want to talk to."

He grinned. "You take the fun out of it."

"Well, I'm serious! My project was to wow the San Diego screen industry, and that stupid explosion messed it all up. I've got nothing to look forward to but the same faces I grew up with until it's resolved. You're my vicarious look into screencrafting. I want to know everything you're doing."

"This is hardly what you need. This is news, and maybe background captures. Melear Aircraft could be doing corporate fundraising more than anything. It's minor."

She reached across the tiny table and poked him in the chest. "*You* are going. You *are* going to do your best, right?"

"Well, yes. If it's important to Uncle Jason, then I have to do my best."

"You're going to capture the scenes dramatically. You're going to mine raw events for eye appeal. You're going to build a library of scenes that you can edit into a feature. That's all standard stuff. It's stuff I should be learning. I should be going with you and getting my fingers in the process. Diana Jameson would have."

She sat back down and sulked. He remembered their first meeting when she said she wanted to be like that historic figure in the screen industry. He knew the feeling. He felt the same way about Uncle Jason.

"I'd take you with me if I could, but you're going to the Carolinas."

She pouted. "I could sneak out."

He shook his head. "It wouldn't work. First, you're a famous person. Your father wouldn't let you vanish off the train without tracking you down. Didn't you say that there's probably someone already on the train watching out for you?"

She raised her chin, "I've been sneaking past those guys since I was eight."

"And if you did, they'd ask themselves where you went. My name would come up, and five seconds later, they'd know I took the same train. Your family plane would land in Midland shortly thereafter and take you away."

He shrugged, "Besides, you'd never work behind the camera."

"And why is that?" She crossed her arms.

He smiled. "Because you're too beautiful. Before you say a word, the instant you walk into a room, every man looks up at you. Conversations stop. Thoughts get jumbled. You are one of the Beautiful People, and it definitely works as advertised.

"You would disrupt every attempt to capture events. Even without makeup, every eye in the place would turn to your face."

She stared down at the table. "I don't wear makeup anymore. This is part of the BP package."

He looked closer at her flawless complexion, her clear blue eyes, and her sharply defined brows. "Must save time."

She glared at him, a perfect golden lock of hair straying over her forehead. "I have to be able to function. It's not really that bad, is it?"

Samuel hesitated, then said, "It's pleasant, and stimulating, being in your presence. Addicting, almost."

He shifted in his seat, unlatched the window glass, and took a deep breath of the hot, arid outside air to clear his head. She was frowning when he sat back down.

"I'm not doing anything to the air in here!"

He nodded. "I didn't say you did. Is that a BP thing? Baron Jenner implied that it was."

She nodded, the frown deepening. "It can be, but I have to activate it. It's not autonomic." She sighed. "I wanted... I wanted to *work* with you. I didn't want some chemicals meddling with your brain."

"That's good to know. I just don't really trust myself—not here, in private, with you."

"You haven't even tried for a kiss. Most guys would have, by now."

He nodded, a sad smile barely making its presence felt. "I've moved too fast in the past. I've sworn off."

"Oh? An old romance."

He laughed. "Maybe on my part. She had other plans."

She leaned closer, the frown vanishing as if it had never been. "Details. I want dirt."

He shook his head. "No dirt. I was haole and she was very much a part of her ohana. We were friendly enough, but that was all, for her."

He straighten up. "But enough of that. I came to the mainland to learn my trade. Getting side-tracked is not on the menu."

"Well, that's fine with me! Isn't that what I've been saying all along? Why can't we do this assignment together? Just assume I can slip free of Daddy's spies."

If he told her his true feelings, it wouldn't go over well.

He scratched at his eyebrow. "What would you do? Be my pack mule? Carry my gear?"

"I have a professional camera on my handset! I could take alternate views."

"Okay, show me what you've done."

She fumbled with her luggage and hauled out a larger portable. She tapped the screen and saw the deadly crawling text of low bandwidth.

"Hang on, I've got some things in the cache." She tapped and scrolled. "Here."

It was collection of short captures, most two or three minutes long. He watched the collection of party shots—all with bad lighting and horrible sound, without showing his expression.

"Wait. Stop and go back." There was a sunset on a beach.

She looked at his face. He pointed. "Can you edit this sequence?"

"Yes." She brought up the controls.

"Okay. Zoom in and bring this man sitting on the chair to this spot in the frame."

He coached her into moving the center of attention away from the sun to the man watching it. Then they adjusted the brightness to tone down the sun's glare and bring up the range of colors in the sunset clouds.

"Mark that frame, and now move on a few seconds."

By the time they stopped, they had trimmed half the time off the capture and dramatically improved its impact.

She sighed. "All my stuff is junk, isn't it?"

"No. There are bits of goodness in there. All my captures have to be edited like this before I can ever turn them loose on the Net." He gestured at the screen. "This is yours, just cleaned up a bit."

"But I should have framed it better to begin with, and paid more attention to the lighting. The edited version is great. It's a shame I can never show it to anyone."

"Why?"

She grimaced and tapped the image of the seated man. "That's Daddy, and he never lets himself be visible to the public." She gave a short laugh. "He wants to be like the Gnomes, I think."

Outside, the light was fading. "How many captures do you have?"

"Um. Maybe a hundred or so."

He shook his head. "If you want to do good work behind the camera, you need to do a lot more than that. Are you sure you really want to be involved in that part of the process? You're already on the fast track to be in the focus field."

She shook her head, her lips tight. "No. I'll enjoy that part, but I *need* to know how everything works. I want to be the chess master, not the pawn."

"It takes work."

"I know."

He nodded at the glow on the horizon. "And I have to work tomorrow. I want to be there to watch you get better, but this assignment isn't the time to start." He paused. "I had better go to my cabin now. I want to be rested when I show up."

"You have other options." She took his hand. It felt warm and soft and he wanted to hold it longer.

"No. I don't." He let her go.

Midland

Lit by the dawn, the boat looked like any normal fishing trawler, swaying in the waves. It was anchored just off a two-hundred foot long island, barely a rock, just east of Grenada in the Caribbean. The captain scanned the water with his binoculars, looking for the tell-tale burst of vapor, hardly different from what a tiny whale might blow.

What he wasn't expecting were the visible ripples in the surface, as something very fast moved just under the surface like a torpedo. He smiled, and slapped a lever, lowering an underwater hatch.

Before long there was a thump under the hull, and he moved the lever back.

Ducking down below, the captain turned on the lights and saw, above a face with no nose, eerily nonhuman eyes staring back at him through the aquarium tank. He gestured a question to the numal merman with hand signs and his partner gave him a thumbs-up in return. The captain reached for the feeding tank, then stopped when Abel 8 grinned back at him and took out a bite from the parrot fish he had already snagged for himself. Those sharp teeth made short work of the fish, bones and all, and the captain was sure his merman was laughing at him. Fresh fish might have been a good training treat, but when Eight was out in the open water, he was a capable hunter on his own.

Abel 8 picked up the laminated images of the ship that detailed where on the hull to place the sticky metal plate. He put them in the slot where his human could reach them. He was done with that task. Abel 8 enjoyed watching the land person, with legs that worked funny, and the strange appendage in the middle of its face. The ridiculous human was nearly his only entertainment. How long would it be before they went back to the island where his brothers and sisters lived?

Ten minutes later, the captain watched the puff of smoke on the horizon, and heard the muted explosion several seconds later. He went to the comm unit and sent the code for unqualified success.

...

Rachael didn't acknowledge his morning call, so as the Midland station approached shortly after lunch, he composed a message:

Sorry to miss you this morning. I just wanted to let you know, in case you didn't see the news—there has been a second suspicious ship explosion, just like with the Queen Helen, this time off in the Caribbean. The news commentators are linking it to the blimp that was shot down with a rocket. They think it's Australian retaliation. If so, it's an act of war, and not a criminal act. That should take the San Diego police out of the picture, and put it in the laps of the royal courts. You might be back in the California social whirl sooner than you thought.

Keep me informed about your movements. I'll want to see what you've been doing with your camera.

Until then, Samuel.

...

Whether it was an ocean liner or a passenger train, disembarking was rife with frustration. He had more luggage than he liked with the addition of his uncle's capture gear, and unloading on schedule was always urgent— even more so on a train than on the liner.

He was instantly hot and sweaty as he rolled his bags out onto the platform. He turned and counted down the cars and windows. Rachael's window blinds were closed, but he waved at her anyway. He might have imagined it, but it looked as if the blinds moved.

"Mr. Bolls?" A short bald man called his name.

"Yes, sir?"

"No 'sir' about it. I'm Marcos López, come to pick you up."

"Thanks." Marcos waved him toward the exit, but didn't offer to help with the bags. That was fine with Samuel. The VIP treatment in San Diego had felt a little strange.

They loaded into a utility van showing a logo on the side with 'Melear Aircraft' and an airplane image. Airplanes were rare enough that he was tempted to stop and capture the image right there, but he decided it could wait until later.

Aircraft had suffered from the popular distrust of high altitudes—until the past few years, at least. From the little he knew about the craft, a lot of the new developments were reinventions of pre-Star designs. He had seen bamboo and cloth gliders flown near Haleakalā on Maui, but the ones in the news were all smooth and metal and breaking new speed records.

I'd love to get a capture of a new plane in flight. How can I do that without just getting a blur in the sky?

There was also the question of what kind of an assignment this was supposed to be. Was it news event reporting—or a commercial PR process? Uncle Jason had told him to ask Mr. Melear.

He didn't have much time to think about it.

Marcos waved as he drove. "The train station is close to the airport. It's halfway between Midland and Odessa. Neither city wanted to let the other one get the station, so they split the difference."

He turned onto a curved road. "This airport is pre-Star, and you'll see a lot of old vintage planes. Not many of them fly, but this was something of an aircraft museum even before everything got fried."

The driver had become animated the instant they came onto the airport grounds. Samuel got the feeling that he gave this tour a lot.

"See that B-25. It's a bomber. It saw service in the war with Japan."

"When was that?"

"Oh, long before the Star."

Samuel had seen the ship graveyard at Pearl Harbor, so he had some sense of the time the man was talking about. *Ancient stuff—back when people made huge ships and great metal planes.* Even the Queen Helen had not been the size of some of those derelict ships in the harbor.

One of these days I need to read the history of that time. It had barely been taught at school—no more than a day or so, lumped together with the Greeks and the Romans.

As they walked into one of the large hangars, Samuel was still trying to digest the strange planes, especially the ones with gun barrels sticking out from their bodies. The idea that those old wars were violent times, with bullets flying around like bees, was gradually creeping up on him.

Bill Melear was thin, but he seemed to be made of springs—always turning about, shouting at workers up on the wings, or dashing across the waxed and polished concrete floor of the large open-spaced hangar to adjust some machine himself. Samuel waved off Marcos when he offered to make the introductions.

"Just a minute. I want to see him in action."

His handset was in a forward-facing shoulder pocket, and he set it to record. As long as he didn't wave his hands too much, he could get a good capture just by walking around.

There were at least three planes in the hangar. There could be more, hidden in the tangle of hoists and carts and cranes. It was a huge open space, and he could imagine it filled with twenty planes or more. He was out of his element. He had trouble focussing his attention, and thus the camera's. There was activity and noise coming from all directions. There were even birds chirping from the rafters above.

"Marcos, these three planes look like different types." He had to talk louder to be heard.

"Yeah, it's a madhouse. Bill wanted to clear the deck for his test flight, and he's rushing to finish off some of the jobs in process."

"Can you tell me about this new plane?"

He chuckled. "Sure, but then Bill would shoot me. It's his baby. Ask him."

Samuel nodded and began walking toward the man. Melear had his arms out, fists at his waist, watching like a hawk as a plane was being moved inch by inch up closer to the wall.

Abruptly he turned, sized him up and said, loudly over the noise, "Samuel Bolls. Marcos giving you the tour?"

"Yes sir!" He had to shout to be heard.

"Hang on until I get this Beech parked, then we'll talk."

By the time they moved to a little office, one of several along the southern wall, his ears were ringing.

"Have a seat." Melear gestured, still talking loud.

The room was decorated with photos of hundreds of planes. There were two drawing boards against one wall and three high-end displays along another. The desk was cluttered.

"Jason said he was sending his nephew. What do you know about the project?"

"Practically nothing. It's some kind of new airplane. Uncle Jason said to follow your lead."

He nodded. "He called last night and said you were competent. He also mentioned that you were interested in the Gnomes."

Samuel winced. "Well, it's been a hobby. Every time some new tech shows up, somebody claims it came from the Gnomes. Either that, or it's re-discovered Techno stuff."

Melear frowned, "With good reason. I've been working all my life, re-inventing things that some Techno wizards had already worked out before the Star. I was starting to think that there was nothing new to be discovered. Maybe they had invented everything that could be made and the Star was just destined to set us back a few places on the board."

He shook his head with a smile. "But that's just frustration talking." He sat down in his chair and propped his feet up on his desk.

"Tell me about yourself. News reporter, are you?"

"Some of that." He smiled. "It seems to pay the best, but I've been growing up watching Uncle Jason's screens. Romance, comedy, maybe an occasional documentary—that's what I'd like to be doing. Showing things to people that they've never seen before."

He nodded. "How are you at keeping secrets?"

Samuel frowned. "I... have a few, I guess. But I'm not interested in blabbing everything I know. That's not good storytelling. Nobody wants to watch a second-by-second replay of what happened. It's always a process of showing what contributes to the story, and leaving out the boring and the side trails. I'm still learning that."

"What if something wasn't boring, but needed to stay secret?"

Samuel knew Melear was looking for a certain answer, but he didn't know what to give him. He shrugged. "I guess if I thought it needed to stay secret, or I trusted the person who thought it should stay quiet..."

"I guess that's all anyone could ask." The man was frowning, thinking.

Samuel held up his hand. "Wait a second." He fumbled with the handset, turning off the capture. He shrugged, "If you're going to be talking secrets, I guess I'd better not be recording."

Melear chuckled. "I'll never get used to how small cameras can be. Thank you."

He got up and moved to the front of his desk, sitting on the edge. "There's a secret Jason and I share. He said you could be told. I hope he's right."

"When we were ten-year-old kids, we met the Gnomes."

Discovery

Thirty-eight years before:

"Bill! Jason! What are you going?"

Jason looked up innocently, "Canoeing, Mr. Mendoza. We're supposed to meet down at the lake."

Their cabin counselor frowned, but nodded. "Okay. But you two are restricted to the cabin when you get back—until your bunks are made and all your gear is stowed. I'm not going to clean up this mess for you. You've both got two marks on the board already."

"Oh, we'll get it all straightened out before inspection, no problem."

"You'd better." He looked at Bill and gave him a glare for good measure. Bill was the quiet one.

They were halfway down to the beach when Bill asked, "The canoe practice is supposed to be back by the dock."

Jason shrugged, "Yeah, but its only going to be safety stuff—like how to put on life jackets. I had it all before."

Bill grumbled, "I wish I had come last year. Where are we going?"

"I found this place. Come on, and stay low!"

The wire fence keeping them in was marked with the Texas Royal Cub Scout logo, but the little feeder Jacob's Creek that trickled into Canyon Lake had eroded away the soil below one of the fence posts. It took little effort to crawl underneath and into the wooded lands just south of the little town of Wimberley.

Jason whispered as they vanished into the tangled undergrowth. "My dad was a real Cub. He could go out into the woods and live for weeks off the land, he told me." He saw Bill's expression and added, "That werewolf stuff is just legend. Cubs were real people."

Bill said, "My dad is an engineer. He rebuilt the Buchanan Dam. He and some other guys."

They scrambled over a downed set of trees. "This is different from last year. I bet they had a flood."

"Where did the werewolf legends start?" asked Bill.

"They're really old. I've seen some pre-Star films they salvaged in Austin. One of them had werewolves. France or someplace like that."

Bill pointed. "What's that?"

They climbed up the muddy slope of the creek bed. It was a metal cylinder, too large to move, with some funny marks on it.

Jason had a wide grin, "This is Techno. Has to be. We can sell it on the Net."

"Is it ours? Who owns this land?"

"It's crown land... probably. But nobody knows this is here. Found treasure. The flood washed out this slope and uncovered it. Who knows how long it's been here?"

Techno salvage was a popular, and sometimes profitable game on the Net. Jason told about the burned-out cabin in the woods his father found with an intact, but Star-fried car in a detached garage. He sold that. Bill had heard that old computers could be sold for parts.

They paced off the location of the cylinder, back to the fence line, and then went back to the cabin.

···

Bill Melear chuckled at the memories. "Of course, old Mr. Mendoza had discovered that we'd snuck out of the camp and confined us to the cabin. It actually worked out well for us.

"Jason had always been a Net junkie, even back then. I don't know how he'd managed to smuggle a Net box in with his gear. Those things were huge back then. He dug down into his duffel and when we turned it on, it was clear we were out of signal range. That didn't stop Jason. He had a spool of wire and we stretched it all across the cabin to make and extented antenna. It was just enough to pick up a minimal signal.

"It was a simple, standard Offer. We described the metal cylinder in detail, and the funny markings on one end. We didn't say where we found it, or in what condition. We didn't add our names, so it went out anonymous under Jason's Net ID."

He shook his head. "You know, when you're a kid, sometimes you play make-believe games. Storm the castle, fight off the Hunters—things like that. At the time, it seemed like one of those. We were going through the motions, but I never really believed anything would come of it.

"Morning was just another day, Jason quickly strung his wire antenna and checked his account, but there was no response. We took it down and went on with our camp activities—a rope maze, if I recall. Later, I had a moment to sneak down to the cabin, and that's when it got weird."

···

Bill ran into the cabin and grabbed his belt knife, then paused and dug down into Jason's duffel.

How did he turn this thing on?

He clicked the switch and the lights came on. After a moment, the call light also lit up.

A call! Is it a reply to the Offer?

He tapped the read button, but was immediately asked for the Net ID. But he didn't know Jason's number. Quickly, he spread the cover over the device and hurried out to find Jason.

As soon as they were able to sneak away from the pack, they went back at the cabin.

"Are you sure there was an answer? Did you string the antenna?"

"No. I turned it on and the call light—the green one, came on."

"That shouldn't have happened, with no signal."

They uncovered the device and flipped the switch.

"There is signal! There wasn't any last night." He tapped the long ID number.

The message appeared on the little screen:

Offer being considered. Meet outside the camp gate ASAP.

Bill asked, "What's 'asap'?"

"As Soon As Possible. I'm confused. How do they know where we are, or who we are? We didn't include our names."

Bill shook his head. "Doesn't matter. How do we get outside the camp gate?"

Jason checked the time. "It's nearly lunch time. I think they leave the gate unlocked so visitors can get in and out. It's worth a shot."

They hurried over to the entrance gate, staying in the shade of the Live Oak trees until it appeared no one was watching. They slipped through the opening and ran down the road. There was a black van waiting in the shade.

"Is that them?" asked Bill.

"And who are they?" They slowed to a walk. As they reached the van, two very short men stepped out from behind the van. The boys stopped in their tracks.

The man on their left asked, in a voice too low for his size, "Are you the ones who made the Offer?"

Jason nodded. "Yes. Who are you?"

"We are interested in your salvage."

Bill watched them carefully. The quiet one looked almost identical to the one who was talking, down to their simple brown suits and sunglasses. They wore matching golfer's caps.

"We want a million dollars." Jason said boldly.

"That is impossible. We offer two hundred."

"Not enough. Who knows what's inside—it's Techno. It could be worth ten million."

"Show it to us. We can assess how much it's worth."

The boys hesitated. Bill spoke. "We know its location, but we have not removed it. It was too large."

The quiet one spoke for the first time. His voice was slightly different, more mellow. "Please describe the device, in detail."

Jason was excited, and could hardly stand still. He blurted out the description, adding all the details, from mud stains to how it leaned against the slope."

"So, you think it is metal, but you are not sure?"

Jason thought about it. "It was like an old pre-Star refrigerator, you know? When you touch it, you know it's metal, but maybe there's a coating over it?"

"Describe the markings."

Jason tried, but they were just strange circular markings to him.

The low-voiced one said, "We will pay two hundred dollars now, in cash, for the location of the device." He pulled out a wallet and removed two bills, spreading them like a 'V'.

Bill nudged Jason, and whispered, "Take the money."

Jason was sweating. "But it could be worth so much more!"

The mellow-voiced one said, "We all know how difficult it would be for boys of your age to deal with larger quantities of cash. It would be unlikely your parents would let you spend it. Let me make an additional offer.

"Once we take possession of the device and assess its value, we will offer you a line of credit when you become adults." He produced a pen and a notepad. He scribbled and tore off the sheet. "This is a code number. Use it when you request credit." He held it up in his other hand, opposite the money.

Jason looked at Bill, and then sighed. "Okay."

He pulled out a folded and smudged sheet of paper where they had written the directions back to the cylinder. Solemnly, they exchanged the map for the payment. Without another word, the two small men stepped back into the van and drove off. The boys stared at their hundred-dollar bills.

Jason asked, "What's a line of credit?"

...

Samuel shook his head. "It's a good story, but it doesn't make sense. Net boxes, even the originals, kept the identity and location of the sender secret. From what I understand, it's wired into the protocols, and no one can override it or decode it. How could your Gnomes locate you?"

Bill Melear nodded. "I've thought long and hard about that. I have to conclude that the Gnomes, if that's what they were, had a tricked out Net relay in their van. That's the only explanation for the signal strength when their van was close, but none when it wasn't. Maybe they already knew about the device, what it was, and roughly where it would be. Maybe they could detect when the relay was active. I don't know. That's not my field. I do know two things, though. The device was gone within hours. They had moved in with some tracked machinery and lifted it out. And I also know that line of credit was good. Both Jason and I owe our fortunes to it."

"What? Explain."

Melear gestured at the hangar around him. "Starting a new business, or a screen project like Jason's, requires a lot of up-front cash. So, you have to borrow the money, and if you are successful, you pay it all back later with the profits.

"The catch is that bankers don't like to loan money to young unknown and untried entrepreneurs. It's very hard to get that first round of money to prove yourself in the first place.

"Jason figured it out. He had a big screen project that needed funding, and his usual sources just weren't forthcoming. He was desperate. So he applied to the Gnomes for an equivalent value of Net Credits, using the code we were given as kids. Amazingly, the loan went through instantly. He converted the Net Credits to the cash he needed for his screen project. It was a big hit, and he took profits and paid it all back."

Bill Melear smiled. "Jason met me at a restaurant and confessed it all. I was hard up for cash myself. I was trying to build a jet engine with current technology that could be used on the old pre-Star airframes. I had long ago lost my copy of the code but Jason shared it again. I followed his steps and soon had the cash necessary to build my engine. It was the cornerstone of all that I have done with Melear Aircraft.

"I have to believe that we saw the Gnomes that day. Your uncle is really the guy that popularized that name for them with his stories. But we're not telling anyone what we saw that day, or the secret of the line of credit. That's too dangerous. Jason was alway threatening to make a fantasy story that told our tale, but he never did. I was surprised when he suggested I tell you."

Samuel shook his head. "I don't think I could tell your secret if I tried. No one would believe it."

Melear chuckled. "Welcome to our world. But maybe with this under your belt, you'll be able to understand my new project. After all this time, I think the thing we sold to the Gnomes has finally appeared."

Delivery

Caleb was on edge, and the cattle picked up on it. He had to keep the cross ropes up longer than he had planned, but it would not be wise to ease off on safety, just when they were in sight of their delivery.

"Are you sure?" he asked Saul. Through the clear skin at his feet, he could only see an endless patchwork of fields. Central Mississippi had brought to mind a great river, but all he'd seen since they left the desert lands were fields and isolated patches of trees.

"Leave it to the captain. She has all the maps. I'm sure she's in contact with the client. We've got guaranteed water. That's all I'm worried about."

Caleb frowned. "I can't understand how she could navigate with this maze below. There are no landmarks."

Saul chuckled. "Captain can navigate anywhere. She's got the pigeon mod." He tapped his head.

"Oh. I didn't know." He had heard of the gene mod that gave an extra navigation sense to people. He'd thought that was something he would like—especially if he were going to be an airman all his life. It would give him an edge, and maybe get him out of the cow dung and up onto the captain's deck.

"Prepare for landing," she called out, her voice carrying the whole length of the *Lance*. The cattle mooed.

He checked his feet and moved to the leading edge of the cargo platform. Below, the checkerboard was coming at them. In one of them, there was a large 'X' marked with a dozen or so white sheets. They landed belly down on the mowed field. A couple of the crew were already out the nose ports, attaching landing lines to a large farm machine of some kind.

"Hold for gas release!" They couldn't unload immediately. It would be like dropping all the ballast water at once, and more. The *Lance* would likely drag that farm gear aloft, or more likely, snap the line. Extra precautions had to be taken, releasing that much hydrogen into the air. Four percent hydrogen in the air made a fire hazard. Eighteen point three percent made an explosion hazard. That was drummed into him dozens of times during his airman training.

Up above, on the spine of the *Lance*, a trio of holes slowly opened up. They were biological valves, stomata of the giant leaf, slowly allowing hydrogen to escape straight up. Luckily, the day was calm. With a side breeze, the hydrogen had the chance of being captured by a side-draft and concentrated close to the skin. With the calm, they could vent hydrogen faster.

The ballonets were expanding as the *Lance* attempted to pump more air into them, trying to make up the internal volume lost by the hydrogen. But it couldn't keep up, and the airship was visibly sagging from its normal shape.

Caleb was laying out the ramp, boards that had been stacked double around the edges of the corral, now overlapping to make a path for the cows to walk without punching through the blimp's skin.

And then the mouth opened up. It wasn't a real mouth, of course, but three layers of skin overlapped on the lower, leading edge of the blimp, all securely fastened together in flight. But now they were laid out, and rolled up by the ground crew.

"Okay, girls." Caleb jumped back on the wooden deck and began opening up the rope gates. "Time to move out."

Saul and Danny were positioned on either side of the ramp with prods to keep them moving in the correct direction. The cows started slowly, and Caleb wanted to keep it that way. This was no time for a stampede.

Maybe they remembered loading up. In any case, they behaved themselves. He had to round up a couple of reluctant ones, but soon they were out, and it was like a great weight had just dropped off his shoulders. His job was done. He would likely be dead weight on the returning leg of the flight. There was no cargo to pick up. Maybe he could sleep.

He walked down the ramp and stood on solid ground for the first time in ages.

"Okay, your money has been transferred. Now get out of here as quickly as you can." The farmer's accent was strange, and he sounded abrupt and worried.

Captain Kelly said, "Hold on there. We need to refresh our water. We can't even lift off until that is done."

"I can't help that! You shouldn't have come down in broad daylight like this. Someone is sure to have seen you."

"You promised fresh water and a safe landing zone."

"I did that! But things have changed. You Australians have gone crazy, sinking ships—killing people. My neighbors aren't going to take it kindly, you're being here. Get your water and be gone. I'm not going to stay and get caught in the crossfire."

She yelled at him. "There's no crossfire! We don't have guns. We aren't killing anyone. You northerners are burning blimps and killing us. All we wanted to do was deliver your cargo, and now one of my best friends is dead. Don't call us crazy! You're the ones who started it."

"Get out! Get off my land!"

She screamed. "We can't! Not without the water you promised and are contracted to deliver. If you don't want your farm burned to ash by your bloodthirsty neighbors, you'll help us replenish our water!"

Caleb started lifting the boards and stacking them. It sounded like there was no time for enjoying the fresh air and sunshine.

He frowned. Captain had never lost her temper before. Had that been building up?

She saw his stacks. "Dump the boards. Get rid of all you can until it's time to lift off. We need to get aloft as soon as possible.

He nodded, "Captain." He ran back inside and began cutting the fasteners, and carrying boards outside.

The farmer showed them how to work the water pump and then drove off, leaving the cows to fend for themselves. At least the green girls were happy. They had fresh forage and room to move.

As soon as they got the big fat water hose up into the ballast trough and started the pump, they began purging the dregs of the old salt water. It would probably hurt the farmer's soil, but that couldn't be helped.

Caleb worked single-mindedly, sweating as he stacked the boards high.

He'd just started a new pile, not as tidy, when the call came. "Sealing up!"

He paused and set the board down. He took a moment to look around. The water in the ballast trough was full, and a couple of the ground crew were pulling the hose out.

The sun was shining brightly, and that was their only salvation if, indeed, farmers with guns were coming. The *Lance* was busily splitting the fresh water into hydrogen and oxygen, and the blimp was slowing regaining its shape.

Captain yelled to the ground crew, "Drop the line the instant we begin moving."

Caleb sat down on the platform, still mostly intact in spite of all the lumber he'd dumped on the ground. He could only pant and try to catch his breath.

He thought about her order. Normally they waited until they had more than enough lift so that they went up fast, to clear any obstacles.

I guess we could move early. The land is flat enough that we're not likely to run into anything if we drift off at ground level.

Down below, he watched the contact area between the ground and the blimp shrink steadily as they lost weight. Danny was walking the perimeter of the platform, his patch kit belted around his waist, looking out for any punctures from rocks or sticks on the under surface. Blimps liked to land in the water or on smooth, paved surfaces for a reason.

The Healer abruptly lowered himself off the side and applied a quick patch. It was probably just a precaution. In any case, the *Lance* would heal itself from minor injuries.

He climbed back up onto the platform. Caleb nodded. *Better to be safe than sorry, if the skin is damaged. Walk carefully for a while.*

Then the *Lance* reached neutral buoyancy. The rope that had been looped through the farm machine slipped free and they drifted upward a couple of feet.

"Dump ballast," the captain called out. "Three seconds."

That made a difference. They started upward at a respectable climb.

Caleb nodded, "Leave it up to the captain. She knows what she's doing."

Back in the air again. Caleb relaxed, and realized he'd been tensed up the whole time they were on land. In spite of the fresh air and sunlight un-tinted by the blimp's green skin, he was more comfortable in the air, moving with the clouds.

Down below, the fence line, dotted with trees, moved slowly beneath them, followed by a ditch with flowing water. Shortly, he knew, it would all be just anonymous patches of color, but for now, each field was distinctive.

Then there was a road, a truck passed by underneath, and a car. It stopped.

Crack! The board three feet away from him splintered into pieces.

"Gunshot!" someone called out.

There was a zip noise, like a passing insect, only gone in an instant. Caleb froze, not sure where to dodge. He screamed, "Second bullet! Just missed me."

The captain was calling out orders, moving them and dumping another second of ballast water. They surged under a few seconds of full power, and then abruptly, she called the engine to full stop.

Danny came running to where Caleb sat. He looked upward from where he stood. Handing Caleb a patch bag, he said, "Here! You're on my team now. Look up."

He did, and followed Danny's pointing finger. "That second bullet went straight on through, up through the hydrogen bag. I have to patch the outside. You crawl through the plenum and patch the underside. Nothing but your uniform. Empty your pockets and be gentle. The plenum skin isn't very strong."

Caleb nodded. He stuttered, "Ah... are there going to be more bullets?"

Danny was solemn. "Not our business unless they come. Then we'll patch them. Get!"

Caleb blinked and then nodded. He dumped his tools and checked his pockets, then made for the rope ladder.

The captain nodded as he hurried up and then opened the flaps that secured the plenum layer that ran the whole length of the ship. All the control lines from the pilot's console to the engines and the fins ran through this little oxygen-filled layer between the hydrogen bag and the cargo bay. It was barely tall enough to crawl through, but it thinned out to nothing the farther from the center line it got.

He was going to crawl toward a bullet hole, a weak spot, on his belly.

I am not afraid of heights. I am not afraid of heights.

Moving slowly, to make sure he put no excess pressure on the thin layer holding his weight, he gauged his distance by looking down at the wooden platform below.

Behind him, he could hear the captain talking to the engine crew. Danny was there, at the aft where the engines were mounted, already making his way outside through an access flap. He would have the tougher task—free-climbing up the spine of the blimp to find the exit hole and patch it.

But he likes that.

Caleb slowed down, knowing he was getting closer to the hole. There was a chance the hole below him would split wider and drop him. It was an even bet whether he would smash against the boards or miss them and punch his way through the belly of the *Lance*, falling all the way to the ground below.

Go gentle. He saw the lower hole first, but that wasn't his first priority. Just above it was the puncture into the hydrogen bag.

"I found it!" he shouted, but his voice came out in a squeak.

The captain yelled, "Gas talk! Hydrogen in the plenum. Caleb, I'm sealing you in for now. Get it patched."

"Okay!" he squeaked. The captain's voice had been affected, just slightly, and that was a bad sign. When your voice went high-pitched, it was a sure sign that the air had enough hydrogen in it to be explosive. It had to be sealed away from the electronics in front. It would also have been bad, if air had been leaking into the hydrogen bag, but it was less urgent.

He was suddenly aware that his ears were ringing and the world seemed a little woozy. He was short of oxygen. Training told him to breath deeper and faster than he would normally. Breathing reflex was controlled by too much carbon-dioxide, not by oxygen need.

The patch bag resisted his fingers for a moment, and then he pulled out one of the circular ones and he peeled the protective layer off the sticky side and slapped it firmly against the hole above him.

He breathed deliberately for a moment before patching the hole below him.

"Patch done!" he squeaked, but he wasn't sure it was something they could understand.

He had to back his his way toward the captain's deck. It seemed to be too complex an operation to turn around. He edged backwards, and then paused to rest. The last clear thought he had was how nice and smooth the blimp's skin was against his cheek.

Going Dark

"Your Grace, another one."

King Thomas sighed, "How bad?"

"A shooting, after a successful delivery. Holes patched. One crewman had to be rescued when overcome with hydrogen leaks."

"That makes how many attacks?"

"Eight today. After the ocean vessels went down, public sentiment up north got nasty. Even government orders to allow the blimps safe passage isn't stopping random violence. Several blimps have reported parties of armed gunman following their movements. One has requested permission to turn off the Net relay."

"We wouldn't be able to track him then. Everything runs through the Net interface."

The admiral agreed, "I don't like the idea either, but people on the ground in rural areas can easily detect a blimp in their area by the increase in Net bandwidth. For them, it's an early warning system giving them time to get their guns and start hunting Aussies. I'm inclined to give the captains that option."

One of the consistently profitable side effects of the Blimp Feet, was the Net traffic through the relays each one carried. At a high cruising altitude, a blimp could relay signals from a city many miles away, and the fleet of blimps would automatically network with each other to relay connections across hundreds or thousands of miles.

Thomas asked, "*Can* they turn it off—without cutting cables?"

"I had to check that myself, and yes, there is a diagnostic mode that turns off the external radio transmitters. The Comm officer on each blimp could enter a code to turn off their signal, and another code to turn it back on. I looked for a way to restrict traffic to and from Fleet HQ, but the relays are too promiscuous for that. Net traffic for one is Net traffic for all."

"Okay, then. You're right. Notify each blimp that they have that option, but if they go dark, they should attempt to turn it back on for a short time twice a day so we can know they're still alive."

···

Baron Jenner had the latest court update on one screen, and compared it to his own shipping fleet reports on another. The situation was deteriorating rapidly. King Thomas was absolutely vindictive. Every incident with the blimps immediately turned into a disaster for a Jenner ship. Maybe the king thought he was targeting the countries that were taking action against his people, but in reality, it was all turned against Jenner Shipping. Half the countries on the oceans had leased their fleets from his operation. Jenner shipyard at Bremerhaven was the premier shipbuilding center of the world.

As he sat there watching his screens, some of his ships were sinking, others burning at port. Other countries had also contacted him regarding ship availability in case there was to be an attack on Australia. There could easily be a multi-national effort to stop the conflict.

I can't let Thomas continue this extortion. And only I can throw a roadblock in his plans.

···

"We'll have to flush the plenum several times to make sure the hydrogen is purged." Captain Kelly was holding the air hose as Ray, the Comm officer, was sealing the flap to the plenum tightly around it.

Caleb asked, "Is Danny okay?" His head was pounding.

"Yes, the *Lance* is patched. He's taking his time getting back."

"The shooters?"

"We're out of range."

He tried to move, but his legs were rubbery.

"Just take your time. Breathe some good air."

He nodded.

A moment later, Saul poked his head up, a big grin on his face.

"Hey, kid. I've got something for you."

"What?"

He handed him a little lump of metal. "The first bullet that hit next to you. I thought you might want it."

The captain asked, "No signs of any other bullet holes?"

Saul shook his head, "No. Just those two. The one that went all the way through, and the one that splattered the boards."

Ray was back at his console. "Captain, Fleet has authorized us to de-activate the Net relay, if it is a danger to us."

She nodded. "About time." She looked at Grant. "What hazards would we face if we turned it off?"

The pilot shrugged. "Are we still planning to follow the river south?"

"Unless there's a good reason not to."

"Then I say turn it off. We'll lose map updates and weather reports, not to mention the news, but that great big river is hard to misplace. Turn it back on every hour or so to make sure we're not missing something, but I'd rather stay high and invisible if we can."

She agreed, "My thoughts exactly. We can do without the news for awhile."

Caleb fingered the mangled little lump of metal. Maybe he would like to know what was going on in the world, but it wasn't his place to offer an opinion. He was on the captain's deck by invitation only, and he planned to stay until told to leave.

...

The *Divine Chariot of the Gods* wasn't its original name, but when Joe Rather had the opportunity to purchase a second-hand blimp, he couldn't leave it with the original name. For one thing, the name its previous owner had given it couldn't be spoken in polite company. The *Chariot* was small, one of the early-generation commercial blimps, and didn't have the speed or lifting capacity of the latest green giants from Australia. It was originally designed for a crew of five, but Joe had his own way of doing things.

He kicked the metal plate on the console and his chair slid around on rails to the comm station. Carefully, he composed an Offer, phrasing it to keep his expenses down. He requested two experienced blimp linemen to be picked up and returned to Dakar after a short job to last no more than two weeks.

He scooted over to his weather and navigation desk and double-checked his arrival time to the west coast of Africa, then rolled back to finish off the request. He was still just barely past the Central American coastline, and with that hurdle passed, he had nothing to do but stay on course. He sent off the message and then checked his current course and speed.

Locking the chair in place, he got up to stretch his legs.

Flying a blimp was never designed to be a one-man operation, but he'd proved it could be done. He didn't even need linemen when he was making deliveries to established ports. Unfortunately, the big ships would easily outbid him there. He made his nut with oddball, unscheduled, point-to-point deliveries like this one.

And it had been a lifesaver. He'd been stopped at Honolulu when the *Southern Star* went down and all the requests for deliveries to the mainland dried up. He'd been living at the comm terminal, just hoping for anything he could bid on. He had to have a paying job quickly, or port charges would wipe him out. Disastrous measures had crossed his mind, like "losing" the *Chariot* in a windstorm and getting a ground-side job. He wouldn't even be able to sell the blimp in the current market. They were living creatures—you couldn't deflate it and park it in storage until things got better.

The *Chariot* would live or die by the jobs it could handle.

When this one had popped up, he'd bid blind, not taking the time to calculate expenses. The Offer closed almost instantly, taking his bid. He probably could have charged more, but a job was a job.

After scratching his nearly bald head over the sketchy details, he had picked up a couple of out-of-work linemen to fly with him over to the coordinates on Kaho'olawe and together they positioned the *Chariot* over the sealed container and attached it to the belly harness. The bigger blimps could swallow their cargo whole, but he had to make do with hopefully weather-tight containers. It made ballast resupply a tricky maneuver, hovering just above the water, keeping the cargo out of the drink, while the siphon hose gulped up the water. That was another of the reasons Joe preferred an established port where resupply could be handled under controlled conditions.

He'd paid off his linemen and let them down by ladder. After that it was smooth sailing.

Fleet channel was disturbing. Yes, he was part of the Australian blimp fleet, but he was born in San Diego. If this developed into a full scale war, he just might be faced with the choice of moving to the blimp-friendly territories or giving it all up. Joe didn't really like either option.

Nor did he take the option of turning off his Net relay when the word came.

I'm just going to stay high. I'm past the Americas, and Dakar is listed as a friendly port. Nothing can reach me here.

He went to the pantry to fix a lunch.

In the featureless cargo container, slung beneath the blimp, a Net controller received an anonymous coded message. It translated the command, checked the altitude and then pulsed a voltage spike to the detonator.

···

Fleet Admiral Dale grunted and griped at no one in particular. Everyone listened.

"I hate it when a blimp goes off-line. Each time the dot on the screen vanishes, I tense up. I know it's likely just some captain taking precautions, but I can't help fearing the worst."

A young lieutenant hesitated, then she said, "Sir, I could make a list of blimps that haven't reported their location in several hours."

He nodded, "Your name?"

"Lieutenant Glynde. Assigned here last week."

"Okay, Do that. Give me a list, about once an hour, ordered by how long they've been silent."

She winced. That was more work than she'd intended. "Yes, sir."

Demo Time

Samuel checked the framing on the second camera his uncle had sent. It was on a tripod taking a broad view of the demonstration Bill Melear was setting up.

The aircraft designer was making some adjustments in the foot-long, hefty-looking metal cylinder he had set up on a tripod of its own. Samuel moved in closer with his handset camera.

Bill looked his way and grinned. "Are you ready for the show?"

"Yes. Go ahead and tell me everything, even the stuff you explained to me before. Anything you forget, I'll add as voice-over in the edit."

Bill grimaced. "The public stuff, at least."

"Right. But you can cut stuff later, too. Don't edit yourself too much when you're talking. Talk to me." He tapped the handset with his fingers. Bill nodded.

It had taken a couple of days, fitted into Bill's heavy schedule, before they agreed what kind of message they wanted to present to the world. Bill had just wanted his project documented. Samuel wanted much more, with a teaser presentation to get the public's initial interest, real-time coverage during the main event, and then a two-hour, in-depth presentation for the people that were really interested. Bill had to be the face of the introduction. He had the reputation and the expertise. He had flown the first faster-than-sound, post-techno plane. If he said this new thing was more important than cracking the sound barrier, people would listen.

Samuel already had the capture running, so when Bill took a deep breath and put on his salesman smile, he was ready.

"Hello, I'm Bill Melear of Melear Aircraft, and I'd like to show you something that's been sitting in the laboratories for a decade now—and it's something marvelous.

"When my plane, the *Black Lightning*, broke the sound barrier a few years ago, the commentators said that we had finally matched the Techno age and that we were no longer living in the shadow of the past. Well, anyone in the aviation industry knows that was a bit of hyperbole. The skies are not filled with supersonic planes like they were before the Star. They're filled with blimps." He chuckled, and Samuel made a note to edit in some sympathetic laughter from the imaginary audience.

Bill shifted his posture a bit. "About thirty years ago, someone found a Techno device unlike anything we know about. It must have been just a laboratory prototype back when the Star happened, because even though we've recovered so much of the Techno's science that was lost, I haven't been able to find a hint of anything like this."

Samuel smiled when Bill's real grin came back. The man was a much better communicator when he was talking one-on-one rather than speaking to an audience.

"Now, I'm an engineer, not a scientist. This gadget has been in the hands of a couple of PhDs at the University of Texas for a number of years now—Amanda Bate and Frank Nance. Maybe they understand the deep physics of it all, they're certainly the only ones who know how to make the devices. I'm just lucky enough to have licensed a few of the units to play with.

"Let me show you a few things."

Bill stepped aside and pointed to the cylinder positioned between two stacks of bricks. "That's the Nance-Bate Momentum Field Overlap Generator, and believe me, we need a better name for the thing. It's set on 'push'. Watch as I pulse it for a fraction of a second. Three...two...one..."

The device was completely silent as it hurled bricks twenty feet in both directions. They crashed onto the asphalt, some of them cracking and shattering.

Bill shrugged. "As you can see, with no fuss or flame or explosion, the device pushes equally in both directions. According to the experts, the push follows the old tried-and-true Conservation of Momentum: mass times velocity equals mass times velocity. So, let's see what happens when the masses aren't equal."

Samuel kept recording as Bill moved the tripod a few feet to position it next to a larger pile of bricks. He patted it. "Five hundred pounds. And on the other side..." He reached into his pocket. "A baseball, which weighs about a third of a pound."

He set the baseball resting on the rim of a small drinking glass, and held the glass gingerly by the base, positioned right in front of the cylinder. With a control in the other hand, he said, "Three...two...one..."

He pushed the button, and the baseball zipped away. Samuel tried to track it as it arched across the landing strip and started bouncing away, hundreds of feet into the distance. He panned back to Bill, rubbing his hand. "I barely held on to the glass this time. I shattered three of them while practicing. But you can see. The bricks barely moved, and almost all the energy went into the baseball. MV equals MV."

Samuel zoomed closer to his face. Bill was thoughtful. "The scientists were more concerned about the theory of how it all works. The engineer in me can see many practical uses, not all peaceful. But maybe we don't need a silent way to knock down buildings or a smokeless cannon. Let me show you what I'm really excited about in the next demonstration."

He paused, and then signaled to Samuel that he was done. "You can take a break. I've got to bring the gear out from the hangar."

Marcos appeared from nowhere. He must have been waiting silently for the capture to finish. "Excuse me, but your other equipment has arrived." He pointed to the hangar where a man waited with several bags.

"What?"

Marcos shrugged. "A guy wearing Bolls coveralls showed up and said he was your pack mule."

Samuel nodded, trying to keep his suspicions from showing on his face. "I guess I'd better go see what my uncle sent me then."

···

His pack mule was leaning up against the wall, looking bored and disinterested. The height was about right, but the hair, poking out from beneath a faded cap, was a drab brown. The chest was flat and the small man looked about twenty pounds overweight.

Samuel cleared his throat. "I understand you've brought me more equipment?"

He straightened up abruptly, as if startled. "Yessir. A Clearstone wide-angle, a Teleview extender, a bounce lighting kit, an extra memory buffer, and a Mark III edit station."

Samuel nodded with a wry smile. "Good job, Brighteyes. What is your name... today?"

Under the carefully applied makeup, her face reacted, clear blue eyes widening. She fumbled and found sunglasses in a breast pocket, and put them on. Clearing her throat, she replied in a voice that sounded close enough to male that it would raise no suspicions, "My name is Clark. Clark Peterson."

Samuel was really impressed by the masquerade. If he hadn't been clued in by the pack mule reference, Rachael might have fooled him, for a little bit.

"Okay, Clark, take the wide-angle over to the camera on the tripod, move everything closer to where Mr. Melear is setting up the next demonstration, keeping the same field of view that I used before, and begin streaming its memory to the buffer your brought. And I'll need it ready to capture as soon as the demo is prepared, so you don't have much time."

"Yessir." She grabbed the buffer and the lens and hurried over to the camera.

I'll need to warn her not to run. Her hips sway too much. He shook his head with a smile.

Of course, he'd need to talk her into leaving as soon as he could. His reason for staying clear of her father's investigators was still valid, even if she did look mostly like a smallish middle-aged man.

And I need to prep my own camera.

He walked slowly back to where Bill was working, trying not to pay any attention to Clark's work. He made sure his captures were streaming over to the buffer in his bag and then put his full attention on Bill's equipment.

...

Bill looked serious as he faced the camera. "And now we get to the real point of these demonstrations." He gestured at the setup. "This time, I've got a large block of lead clamped to one end of the device, and the other end is aimed out across the open sky of the landing strip. I want to make sure that there is nothing but air in the other half. And notice that I've got the Nance-Bate Generator strapped to a wheeled cart, instead of perched on top of a tripod.

"Ready? Three...two...one..."

Samuel had been coached ahead of time, so he was able to pan the camera to follow the cart as it lurched as if struck by a giant hammer and rolled several dozen feet before coming to a stop. In the other direction, Marcos was chasing his cap after the sudden gust of wind stripped it from his head.

Samuel glanced at where Clark was standing. She looked at the frame in the editor and gave him a thumbs-up. The wide-angle had gotten it all.

So he panned back and zoomed in on Bill, gesturing at the cart.

"This is what I had hoped to see when I first heard about this device that could push matter from a distance. By clamping one of the masses to the device, it could propel itself.

"You see, I am probably the world's leading authority on modern jet engines, and I have to admit that we have yet to be able to match the raw power that the Techno era could achieve. We just can't make the metal alloys that they used to create their versions. I've tried all my life to come close, but with today's materials, we run up against limits on the heat of the exhaust, and the strength of the spinning turbines. We can't yet duplicate the old engines or match their power.

"So you can understand my excitement when I heard of this new technology. I'm an engineer—an aircraft designer. I've acquired and tested a much bigger version of this gadget, one with enough power to push a large jet plane through the sky, one that has no moving parts and operates with no roar of flame. I'm going to fly a plane like the world has never seen. And I'm going to make history doing it."

Training

Danny was waiting for him at the bottom of the ladder when the captain finally shooed Caleb off the command deck.

"I thought you'd still be up on *Lance*'s back."

Danny gave him a half-smile, "Some other day, when we're not being shot at. I needed help. Since you're now useless with no cattle to tend, the captain gave me you for grunt labor. Come on."

They headed over to the now-vacant cattle platform. Danny gestured to the splintered board where the bullet came through. "The *Lance* has been irritated."

"A bullet would irritate me too."

Danny shifted his weight and stared up at the gas bag above them. "It's more than just a couple of holes. I know the people who designed the blimps in the first place were just attempting to make a flying machine that would grow, but their raw material was alive." He knelt down and spread his hand on the skin below. "The 'ancestors' of the blimps had their own ways of dealing with injury, and not all of those traits have been bred out of the blimp design. Come here and feel this."

Caleb frowned and went down on his knees. As he spread his hand over the smooth skin of the *Lance*, he felt it. "Bumps. I don't remember feeling bumps before."

Danny nodded. "That's one of the stress reactions. It wasn't just the bullets coming through. We belly-landed on an open field and there were probably many pointed rocks and twigs and stuff that were jammed up against the skin. The bullet shattered the wood and dropped splinters all over the place. The crew were all running full tilt from place to place. Even the adhesive of the patches, as mild as they are, are probably contributing to the stress chemicals in the ship's skin. Those bumps are reactions as the blimp is trying to heal itself, and feeding different hormones and nutrients to where they are needed."

He looked Caleb in the eye. "Many, maybe most of the injuries will heal up by themselves, but we have to help. Natural plants and animals have had millions of years to work out the glitches and fine-tune their stress responses. The blimps have only been alive for a blink of an eye, and the scientists who created them were only human. It's up to you and me to inspect every inch of the *Lance* and find all the irritations and do our best to fix them."

Caleb noticed a splinter of wood next to his hand. He picked it up. "Every inch, you said?"

"Every inch."

Caleb looked down the length of the ship—hundreds of feet of uniform green. He sighed. "And I thought I'd be able to catch up on my sleep."

...

Samuel pointed to the company parking lot. "Clark, I've arranged a room for you at the place I'm staying. Take the data packs and the edit station and load them in that white-sided truck. Get your gear as well. I'll meet you there as soon as I check tomorrow's schedule with Mr. Melear."

"Yes, Boss."

He sighed once Clark was out of sight. Today had been his only chance to punish her for this prank. She'd obviously put a lot of effort into the masquerade, not to mention money for some expensive gear, but showing up at the work site with no warning was a ridiculous risk. What would Bill have said if she hadn't been able to pull off her old-man disguise? And what would he have reported to Uncle Jason?

Once they were in the truck and out of sight, he was sure Rachael was going to let him have it, but the workload he'd given her wasn't much different from what he'd have expected from a real assistant.

He remembered his first days on a capture, back when he'd wrangled an after-school job at the Honolulu News Service. The new guy always gets tested to see what he's made of. And when the new guy was a white haole in a family-run business, it was extra special. For days they'd had him hauling equipment, emptying the trash, and even cleaning the bathroom before they realized he was sticking.

Rachael did a good job. No complaints.

He confirmed that Bill would be busy on his other projects until mid-afternoon and then went to the truck. She was sitting in the passenger seat, fast asleep. He was two miles down the road before she stirred.

"Oh. Where are we?"

"Heading to the motel. I've booked you a room near mine."

"A separate room?" Her normal voice, rich and resonant, was a disconnect from the Clark appearance. She looked very much like a girl in a costume when she spoke that way.

He nodded. "We're on an expense account. Workers on a job like this would have their own rooms." He grinned. "Or at least, I would have a room of my own. If I had a bigger crew, maybe they would double up."

"Because you're so special."

"Exactly. The nephew of the big boss."

"You're enjoying this too much."

He frowned. "No, I'm scared this will blow up and cause a problem too big for me to handle. Jason Bolls has a lot of pull, especially in San Diego—but it's nothing like the power your father could apply. He could make me vanish if he wanted. If you're staying here, it has to be as Clark, and he has to be invisible, just like today."

"Hmm." She stared at the windshield. "You're no fun." She began rubbing her upper left arm.

"Problem?"

"It's just sore." She glared at him. "No problem."

"Well, put Clark's voice back on. We're here."

They checked in and got the key for Clark's room. They loaded the equipment on a luggage rack and wheeled it down the corridor.

"I'll want to do a rough edit of what we shot today, but after we eat."

"Room service?"

He shook his head. "I don't think they have it."

She looked startled. She took a breath, "Okay. I was looking forward to..." She whispered, "This outfit chafes."

He nodded, "Okay. Go get comfortable. I'll pick up something at the restaurant and drop by a little later."

She smiled gratefully and vanished behind her door with her bag.

He took the time to verify the screen captures in the datastores before he went to pick up a couple of steaks from the restaurant next door.

The news reports playing for the customers made him sorry he'd come. Europa declared its borders closed to all airships, although King George declared that all blimps still on the continent would be allowed to leave unmolested. The news commentators were making their own guesses on how Australia would react, and whether any of the other nations would follow Berlin's lead.

Samuel was happy to walk out with the food and leave it all behind him. There was a scrolling death count below the talking heads, and he was shocked how bad things had gotten in just a short time. He could never have imagined a war, just a week or so ago. Now it was saturating the news reports.

...

"Out!" King Thomas ordered, not even looking as his old personal servant Emanuel Busby bowed deeply, leaving left the study. The door closed with a solid click. The silence of the room was comforting, a result of thick walls and strategic use of tapestries. It had been built with the idea to keep distracting noises out. Today, it kept the chatter of the world in.

One entire wall had been covered with displays. Not as tidy and organized as the huge one he'd seen at fleet operations, but it gave him the pulse of the moment. There were news screens from all over the world. One row was a direct connection to his own secret army.

King Thomas waited for the official notice to arrive from the European Embassy before preparing his statement. It was a matter of self-control. This conflict was escalating much more rapidly than any he had studied in history. Part of the reason was the instant communication between heads of state, although he suspected he was the primary driver. He had seen this war coming for years and he had his assets already in place. He could react almost instantly to every attack by the northerners.

But maybe I should slow the pace down. I may have a finely tuned machine, with immediate reports and quick response, but the northern courts blundering all over the place.

He had to keep the end-game in sight—a free and open world where everyone wanted to buy Australian. Too many deaths and that couldn't happen. But neither could he let any idiot out there shoot down his blimps for fun either. He had the responsibility to protect his people.

Listening again to King George's latest message gave him an idea.

Inspection

If the steaks in the pressed-cardboard take-out containers weren't slowly getting cold, Samuel would have taken a moment to stop and get a firm grip on his feelings about Rachael. As it was, he felt like he was sliding down a chute, heading into the dark.

Maybe she was just determined to learn the craft. For certain, she didn't really understand when someone told her no. He would have to make her understand. This game was too dangerous. If not for her, then for him.

On the job, pretending she was Clark, it had been easier to keep his mind on the job, but once they were behind closed doors, there would be different rules.

I have to keep this all on a business footing. She's a trainee. That's all.

He took a deep breath, shifted the food, and rapped the door with his free hand. After a moment, the door clicked.

He opened it. She was out of sight. "Clark?"

"Come in," she replied in Clark's voice.

With the door closed, she appeared, draped in a drab terrycloth robe with her hair wrapped in a towel. She hadn't been kidding. Right out of the shower, and she needed no makeup.

"Sorry, I didn't want to be seen," she spoke quietly in her own voice.

"No problem." There was hardly any furniture. He set the steaks down on a dresser top that had seen its share of use. "Don't take too long getting dressed. I think they're getting cold."

She opened one of the containers and breathed in. "I'm starved. And this is it. I only brought Clark's clothes." She moved to the bed and sat against the pillows, sawing at the steak with the cheap knife.

Samuel took the chair and tried not to pay attention to her legs. "Okay, tell me the story. How long before your body guards show up?"

She waved the fork and mumbled. "'Sokay." She swallowed. "I've got it covered. You said I was too pretty. I'd be a distraction. You have to admit I've got that covered. Clark is just another guy."

"But when you went missing, they must have started tracking you down."

She waved the fork and swallowed, then said, "But I haven't gone missing."

"Don't tell me you told them you're here!"

"No. They think I'm in Dallas. I got off the train there. Once the war news started, I send a message to Daddy telling him I didn't need to hide from the police anymore. It was your idea that the bombing was war-related. I told him I was staying with Ellie Poutron, an old friend of mine from school. As far as they know, I'm still there."

He concentrated on his food. "What does she know?"

Rachael laughed, and it was like a soothing, warm drink on a cold night. "Ellie knows she's got a once-in-a-lifetime opportunity to shop on my bank ID, and that all the clothes, shoes, and jewelry will stop if she blows the masquerade. All she knows is that I'm chasing a San Diego boy and she saw none of *this*." She fingered the worn robe with a frown. "She probably would have blacked it out of her mind if she did."

"So she doesn't know where you really are?"

"No. And I've left no money trail either. I've got a small stash of Texas bucks instead of using my ID, and I've been frugal since I left Dallas."

"San Diego boy?"

Rachael blinded him with her smile. "Not you. Wes Bertram. I met him on the Queen Helen—even mentioned him to my father before I ran into you. He's the son of some baronet or another—someone on Dad's approved list. Once I had this idea of doubling back to Midland, I called him up and chatted a couple of times. If I read him right, he'll brag about it to his friends. A false trail for the bloodhounds if Ellie drops the ball."

He just shook his head. "It sounds like you've done this kind of thing before."

She showed wide, innocent eyes as she ate another bite.

Whether it was their hunger or restaurant's unexpectedly good cooking, they finished their plates quickly. As he bundled up the trash, she asked, "What's the point of this thing we're capturing? I didn't follow the technical stuff."

He settled as comfortably as possible in the hard wooden chair. "You have a jet plane, according to rumor. I would have thought you would have been the first to appreciate the possibilities of more powerful aircraft."

She nodded. "It's nice—being able to cross the continent so fast. But we can already do that. A new engine wouldn't make that much difference—not a historical shift."

"I've never had the opportunity to fly. And I notice you took the train this time."

Rachael settled back against her pillows, staring at the ceiling. "I guess more planes would change things. I can't always fly when I want to. Dad's company always has first priority. And it would have been really nice to fly to Australia, but Dad said I had to take the cruise."

"I hear there were a few passenger blimps."

She sniffed and shook her head. "I checked. What berths available were hammocks with a curtain for privacy. If I were going to be traveling for days on end, I'd need room to walk around, and more to keep me busy than reading books on my handset."

He chuckled. "At least the bandwidth would be better than on the train."

Rachael's eyes scanned his face. "The train was bad enough before we connected. I don't do well in a cage by myself."

She unwrapped the towel around her hair, and fished for a brush. It was still tinted brown.

Samuel had trouble keeping his mind on their discussion as she turned from chrysalis into a butterfly. He was intensely aware that her robe was shifting loosely over her body as her arms moved and as she tossed her head from side to side. He could feel himself slipping.

"What was it like?"

"What?" she asked.

"The treatment in Australia."

She didn't meet his eyes. "If I had known in advance, I might not have gone through with it." She shook her head and her hair settled into place with no stray locks. "There were the usual medical tests, making sure I was free of any diseases before they started. There was a sinus issue they worked on for a week or more."

She straightened the collar of her robe and stared at the wall. "They put me to sleep for the worst of it. I know they shaved my head and made some minor surgical changes. It was all spelled out in the contract, and they captured it all, for my safety, but I didn't want to watch it. When I woke up, I had to learn to walk again. I was weak and everything was different. I also had to learn how to turn the extras on and off. They had me watch instrument traces until I could change how I smell and all the rest."

Samuel suddenly realized he could smell an elusive perfume, very faint, that was at odds with the worn and utilitarian motel room. It had to be her.

"After that, there were the social training sessions. It was like charm school, with extras."

"They taught you how to seduce."

Traces of a frown and then a smile flickered across her face before she looked at him. "Lots of social interactions. My mentor, Julia, hammered away at the art of subtlety. With power comes hatred. I was used to being resented for my money. I had to learn how to deal with being beautiful as well."

Samuel nodded. "Do you have a picture of you, before the changes?"

She looked aside, "No! All gone. I've wiped them."

He didn't believe her. It was very hard to track down every image of a person. Impossible really, since there were private captures secured behind other Net IDs.

"Well, if you run across one, send it my way. I'd love to know what the differences are."

He stood up. "I've got more work to do on the data tonight. I've got to find some teaser images. Something to compete with war news reporting."

She asked quietly, "Is it my alterations? Is that why you're so... distant?"

It took a moment before he could put his feelings in order. "I don't think so. I have to be careful—that's a given. If you were just some random girl I met in Midland, I'd still go back to work and sleep alone.

"I know what you mean, about being an outsider because you are different. I started screencrafting when I was in my teens, amateur stuff, but even when I got a professional-quality handset, I had to fight hard for every opportunity. I was the last choice—the guy with no family connections and the wrong skin. Everything I crafted had to be dramatically better than the competition, or it would never be used. I scrambled for every opening for years before I decided that the islands were a dead end for me.

"Then I arrived in San Diego, and everything turned on its head. Suddenly, I had the family connections, and opportunities fell in my lap before I was ready." *And girls who see me as an opportunity are suddenly interested in me.* "I'm on trial here. If I can impress Uncle Jason, it will make my career. He sent me here with no backup, and I have to believe it's to see whether I will fail or not.

"But I'm distant because I have to be. I can work with Clark, in public. I can't be distracted, and if I get too close to you, I will be. I'll come here for a meal, but no more...."

He wanted to say more, but turned toward the door.

"Call me in the morning when you get your Clark face on, and we'll have breakfast next door. We'll need to discuss tomorrow's scenes."

Her scent trailed out behind him as he left.

Alone in her room, Rachael stared at the closed door and whispered, "So I guess I'm on trial, too."

...

Wizzer scratched his whiskers and asked, "So you're Danny's new slave. Does that mean you'll want to go for a walk outside, too?"

He gestured at the rear access on the upper side of *Lance*'s tail. The ship healer had to strap on his safety harness and crawl out on the external skin at a moment's notice. It was currently tied open to get the maximum ventilation, and would remain so until the captain was totally certain the hydrogen leaks had all been dealt with.

Caleb shivered at the untainted blue of the open sky. "No, not this time. I'm supposed to inspect all the connectors." He looked up at where the plenum's rear opening spilled various cables into Wizzer's domain. "Could you show me where all of these go?"

The engineer set down his mid-sized computer, still showing some girl with red curls, and dressed in a remarkably tight version of a fleet uniform. He grinned at Caleb. "Hey, with the Net relay down, I've got to stick with what I've got in the cache, don't I?"

He smiled, "Sure. I just wish I had thought of that." Not that he'd been able to afford a handset of his own. It was on his list when they returned home and he was paid the completion bonus. If he did a good job helping Daniel with the ship-healer job, it might even pay more. He remembered something about changing job descriptions in the contract, but he didn't have a copy with him on the trip.

Wizzer stepped over to the plenum. "You know how all of this works, don't you? These fat ones are the low-pressure hydrogen feeds from the lift bag. The engines suck as much of the hydrogen as they need, based on the engine thrust. The green lines are return water, generated by the fuel cells on the engines."

Caleb ran his hands along one of them, to where there was a Y-splitter. "Branching to..."

Wizzer smirked, "Your cattle watering troughs, the faucets in the break room, anywhere where we need fresh water. There's a small reservoir amidships, but at cruise speed we're always generating new water faster than people can use it. The excess goes back to the ballast trough, of course, because the *Lance* never gets enough."

Caleb pointed, "And the little black ones are control signals, right?"

"And a power feed to the rest of the ship. The fuel cells generate electricity for everything, not just the engines."

Caleb followed the lines as they branched out of the plenum and down to a portal through the skin. Wizzer watched to make sure he didn't tug at anything.

"The skin is thicker here." It looked healthy enough. There was no sign of the irritation Danny had him checking for.

"Yeah. I don't know whether baby blimps grow thicker tails naturally or whether it's just an adaptation to the engine saddle that holds everything in place. As long as my engines ride stable and true, I don't care."

The spinning propellers were visible through the hull, held off at a distance by a criss-cross lattice of aluminum beams that fitted comfortably across *Lance*'s tail. The engines and fuel cells rode in opaque silvery bulbs in front of the blades.

Caleb asked, "Do you ever have to go outside?"

He nodded. "That's why they pay me. Of course, I stuck to the rigging. It's not bad climbing over there to check the lubrication and to monitor the vibration. All the serious work is done at port, where we can wheel an undercarriage in place to support the engines. At least I hope that's where it happens. I'm trained to do more serious repairs while in flight, but that's to be avoided. It's bad enough to crawl over there when the blades are a whirlin' to check for vibration."

"Do you ever worry about falling?"

Wizzer's face twisted in thought, "Not much. I dropped a wrench one time. Watched it spin in the sunlight as it arced away behind us. I try to avoid that. They're expensive."

Caleb checked the access membranes as well, but it was really to get a good look at the sky above, not filtered by the green skin. It was very bright, and intensely blue. There were clouds in the distance, and below in the haze, the wide Mississippi River wound back and forth like a wounded snake. Sounding like a giant swarm of mellow bees, the propellers hummed, pushing them south.

Value

The mid-sized blimp *Muldjewangk*, laden with one of the last shipments of electronics from East America, shook with the echo of distant thunder. Captain Stedman was monitoring the weather reports from Jamaica as the early-season tropical storm was moving into the Caribbean area. He grinned as the growing tailwind from the western edge of the storm increased his speed and reduced his need for another water stop.

"Captain, Fleet Command has a message." Navigator and comm officer Neale pushed back from his display to let the captain read.

For: 98459931 – Fleet Ship Muldjewangk
From: 73487881 – Fleet Admiralty
Content: Your assistance is requested. Small independent transport "Divine Chariot of the Gods" 77939326 working out of Honolulu has failed to report its location, last pinged in your area traveling due east. If the craft is detected, report coordinates and bearing.
Continue watch while north of equator.
End of message

The captain sighed, "It looks like another item for your list, Neale. Update the rest of the watch rotation."

The navigator nodded. "Do you think it's another downed blimp?"

"Hard to say. Those small transports are getting old now. It could have been weather, or even a sloppy crew who turned off their router and forgot to turn it back on. All we can do is make note of any blimps we pass and record the registration number. For the duration of this mess, let's log all the blimps we see, at least those twenty miles or more from port."

"Aye, sir."

The blimp shook again with another gust of wind, and both men turned their attention back to keeping the *Muldjewangk* safe in the marginal weather conditions.

On the skin, there was a splattering of light rain. Tiny, almost microscopic hairs trapped water droplets and the ever-thirsty numal drank fresh water into its system.

There were other particles in the air as well—dust, pollen, and spores. The blimp managed to leech some minerals from the dust, but the pollen and spores found the engineered skin too impervious. There were no pores to latch onto, no soil from which to sprout. They were natural lifeforms, bred to find a natural place to grow. Time would shake them free.

All except one kind of 'spore'.

...

Bill Melear shook his head firmly, "No. The record-breaking flight must be on the twelfth on the month. All the tests leading up to it are scheduled to make that happen."

Samuel shrugged. "I'm just trying to maximize the public attention. With this war news taking up all the first clicks, it will be hard to build the people's interest. We can't just spring the main event and expect anyone to watch. I have to stage screen releases just like you have to stage your tests. My problem is that anything I put out there might just be usurped by a political change or a flaming disaster. I have very little flexibility in case of problems."

Bill nodded. "Sure, but if you mess up, I lose attention; if I mess up, I die."

"Why does it have to happen on the twelfth? What if the weather changes? I hear there's a hurricane brewing down south."

The pilot chuckled. "Texas is big, and the hurricanes tend to veer off to the northeast. But even if there is cloud cover, I'll need to fly on the twelfth."

"Why?"

Bill glanced at Clark, who was within earshot, but apparently checking something on the datastore. "Samuel, I'm sorry about this, but it has to do with physics. Yes, I could probably achieve the first flight on any day, but to attain my real goals, everything has to be aligned perfectly. It's either the twelfth, or I wait a whole month after that."

Samuel shook his head, "That would just give the same problem a month from now. Can you give me something? Right now, I don't have enough information about what exactly your history-making flight is going to accomplish. I can't build an attraction out of what I have now. Sure, airplane fans and a few die-hard news addicts will watch, but I don't have any zing for the wider audience."

Bill lowered his voice. "It's a secret because I can't afford let my two competitors, nor the government, understand the true range of what I'm trying to accomplish. It's even worse, now that people are talking war. I've gotten feelers from the Texas Court already about equipping airplanes with guns to shoot down blimps. I wake up in the middle of the night, afraid they'll show up and order me to drop everything and make some blimp-busters for them."

"Just tell me, in confidence. Something to give me ideas. I'll run everything by you before it's released."

Bill thought for a moment. He reached for his arm. "Come with me."

They went into his office and closed the door.

...

Marcos López watched from the workbench nearby where he had been re-racking some tools, thinking about what was going on. He had been just close enough to catch part of the conversation—Bill's voice carried. But the boss had been more closed-mouth about this project than anything else they had attempted. Bill had some special plan that he hadn't been ready to share with anyone, not even him. That he was apparently ready to spill details to the camera guy was a little disturbing. How could he not trust his own crew first?

And that Clark guy was watching things as well. He was a little creepy. He spoke to no one, and he didn't act quite right. Bill seemed to trust the kid—or at least he trusted the kid's uncle. But this assistant showed up unannounced, and even the kid seemed surprised when he arrived.

Could Clark be a plant? Could Fremont Aeronautics have sent him here to spy on the new project? Things had been pretty tense back when they had competed to get the contract for the Olympian Court. He always thought Bill had lost the bid by a suspiciously slim margin, as if someone had known his bid before-hand.

Marcos nodded to himself. He wouldn't let Clark out of his sight—and certainly never leave him alone close to the plane.

Twenty minutes later, Bill left in a hurry to deal with a hydraulic issue on the plane. Samuel came out slowly, lost in thought. Marcos watched and waited.

...

Prepared this time, they went to the restaurant. She vanished into the men's restroom to make 'adjustments' before they ate.

She smiled, looking more comfortable, when she returned to the booth and sat across the table from him.

"Well, Samuel, what did Mr. Melear tell you?"

He hesitated before answering. "It really is a big thing. And the secrecy is valid. I can't even tell you. His own men don't know the whole story, and I can understand why he's playing it close."

"Now I really am curious. Can't you give me a hint?"

He wasn't very talkative. They ordered and ate quietly, looking up at the public terminal on a pedestal a few feet away that was seemingly dedicated to news reports. Two more blimps had come down in North America. There was a map showing reported blimp sightings, but image captures by the public showed that the airships were staying at high altitudes and hiding in cloud banks.

Clark mumbled, "I don't blame them. If I were up there, I'd stay out of sight."

He whispered, "We'd better not make too many comments where they could be overheard. We're strangers here, and the Australians are getting very unpopular. Every sailor that dies fuels a fresh wave of resentment."

"It's okay. I looked. No one is sitting close to us."

"Better safe than sorry." He'd learned to keep his opinions to himself long ago. It wouldn't take a second for a wrong word to change them from strangers to enemies.

The food arrived, and she watched him eat.

"Yes?"

Her grin looked strange on Clark's face. "I thought it was a brave choice—fish in the desert."

Samuel poked at the rubbery flesh with his fork. "I didn't think about it. I always had fish at home. I guess they have trouble getting fresh fish delivered here. But it's edible."

They paused when the new screens flashed and the endless commentary was put on hold by an announcement by King Thomas of Australia.

Clark frowned, trying to understand, she asked, "Does that mean it's over?"

Samuel shook his head. "No. He congratulated Berlin for taking measures to stop random shooting at blimps, but the rest makes no sense."

She toyed with her potatoes. "What does 'We will assist Europa in its desire to close its borders' mean? I took a class in reading faces, and that wasn't submission. That was the look of a man moving a chess piece and saying 'Check'."

"You're right. Australia is making another move, and they're happy about it. That can't be good."

On the screen, a commentator was making the same guess.

Samuel gestured toward the terminal in frustration, "See! That's what I have to deal with. I'm supposed to come up with a teaser campaign that can survive these random political explosions? If I had scheduled a tag for this evening, it would have been completely wasted."

"I don't know. More people would be watching the news than they would normally."

"But they would tune it out—ignore it completely. They would be thinking about this stupid blimp war."

"Make it tie in, somehow. If people are thinking about war, you'll have to use those words. Make them think it's related, even if it isn't."

He was still irritated and it didn't help his appetite. He dropped his fork onto the plate. "That's a dangerous game. If you promise one thing and don't deliver, all people will remember is the lie, no matter how spectacular the screen is."

...

After dessert, they left for their respective rooms. Samuel opened up the notebook on his handset and played with teaser ideas.

Rachael shed the Clark disguise and relished her unbound hair and clean skin. She eyed the old robe and the Clark clothes with distaste. When she had been fresh with excitement at the grand deception she was planning, it had been easy to forgo the creature comforts of good clothes in favor of authenticity, but normal-people clothes were rough and irritating. She didn't really have much experience with coarse fabrics, but surely she would get used to them?

She dug out her handset from where she hid it deep in some smelly leather men's shoes. No matter what the masquerade, she couldn't do without her handset.

Midland had decent Net coverage, and there were dozens of messages waiting for her.

Ellie sent her a chatty update from Dallas, showing off the things she had bought, bragging that her Texas friends were getting very jealous of her close friendship with the generous 'shy school buddy' that was staying with her.

Most of the other messages from friends didn't appeal enough for her to view. When her life got back to normal, then she'd catch up.

But there were also five messages from her father, with progressively demanding leads. She frowned. He could find her, if he decided to, no matter how devious she'd been. Maybe she should call him back and settle him down.

But what to wear? Did she have anything?

She looked around her ugly room. Even the nicest paintings on the wall were cheap copies. The walls were rough with chipped paint. One glimpse of this place and he would be sure she had been kidnapped.

But some of her lessons with Samuel had to do with lighting. She rummaged through the trash until she found some reddish packing material, and carefully stuffed it around the lamp shade, until the room took on a pinkish cast.

Maybe that will cover up the yellowing plaster a bit.

She double-checked her face and hair. Dad had never bothered noticing her hair color, not even when she had been in her purple-and-orange phase. The blonde that had come from the Australian vats wasn't any more natural to him than this brown. Clean and brushed was enough. Maybe her eyes showed just a little how tired she was. The days had been long, and she wasn't used to drudgery. Sports and shopping had been her exercise of choice.

But I'm learning. I like it.

She slipped between the sheets and examined her handset. She smeared a little spit over the handset's lens, just enough to make everything a little blurry, and then propped it up on her knees. She adjusted the sheets carefully, then took a deep breath and slow-tapped her father's entry.

"This is Nue House." A rotating logo for the company appeared on the screen.

Rachael smiled, "Hi Columbia, it's good to hear you. I'm just calling to check on Daddy."

"It is good to see you, Miss Rachael. I will see if he is available."

The Nue House amanuensis was only in her forties, but she cultivated an older voice. In a rare moment when they had met at the house, she admitted she did it to add distinction to her presence. There was a faint hint of classical strings in the background while she waited.

The the image faded to a darkened silhouette. "Rachael, why have you been ignoring my calls!"

She gave him a tolerant smile. "Daddy, I called to see you. If you want my image, you've got to do the same."

He grumbled, then reached over to turn up the lights. His thinning hair looked like it was trying to escape in all directions. He blinked his own tired eyes at the brightness.

She smiled, "Much better. I just had a moment alone tonight and felt like checking in."

"Where are you?"

She looked around. "Some hotel in Texas. Hardly first class, but it will do."

"I want you to come on home. With all this war talk, it's dangerous for you to be out there by yourself."

She put two fingers to her lips and looked down. "Well, I'm hardly alone."

He sighed loudly. "I knew you'd get yourself in trouble. Who is he?"

"We'll deal with that later. How are you holding up?"

"I'd do better if you were here, where you belong."

Dismissing his worries with a wave of her fingertips, she shook her head, "There's nothing I can't handle. Isn't that why you let me go to Australia, to help me take care of myself?"

"That's just the point! My people are telling me that the anti-genie sentiment is at an all time high. If you show off your abilities, it will paint a target on your back. You dealt with the Aussies. To some people, that makes you an enemy."

She was quiet for a moment. Daddy was seriously worried about her. "I saw some of that back in San Diego. I've even been playing with makeup, to tone down my dazzle. You may not realize it, but I'm not an idiot."

Quietly, he sighed. "I never thought you were an idiot, just willful and spoiled. I'm glad you're thinking about these things."

"Willful enough that I'm not ready to go hide in the Carolina house. You know what I want to do. I really should head back to San Diego and make my industry contacts. I'm bored with the shopping. Don't you want me to get back to business?"

He sniffed. "Not bored enough, from the look of these bills."

"You know, Daddy, something just occurred to me."

"Oh?"

She frowned in thought, and talked with her hands. "If being me, as I am now, all shiny and new, is a danger in this political climate, maybe you're putting me at additional risk."

"What? How do you mean?"

"The safest I could be, for a while at least, would be to drab myself down and pretend to be a normal person."

She watched as he absorbed the idea. Then she added, "But you'll have to call off the dogs. Nothing could point eyes at me more than people following me around, asking questions.

"Daddy, I've still got the 'X' number memorized, and ready to go on my handset. At the slightest hint of danger, I can call them in."

Since the kidnapping attempt when she was twelve, she'd been carrying her emergency call number. It would alert Nue's private security and give a beacon to her location.

"I don't know."

Rachael could see him consider it. "Just tell them to take a break and enjoy Dallas. I'll call if I need them, and I'll call you if I move back to San Diego. Until then, I'll try to keep a very low public image. At least until this war scare stuff goes away. How about that?"

He mumbled, but she knew she'd made her point.

"Thanks, Daddy! You're the greatest."

She closed the call before he could talk himself out of it and settled down into the sheets.

I wish I could get Samuel over here and share the good news. She shifted in the bed, then shook her head. She wasn't going to get him to sleep with her, not until some things changed. He had his barriers up, and without a full chemical seduction, he wasn't about to budge.

And that would put an end to my training. I'm not after a tame puppy, no matter how comforting that would be.

She'd just have to work at it day by day, doing her job and making herself valuable to him.

That would be so nice—to be valuable to someone.

Alligators

Baron Jenner paced his massive office, glaring out from the thirtieth floor overlooking the San Diego harbor. Down below, he could see his Queen Helen in dry dock. For years, he had lived aboard his ships, in a set of nicely-appointed suites. They weren't close to the size of this whole-floor office he had set up in the glass tower, but the decks and the open sea had been his as well. He felt cooped up.

It would be nearly a year before the QH would be fully repaired and ready to take her place on the waves. But would he be able to go back to the way things were before?

Here on land, his business empire spanned continents, linked by the Net, and critical data flowed freely. Paradoxically, the hated blimp fleet with their wide-ranging Net relays had enabled him to keep his domain under control. If the blimps came down for good, as he hoped, then so would the range of the Net.

He shook his head. Ships made no money on the ocean, nor sitting at the dock. Only loading and unloading cargo and passengers produced any revenue. He might be condemned to live in office buildings forever. He loved the sea. The idea seemed like a death sentence.

But he had planned this. He had to do it.

A large display on one of the interior walls began flashing, drawing him out of his fidgets. He walked close and tapped a control pad.

A call had arrived from his Lisbon Port Commander. As he scanned the ID information, he tapped on through. He barely knew the man. They'd only talked briefly at a company conference a couple of years ago. Was there unusual blimp activity? His spotter network was on high alert. Maybe...

"This is Jenner. You have information for me?"

The dark-featured man with a tall face nodded. "Lord Jenner, a situation is developing here in Lisbon. Beginning about two hours ago, ships are stalling out in the narrows. I've had to wave off all arrivals and halt scheduled departures."

"What is it?"

"There is some kind of plant growing in the narrows that fouls the props. My men say it's like kelp, long and ropey, but like nothing they've seen before. It's very fast-growing. There was nothing noted yesterday, and now it has blocked off the harbor."

"A numal."

"I believe so, yes."

After getting the particulars sent to his staff, all of his port operations were flashed an alert. Unfortunately, he had to do more.

I knew it would come to this. He took a moment to put on his diplomatic face and then initiated a call to Berlin.

More quickly than he had expected, he faced the Duke of Lorraine. They hurried through the formalities.

Jenner put it simply. "King Thomas has revealed what he meant by helping Europa close its borders. He's going to to block all of our harbors with this numal kelp. I'm sure it just showed up in Lisbon first."

"Do you think he seeded this earlier? Back when there was blimp traffic?"

"I don't think so. A fast-growing numal like this had to have been seeded recently. Clearly Australia isn't limited to blimps. I've checked the attacks on ships against known blimp traffic, and it's plain that he is moving his pieces with normal watercraft."

The duke nodded, "We are aware of your intense interest in blimp traffic. Do you have any information on Australian ships?"

"Not enough. The Real Time registry only logs merchant ships that arrive at the known ports. There are thousands of smaller fishing vessels and private craft that go unreported. All it would take is a small craft to sail into a harbor and toss the seeds into the water."

"Your suggestions, Jenner?"

"My people only report the kelp in Lisbon. King Thomas is giving us a moment to appreciate his plan, otherwise we would have seen something showing up in the other harbors."

"His plan?"

"Isn't it obvious? He wants parity between airships and ocean-going vessels. He's wanted that from the start. When the first blimp went down, he bombed the Queen Helen. After that, it was always tit for tat. One airship down, one ocean ship of related capacity down, as well. King George blocked airships from Europa and now King Thomas is saying that he'll block Europa from the ocean.

"The only way we can stop him to prevent him from seeding the other harbors. You will have to control the sea. Not just the harbors, but all close access as well. You have to be able to interdict the small vessels he is using to place his weapons.

"I have spent considerable resources all around the world to keep track of the blimps. Most of it is simple—a person with binoculars and a number to call. You're going to have to do the same, only watching the waters from shore. You'll need fast boats with armed crews to investigate each suspicious vessel. Get some airplanes as well, something to see beyond the horizon, so your military boats will have time to get into place.

"My people are already investigating the kelp. Maybe we can poison it or send fishing trawlers to rip them from their location. I don't know. But we can be confident that King Thomas has been planning this attack for a long time. It takes more than a couple of weeks to engineer a numal like the kelp. He probably has other weapons ready to use."

The duke nodded solemnly. "It's a shame this couldn't have been resolved earlier—before the blimps burned and the ships were bombed."

Jenner said nothing at first. Diplomacy wasn't his game. He'd been in this battle for years, and the escalation to bloodshed was just a change in degree. And unless his plans had gone seriously off, it was far too late to resolve this nicely.

He stood a little taller and leaned closer to the screen.

"This will be a matter for the World Court to address one way or another, certainly. Everyone is watching Berlin and Sydney. If there are seeds for Lisbon and seeds for Bremerhaven, then likely there are seeds for New York and Georgetown and Capetown and San Diego. Any nation that dares stand up to Australia can be shut into its own borders with no choice but blimps to move its goods. The way King Thomas wants it, every nation on the globe will be have to pay him for the lifeblood of commerce. Why else has he invested in the research to create this weapon? It's only use is to beat other nations into submission."

...

"That's it," Samuel said, talking over the news reports showing captures of ships dragging up enormous green fronds out of Lisbon harbor. "We'll have to tie our tags into the war news, somehow."

Clark sat in a chair against the wall, saying nothing as Bill and Samuel worked out a schedule for the upcoming tests, trying to decide which ones would be enticing enough to the average person to be worthy of a capture.

Marcos rapped at the door. He nodded to his boss. "You've got a priority message on the company ID."

Bill sighed and headed out the door. "You two work it out. I've got a business to run."

Samuel swiveled his chair face his assistant. "Any ideas?"

Clark spoke softly, testing her voice. "Hmm. Yes, actually. We've got strange new devices, a mystery you're not willing to share and a hard deadline. I had trouble getting to sleep last night, and one of the reasons was that question; what happens on the twelfth? Drop the right tags into the news. Make everyone want to know what happens then."

He nodded, thinking it over. "How good are your voices?" He scooted his chair closer.

Clark looked at the door then repeated "On the twelfth" in different voices, keeping them soft. A couple of them cracked, but Samuel's face was shifting from a frown to a grin before she stopped.

"I think we might just have something."

Bill came stalking back in then, his face a thundercloud. "That's great, but you are on your own. No more narrations. I just won't have time for it. The test schedule is still on, but Texas Court has just usurped three of my contracts. They want all my available planes to watch for Australian attacks—security flights they're calling them." He shrugged. "It's royal prerogative. They'll pay, but I've got penalty clauses in my contracts and angry customers to deal with."

He put his hand on Samuel's shoulder. "You know what I've got to deal with. Go with your gut on the screens. I won't have time to check your work." He nodded to Clark and then walked out in a hurry.

Samuel whispered, "Let's move back to the motel, where we can work in private." They packed up and headed for the car.

...

Marcos watched them leave and then let himself into Bill's office.
"Uh, Boss?"
"Yes." He didn't look up from the contracts he'd pulled from the files and spread out on his desk.
"I think there's something wrong with Clark Peterson, the camera assistant."
Bill didn't look up, "Yes, she's a girl dressed as a man. None of my business. She's Samuel's problem."
Marcos raised his head a fraction. He suddenly had a different perspective on it. What was going on? Was it a secret girlfriend?
"You're sure the kid knows?"
Bill nodded. "It's obvious. They're playing the game together. As long as the job gets done, I don't care."
Marcos nodded. "Okay, I just wanted to make sure you were aware."
Bill pushed one of the contracts his way. "Get Victoria Agriculture on the screen. I have to break the bad news, and I want them to hear that they're not getting their jet as soon as possible, and from me."

...

Admiral Dale was watching the Lisbon news on the private display near his desk.
This has to be King Thomas. I know he was responsible for those ship sinkings too. It looks like he's been preparing for this.
Good that he was prepared—but the secrecy involved! No one at court was aware of anything like this.
I'm responsible for the fleet. How could I be kept in the dark all this time?
The king is the king. Keep my mouth shut.
But how many of my blimps were burned in reaction to his attacks?
Lieutenant Glynde stood at attention at the entrance. "Sir. The *Muldjewangk* is reporting in. Technical problem."
Dale shook off his dark musings. "Details."

She began reading from the terminal in her hand. "Captain Stedman reports that the blimp began having trouble maintaining altitude shortly after passing over Panama. They had been on course for the Galapagos, when they determined that they might not make it. They changed course for Buenaventura. The cause of the problem is an undetermined hydrogen leak. They reported in because they were headed for an area with weak Net connections."

"Why do I remember the *Muldjewangk*?"

"Sir, they were one of the half-dozen ships you ordered to be on the lookout for the missing ship, *Divine Chariot of the Gods*."

"Right. So, they were likely in the same area, and now they've sprung a significant gas leak. Leaking faster than they can regenerate, it seems."

"Yes, sir."

"Do we have an idle blimp in rescue range, in case they can't patch their leak?"

She sighed. "Several. The west coast of South America has been relatively friendly. Several blimps that were diverted from North America have sheltered in those harbors."

"Choose one with a backup shortwave Net radio and order them to make contact. I want a full report on this hydrogen leak, even if it's something trivial."

"Yes, sir."

...

Caleb was happy to be ordered back to the command deck. He was the only one with a smile on his face.

Captain Kelly explained. "Louisiana sent an alert to all the blimps in the area, changing the allowed places where we can land for water. It's a reaction to the kelp infestation over in Europa—they're afraid blimps might seed the kelp, but after their previous claim that they're friendly to us, they can't just wave us off, not without evidence that we're doing something bad.

"It's all political, but instead of landing somewhere with port facilities, we've been directed to Lake Calebasse, which is almost a swamp. So, no shore leave, and no fresh food. Add to that the wind gusts from a storm churning away in the Gulf of Mexico, and we're on a tight schedule."

She pointed to the starboard side of the deck. "For the next four hours, I want your nose to the skin, watching for anything that might be hazardous. Report boats, floating logs, even alligators." She gestured with outstretched arms. "This is your angle of view, and I don't want you getting distracted. You see anything, call out, but keep your eyes on the water. Got it?"

"Yes, Captain."

There was a swivel chair bolted to the deck that was ideal for his position. He strapped in and watched as the *Lance* penetrated a low-level cloud layer. The ground below looked like an endless flat forest, but water glistened through the gaps. If there was dry land down below the tree cap, it was hiding very well.

The deck shook, as a gust of wind shoved at the blimp. The captain spat out a change of course and the landscape below shifted slightly.

Caleb wondered about the kelp. He hadn't seen any reports first-hand—he'd been too busy helping Danny. Still, the idea that people were fighting with plants rather than bullets seemed like progress to him. He felt the hard little lump in his pocket. So what if ships couldn't sail on time? It was better than explosions. Maybe everyone would be a little better for a few delays.

The trees opened up to a river for a few seconds and then the view was back to solid trees. The *Lance* seemed just a thousand feet high, moving quickly to some place the captain could feel in her head.

More mud patches. Not something to report, but he did peer closely, looking for alligators. They hadn't been this low in some time. Not since that midnight watering stop in the middle of the Mississippi River, on high alert for a spray of bullets.

At least this time they were in officially friendly territory, and it wasn't a bad thing that he saw no signs of roads or human habitation. The water looked muddy, but maybe it would be better where they set down.

And the water patches were coming more frequently.

"That's a canal."

"Caleb, did you say something?"

"No, Captain. I just saw a straight-edged channel and thought it was a canal."

"Fine. There will be several of those." She raised her voice. "Expect the lake waters in three minutes. Grant, take us down to two hundred feet."

Right on cue, a broad mud-flat led to open water.

Caleb called out, "I see a blimp."

"What class?"

"Um. Mid-size. It's not wearing its numbers."

She said evenly, "Neither are we. Keep your eyes sharp."

Shortly, everyone swayed in their chairs as the *Lance* touched water and came to a stop. The captain's orders sent people running. Caleb watched the waters. There were three blimps visible on his side, off in the distance.

"Two small craft approaching!"

The captain peered at them through binoculars. "We may get some fresh provisions after all. Ray, check with port operations and get the ID of Port Sulphur Market."

Shortly, Ray was chatting away with the closer boat and making arrangements for a quick delivery. The second boat changed course and moved off to service one of the other blimps.

It was a busy four hours. The ballast water was flushed and replaced with the brackish waters of the lake. Several crates of food were loaded through a waterline hatch. Danny recruited one of the others to put the ID banners back in place.

Caleb would have liked to help with that, but he already had a job, watching for alligators.

Actually, he was watching for ripples in the water. Wind gusts stirred the surface of the lake before they hit the *Lance*, so he was the early warning. The blimp wasn't anchored. They stayed roughly in place with the engines and steering vanes, nose pointed into the wind. For the most part, it worked, but the gusts came from various directions, and at least when the supplies were being loaded, it was a very tense game, anticipating the winds and trying to push at just the right moment.

Saul came up on deck with a bunch of bananas and shared them around. He stayed and watched through the final preparations and heaved a sigh of relief as they lifted off and rapidly gained altitude, turning downwind, heading out over the gulf coast waters.

"I'm glad we're done with North America. I used to like the place."

Caleb asked, "Are you sure we're done?" Out his starboard view, they appeared to be paralleling the coast, heading west.

The captain peeled her banana, able to relax a bit now that they were out of shooting range. "The plan is to let the storm winds push us around the coast line. Depending on the winds and the mountains, we'll cross Mexico to the Pacific and then ride the trade winds all the way to the Solomons.

"So, while not strictly true that we're done with North America, we shouldn't have any more troubles."

Watching

"Any screen producer can sell tags, but it's the low-profit screens that really need to sell them. It's a way to increase income for screens that can't demand a high per-view rate."

Marcos seemed puzzled, "Like the news?"

Samuel nodded. "Yes. Right now, with everyone addicted to the war reporting, maybe news could have demanded a higher viewing price, but to build a reputation, news screens appear in the Queue on a regular basis, once an hour, once a day, or whatever. People subscribe to their favorite news on a yearly or monthly basis to get a cheap rate. Most days, news is just junk, so they couldn't sell it for much. It's the disasters and drama like this war that come along unpredictably that allows news organizations to make a living."

Marcos asked, "And they buy tags?"

"No, they sell tag time. People like us, who want to advertise something, create the tags and pay the news company for the opportunity to include our tag into their screen."

He frowned, "Bill is paying for this?"

Samuel shrugged. "We're sharing the cost. It's part of my contract with him. We share the promotion costs, but we also share the income when people choose to view our finished screens."

"Just the screens, though?"

Samuel chuckled, "Just the screens. I don't have any claim on your inventions or your products."

Clark muttered, "It's almost time."

"Right." Samuel tapped the news link and the real-time screen appeared on the big terminal in the break room. There were just the three of them. Bill was working day and night to get all of the projects completed and he was driving his crew hard.

"...with the simultaneous outbreak of the kelp infestation in Navalo and Barcelona harbors, it shows that not only is Australia increasing its efforts to blockade ship traffic to and from Europa, but also that there is more than one source of infection seeding the prime harbors.

"Coming up in a moment is Sir Francis Clayton, with his insight on what Berlin's options will be."

Samuel tapped the sound a bit louder.

A smiling woman in bright clothes breathed in the fresh scent of her custom garden plants.

Samuel shook his head. "That's a mistake. They shouldn't be advertising gene-modified plants right now—not when everyone is worried about the kelp infestation."

Marcos shrugged. "Maybe their sales are down."

"Of course. But their best bet is to wait it out—not tie their product to weaponized plants in the public mind."

The screen changed. Samuel whispered, "This is it."

The image was of a lone dark dot, so high in the blue sky that even on the large display you couldn't make it out. Then a voice whispered, "That's not a blimp. It's so much more. For all of us, on the twelfth."

And like that, it was over. Another tag started, promoting a romance feature.

Marcos sniffed, "Short."

"It had to be. That one will show several times today. News addicts will see it over and over again. They'll pay attention, because we mentioned blimps. We'll change it several times between now and the flight, always keeping a little secret, and always ending with 'on the twelfth'."

"Do you think anyone will pay attention?"

"Some will. Some will even figure it out. I hope. But if anyone calls here about the tag, you'll have to send them through to me. That's what Bill and I agreed to."

Marcos nodded. "Sure. I'll make sure everyone gets the word." He had a thought. "Oh. What if people show up on the twelfth? We're not really equipped to handle crowds."

"We'll deal with it. I'll ask around. You have parking space. All we'd need are people for crowd control."

"Bill won't like it if tourists get in the way."

"We'll have it figured out, on the twelfth."

"On the twelfth."

...

"The *Tasmania* has scouted the whole Buenaventura area and has seen no sign of the *Muldjewangk*." Lieutenant Glynde read more details from her terminal, not meeting his eyes.

Admiral Dale glowered at the big map. "Give them the last known check-in coordinates from *Muldjewangk* and ask them to fly the route. No, *order* them to fly it. I have to get some data on this. And tell them to report in frequently. I don't want any possibility that they drop off the map as well. There could be an advanced aircraft in the area."

"An aircraft, sir?"

"Yes, did you see that cryptic thing on the news report? It looked like an aircraft to me. I almost remember seeing it before, but I can't put a finger on it."

"I didn't see it."

"Watch it. It's a tag after the hourly news. Someone is preparing to announce something new, and they're saying it's *not* a blimp, like that's important."

"Yes, sir."

She left. Dale looked down at the last report of missing blimps. It was too early to be sure, but the numbers seemed to be going up. There were too many to be simply missed check-ins. The enemy was up to something, and he had to figure it out quickly.

...

Baron Jenner frowned at the report of strange blimp traffic off the western Columbian coastline of South America. His spotting network reported that several blimps, after having already negotiated tethering locations in Tumaco, had suddenly put to the air and then headed northward.

Could this be it? Blimps leaving North America might have picked up spores from the hurricane. But why would they head north? Rescue missions?

It didn't matter. Regardless of what was happening, he had to forward all these reports to Berlin. Let them make their own tactical assessments. He had to give up his raw data, but they didn't have any claim on his private insight.

It doesn't matter that I'm fighting on their side. It was a personal initiative, and even if it works out perfectly, the Court will want to have a scapegoat handy to ground all the public outrage. I'll never be called a hero for this. I knew that from the beginning.

But I've covered all my tracks. There's no way I can be linked to this.

Berlin probably had no interest in the blimp deployment going on in South America. They were mobilizing all efforts to attack the kelp infestations.

King Thomas has his eyes on Bremerhaven, I'm sure. Either he only has a few seeding ships and they're taking their time, or he is attacking the harbors slowly to build panic. But my shipyards are the heart of the merchant fleet.

If the shipyards were compromised, it could take years to develop equivalent capacity to produce and repair ships.

Jenner looked out over San Diego harbor. Europa would hate to give up its preeminent position in world shipping, but a strong Californian push to expand its production might be the smart move. It would take several places like this to replace Bremerhaven, but his facilities were too concentrated.

He went to a terminal and reviewed his ships. Slightly more than half were at sea. Thirty percent were idle, a drain on his resources, but when the blimps were gone, his ships would be in high demand.

It would be expensive to fuel them up, gather crews, and put them to sea without a cargo, but just how dangerous was this kelp? Surely the port authorities were trying everything.

And if it comes to that, the same kind of engineered spore that I've set loose on the blimps could be created for the kelp.

But he'd burned those bridges. The anonymous genetic engineering team that had worked for him had been paid off. They'd never known who he was, and all communications had been destroyed. The one time use Net IDs he'd used to coordinate with them were long gone and unusable.

No, Lisbon was dumping truckloads of arsenic into the bay and Barcelona was using dredges to carve pathways through the kelp beds. Surely they would find some solution. *Hmm. I wonder if King George would be interested in an instant navy—if he paid the expenses to equip the ships and find the crews?*

...

King Thomas was watching real-time coverage of the trucks on the Lisbon-Tagus Bridge, backed up to the guardrails with chutes dumping poison into their waters. He shook his head in amazement.

Maybe I should send them a message. Anything as quick-growing as the numal kelp needs lots of sunlight and nutrients. It's going to starve out shortly, but that poison is going to haunt you for years.

But it wasn't his fault he was jousting with idiots. They should never have started this in the first place. He was in the position of the seventeenth-century explorers with guns, moving against the aboriginals with spears. His technology was so much better than theirs—the end was inevitable.

It's a kindness if I can overwhelm them—convince them to give up sooner rather than later.

He had a fallback—just let their numal crops start to fail because of their own foolishness, and they'll realize how dependent they already had become on Australian technology. Starvation would trump their pride. However, a few quick shocking defeats, and the Europeans could make a political compromise that could shortcut the whole process. And if Berlin led the way, the rest would follow.

His bag of tricks had a number of things left to try. Some, like the blimps, took years to put into play. Others, like the ship bombing or the kelp, could be set in motion in hours. Some took just a little longer.

His world clock showed it was dawn in Bremen on the Waser River. Three of his mermen had towed containers of a numal algae seventy-five miles from their host ship just outside the Bremerhaven harbor upriver to the city of Bremen. When sunlight hit the waters in Bremen's waterways, there would be a quick bloom and then it would begin to drift downstream. Once the salinity reached near ocean levels, this algae would clump together like gelatin.

Matured, this numal had a special trait, just for the shipyards.

He smiled and wondered just how fast they would clean up this gift.

Good spirits never last. A call from the fleet flashed in the corner of his display.

He sighed. *The admiral never brings me good news.*

...

The streets of San Diego were still bright with theatergoers and nightclubbers. Baron Jenner observed, but never joined the throng. Too many years where he'd lived at sea, more as host than partier, had left him a hermit in spirit. Over the past few days, he'd never strayed more than a few steps from his office displays. His sleep cycle was completely disrupted. Events in Europa and South America were demanding immediate attention. He was catching what sleep he could in his office chair.

He wasn't surprised at all when there was an urgent call from Bremerhaven.

The portmaster was apologetic for calling at the late hour in San Diego.

"I was up. Go on, what is happening?"

"According to your orders, we have set up observation posts all around the shipyards, even up the river as far as Bremen. Early this morning, the post reported a strange effect in the water."

"What was it?"

"Let me show you. Here is a screen capture taken from our Bürgermeister-Smidt_Brücke station."

The image showed three distinct ripples heading downstream. They could have been fish, but if so, they must have been dolphin sized.

"Have any of the other posts reported them?"

"We have sent an alert, but thus far, nothing has been seen."

"Thank you for your diligence. Even if they are just stray fish, we can't ignore them. Put some crews in boats and scour the Bremen waterways. Look for anything suspicious. If we have been left kelp seeds, maybe we can root them out before they take hold."

Within another hour, the observation was sent to all the other harbors at risk.

Jenner sent the news to the Duke of Lorraine in Berlin as well.

"We can't ignore the possibility that kelp seeds are being distributed by trained fish. If this is the case, then they could be released farther away from shore, and out of our normal search range. This is not good news, but it is better news than searching blindly. If something Australian shows up in Bremen, then we will have a firm lead on how these numal weapons are being delivered."

The duke took the news and promised to spread the word to others in the World Court.

"Jenner, the king is also interested in your proposal to... I don't know the word... 'field' a navy. You weren't the first to make that suggestion. Thus far all of the explosions, fires, and disasters have happened up here in the Northern Hemisphere. The idea of sailing an overwhelming force into Sydney Harbor and making King Thomas listen to reason has its appeal.

"There are problems, obviously."

Jenner leaned forward, "Right. All available ships are unarmed. Someone would have to design and manufacture weapons; deck cannons and torpedoes probably. Crews would need to be recruited and trained—not the least, competent navigators and captains."

The duke shook his head. "No. The most driving need is an admiral—someone who can make all the other things happen. We're looking at you."

Jenner frowned at the screen. "I'm an administrator, not a military man. You'll need someone with real naval experience—someone the captains will all obey with confidence, not someone more concerned with the budget."

"Jenner, none of us have military experience. We've been a nation of peace, and proud of that. One of the strongest of our claims to power is the moral authority we've managed to show. We are different from the pre-Star nations who were constantly at war, killing each other.

"But we lose all of that if we allow a rogue nation to destroy our shipping and starve our populace. If a power-mad king from halfway around the world is free to throw his weapons at us and we do nothing to stop him, then someone will take our place—someone whose moral authority will be based on the willingness to kill.

"I say putting a merchant in charge, a man who has dealt peaceably throughout the whole world all his life—that's the man we need to run the navy. And it doesn't hurt that no one is more familiar with a fleet of ships than you.

"Think about it. But we'll need to move quickly, and we need the right man to give the orders."

When the screen went dark, Jenner stared at it still. This was not how he wanted this to go.

Credit

The power converters were lined up in a row, each the size of a large truck, taking up a small hangar next to the main Melear Aircraft facility. Clark touched the metal.

Marcos nodded. "It's spinning. It's like a huge motor-generator." He pointed at the electrical connections. "We're connected to the municipal power grid, and we've been buying electricity like mad for the past month. Energy gets loaded into Nance-Bate accumulators, which we can then load into the new plane."

Samuel asked, "So, they're the batteries that will power the plane?"

"Umm. Not electrical batteries. They store energy, but in the push-pull form already. It turns out that you can store much more juice per pound in that form than you can with batteries. Plus, if you tried to run the plane on electricity, you'd need one of these converters on the plane. Pre-converting electricity on the ground saves a lot of weight."

Samuel gestured and Clark went to set up the camera. "Could you give that same explanation once we've set up the capture?"

Marcos shook his head and waved away the suggestion. "Oh, no. I couldn't do that. You can show me pointing, but I can't talk when the camera is running."

"Are you sure? You explained it to us plainly enough."

"Yeah, but you and... Clark have been around. I couldn't talk to strangers. I'll point and look sexy for you, but you'll have to talk over it or whatever you screencrafters do."

The little lines between his eyes and the tightness of his lips didn't give Samuel any hope that he'd change his mind.

"Okay, but go ahead and tell me everything. I'll record it here, transcribe it and get someone else to do the voiceover. I can't use your voice without your permission."

Marcos sighed with relief. "Good. Are you recording?" Samuel tapped his handset. "Okay, then take a look at the different sizes of the accumulators. These little ones are what powered those first demos."

He talked quite a bit, and let his worry about the expenses color his enthusiasm for the technology. Melear Aircraft was burning through their reserves, and what with the cancelation penalties for the confiscated planes and the government's notorious delays in paying their bills, Marcos wasn't sure even a successful flight would keep the company from sinking under their debts.

Then Marcos frowned. "Um. Let me go check some things. I'll be back in a minute."

Samuel turned to Clark as he left. "Are you ready?"

"I've been running a capture for the past ten minutes. His body language was great. I'm not sure the audio is usable, but we weren't going to use that, were we?"

He smiled and moved closer. "We've got to respect his wishes, but I agree with you about his emotions. Show me what you've got."

They huddled over the display, and she was right. Marcos gestured with his hands and his feelings were all over his face as he explained things to Samuel.

He backed up the capture and ran it through again, stopping at several places. "You've gotten much better at this. I like this lighting. Why did you set it down?"

She shrugged. "Just the feel of the place—in a metal cave with giant machines rumbling away. It needed to be darker."

He nodded. "Take another scan of the electrical wiring up there. It's heavy duty. Much heftier than you would think at first glance. See those insulators?"

She nodded and moved the tripod over to get a better angle. As he turned his head, he saw Marcos watching them.

"Back so soon?"

"I was quick. What are you doing?"

Samuel explained. "Come look at what we've already got. The audio will be replaced with a voice-over, like you wanted."

Marcos laughed uneasily. "I look like a windmill, flapping my arms like that."

"Oh, it's great. It shows your emotions. I wouldn't have it any other way. If you don't have any great objections, we'll use this, interspersed with closeups of the equipment and other things."

"I guess." He sighed. "I don't understand what you and... Clark are doing, really. But you can use it."

"Thanks."

"One last question?"

"Sure."

Samuel pointed to the accumulators. "The big ones are only seven or eight times larger than the small ones, and you're charging several of them. Why aren't you making one really big accumulator instead of a dozen of these? I would think it would be more efficient."

Marcos shrugged. "We don't make 'em. All this is Nance-Bate equipment, designed for the power companies. They use them to store power for when the wind doesn't blow on the windmills and the sun doesn't shine on the solar power fields. That's where they're making their money. A power company will set up one of these converters where they need steady power and pump juice in or out of the accumulators as necessary. In a pinch, they can also truck the accumulators from place to place.

"We're an aircraft company. None of this is our invention. We're just using it for our own purposes. When Bill designed the new plane, he had to make everything fit around these accumulators. Get him to show you the designs sometime."

Samuel had a tight smile, "I will when he has time."

Marcos sighed. "Yeah. I know what you mean." And then he left.

Clark waved him closer when they were alone. "Are we done here?"

"I think so. Unless there are any other angles you think we need."

She shook her head. "We can come back, if necessary." She stared off at the cameras.

"Problem?" Something seemed off, underneath the false voice and old clothes.

She sighed. "Marcos looks at me funny. He doesn't look my way, even when he's talking to me."

"I've been getting the same impression. I pay attention to the way people talk. Texas is all a foreign land to me. Even California was strange. The people on the ship were an amazing mix.

"So, Marcos has been my sample native-Texan and I've been listening to how he talks. One thing stands out—he'll use *he* and *she* all the time when talking about people. But not with you. Every time he refers to you in a conversation, he hesitates slightly and says *Clark*. I think he knows or suspects that you're female, and isn't a good enough liar to fake it smoothly."

"Oh, no. What will we do? What did I do wrong?"

Samuel took her hand. "It may not have been your fault. I know I have grown comfortable with your costume, but I still think of you as Rachael. Maybe it's the way we work together. Maybe we whisper together too close together like a couple, rather than how two men would talk."

"I've not been comfortable," she grumbled. "I've caught myself sitting like a girl, and having to readjust the way I stand all the time. No one said anything, so I thought I was getting away with it."

"I'll have to talk with him—see if it's just him with suspicions, or if the whole crew are watching the way you sway."

Rachael pulled off her glasses and glared at him. "That's not helping. I've still got to pack up for today and now you've made me self-conscious about the way I move."

He let her go with a hands-off gesture. "Let's move the individual crewmen interviews up a day."

"Do we need them?"

"If this is a historical event, then yes—every person here is of interest. Maybe we won't include them in the main screen, but if there are follow-up documentaries, they will be essential. Every person's life is valuable, but it's rare to get the chance to be seen and have a chance to shine. Everyone deserves credit."

"Tell me about it." She began packing the camera in its case.

"What?"

"Nothing." She was frowning down as she roughly stuffed it into its protective container.

He frowned. "Come on. There's no one around. What's on your mind?"

She stopped and sat down on the fold-out stool she used when waiting between captures. "I'm doing good work here. You've said I was."

"Right. I'm trying to be as honest as possible. You need feedback more than anything right now to develop your skills."

"That's fine, but I'm getting no credit. We've put three tags out there to a world audience, and I did half the captures and all of the voices. And we've stripped the metadata so no one knows."

It hit him in the gut. He remembered the day when his first captures were used on the Honolulu news coverage of the Polynesian Jubilee Parade. He'd raced home after work to pull a copy for his private files. He'd opened up the metadata to see his name in the credits, and "S. Bolls" wasn't there. There was the company, the old-time camera guys, the audio mixer guy and the editor, but his name was nowhere to be seen. He viewed the screen again, just to make sure, and there it was, his capture from Ala Moana Park as the floats moved down the avenue.

And there was nothing he could do about it. He was little more than a freelancer, and the verbal contract he had with the company had said nothing about putting his name in the credits. They'd paid for his capture—a token amount, but he'd been happy because it would be his first professional credit—and that had been taken away from him.

It was a bitter learning experience, and one that had left its mark on every contract he'd negotiated from that time on.

Probably the news editor hadn't given it any thought. He was under a deadline and just imported the company template credits into the metadata.

And now he'd done the same thing to Rachael.

He pulled up a packing crate and sat down. "Okay, I understand. My fault. The air of mystery about our tags meant I stripped everything but the audio and video. No location tag, no timestamp, no credits of any kind. I couldn't have done it any other way without reducing the impact of the tags.

"But starting in two days, we're moving to a fifteen-second tag, with more data and more hints. How about when we add the credits, we mark them for the 'On the Twelfth' tag series? That'll pull the early ones all under the same umbrella."

She looked up and nodded. "I'd like that."

"Now the question is, do we use 'Rachael' and blow the whole disguise thing? There's always the possibility of a pseudonym, but I know I wouldn't be satisfied with that."

Rachael frowned, and the Clark makeup showed some cracks. "I hadn't thought of that. How much problem would that cause?"

"At worst? Your father would be notified, and know your exact location. Bill Melear's crew would feel betrayed and it could put the whole project—at least our part of it—at risk of being cancelled. Imagine a crew of private security guards walking in here and dragging you off. My uncle would be upset that I betrayed his friend." He had visualized it all in his dreams. He shrugged. "It could be bad."

It might mean the end of his career, and he couldn't imagine anything worse than that.

...

King Thomas had them all queued up in a loop, and he played them over and over.

"That's not a blimp. It's so much more. For all of us, on the twelfth."

There was a black frame from the splice. And then there was a closer view, clearly a jet plane, moving quickly across the frame. *"Can you imagine something that no one in the world has seen? We will, on the twelfth."*

Next, there was a clear sky, only wisps of clouds with a low rumble, and then an echoing boom. *"Years from now, we will all remember what we saw, on the twelfth."*

Thomas tapped a secondary terminal. "Is this all of them?"

"Yes, your Majesty, but they seem to be changed frequently. I would expect a new version shortly."

"No embedded information?"

"None. They are being deliberately mysterious."

The king sat back and pondered. It was obviously a new airplane, possibly supersonic if that boom was an indication. And either the promotion was going over the top, or the owners of that plane had significant plans for it. On the twelfth.

He smiled as the catch-phrase intrigued him.

It shifted to a frown as he leaned over and queried all the aircraft developers.

The first one on the list looked ominous.

Melear Aircraft, based in Midland Texas. He was the one who first broke the sound barrier.

A few more queries brought up some historical images of the plane. One of the frames looked almost identical to the plane in the tags. Did he have a new version, perhaps one more suited for practical use?

The timing was suspicious. The twelfth was only a week or so away. Building a plane took months or years, and a public announcement wasn't likely planned until the plane was completed and tested.

He checked more database entries.

Oh, my. Greater Texas has submitted a voucher for payment of three new airplanes from Melear Aircraft, to be picked up next week.

And Texas was just north of where those blimps vanished. *Has Texas developed itself an air force, with supersonic planes to sweep the blimps out of the sky?*

It made sense. A very fast-moving plane could approach a blimp from above and set it ablaze before the crew had a chance to report in. If it went down over the ocean, there might be no evidence left for searchers to find.

I'll have to get a closer look at these Melear planes before the twelfth. Who do I have in that area?

Gray Spots

"Caleb! Wake up." Saul pushed aside his curtain. "Come on, Captain wants you on deck."

Caleb barely glanced at the timer. He'd gotten six hours sleep. in spite of how he felt, he couldn't even complain. It must have been accumulated exhaustion that was wiping him out.

"What's she want?"

"I don't know. Get dressed and report."

Caleb rolled out of his hammock and slipped on his shoes. It was daylight, and he blinked his eyes to clear his vision.

Below his feet, he could see mountains, moving by fairly quickly. He frowned. Last night, when Captain Kelly was discussing their route, she'd said they would cross Mexico at the "ankle" before they reached Yucatan, which would take them over flat terrain most of the way to the Pacific.

Probably the hurricane. Change in weather was always the wild card in navigation, he was learning.

He bounced softly on his way down the slope, and then abruptly came to a stop. His heart beat strongly enough to feel. *What is that?*

He backed up a few feet until he saw it again.

"Danny!" He called out as loud as he could. "Get Danny Lane here immediately."

He stood quietly, trying to understand what he was seeing. Danny came up. "What is it?"

"Danny, look here," he pointed. "What's this gray patch?"

It was in the skin of the *Lance* itself, a circular patch about as wide as his hand, only the color was different and the texture wasn't nearly as transparent as the skin next to it.

"I don't know." He opened his patch kit and spread out flat on the surface. "Move back out of the way, I'm going to make a cut."

Caleb didn't have to be told twice. If the cut suddenly ripped wider, they could both tumble through and fall to the rugged terrain below.

Danny carefully taped a broad ring several inches away from the gray patch—to strengthen the area, he guessed. Then he took out a razor-tipped blade, cut the gray patch free, and placed it in a sealed bag. He finished with a large patch, much like what they'd used on the bullet holes, only with a big X of cross strips to secure it all in place.

Caleb forced himself to ask, once Danny had gotten to his feet. "What is it?"

Danny held the bag and shook his head. "I still don't know. But I don't like the looks of it. Something infected or denatured the skin. I suppose it could have been a splash of acid or something. I can't tell if it originated from the inside or the outside. I'm going to have to look at my references. Can you help me search the skin again? If there was one, there could be others."

"I'm already late. Captain called for me."

"Well, let them know we've got a weak spot to watch out for. It will take some time to heal."

"Right."

When he reached the captain's deck, he told them what had happened.

She frowned. "That's unusual. For now, take a seat. We have an order from fleet to be on the lookout for fast-moving airplanes, possibly flying in this area, and possibly shooting down blimps. If you see anything, yell the alert, and Ray has orders to report it instantly, even if we're under attack."

Looking over at Ray, she said, "Take over while I go check on Danny."

"Yes, Captain." He moved over to the pilot's station and trimmed their airspeed slightly.

Caleb scanned the landscape, looking for anything above the horizon. Realistically, he wasn't likely to see anything coming up from below.

"Where are we?"

"South of Oaxaca. We've still got another fifty miles to go before we reach the Pacific. There's been no reports of locals shooting at blimps here, but Mexico is still listed as unfriendly."

"What about this airplane? Did some other blimp report it?"

Ray didn't look up from his display. "Not that I know about. Captain doesn't take it seriously, but it was an order from fleet. That's why you're here."

Caleb understood. He was the least valuable crewman, so his time was easiest to waste. But he didn't mind. He liked it up on the captain's deck.

"Just out of curiosity, should I see some airplane bearing down on us, what could we do?"

Ray laughed. "Pray and report it to fleet. Blimps don't dodge and weave very fast."

Caleb eased back in his chair and concentrated on the band of light just above the horizon, up to where the blue shifted to a darker hue. There were clouds, and occasional birds, but nothing sinister that could be an approaching airplane.

"I should probably be looking behind us, if they're chasing us."

Ray mumbled, "Captain already gave Wizzer a heads-up."

Staring through the clear skin at terrain gave him a pleasant view of the Mexican mountains. A prominent river deep in the V-notch between ridges was heading south toward the coast, and the *Lance* had settled into place three thousand feet above it, nearly even with the peaks on both sides.

"How did you get this job?" Caleb asked. Ray was in his late twenties, and while he normally manned the communications terminal, he was obviously trained to fly the *Lance* as well. It was the kind of position he wanted for himself in a few years.

"Worked my way up. I was ground crew at Brisbane. Took a cargo specialist berth on the *Rockhampton* and when Captain Kelly posted for a crew, I applied. Been on the *Lance* ever since." He grinned. "What're you thinking? Gunning for my chair?"

Caleb laughed. "Maybe someday."

A little while later, the captain came up the ladder. "Ray, call fleet."

He moved to the terminal and opened a voice call.

"This is Captain Kelly of the *Lance*. We're ten miles north of Cometa, Mexico, reporting damage to the skin membrane. In the past hour, we've detected and patched three gray blemishes. Ship's healer suggests that it's an infection of some kind. Patches are weaker than normal skin and may be causing gas leaks."

Caleb felt a shiver as she described the spots in detail. He blinked as he looked down at the ground below, becoming less rugged as they approached the coast. *What was that?* He blinked again, and shifted his position in his chair.

"Captain, there's one here. And it wasn't here a minute ago."

It was a tiny dot, smaller than the tip of his finger, but if it had grown that large in the length of time since the captain had arrived, it must be growing fast.

She modified her report.

"Caleb, go call Danny. Get this patched and go full-time watching the skin."

He was down the ladder as fast as he could go.

...

Admiral Dale stared at the others around the table.

"We've got three reports of gray spots on blimps—four if we include the report of the unexplained hydrogen leak. All passed through the Gulf of Mexico, but none had any close contact with each other. I'm open to suggestions."

Dr. Tuck tapped the papers before him. "We've never seen anything like this before. The exterior blimp skin is deliberately fine and free of micropores. From the beginning, we've known that any infection would compromise the ability to contain the gasses. Other than the hygroscopic tendrils and the gas pores in the interior of the gas bags, the skin is impervious to all known fungal spores and bacteria. The first generation blimps had a problem with mold in the ballast trough, but that has been corrected years ago. The *Lance*, for example, is one of the latest models and has no known vulnerabilities."

Captain Ross asked, "What would it take to find out what it is, rather than what it isn't?"

The doctor wrinkled his nose, "A sample, of course. If we had a sample of the affected skin, then we could examine it in detail and determine what was really happening. Could we get one of the blimps to come here?"

Ross shook his head. "If this is an infection, probably airborne at that, then I don't want any of those blimps anywhere near Australia."

Lieutenant Glynde added, "They wouldn't make it, in any case. From the time the blimps went through the Gulf of Mexico until the time they dropped off the map, none has traveled more than a thousand miles."

"Then fly it here in a sealed container on a jet."

"Yes, Doctor," sneered the captain. "Do you have a jet?"

There was a moment of silence and they all looked at Admiral Dale.

He sighed, "No, I don't have a jet either. Lieutenant, get on the Net and find someone who will fly a package from the Pacific coast of Mexico to Australia, either in one jump or two, at the fastest available speed. Once we've got an airport identified, then we'll get the *Lance* to fly close and meet a courier. They've already got a bagged sample, according to their report.

"But Captain Ross is right. Until we have more information, we'll need to quarantine affected blimps. From now on, any infected ship gets told to wait at Buenavista or in that area. We already have affected ships there. Also, send out a fleet-wide warning to avoid the Gulf of Mexico until further notice."

Ross grumbled, "That may not help. With the hurricane in that area, any airborne spores or whatever are likely being spread far and wide. My gut tells me, we're dealing with a targeted biological attack."

Dale nodded. "We can't rule anything out, but I've got that feeling as well."

...

The report from his admiral caused King Thomas to alter the instructions to his agent in Texas.

So the planes aren't shooting down the blimps, they're spraying them with some infectious agent. How long would it take for a fleet of jet planes to circle the world and infect every blimp in the sky? They could even pass over the east coast blimpyards and wipe out the next generation. Fleet is trying to identify the poison. I need to destroy the enemy's ability to deliver it. Maybe it's time for some good old fashioned explosives.

He pulled up the Net ID of his agent and sent the new instructions—destroy every plane in Midland beyond the ability of the engineers to rebuild them. Time was critical.

Once that's done, I'll need to determine if it's just Greater Texas that's trying to wipe out the blimp fleet, or if it's a World Court plot. It will be a lot easier to punish Texas than it will be to send the message to the whole world.

He was a little uneasy, sending an attack so deeply into Texas. The sky was his, of course, and he needed to defend it. He was well on his way to owning the seas as well. But sending a ground force felt so much like the old pre-Star warfare. History warned that taking another country's soil was a lot harder than many leaders had been able to handle.

I don't want to own their land. Controlling the shipping is enough. If they had just played fair from the beginning, none of this would have happened.

Interviews

Samuel rapped on Clark's door. A muffled voice said, "Come in, I need your approval."

Puzzled, he tested the door, and the latch wasn't engaged. He pushed on in.

Clark turned, and it was Rachael. Yes, she still had her hair under the cap and still wore the worn coveralls, but she had breasts. In fact, she was completely girl-shaped under the drab.

Her eyes were Rachael's blue, but the face was colorless, more like a normal person.

After having gotten used to the Clark wrapper, Samuel felt a surge of appreciation, even though this was a toned-down version of the true Rachael.

"What's this?"

She nodded, smiling at his reaction. "You said we were at risk of making the Melear people feel betrayed. Well, today is all the interviews—one at a time in the break room. It's the perfect time to come clean and ask them to be part of our little conspiracy."

He felt a little silly, with a stupid grin on his face. "Umm. What about your father? This will blow your cover."

She put her hand to her chin. It looked adorable. "Possibly. But I have been talking with him, more than once, while we're here. He's worried about the anti-genie sentiment that's being stirred up. I promised to be less attractive, more like this, and he seemed to be content with it." She gestured at her outfit. "I've aged my face and I'm already staying out of the public. I'm either at work or that little dump of a restaurant. No one will notice me.

And I've made it plain to him that I will be working in the screen industry, no matter what he wants of me."

"Tsk. I'd hardly call it a dump. They serve good food."

She glared, "You know what I mean! It's not fancy waiters and elaborate furnishings and a place where people go to be seen."

"Just a real restaurant, then?"

She took a deep breath. "Okay. I'm rich and spoiled. And... the food is good. Satisfied?"

He gave her one nod. "If you're really going to work in this industry, you'll eat at much worse places."

"But what about the costume? I really need to know whether to go with this, or to put the wraps and padding back on. I'd really love to be able to breathe all day. What do you think?"

He paused for a moment. "What's the cover story? What will keep them satisfied with keeping it a secret they can't share? I'm sure Midland has a news company that would love to boost their clicks with the story of a glamorous international heiress slumming at the airport. We don't want to dilute the event we're building."

She tucked at a wisp of her restored blonde hair escaping from the edge of her cap. "I've been thinking about that."

...

Marcos stood there with an open mouth. Samuel turned and looked at Clark, as if he wondered what the fuss was about.

"Oh, I thought your already knew Clark was female."

He swallowed, nodded, and said, "Well, yes, I did. Bill knew before I did. It's just... she's more...."

Rachael whispered in her normal voice, "Sorry. The wrappings were getting to be too much, and since you already knew..."

"Yes. Fine. No problem. So... what's your real name?"

She gave him a bashful look, "Maybe we'd better stick with 'Clark Peterson' for now... or just 'her' for that matter. The whole reason for the masquerade was to hide my job from my family. I still can't risk someone mentioning my true name to the wrong people. I just didn't think we needed to hide it from you."

...

"Manny. Manny Gonzales." He eyed Clark as she took a comb to his hair.

"Sorry about this. It's a historical record and you don't want your wife fussing about your hair all your life."

"If that day comes. Hey, what's the story? Clark ain't a girls name."

She beamed a smile designed to warm him up inside. "I'm hiding out while I learn my trade. Gotta keep it from my family."

She moved back to the camera and asked, "Manny Gonzales, what is it that you do here at Melear Aircraft?" Samuel had left her to do all the interviews while he went to edit the last set of tags. She was a little nervous, but it was fun.

He shrugged. "I bend metal. I take apart old pre-Star airplanes and put them back together better'n the original engineers."

...

"Matt James, electrical engineer. Of course, I suspected you were a girl. Larry was thinking you and your boss were lovers, but he didn't guess the truth, eh?"

She adjusted the pens in his pocket. She whispered, "Samuel is a bit of a stick-in-the-mud. But I'm working on him." She winked and moved back to the camera.

"Mr. James, can you tell me about what's been special about your work with the new plane?"

...

"Larry O'Neal, machinist." He was inspecting her as closely as if she were one of the turbine blades he worked on. "You're not quite what I was expecting, up close."

She smiled, "Sorry to disappoint."

"Oh, no. Just gossip. Hey, Marcos was thinking you were a spy for one of the other airplane companies."

"No, just anxious to get your story captured for the history books. Tell me about yourself."

...

"Chuck Haywood, engine specialist—although I've been really stretching it on this job. The Nance-Bate engine is hardly a jet turbine." He frowned.

"I'm a little uncomfortable with this. The secrecy is pretty tight. I don't know how much I really ought to be telling you."

She nodded seriously. "I completely understand. I've been wrapped up like an Egyptian mummy since the day I arrived, trying to keep my job a secret from my family. Today is exciting, making the decision to drop the disguise for you guys. But it's a little dangerous if the news got out. It would be a distraction from the project.

"But honestly, I'm not too interested in your technical details anyway. Eventually Bill Melear will sell or release what he wants, and that's not our decision as screencrafters. What I would like to capture today is the human interest. How do you feel about your work here? Pleased, frightened, disillusioned—what would you tell a grandchild about your time here?"

He nodded. "I'll trade you. Secret for secret."

She hesitated. "Okay."

He looked at the door, just to make sure there was no one listening. "The guys have been chatting—gossip if you will, and it's exploded since you started talking today. I've been listening, and one thing doesn't quite ring true. Why are you really here? Surely there are a lot more comfortable assignments where you could learn your camera work. Why here?"

She glanced at the doorway, and tugged her cap off. She straightened and re-wrapped her hair as she talked. "I'm famous. Not for anything I've done, but because my father is very rich."

She could tell that he probably believed her, but there was no recognition. Probably he paid no attention to the gossip news. "As a result, I've been protected, protected from my own incompetence even. I could hire great instructors, but I'd never know if my work was good, or if they were just protecting my feelings. Money can keep truth at a distance."

She felt a wave of relief, putting this into words.

"Samuel didn't know who I was when I met him. I'm sure he likes me, but he took extraordinary steps not to fall for me. He's struggled to keep us on a professional setting at all costs. And he tells me my mistakes.

"If Samuel gives me a compliment, then it's real. If I'm doing it wrong, he points it out, quickly and with no sugar topping. I've learned more by being around him in these few days than I have from any other instructor in years.

"So if Samuel scores a secret assignment in the middle of the desert, then I'll find a way to be his assistant, even if I have to wear this stupid cap and hide behind clothes that chafe and pounds of ugly makeup on my face."

Chuck nodded. "Good enough."

He straighten in his chair and faced the camera. "Although this project has been outside my field of expertise, I find it one of the most fascinating opportunities I've ever been given."

···

The overhead lights turned off with a click of relays that echoed in the huge hangar. In one of the little offices, Rachael stirred from her sleep, head resting on a table across from where Samuel was making his final adjustments to the tags.

She sniffed, and stretched back in her chair. "What was that?"

"It's late. We may be the last ones here. You conked out on me."

"Sorry. For some reason, those interviews took a lot out of me."

He nodded, not looking up from his terminal display. "You were acting, playing a role all day. Adrenaline was spicing up your performance, keeping you on track. But when it was done, you faded. I've seen it happen before—to me and to others. Every time you're putting yourself out there to be judged, it takes a toll."

"I hope I didn't flub the lines."

"I'm sure you did fine."

"Have you reviewed my captures?"

He shook his head. "Not yet. I'm still focussed on these tags. Two days from now Bill is rolling out the new plane and I have to be done with these before then."

"What happens then?"

"The rollout? If I understand it, they'll fire up the engines and taxi the plane down the runway. If everything goes as planned, he'll lift off and fly a big circle and land again. He's naming the plane then, as well. But that's a big secret."

Samuel looked up and met her eyes. He gave a little smile. "That's what I'm worried about. It will be my first and only chance to get real captures of the plane in the air, not just these old historical images we've been using. I've never done that before, and I won't have a second chance."

"I'm sure you'll do fine."

"You'll be behind a camera, too. We'll be editing the best captures into a ten minute feature to be made available on the eleventh. Sort of a super-tag. We have to get the whole world primed to watch on the twelfth, real-time."

She nodded. "And then the documentaries."

"Right. Cross your fingers that Bill is on top of his game, or all our work might be a case study in how to build a failed event. You might not want Rachael Nue's name on these."

A confident smile lit her face. "Yes, I do. No matter what." She reached across the table and took his hand. They said nothing for a moment.

And then, outside in the hangar, there was the clatter of metal as something like a bunch of wrenches was spilled. They barely had time to flinch at that noise when a gunshot echoed through the building.

Spies

"Camera!" shouted Samuel. After a frozen second, she nodded and grabbed for the unit she'd been using for the interviews. There was still plenty of memory left. Tripod? No. Lights? That would just make them a target. She set it for maximum light gathering. With just their office lights illuminating the whole space, the image would be horrible.

Samuel knelt down at the doorway, holding his handset out around the edge. She saw that, even under this dangerous situation, he was careful to hold the camera steady and level.

There were three more gunshots—flashes of light in the darkness.

Across from them, Bill Melear's office opened up, spilling light, doubling what little illumination was available in the hangar. Bill and Marcos were both there. Marcos pointed their way and then tugged Bill down and back into the office.

There was a yell, and then someone began scanning the place with a flashlight.

Samuel whispered a narration, "I see two men with guns, an overturned tool cart, and what is possibly a body on the ground beside the tool cart. The two are gesturing hand signs between themselves. They appear to be searching for any other threats.

"One of them is now on his knees, searching the body or checking for injuries, I can't tell which."

Rachael, conscious that Samuel's little handset camera likely had better low-light response than hers, decided to scan the area, sweeping the hangar and zooming in on Melear's office, showing them watching the events fearfully.

From the darkness, a voice called out. "It's safe. Miss Nue, could you please stay clear?"

Marcos moved quickly across to the far wall and threw the light switches. The hangar lit up.

Samuel looked up at her.

She nodded. "Daddy's security guards. I recognize the voice."

They got to their feet. She shifted the camera to her shoulder.

He put out his hand. "Shouldn't you stay back, like they said?"

"I've been disobeying that guy all my life. I'm not changing now." She reset the light setting on her camera and then stepped out.

Samuel hurried over to meet Bill and Marcos. He whispered and pointed at her. They all went to where the others were examining the body.

As she approached, a familiar face showed his resignation as he saw through her makeup and costume. "Please. I don't advise coming any closer."

"I have to. Cameraman." She aimed past his hand and saw the black-clad body, face marked with camouflage staring sightless up at the ceiling. There was a gun just inches from his outstretched fingers on the concrete.

"I'm Bill Melear. This is my facility. What's going on here?"

The lead guard nodded. "Yes, sir. I recognized you. We apprehended a saboteur entering the area. When he shot at us, we returned fire and brought him down."

Marcos asked, "Saboteur?"

"Yes, sir." He pointed down at a small device lying loose on the floor. "That is a Hi-B, high brisiance explosive device, with a remote control detonator. We've de-activated it. There are several more with two other individuals that we have restrained in the parking lot outside."

"What were they trying to do?"

"Unknown, sir."

Bill asked, "Why are you here?"

He looked over to where Rachael was trying to maintain her composure. She'd had to turn on the anti-shake circuit. Blood was seeping across the concrete. She'd never seen a dead man before.

"We were hired to protect the safety of our principal. I have also been ordered to preserve her privacy."

Bill nodded. "I understand. I recognize you, too. You were with Mr. Nue when he picked up his plane, weren't you?"

"Yes, sir."

Marcos asked, looking up from the dead man. "What do we do now? Call the police?"

"Soon, but we were not expecting their arrival. We only took action when it appeared that our principal might be in danger. There is still the possibility that one or more bombs were placed on the airplanes parked outside. We have the remote detonator, but the planes need to be inspected."

"Yes! I'll get a light trolley."

The guard put up his hand. "We can do this, sir. It might be dangerous."

Marcos tightened his lips. "The planes are my business. You'll need my eyes." He moved over to the wall and lit up a small wheeled lighting cart.

Bill said, "I'd prefer to minimize the public knowledge of this. Anything that delays our new plane's launch would be disastrous. Almost as bad as if the explosive went off."

The guard gestured to his partner and he followed Marcos out the hangar door. Rachael took a step to follow.

The guard shifted the gun into his other hand and held up his hand, to her, "No."

She paused. "It's my job."

Samuel said, "I'll go with her."

He sighed, locking eyes with Samuel. "Keep her at least fifty yards away from the planes and the black mini-truck. I'll be there shortly."

...

A Ranger car pulled into the parking lot thirty minutes later. Rachael zoomed in on the rearing stallion emblem on the side. One man in a western hat got out. He had a gun at his belt.

Samuel tapped her on the shoulder. He spoke quietly. "It's all over, but we'll be stuck here for hours yet if this plays out like other crime-scene investigations I've been at. There'll be nothing to capture that I can't get with my handset. Take the camera back to our office, make sure everything is uploaded, and take a nap. It's going to be a long night and we'll have to take shifts."

She nodded and left.

Ranger Tom Craddik examined the body, and the explosives—the one from the hangar and three others. Those had been magnetically clamped to the engines of the planes awaiting pickup by Greater Texas. Pilots were scheduled to arrive within hours. If the Nue family guards had not been in place, Texas would not have received its planes.

The two other saboteurs, still bound hand and foot, refused to talk, but a piece of paper in the dead man's pocket had a list of all the planes Melear Aircraft had sold in the past year, with checkmarks by the ones that had been marked for destruction.

Bill looked it over. "All but one. They didn't know about our newest prototype."

Samuel made non-commercial copies of the firefight captures for Craddik, and after a whispered request, for the guard as well. By dawn, the body had been removed and Marcos had manned the mop himself to get the bloodstains up from the concrete floor.

...

"Rachael? It's time to wake up."

She groaned and followed him out to the car. "I expected the Ranger would question me."

"Relish your life of privilege. Since you were with me every instant of the fight and we had a capture of the whole thing, I was able to answer everything he needed."

"Who was it?"

"Marcos seemed to suspect business competitors, but the others were more inclined to blame Australia, what with this war scare."

"Australian spies. They're after the new plane?"

"No, they were going to bomb the ones Texas just bought. Protecting their blimps, I guess. Who knows in this crazy business?"

She frowned, "I'm surprised Ben let me go."

"Ben?"

"The guard. Ben Mason. The other is Ira Green. They've been with the family longer than I have."

"Closed-mouth sort. I'd been labeling them Guard One and Guard Two. But they know their business."

"Yeah."

He glanced to the side, where she was staring at her hands.

"Lucky they found you."

"Right."

"They must be expert detectives."

She winced. "I told Daddy where I was."

"Oh?"

"Yes. Last night. I mean the night before—after we talked about how bad it would be if the guards stormed the hangar and took me away. That night I called Daddy and explained how important this new job was to me, and how serious it would be if the guards caused any trouble. As a gesture of good faith, I confessed that I was in Midland, not Dallas, and begged for him to let me stay put and finish the job. I guess the guards arrived yesterday and set up surveillance."

"Sounds like your father deserves an especially nice birthday card this year."

"Yeah." She started shivering.

He put his arm around her. "It's okay. It's all over now."

They arrived at the motel and when they stopped at her door, she asked. "Samuel, could you stay with me?"

His eyes looked sad and tired, she sounded distressed, but right now he couldn't tell if it was another of her endless ploys. "I really need a shower and at least six hours of sleep, and then we'll have to go back to work. Things are really starting to accelerate now."

"Please, I just need someone to hold me, for a little bit. Nothing more."

He sighed and nodded. They went in and bolted the door.

She shed her cap and kicked off her shoes. He eased down on the bed beside her and closed his eyes as she snuggled close, breathing onto his chest. It had been a long day, and nothing could be more comfortable.

...

King Thomas waited for hours. There was no signal from his Texas team. Local news reports said nothing. He desperately wished for eyes in the area, but he had pulled in everyone within five hundred miles of Midland to execute the attack.

Pre-Star generals would have satellite cameras in orbit above and drone airplanes to watch the attack. Pre-Star networks could be hacked for information. It's so hard to find out anything now.

He pulled up the fleet's map of blimps. He growled in frustration. North America had been emptied of blimp traffic, other than two still left in Louisiana. What was more, the admiral had ordered all blimps out of the Gulf of Mexico. Even the remaining two were scheduled to lift off and take a northerly overland route to the Pacific. Their status report showed them taking on extra water to minimize the possibility of being shot at. They'd stay high and out of sight for as long as possible.

I have to find out what's happening in Midland.

He keyed a Royal order. The admiral didn't like him going around fleet channels, but his need for information was urgent. Besides, they would just be shifting their course by a few hundred miles and dropping down for a quick inspection. It was hardly different from what they'd planned already.

Of course, he'd order them to report to him only. Everything had to be tightly capped.

RIP

The harbormaster stood at attention in the display. "It's certain. The algae patches are unsightly, but innocuous as they drift downstream from Bremen, but once they reach the vicinity of the shipyards, they clump up into green balls. The denser they are, the larger the clumps. We didn't worry too much about that, since we could motor right through them with no obstruction. They didn't clog the propellers like the kelp.

"But then, one of the harbor patrol ships ground to a halt and had to be towed to shore. The propeller shaft was coated with the green blob, and it had eaten into the steel. Out of balance, the shaft bent and everything jammed."

"The algae eats steel?" Baron Jenner asked.

"Yes. Definitely. I sent crews to scrape the blobs off of metal surfaces. Everything that was iron—boat hulls, marker buoys, anchor chains and even dry-dock gates, they all show signs of corrosion, as if treated with acid."

Jenner felt his heart pounding. "How many ships? How much equipment has been exposed?"

The harbormaster shook his head. "Perhaps a hundred vessels, of all classes. All of the channel-facing infrastructure. Plus, fresh algae is arriving constantly from upstream."

"How difficult is it to clean off the blobs?"

He shrugged. "High pressure water hoses get the most of it, but the corroded surface has to be scrubbed out by hand to get every last trace. But if the metal surface goes back into the waters, more blobs stick to the cleaned surface."

The conference went on for hours. Some of the danger went unstated, but everyone could put the pieces together. The word was out. All ships in the area were diverting to other harbors. The Bremerhaven waters were to be avoided at all costs. Nor were other European ports willing to take ships that might have been exposed to the green blobs. It was still unknown if a ship carrying the corrosive material could infect other waters. No port would risk that.

A large portion of the ships that he had intended to sell to the European government were either sitting in the water with their hulls being eaten away, or safe up on dry land, with no way to put them in the water without subjecting them to the attack. Even the dry-docks could be compromised if the gates couldn't be kept clean.

Everyone was in agreement that it was hopeless unless the algae bloom upstream could be eradicated. Floating booms were ordered to try to contain the early-stage version before it could reach the shipyard.

Cleanup was hampered by the lack of manpower. The most experienced crews had been sent to kelp-infested harbors on the southern coast to deal with that issue. Jenner had to move people away from where they were needed to where they were needed more. Finally, he left his people to do their jobs.

It's come to this. He shook his head, almost exhausted dealing with the constant calls for his help. His people needed a dozen of him. He needed thousands more of them.

He composed himself and sat in silence, looking out over San Diego. Then he tapped on his display.

The Duke of Lorraine's assistant appeared.

"I need to speak with the duke concerning a previous offer."

...

Captain Kelly frowned at the Salvadoran coastline thirty miles off the port side. "Something is wrong. We're losing altitude."

Grant tapped at his display, reading the barometric altimeter. "You're right, unless we're entering a high pressure zone." He turned on the laser echo altimeter that they had deactivated to avoid detection. "Definitely. Dropping a couple of feet a minute." His hand hovered over the controls that would feed more water to the *Lance*'s tendrils to increase the rate of hydrogen production.

"Hold off," she ordered. If we've got a hydrogen leak, I want to know how bad it is. Monitor our rate of fall."

She went to the ladder and scanned the interior. Looking through internal layers of skin, she could see the minuscule image of someone, probably Danny, working on the outside of the hydrogen bag, up on top.

Down below, Caleb was kneeled over, applying a patch. There were dozens of white X's, and just an hour before Danny had grumbled that he was running out of patches in his kit.

She inhaled sharply. From this vantage point, the patched places formed a definite pattern. She looked up, wishing for binoculars. The patches on the top side were barely visible, but maybe they showed the same organization.

"Caleb! Come here."

"Yes, Captain!" he yelled back, but waited to finish his latest repair before heading to the ladder at a run.

She waited for him to reach the top before speaking. In a low voice she asked, "Caleb, look at your patches below. Can you see a pattern?"

He held on with one hand and leaned casually to look below. "Um. Yes. Maybe. They seem to line up on one of the major veins."

"Good. I have a job for you. Go aft and get close enough to Danny to report the pattern we see here and to also tell him that we're seeing a distinct and growing hydrogen leak. Leave him your patches and tell him he is to keep patching the main bag until his supplies run out. We need to stay in the air until we can reach land."

Caleb's face paled. "Yes, Captain."

"When you've relayed the message, report back to me. I'll have a task for you. Hurry."

He nodded and skimmed down the ladder fast enough that she worried about his hands.

"Grant? How's the elevation?"

"Down five more feet. Definitely losing gas."

She sighed. "Okay, open the water feed. We'll need all the lift we can maintain. Plot your best course for land."

He met eyes with her, then nodded.

She went to the communications terminal and called Fleet.

"The is Captain Kelly of the *Lance*. We are losing hydrogen and will be unable to make the Nicoya connection as ordered. We are diverting to the Salvadoran coast at best speed. Spots are appearing all over the ship, most noticeably along the major veins. Our patching supplies are depleted."

She attached co-ordinates and bearing, and sent it off. There was no need for a response. Fleet was overwhelmed. She'd seen more than a dozen "assist if possible" requests in the queue pointing to other blimps. The *Lance* would be just another on the list. More blimps were in trouble than ones available to come to their rescue.

···

Caleb located Danny's position before he reached Wizzer's engine room. He was nearly a third of the way forward. Any hope he could yell that far vanished as he approached the rear hatchway. The engines were spinning at full speed. Wizzer frowned and cupped his ear when he shouted, "I've got to go topside!"

The engineer grumbled, and Caleb was just as glad that he couldn't make out what he was saying. Wizzer shoved a safety harness was shoved his way, and after a moment's hesitation, helped him secure it and take up the slack to fit his smaller chest size. The safety line looked far too thin to hold his weight, but it was probably the best stuff in its class—not the simple hemp ropes he'd used to keep the cattle in control. Wizzer checked the spool and gave him a thumbs-up.

Heart pounding away in his chest, competing with the powerful roar of the engines, he crawled up on hands and knees, out of the hatch and along the ridge-line of the *Lance*. There was a major vein between his right hand and his left, and it was disturbing how many places had been patched nearby.

By the time he'd crawled fifty feet, he saw Danny working downslope on the right. In addition to his safety line, Danny had a dumbo—a hundred-pound sandbag that draped off the left flank of the blimp—a counterweight to the line that kept him from sliding off the side.

I don't have one of those. I have to stay on the ridge-line.

"Danny!" he yelled, but there was no response. The healer was working intently on a patch.

Caleb looked up, and suddenly it hit him like a slap in the face. He was out in the open, naked to the sky, with probably two thousand feet of fall below. The *Lance* was nosed over toward the shoreline, but they didn't appear to be making much headway. Bands of clouds—clearly curved, the edges of the storm still on the Gulf side of the isthmus—dominated the sky. Between the gaps in the clouds, a volcanic peak rose much higher than they were.

A gust of wind shook the *Lance*, and he lay face down, hugging the skin. It seemed to ripple beneath him. Fighting the urge to close his eyes and freeze, he raised his head. "Danny!"

This time, he looked up. "Caleb?"

"Captain sent me!" He held his patch kit. "Patches. Losing hydrogen. Keep patching until you run out."

"I know."

"Most spots near the vein!"

He looked around him. "Not good!"

Caleb unfastened his kit. "Patch kit?"

Danny pointed along the dumbo line. "Loop it."

Caleb nodded, fishing the strap under the line and latching it. He pushed it, but it wouldn't slide.

Danny yelled. "I'll get it later. Go back inside."

With a little wave, he turned around and began working his way back. The roaring fans were intimidating, and from his view on the ridge-line, the *Lance* was bending a little, every time a wind gust hit them.

The safety line was reeling itself back into the hatch every time he inched closer. *That's good. I'd hate to get it snagged in the propellers.*

He took one last look back along the flank of the *Lance* before he went inside. A break in the clouds let the sunlight play over the skin. There were hundreds of unpatched gray dots everywhere.

...

She was waiting for him at the cargo platform. "Caleb, we're going down. We're losing hydrogen faster than we can make it, and what's worse, the winds are coming from shore. The engines can't push us as fast as we need. We'll be in the surf before we reach land—unless we can lose weight."

She pointed at the wooden platform. "Break this down, and dump it."

"Out the hatch?"

Her face was as solemn as he'd ever seen it. "No need." She pointed off to the side where several of the patched holes had ripped, linking to form a six foot long gap to the open air below. "Dump everything there. No matter if it rips wider, the *Lance* is doomed. The only question is whether she'll take us with her."

Without another word, the captain carefully made her way back up to the command deck.

Caleb went to the tool bag and pulled out a large hammer and a big knife. Normally, the knife would have made him uncomfortable, but today he had to numb himself to many blimp instincts. He kept his eyes on the wood and tried to ignore the rippling green skin around him. The *Lance* was dying, and he could almost feel her cries. The ballonets were full and stretching, trying to make up for the shrinking hydrogen, but it wasn't enough. The sides were becoming wrinkled and flattening.

Seth jumped up on the platform beside him. "Tell me what to do."

"Get a knife and cut the lashings." The man nodded and went for the tool bag.

Blimp rules had kept nails from being any part of the platform construction. There were a few bolts in key positions in the framework, but everything was held in place with straps and ropes. Caleb cut the boards free of the framework, giving them a whack with the hammer when they stuck. He almost froze up when he held the first board over the edge. He grit his teeth and shoved. It fell a little short, but it made no difference. The tear opened with an low-pitched rip, and the board tumbled free, vanishing in the cloud layer below them.

Seth came up behind him, his forehead deeply wrinkled. Without a word, he tossed another board. The tear widened another few inches.

Six more boards went through the gap, and the captain yelled from above. "It's going too slow. Caleb, Seth, go around the edges and cut the bottom out." Then she vanished back inside.

Seth met his eyes. "Start on the side with the rip?"

Caleb couldn't talk. He hadn't reached that point where there was freedom in destruction. He was still hurting the *Lance*. But he nodded.

They pulled out their knives. Seth went aft and Caleb went fore, holding onto the platform's framework for support while cutting away the skin that was holding it in place. As a child, he'd seen an animated screen with a character sitting on a tree branch, sawing away at the base of the very limb where he sat. It was the same thing. Any instant, the weight of the platform could widen the tear uncontrollably and take Seth and him right out of the blimp to crash into the waters below.

He rounded to the leading edge of the platform, where most of the floor boards were already gone from when they had unloaded the cattle. With every gust of wind, the platform was rocking, still attached on the port side but waving free on the starboard.

"Hang on!" yelled Seth. "I'm cutting through the ballast trough."

That was the strongest part of the blimp's skin, where it had folded into a thick-sided container. But it had to go if they were going to cut the platform free.

He was already around to the port-side corner when there was a strong lurch, almost throwing him free.

Is it going? He should jump free to try to reach the side.

But the rip noise was coming from above. He looked up.

The ridge-line of the main hydrogen bag, where he'd been just recently, was opening up like a zipper.

Bam. Rip. And Danny, a wide frozen scream on his face, fell though the hydrogen bag and ripped through the plenum like it wasn't there, hitting the platform once and then bouncing on through the hole in the floor. The dumbo and its line followed. The safety line, still attached to Danny, cut through the plenum like a knife.

I'm falling. He gripped the framework of the deck. Everything was falling. There was the sound of twisting metal and the dying sigh of the motors.

Don't Rescue Them

Samuel struggled out of a solid slumber, puzzling out a vaguely floral scent and a warm bundle in his arms. There was a tickle on his face, a strand of hair. And it was daylight.

He opened his eyes and focused on Rachael's clear blue ones staring back at him. He couldn't move without pulling her closer, and that seemed right. Her lips met his and only a moment later did he gently pull back.

"Why am I kissing you?"

She smiled, "Careful planning, endless patience, and exquisite timing."

He was awake, but not fully alert. What she said sounded right.

"You smell clean."

"I didn't want you to wake up to Clark's face. I've had a shower. You still need one."

It occurred to him that the bundle he was holding was very smooth. Round, warm, and smooth. He stroked, and then stopped. Perhaps that wasn't a good idea. It seemed nice, though.

Her smile was playful, as if she were reading his mind. "You could use my shower, if you want."

He frowned, suddenly worried. "What time is it?"

"Six hours since you fell asleep. Six hours and thirty seconds since you put your arm around me. Thank you for that. I needed it, after what happened last night."

She smiled again to lighten the mood. "While I haven't subjected you to my evil genie witchcraft—nor the guys at the hangar either, for that matter—I do have an excellent internal alarm clock. You said you needed six hours sleep, and you got it."

He remembered saying that. And he did need a shower. His clothes were binding, he smelled, and there were more reasons than one why he shouldn't—couldn't follow through with the temptation on his mind.

Strangely, he trusted her, in spite of the most obvious peril of all—she was rich, powerful, and used to having her way. People like him didn't have a chance against her.

It was so very tempting to give in.

"Set your clock. Three minutes, and then I'm out of here."

"Aww."

He pulled her close and kissed. For three magical minutes, which seemed like thirty seconds, he let himself be a guy holding and kissing a girl who wanted him. His hands mapped what portions of her he could reach, but his focus was on how deeply they could share their breath.

"Mmm." She pushed harder into the kiss.

He reached deep and managed to find the brakes. "Time?"

She nodded, breathing deeply.

He was tingling all over, and he had to break free now. He pushed back, with a lingering touch, and sat up on the bed, careful not to look at her for a moment.

"I'll go clean up and change clothes, and then breakfast?"

"Lunch," she said, from under the sheet.

"Right." He took a few deep breaths, building the will to stand. "We have camera angles to decide."

She said nothing as he got up and walked out.

I guess that went okay. He closed the door behind him and went to his room, wondering if Ben and Ira were waiting just around the corner, watching their every move. *I really want to do that again.*

...

"Don't rescue them." Admiral Dale hated to give the order. His family had been in the gene modification business since the Star, almost. While he owned only a small portion of the blimp business, he had been deep into its operation since his father gave him the grand tour of the seeding yards. He had many more friends in the air than he had at court.

But there was a display now, permanently up on the big map. There were red dots where blimps with spots had gone down, and yellow lines showing their previous routes.

Theory One was that there was a single release of the spores, picked up by the hurricane winds and spread across the Gulf of Mexico. Theory Two was that infected blimps created spores themselves, becoming new sources of the infection.

The yellow lines told the story. There were blimps that were just now showing the gray spots that had never been in the Gulf, but had crossed the path of an infected blimp.

We're spreading into the second generation. Sending a blimp to rescue another is a death sentence.

But all indications were that it was spread by airborne spores. How far would they drift? How long would they be infectious?

They really needed a sample to work with. The *Lance* was down, but there were other candidates to meet the courier plane.

...

Caleb gripped the floating wood. Five feet away, a cross-brace snapped under the load of the collapsed gas bag. The waves splashed higher.

No! The platform is trapped under the skin, and it's dragging me under.

Inflated, the blimp rode easy on the ocean waves, but now, ripped open, it was just dead weight.

The engines! The metalwork riding the blimp's tail was pulling everything under. Maybe the captain's deck equipment as well, but that had been built light.

Panicked, he fumbled at his waist. He'd shoved the knife in his belt when he braced for the crash. The impact hadn't been bad. The blimp had only been two or three hundred feet high when it had opened up. The skin could no longer hold the gas, but it was huge and acted like a collapsing parachute to minimize the speed at which they hit.

He pulled himself around the edge of the platform and hurriedly worked at the job he had started, cutting the wooden structure away from the *Lance's* skin. Only this time, he was jettisoning the blimp rather than the wood.

The force of the engines dragging the skin under helped speed it up, ripping the skin almost as fast as he slashed at it.

Far too soon, the green wrapper that had protected and supported him the whole trip swirled in the water and vanished below.

If anyone is coming to the rescue, they'll never find us. The blimp is gone.

The boards, still stained by cattle droppings, made a broad but shallow raft. The waves ripped over the surface in places. He panted, still gripping the knife tightly.

Where was Seth? Where were any of the others?

Carefully, he moved to the center of the wobbly platform and stood up.

The mountains in the distance looked too far to swim, but he only gave that a moment's thought. He looked for other survivors in the water.

After a minute, he saw someone prone in the surf. There might have been movement, he couldn't tell.

I've got to get to him. He might be unconscious.

He was not a great swimmer, and the waves were fairly high from the winds.

I'll drown. He looked around the platform. *There!* It was just a loose board about three feet wide, part of the flooring that he had been trying to cut loose. It was only secured by a small strand of the rope. He severed it and pulled it into the water.

He fumbled, trying to find the right way to use it. It made it much harder to swim, but he could hang on to it and rest. The platform wasn't drifting away. Maybe they were all in motion in the current, but at least they were all drifting together.

It was Ray, the communications officer. Dead eyes and bloody skin half torn off his scalp left no doubt. He had hit hard and hadn't survived.

Had he been at his station, or running some errand? Where was the captain? Where were all the others?

He pushed away, paddling back toward the relative safety of the platform—his life raft.

Wizzer probably stayed with his engines. The painful memory of Danny hitting the boards hard before being drug under by the heavy weight of the dumbo made him wince. *Danny is gone.*

Ray gone. Seth? Who knows? He tried to visualize where everyone was, but with no luck. He'd been focused on his own task.

The thud of wood hitting wood brought him alert. He reached the platform and paddled around the edge. *Oh!* It was one of the food crates they'd bought in Louisiana.

He towed it around to the shallow part of the platform and pulled it up out of the water. A look inside showed various canned goods, two loaves of bread and three bananas that were going black. He peeled one and ate it down.

Closing the crate, he moved it to the safest position on the crooked raft and sat down. *At least I have a seat.*

The sun angle had changed the look of the distant shoreline, but one thing was clear. It was farther away. Wind or current or both were moving him away from any hope of safety.

Well, that's what a life of adventure is—a greater risk of death. At least he didn't have any family that would grieve for him.

Lightning flashed off to the east, closer to the mountains. Sitting there made him the highest point around. A prime target for a lighting strike, if the rains came his way.

Rain. Water. Fresh water. He got to work. Soon Caleb had the waterproof food crate opened up to the sky, ready to catch any possible rain drops. He had the food bundled in his shirt and securely tied to a cross beam above the level of the waves.

It almost felt like busy work. Was there really any chance that he could survive this? He was alone. Blimp training didn't include being stranded at sea. If the rumors were true and all the blimps were coming down with spots, then no one would be left to come to their rescue.

I guess I need to hope for some boat to find me, and not shoot at me.

He reached into his pocket and pulled out the mangled bullet. *Hardly a good luck piece.* Angrily, he threw it aside. He heard it hit the boards.

I shouldn't do that. Saul gave me that.

Crawling around on hands and knees, he finally found it and put it back in his pocket.

It was a little after sunset when he saw the flicker of light.

The first time, he thought it was just a trick of his imagination. He searched the horizon, a little to the north of east, but with all the waves, he couldn't see anything floating there.

Then it happened again. A light. A moving light. It was strong enough to penetrate the low level of mist caused by all the white-capped waves. How far, he didn't know.

But he had to try. Carefully, he moved his arm from the position of the light, straight overhead to the brightest stars coming up in the southwest. If he lost his bearing back to the raft, then it wouldn't matter what he found.

He grabbed his board and stepped off into the water. He started paddling, riding it like a surfboard—a very unruly surfboard.

The light resolved into a figure, swinging a flashlight, barely staying afloat.

Captain Kelly? And she was holding on to something.

He pushed harder, swinging up closer. She seemed dazed, moving the light by rote, near exhaustion.

"Captain! Grab hold of the board."

"What?" She faced him. "Caleb? Help me with Grant. He's hurt."

One look told him that Grant was drowned. She'd been holding onto a dead man, kept afloat by seat cushions strapped around her with a belt.

"I'll take care of him. Grab my arm."

She was barely able to function. Caleb helped her onto the board while he swam around, collecting what he could. Grant's body was mostly under water, but he checked his pockets. Nothing other than a pen and a soggy wallet with ruined pictures. He kept those, but there was nothing he could do for Grant. It would take a lot of luck just to get her back to the raft.

On the board, the captain had collapsed, finally. Caleb snagged the flashlight before it slid into the sea, and turned it off.

He checked the stars—what showed between bands of rapidly moving clouds. He held onto the board and kicked, like he had been taught in swim class back when he was seven. It wasn't fast, but it was all he could do.

Ten minutes later, the stars were gone and the splash of the waves was joined by warm droplets of tropical rain.

Keep the same direction. Stay on course. It was all he could do.

The captain rolled, and he stopped to shift her back onto the center of the board. *How far have I come? Have I lost the raft?*

The stars were gone, and he'd lost his sense of direction. He clung to the board and rested, with the rain beating down on his back. It was all he could do.

Lightning struck, lighting the clouds like vast blue dragons swirling just overhead. The raft was visible for an instant. He had missed it, passing by the side. He turned and kicked with renewed urgency.

Taking the Wraps Off

Jason Bolls glanced at the blue light and tapped his screen.

"Samuel! It's good to hear from you. How are things in the middle of nowhere?"

His nephew smiled. "Going well. We're gearing up for a real-time event soon."

"On the twelfth?"

Samuel chuckled. "You guessed."

"It was pretty obvious, with what I already knew. You, Bill, and airplanes in the tags. Anything I should know about?"

Samuel lost his smile. "It's getting tense here. Australian spies tried to blow up the place."

"What? I haven't heard."

"It's being kept under wraps. Rachael Nue's security guards caught them just in time. No explosions, but some very nasty bombs had already been attached to the planes. They may not even have known about the new one, Greater Texas had just emergency-ordered Bill's other planes, and those were the ones with the bombs."

"So Miss Nue is there with you?"

Samuel straightened slightly. "Yes, disguised as my assistant, Clark Peterson. You'll see her in the credits before long. She's doing quite well."

"'Clark'. That must be some disguise."

Samuel shook his head. "We were on the same train. I told her she couldn't come because she'd be too distracting on the set. So she ignored me, disguised herself as a man and showed up anyway with a cart-load of very handy camera gear. Maybe I should have run her off, but now I'm glad I didn't.

"By the way, all of Bill's crew are in on it. Her disguise wasn't quite perfect and there were some suspicions, so we confessed. Now she looks like a female camera jockey, but she's doing her job."

Jason was uneasy. "Could she compromise the shoot?"

Samuel scratched his cheek. "I don't think so. She's caked in makeup to reduce the dazzle factor, dressed in old coveralls. The workers here are used to her now, and she's always behind a camera. And Uncle Jason, she's working hard and has talent. You've seen the tags?"

"Yes, once I realized they were yours."

"She did the voiceovers, and about half the camera work. I'm doing the post-processing and editing, but she's putting her fingers in that as well. She's a help, not a distraction."

Jason noticed that there was still a topic that his nephew was avoiding. Honestly, if the girl was behaving herself, he didn't need to know the personal details.

"So things are running smoothly, with the exception of conspiracies on the set and bombs on the planes?"

Samuel nodded. "But I need a favor."

...

Rachael looked up as he came out of the office with his handset. "Any problems?"

Samuel shook his head. "He'll put the tripod mounts on the morning train—not in time to get the motorized mount in place for test flight, though. But we can have that for the main event, with a few days to prepare."

Good news, but it wasn't what she was worried about. "Did you tell him about me?"

He spread his hands. "I could hardly explain about the bombs without bringing Ben and Ira into the story. Don't worry. He didn't order you off the set."

They went back to the airstrip where they had their tripods positioned, doing practice runs capturing the landing and takeoffs. The Texas flight crews had arrived and the pilots were doing familiarity testing with their new planes. Bill wanted them all gone from his landing strip before he wheeled out his new plane tomorrow. He'd confessed to Samuel that although the pilots might be in the way, his real reason for getting them out of sight was that the purchasing representatives might decide to confiscate the new plane as well, once they realized what it could do.

"Here comes another one."

Both of them aimed their cameras at the dot in the sky on the horizon, panning when it came down close, touching the concrete for an instant, and then applying power again to head back into the sky.

They reviewed their captures.

"I could smooth these up in the edit, but these tripod mounts aren't designed for fast pans. See here where it jerked."

She nodded. "And Bill's new plane is supposed to be faster."

"That's what we'll need to show. Let's get ready for the next pass."

···

Captain Bourke of the *Kiwi* chatted with Dibbs on the *Green Monster*.

"I'm not getting any closer. There are airplanes all over the sky. I can stick my nose out from this nice fluffy cloud every so often and get a quick peek," said Bourke.

Dibbs checked his map. "I hear airplanes don't fly into clouds. I hope that's true. Is there any place for me to hide? I should arrive in your area before too long. I'm riding at five thousand feet, and it doesn't feel high enough, what with the airplanes around."

"There are hundreds of clouds in this patch. I'm just drifting with the wind, keeping the engine off unless I need to reposition. The moisture on the skin is helpful. I'm leaking a little."

"Spots?"

"Yeah. I don't have a good feeling about this. If it weren't for the royal order, I'd be churning the props for friendly territory as fast as I could."

Dibbs sighed. "Same here. My healer is doing all she can, but there are too many spots to keep patched. I've got a feeling that before too long, royal order or not, I'll have to set down and go into hiding and practice my Texican accent."

"Yessir, physics trumps royals, no matter what they think."

"Well, I'll look forward to having you close when you get here. For now, its time to report in. For your info, there are three jet airplanes landing and taking off again at the airstrip between Midland and Odessa. Stay out of sight."

...

It was already too late. Hank Baker of Odessa had been watching the airplanes with his binoculars when a patch of green in the clouds caught his eye. It didn't last long, but he was sure he'd seen a blimp. He raced into the house and called the police. They were interested, at first, but when he couldn't identify which cloud held the blimp, all they could do was alert officers in the field and pass the word to the people at the airport. They didn't want do much more. It wouldn't help anything to panic the populace.

Ranger Craddik caught the alert on his handset as he monitored the activity at the airport. Immediately, he rounded up the air crews. There were some hurried debates, but they were there to collect planes for coastal defense, not to play hide-and-seek in the clouds. Before the hour was out, all three planes were refueled and heading east toward Houston. They took routes that kept them clear of any place a blimp could be hiding.

Rachael and Samuel captured it all. She looked at him. "Can we sell this?"

He frowned. "News about Greater Texas buying airplanes? Theoretically, although it's not part of our main job. If it weren't for the other thing, I'd put it in the Queue in an instant. The local news may be covering it, but no one was as close as we were. We should have asked permission before they left, but I didn't think about it."

"Do you usually ask permission?"

He gave a bashful smile, "No. But can we afford to have Texas mad at us, just days before our most critical event?"

She nodded toward the Ranger, sitting against his car beside the airstrip. "Ask him. He's been watching us the whole time. If he doesn't know, he'd know who to call."

She loaded the cameras onto a hand trolley while Samuel went over to check. By the time she was packed up, Samuel and Craddik were talking, and from what she could read from body language, the conversation was something like: "Can we?"—"I don't know. Not my call."—"Can you find out?"—"If you insist."

Rachael wasn't by nature a patient person, unless it mattered. Waiting for a call didn't qualify. The cart was heavy but manageable. The whole airport was deliberately as flat as possible. Once she got it moving, it wasn't hard to steer.

Marcos saw her coming and offered to help. She shook her head. "No. Samuel wouldn't want me here if I can't do my job."

He shorted a laugh. "I find that hard to believe."

She blushed, and was glad her makeup was in place to hide the most of it. "This job is very important to him. You can understand."

He took a deep breath. "Yeah. Sometimes I think Bill has gone off the deep end, but I trust him. He's got something up his sleeve, for sure."

"Keeping it secret from you?"

"Yeah."

"Samuel knows something. He hints. But he's not telling me, either."

"Frustrating."

"Yeah."

Marcos looked over his shoulder. "Have you seen the plane?"

"Just across the hangar. Tomorrow it rolls out, they tell me."

He crooked his fingers. "Come with me."

She locked the wheels on the trolley, and with a skip to catch up, followed him toward the draped-off corner of the hangar.

Marcos was tugging free the tall black sheeting that had been draped from the rafters. "Bill had me put this up the whole time the Texas people were here. He was afraid they'd get sticky fingers, or ask too many questions."

The plane towered over them. Rachael muttered, "It's bigger than Daddy's plane."

Marcos nodded. "Yes, the one we built for Nue Electronics was a business jet. This one is based on an F-111 military jet—one of the highest performance jets of the pre-Star era."

She looked puzzled. "And only one person rides in this?"

"It's actually a two-seater, but Bill doesn't want a copilot. Stubborn cuss."

"I'd love to ride along."

"Wouldn't we all?"

Her handset vibrated. There was a message, "Come set up. We have permission."

"I've got to go. Thank you Marcos. I appreciate the look."

He pointed. "One more thing. When you take its picture tomorrow, make sure you get a good look at these under-wing mounts."

"Oh?"

Marcos nodded, with a worried look on his face. "One of Bill's secrets. The military plane had rockets and bombs attached there. Bill has something, but he's not telling."

She looked at the stubs where something could be attached and nodded.

...

Samuel positioned the tripod so the camera would get a nice overview of Melear's hangar and the airstrip behind it. "I want an intro. Then we'll follow by scenes of the planes flying past, with a voiceover talking about Greater Texas buying them for coastal defense. We need to edit it all together and get it in the Queue in thirty minutes, so we've no time to waste. Do you want to be in front of the camera, or behind it?"

Rachael considered the offer. It would be an great opportunity to get her face before the world. She took a deep breath. "No. Too much makeup, and I'd need a rehearsal. I'll run the camera."

...

King Thomas looped the new screen from Texas.

Coastal defense. That's a logical explanation, but is it true? And "rumors of blimps in the area"—did they actually see the two I sent, or is it general hysteria? Should I turn them loose, now that the planes are gone?

Something didn't seem right. They were still advertising an event on the twelfth. He slowed the images down, and froze on the scene with the young announcer talking in front of the hangar. He expanded the image and adjusted the brightness, bringing up the outlines of the black silhouette. *There is something in there. It's like one of the old military jets.*

I've got to get a look at it. I have to know what I'm fighting.

Celebration

Caleb held her up. "Here, drink this."

She sipped at the can with a knife puncture in the top. It was too dark to read the label. "What is it?"

"Canned corn. Drink all the water. I think you're dehydrated."

Captain Kelly winced after the first sip. "Not the best."

"I don't have a way to start a fire to cook it. But we'll need to eat and drink to survive."

"Here." She handed it toward him.

"No. There is more, but you need to eat first. I wasn't in the water as long as you were. You're too close to exhaustion. Hang onto the empty can; we'll need it."

She nodded, and sipped from the can again. "Grant. Did you find Grant?"

He looked away. "Yes, but there was nothing I could do for him."

Faintly, she asked, "Any of the others?"

He went down the list. There could be someone still alive out there, but not for long.

With urging, she finished the corn. He took the can and smoothed the edges. They had collected a couple of inches of rainwater in the crate, and they would need a drinking cup. He took a look at the remaining food, and then counted the banana as his portion for the day.

The band of clouds moved away, so he put the lid back on the crate and sat there, where he could watch over the captain. Every fifteen minutes or so, he followed her example and aimed the flashlight out over the water. Like he told her, it was possible there was someone still out there, just needing a direction to swim.

By dawn, he was dozing off more than he had planned.

I'll need to take a real nap. One more check to see if she's safe.

He would lash her to the raft if he thought he could get away with it. He looked around in the growing light. Maybe if he salvaged the lashing rope, he could build a shelter. They'd need it when the sun was hot.

He looked over his captain. She looked worn out, but she was breathing regularly. Maybe when she was rested, she'd take over and give him the orders. That's what he wanted.

As respectfully as possible, he looked her over for injuries. She seemed fine—no wounds. But here was one thing that worried him. On her cheek, there were three gray spots.

...

Admiral Dale didn't wait to call a meeting. He showed up in Dr. Tuck's laboratory as soon as there was news. Suffering the indignity of donning protective gear, he entered the sealed room through the double doors.

"Doctor. What do you know?"

Tuck looked comfortable in his gear, but shook his head. "I've never seen such a lethal... organism." He sighed. "I guess I'd call it a life form, but most of it looks like a machine." He shrugged. "I don't recognize the designer. I'd guess one of the anonymous players out on the Net."

"Tell me details. I need to know everything. The more information, the more chance I'll have of defeating this infection."

The doctor shook his head. "It's a targeted weapon. As far as I can tell, it works in stages. The shape of the spore looks like a spear head—an elongated spearhead with slanted bristles. On the microscopic scale, simple mechanical motion from ambient heat causes it to wedge deeper and deeper into the skin. The dimensions of the spear tip and the bristles are exactly tuned to match the structure of blimp skin. It doesn't need pores to enter—it forces its way in until it reaches the cytoplasm.

"In the next stage, there is a band of RNA that is attracted to a specific section of the blimp DNA. There, it behaves like a virus and hijacks the cell to make copies of itself. The newly-created spores travel randomly. Some infect neighboring cells, some reach the skin and force their way out. Careful microscopic examination shows many loose spores on the surface of the gray patches. They're small enough to blow off in the wind and light enough to drift great distances."

The admiral nodded. "Show me. I've got to see this thing."

They went to a sealed glass glovebox container where a square slice of blimp skin was sitting under lights. The green tissue was covered by hundreds of gray spots, many of them merging into large irregular patches. The doctor reached his arms into the box and scraped a dark powder from the patches. The skin tore under the blade."

Dale gasped, "It's so weak."

"Yes. The cells begin to separate. It's no wonder the blimps are leaking hydrogen."

"How long will the spores survive?"

The doctor gestured to the screen showing the microscopic view of the spores he'd just collected. They looked still and dead, but that was just their passive stage.

"I've treated a batch with ultraviolet light and some of them decompose. If no new ones were being created, perhaps they would last a few years. But those on the ground, protected under a rock, for example, could last much longer. Simple atmospheric components; water, oxygen, etc. leave them unaffected. Ozone causes some decay, but at normal concentrations, not enough to be useful."

The phrase that stuck in the admirals head was 'new ones being created'. With an increasing number of gigantic dead carcasses around the world, the concentration of spores had to be increasing.

"Find me something. I need a way to rid the world of these, or the fleet is gone."

...

The reports of blimps falling out of the sky by his spotter network gave Baron Jenner mixed feelings. His plan seemed to be working to perfection, but the loss of the blimps was revealing just how ruthless the Australian leader had become. His own ships were exploding in reprisal, even though King Thomas could not know he was to blame. The kelp was being spread all around European harbors, and his shipyard was suffering from the acid algae in spite of the barricades in the river. East America and Carolina had ordered a blockade against all Bremerhaven ships, not that he could blame them. The algae blobs were relentless. His dry docks were leaking, and cleaning crews could not keep up with the reports.

He had thought the blimps were his greatest threat. It was a wider issue than that. He had to stop the whole Australian biotech industry, and Europa was going to give him that opportunity.

...

Rachael had her arm on his shoulder as she peered down into Samuel's handset screen.

"There it is." He expanded the metadata on the news report about the Texas airplanes. 'R. Nue' was listed as camera operator.

She squealed with glee. "You don't know what this means to me. My name on an internationally viewed screen."

"Don't I though? I had to work my way up, you know."

She squeezed his shoulder. "Thank you."

Samuel tapped over to the listings. "See, here are the viewing statistics. Your Net ID account is now growing, not shrinking. Not many people in the world can say that. Most people just buy their Net Credits. If you really want to keep score, you could set up an auxiliary Net ID and just use it for your screen earnings—you know, to keep it separate from what comes from your family money."

She nodded, tasting the idea. "I like it. Money has never been real to me. I mean, how could it when Daddy buys me everything? But this is real."

"Then do it now. All the work you've done on the Melear project is due to hit the Queue before very long, and you'll want to track all that."

Rachael pulled her handset from her pocket and tapped and slid and confirmed. "Got it. Should we edit the news report? Change it to point to my new ID?"

He shook his head. "Let it go. The real stuff will soon eclipse the numbers you've already got. Besides, editing a current news item confuses some people, whether they can see what changed or not."

"Okay, but I want to celebrate! Can we eat out at a fancier restaurant tonight?"

He shrugged. "I guess. I don't know the town, though. Motel, next door restaurant, and the airport—that's my life here."

She smiled wisely, "I'll find one. Give me thirty minutes to change, and you put on your best interview suit, and I'll find us a place where we feel underdressed. Okay?"

He shook his head. "I'll never understand your life. But okay. It's your celebration. So let's pack up. Tomorrow is a big day, so let's leave everything in good shape."

They secured the camera gear and made sure all the datastores were flushed to the Net. Samuel checked over his project list to make sure he had all the times correct and talked to Bill in person for a few minutes. The boss was so deep in his own checklists that he never looked up. He just waved his fingers and said, "Fine." As far as Bill was concerned, the reporting had been turned over to Samuel and he didn't think about that part of the event any more.

Back at the motel, Rachael made a dash for her room. Samuel took a shower and puzzled over his clothes, not terribly in a hurry for this ordeal. He did have a more formal suit, one that he'd intended to use interviewing with Jason Bolls before his uncle pulled him into his circle too fast to worry about clothes. He fit himself into the tight vest and formal collar without too much effort. He was checking the appearance in his mirror when his handset flickered.

He picked it up. Rachael's image was muted. "Are you ready? I got us a car."

"So soon? And a car? What's wrong with the van we have?"

She laughed dismissively. "Do you need me to straighten your collar?"

He looked at the mirror and made the adjustment. "No."

"Great. Then come knock at my door."

He winced, stuffed the handset into his vest and went outside.

There was a dark gray Bremer waiting outside, not too different from the one that met him at the Queen Helen. He nodded to the driver, and then went to Rachael's door. He knocked.

She opened it up, and it was undeniably Rachael. Her hair was glorious, and her skin perfect. Her eyes laughed as he looked over the slim black dress and tiny shoes, and the long legs in between.

"Miss Nue? He held out his arm. She wrapped hers around it and they strolled to the car.

Inside, he whispered, "I thought you didn't have any girly clothes."

She chuckled, "The instant my cover was blown, I had Ellie Poutron ship me the essentials by the first train from Dallas. And you don't have to whisper. The driver can't hear us through the partition. You have to use the speaker." She pointed to the button. "Sometimes, the passengers will want some privacy."

Either the way she said it or her perfume scenting the air caused him to tingle.

Samuel muttered, "I wonder if this is a good idea. We need to keep our relationship professional."

"Are you thinking of crossing some boundaries?" The way her voice sounded in the quiet interior gave even her argument a sparkle. "Besides, which guidelines are we talking about? The professionalism of the entertainment industry? I've heard tales."

He didn't think too deeply about it. He just leaned in and kissed her.

After a moment, she pulled back with a smile, "Aren't you glad I'm not wearing makeup? You would have smudged it."

The quickness of the trip gave Samuel the chance to pull himself back under control. He had dark suspicions about her perfume, but then she'd said she wasn't using her special skills on him.

The Black Gold Tower was the tallest building in Midland, at sixty floors. The restaurant was at the top, with glass all around, giving a view of the evening lights turning a dusty flat desert into a sparkling modern city. They were seated with a great view, and he pointed out the railroad line and the airport just as the runway lights were turned off for the night. Nighttime flying was pretty rare.

She smiled and nodded when he pointed at some feature, but he quickly got the idea that she'd been up in restaurant towers so many times that all of this was familiar territory. Samuel was the excited tourist. Rachael was more interested in watching him.

He tried to pull his feelings back under control and concentrate on her. And not just on her bare shoulders and form-fitting dress.

"What are your plans, after this job? The twelfth is just five days away."

She sipped her wine, some name she'd rattled off that he'd never heard of. "The project isn't over then. Follow up documentaries, you said, and you've been doing most of the editing. I need to learn more about that."

He nodded, "Yes, but then what? I came to the mainland to learn my craft. I know enough to teach you, but I'd planned to watch Uncle Jason and learn from him. Once I felt ready, there were projects I wanted to tackle on my own—to learn by doing. Jason tossed me into this event alone, but I know there's more to learn from him.

"What I'm trying to understand is your goals. What do you want to do?"

The waiter chose that moment to arrive with steaks that were unlike anything he had eaten before—so tall they threatened to fall over, and the meat was so smooth in texture that he carved it with his fork.

Rachael didn't interrupt his experience until the meat was gone. "Now see why I complained about the motel restaurant?"

He sighed. "This wasn't a steak. It was something different. I can probably still enjoy the other."

She chuckled. "Oh, I did, too. But there is more to life when you can reach the top floor."

Samuel didn't comment, still savoring his meal.

She toyed with a side dish of some vegetable he hadn't seen before. "About your question—I still have a lot to learn. Everything we've worked on has been designed by you. You set the story structure, the pacing, the set pieces. And you seem to do it instantly, with no planning. I can frame a camera and interview someone, but that's just one of the single captures you use to build something better. I want to know how you do it. I want to be as good as you are now." She tilted her head and sighed, "Although I know you'll have gotten even better by that time.

"Then, once I can imagine a finished piece, like you can, then I'll want to build it. Maybe not by myself, because I can see it takes many hands to put it all together, but I'll want to put something out there with my stamp on it—something undeniably Rachael Nue. Something that maybe will last a while and touch many people."

He smiled and nodded as she talked. Her desires weren't much different from his own.

She frowned at her plate. "And I understand that I've got a rich girl's tastes and impulsiveness. If it takes a change.... If I need to be more like Clark Peterson to stay professional and to stay with you to get the training I need, then I'll just have to make the effort."

Samuel rested the tips of his fingers on her hand. "Maybe we can compromise—'Rachael Peterson' maybe."

They chuckled. She nodded. "No sparkle. No rented Bremers. All business on the job."

"Good. But we'll start tomorrow."

She smiled.

After dessert, the waiter invited them to stroll on the roof-top observatory. Samuel took her arm, and they walked up a spiral ramp to a darkened garden with guard rails, to look out over the city. He noted the maze-like garden and several comfortable-looking benches and entertained a few thoughts that were less than professional.

In spite of the city lights, the stars were bright. The band of clouds that had been with them all day had shifted slightly to the south, but he could see stars winking out and back on as the clouds came and went.

"I couldn't see stars like this in San Diego."

She leaned against his chest, staring out over the city. "The closer you get to civilization, the more you lose the beauty of nature."

He held her close and nuzzled her hair. The night was perfect, the girl was perfect, and the rooftop garden had been designed for times like this. As he moved his hand down her side, she pressed closer to him.

"Perhaps... if..."

His hazy, racing thoughts short-circuited when she winced under his touch.

"What?"

"Nothing!" she said hurriedly. "Nothing at all. Go on. I just had my eyes open, and saw something."

"Saw something?" His mood had shattered. Had her eyes open? What did that mean? "What did you see?"

Timidly, she pointed, still clinging close to him. "You can see the clouds, blocking out the stars. One of them is moving the wrong way."

Gently, he turned to see what she was pointing at.

"Sorry," he untangled himself from her embrace and pulled out his handset. He set the camera for low-light exposure and scanned the sky. On playback, it was clear. Dimly lit by the city lights, a blimp was moving upwind, paralleling the band of clouds.

"I've got to call this in."

She nodded and whispered, "Celebration over." But she watched what her mentor had done, and how he had used his handset camera. A real screencrafter always had a camera handy.

That's Not Good

It was rare that Admiral Dale spoke directly with any of the fleet captains, but this one demanded to talk to him personally. He accepted the transfer of the voice call.

"This is Captain Bickford of the *Dancer*. I've got spots. What do I do?"

"Sorry to hear that, Captain. Where is the *Dancer* now?"

"Oh, the *Dancer* is gone. I took her down off Antsirana, North coast of Madagascar, once it was clear she was done for. Got my men off and turned her loose."

"Then I don't know what..."

"Sir, pardon, Admiral, Sir. *I've* got spots. Me, not the *Dancer*, although she had spots a'plenty. On my hands. I can see 'em. Little gray spots just like her hide. I wash and wash, and they won't come off! What do I do?"

After turning the captain over to one of his assistants to do what they could for him, he called Tuck from his lab.

"I've got a report that the infection has jumped from a blimp to its captain. He has spots on his hands. I thought you told me it was blimp-specific."

The doctor frowned. "I ran tests. I applied spores directly to several of our lab-grown tissue samples, including human. There was some cell damage, as the spores did dig into the tissue, but they didn't find a suitable host cell and so died out. You say he reported spots?"

"Yes, gray spots just like on his blimp."

"Well, the circular spots are caused when the spores duplicate and start killing neighboring cells, expanding outward. Just touching the spores might

219

leave a rash or even some hemmoraging, but not spots. This is puzzling."

"Run more tests. I've got a man panicked for his life, and if he's right, then there are going to be more like him."

...

Since he had a lot more lumber than they needed to stay afloat, Caleb began scavenging, removing any of the loose edge-boards and using them to build an A-frame shelter in the middle. When the sun was high and the winds calmed, it was sweltering.

"We need another rain," he said.

Captain Kelly didn't say anything. He was worried about her.

"Captain, how close to land are we?"

She shook her head. Her eyes looked haunted as she huddled beneath the crossed boards.

"Captain?"

She coughed, clearing her throat. "Something is wrong with me. I don't know where we are." Her eyes watered. "It's all my fault. I killed them all."

Caleb was down on his knees. In spite of his instincts to keep her on a pedestal, he held her hand. "No it's not. The *Lance* failed on us. The infection overwhelmed it. There's nothing you could have done."

She coughed again. "I could have kept her closer to land. I should have *known* how fast we were losing hydrogen and adjusted the course accordingly." She stared off in space. "But I tried to follow orders and get to Nicoya Bay as fast as I could. It should have been as plain as day that we weren't going to make it.

"I messed up and I killed them."

Without his captain, he was afraid he was lost forever. Food would run out. Water would run out. The sun would fry them. He was lost in the world's largest ocean, and he didn't know what to do.

"Captain, help me. What can I do?"

She blinked. "Caleb. I don't think there is anything to do. The *Lance* is gone."

"Yes, but we're alive, for now. What action should I take? What are your orders?"

She hesitated, then closed her eyes. The blemishes on her face, the spots, were making her look a lot older. "We'll still die, no matter what we do."

He straightened a bit. "But I need you to give me the orders. Sitting and dying isn't good enough. Give me an order." He half believed it himself, but he definitely needed her to believe she was still needed.

She nodded listlessly. "Okay. We can't go east, back to shore. The current and the wind are both against us. Put up a sail. Let the trade winds take us west, toward home."

...

Samuel and Rachael were at the Melear hangar by dawn, getting the cameras set up on the new tripods. He glanced her way as she lined up a "first view" shot at the hangar doors that would soon be wide open. He was a little grateful for the blimp distraction the night before. They could concentrate on work without any horrible morning-after regrets. Still, he did appreciate the way she looked, even with her makeup to tone down the dazzle. But today was Bill's day to shine.

Samuel was dressed in his narrator clothes, looking presentable enough if he had to step in front of the camera to put a face and a voice on the metal. Hopefully, Bill would be enough.

There was no big crowd. Other than Ranger Craddik, and some of the other workers at the Midland-Odessa Airport who had been promised an early look, it was just the Melear workers, and in the background, a glimpse of Rachael's bodyguards.

Rachael and he would capture today's events, but it wouldn't go immediately into the Public Queue. There was no announcement. It wasn't open to the public. This was just a flight test.

Bill had just frowned and nodded when told about the blimp in the area. "I won't run into him. I'm not taking any chances, not today."

With a metallic rumble, the tall hangar doors began to open, rolling on tracks to support their massive weight. Samuel glanced through his viewfinder, making sure the capture was running. He knew Rachael would be doing the same. They also had a remote camera beside the hangar to get a profile shot of the plane as it was towed out by a pushback tug.

Samuel zoomed slowly in as the streamlined metal appeared. There was a little flutter, a white cloth banner on the side of the nose, obscuring the overnight paint job.

Wheeled stairs rolled up to the side of the plane. It was Bill's access to get in, but also provided him a platform from which to speak.

Rachael shifted the position of her camera, which meant that Bill must be approaching. She would be getting his wave to the people while he concentrated on a lovingly slow pan of the plane itself.

"Go Bill!" someone yelled.

Samuel repositioned his view to the stairs. Bill was dressed in a head-to-toe silvery costume, with a helmet under his arm. He climbed up several steps. There was a remote microphone taped close, but Samuel had only put it there as a backup against stray noise. He knew Bill talked loudly.

Bill glanced his way. Samuel gave him a hand signal.

"Well, it's been a long time getting to this step, hasn't it?"

His workers chuckled.

"I'm not going to talk long. But it's time we gave Mod-F-111-A a real name!"

They cheered.

The gull-wing window of the cockpit opened up and he set the helmet inside, reaching down to the cord attached to the white banner.

"I haven't been the same since I spent one long night dreaming of what could be done with this new engine. There was the chance for faster planes than had ever graced the skies before. There was the chance of clean propulsion, with no exhaust—a scourge of the Techno era at last defeated. But there was something more that came to me that night.

"We can go faster, and higher, than ever before. With the right engine, and the right airframe, we could go all the way up. This was my dream. Humanity could at last go back to space!"

"This is my dream." Bill jerked the cord, and the banner fell away, showing "*The Dream*" in flowing script over a field of stars.

There were cheers and applause. He waved and climbed into the cockpit. Marcos was up the ladder, helping him get secured into place. Soon the window closed down securely. Marcos waved everyone back.

"This is just a simple flight test. But you know from the static tests, it's going to be loud. Everyone get clear."

The steps were rolled back. The tug pulled the plane a few yards more and then detached.

Samuel saw Marcos give Rachael a hand gesture and she nodded back.

What is that all about?

But it was time to shift camera positions. Rachael was already moving to a small platform, just head-high near the runway, where they could be sure of getting fly-by pictures unobscured by vehicles or onlookers.

Samuel tapped his controls and monitored the tower audio feed. Marcos was already on an electric cart, heading in that direction.

An angle presented itself. Handset in hand, he scanned the moving people, everyone with a job to do. People getting ready for this first flight. He panned and zoomed up to see Bill's helmet behind the cockpit windshield.

A loudspeaker clicked on. "Everyone behind the yellow line. If you don't have sound protection, put your hands over your ears."

Rachael and he had been coached. They put both hands to their heads, one over each ear. A high-pitched scream penetrated even through that, and the air around *The Dream* was filled with dust. And it began to move.

The sound, Samuel had been told, was the Nance-Bate engines cycling at a high rate, on and off. The field traveled at the speed of light, so very quick pulses kept the range of the pushing field close to the plane so that it wouldn't knock down people or smash windows all the way across town. Supposedly, once in the air, longer, slower pulses could be tolerated. He would explain it all in voice-overs once he began to edit the coverage.

But now he was experiencing it, and it was deafeningly loud. But the plane was already moving into position for its take-off run. As it turned, the sound was softer.

He carried his camera up the steps and set up opposite Rachael's position.

There was a second of total silence, and then it started up again. The plane pushed across the field, throwing up a huge cone of dust behind it.

In seconds, it was in the air. The nose went up, and the plane climbed.

...

Captain Bourke struggled to keep the *Kiwi* in the cloud layer. "Stay at it, girl."

"Captain?" His communication officer, Larry Halligan, looked up from his post.

"Just talking to the lady, Larry. We're getting in range."

"Yes, sir."

Larry had been the only one who had refused to leave his post when they had touched down in the dead of night before moving back into the clouds. Bourke could see the spots on his skin. He knew he was done for, but the lad was doing it for the king. He had to respect that.

They had dumped everything from the engineer's tools to the food stores to lose weight. It was just the two of them at the controls and a laboring blimp, hurting from her sores and unable to understand what was happening to her.

Bourke had been with the *Kiwi* since she left the surf at Cleveland Bay. They had been around the world several times, and if she were going down, he was going with her.

He closed his eyes, trying to feel how she was doing. The hydrogen leak was sickening. They had started with full ballast tanks, but she was burning water as fast as she could. If it weren't such a sunny day, they wouldn't have made it back to the city. But he could tell she was confused.

The pilot gave his blimp some commands, regulated the water flow, and of course, handled the engines. But a lot of the blimp's actions were bred into her. It was instinct, no matter if some gene engineer had designed it or not. *Kiwi* was feeling her hydrogen bag sag from lack of internal pressure. The only way to keep her shape was to route more and more of the excess oxygen into the ballonets. It was a lost cause, but her instincts didn't know that.

Bourke shook his head and patted the mottled skin gently.

"How's the camera working?"

Larry nodded, "Fine, sir." He pointed to where his handset camera was propped up against the transparent skin, looking down at the Texas landscape. "We don't even need the Net relay. The city's got good enough coverage. What we see though this cloud goes straight to the king's monitors."

"Good lad."

Bourke adjusted their position slightly as they neared the airport. A keen eye on the ground could probably see them now. But any deeper into the cloud and they wouldn't be able to see what they came here to see.

Larry pointed. "Hey, there she goes!"

Bourke could see it. A metal airplane was zipping across the landing strip and climbing. "He's fast." The plane was at their altitude, and then higher within seconds. As it banked and began a slow curve toward the south, the buzz of its engines reached them. "What kind of an engine is that?"

The plane was out of sight, obscured by the spotty clouds and the blemishes on the *Kiwi's* skin. "Did you see...?"

And then, above them, the overstressed fore ballonet, full of excess oxygen, burst with a loud bang, raining shards of its skin into the interior of the hydrogen bag.

Bourke thought, *That's not good.* As leaky as the hydrogen had been, it had still been leaking *out.* The hydrogen inside had been pure. Now it was mixed with a heavy load of oxygen.

...

Rachael panned across the sky following *The Dream's* maiden flight, her eyes glued to her viewfinder. She asked, "Did I hear him right? Did he say he was going to space?"

Samuel smiled, his eyes not leaving his own viewfinder. "Yes. That's at least part of the big secret. The old Techno F-111 planes were built well enough to go into space, but their engines burned oxygen from the air. They could never go that high. Bill's engine can."

"Oh." She was still trying to absorb the idea. Spaceflight was pre-Star Techno mythology—something some people never quite believed in.

Samuel asked, "Do you think we can sell that idea by the twelfth?"

"Well, yeah!"

And then, among the little clouds, off to the edge of town, a giant ball of flame flashed bright—enough light to rival the sun.

"Get a camera on that!" he yelled. He was going to keep trained on the plane, in case anything happened.

Bill had seen it too, because he abruptly pulled up into a steep climb, turning back toward the airfield.

Then the shockwave of the explosion hit, kicking up dust everywhere. There was the tinkle of shattered glass. Rachael stumbled down on her knees, catching the overturned camera before it hit the ground.

Samuel stayed upright, just because of the way he had been braced.

"What was that?" she asked.

He saw Bill's plane swerve in the sky, but then it turned and headed down toward the runway.

"That blimp we saw last night, probably. It exploded."

Fenced Out

"Glynde, come in and close the door."

She did as the admiral said and stood at attention before his desk.

He noticed she was still standing, and pointed to the chair. "Sit."

The lieutenant had overheard bits of the heated discussion as she had waited outside his office. The call from King Thomas had left her curious, but she had not eavesdropped deliberately.

He tapped his desk, and she saw the paper list with markings all over it. She had created it for him—at least the clean copy.

He asked, "You have a better idea of which blimps are in the air and which ones are gone than anyone. Did you know that the king had re-directed the *Kiwi* and the *Green Monster* to go deep into Texas on a spy mission?"

"No, sir. However, Captain Dibbs of the *Green Monster* had reported that he had offloaded his crew near the railroad line in the middle of the night and released the craft to drift on its own. They're stranded on their own, but it was his only choice."

The admiral nodded. It was an increasingly common tale. Blimps with spots were doomed, and it made no sense to risk the crew.

"Greater Texas is becoming more hostile by the day. The *Kiwi* is down, I suppose you know."

She nodded.

"From the news reports, the gas bag detonated, not a simple hydrogen fire like most. The hydrogen bag must have been contaminated with oxygen. Buildings were rattled and hundreds of people on the ground were injured with flying glass. The ship was mostly consumed by the explosion. King

Thomas had ordered it to spy on an airplane. Captain Bourke and his comm officer were on board."

He struck his desk, hammering it with his fist. "How dare he burn my people like disposable trash!"

Glynde took in a breath, but showed none of her own reaction. Words spoken against the king were on the edge of treason, but she had kept her own feelings about this growing global war under tight control for her own reasons. The human cost was appalling.

There was an uneasy silence for a moment, where neither looked at the other.

Then he asked, "How many of the blimps are still in the air?"

She shook her head. "Without a terminal, I'd have to say less than half. The greater share of them report spots."

"About what I had assumed. In another month, there won't be a blimp left alive. The spores are in the winds, and there is no place to hide."

It was an uncertain future, one that made her stomach uneasy to contemplate. With no blimps, was there even a fleet?

When she looked up, she saw his eyes watching her. She straightened.

"Lieutenant, our king has gotten himself into a war, but there are no armies as of old. All he ever had was the fleet and I would guess a private collection of agents around the world that can spread his kelp and what-not. Even the fleet is just a collection of merchants, held together with a rank structure and just a few decades of tradition."

The admiral sighed, "For too long I've been sitting in this nice chair, looking at my pretty displays and taking credit for all the work those merchants were doing. Now it's our turn to bear the load."

He pulled out a fresh piece of paper and began to write. She burned to read over his shoulder, but held her place. After a few minutes, he looked up.

"Lieutenant Glynde, please send this order to all the fleet, even those who have already lost their blimps. Use their personal Net IDs. And do it now."

He handed it to her. She read over the full page and his signature. She straightened her shoulders, and said, "Yes, sir!"

...

King Thomas shook his head, dismissing the raging of the Fleet Admiral.

I don't have time for an admiral that has lost his fleet. That chapter was gone. So there were no blimps left in his armory, he still had other weapons. That was one less call he had to deal with. *Forget the fleet.*

But even with the fleet off the table, he couldn't ignore what he'd seen. Texas had a super-weapon, some kind of fast airplane that could destroy blimps at a distance. He'd watched the plane take off and fly at great speeds.

Then, it had turned directly toward the *Kiwi* and instantly, the signal was lost. Texas news coverage showed the blimp exploding with a force he'd never seen before.

A plane that fast—could it cross the ocean and come here? And what would that weapon do against places on the ground?

For the first time, Australia itself might be at risk, unless he could do something to stop them.

...

They captured *The Dream's* landing and Bill's triumphant wave as he opened his canopy.

Samuel helped with the packing. He sighed, "I wish I could go into town and capture some scenes of the broken glass and panicked people."

Rachael looked up from her camera case. "Could we?"

He shook his head. "Priorities. We're sitting on a unique story here— the return of humanity to space, complete with a backdrop of war unrest, explosions, and spies. We have to do the absolute best in presenting this one tale. The local news and private individuals are documenting the aftermath of the blimp explosion better than we could with our late start. We can't be everywhere."

She nodded. "Three days. Lots of editing. What are the next tags?"

He growled, "I had two ready to go, but I'll need to junk them. What with the world attention Midland is going to get from the explosion, people will be very interested in the plane that was in the sky at the same time. We have to take advantage of that.

"The story of the plane and its speed and performance and the possibility of man in space again—I have to push that out now."

Rachael gazed off into the distance. "Hmm. We have the exclusive capture of the gunshots in the dark hangar. 'Australia sent saboteurs to stop it. Bang. Bang. But it's still happening, on the twelfth.'"

"Hey, pretty good. But we're into longer tags now. Come up with a longer version, and we'll use it."

She returned to winding cables, feeling a glow from his approval.

When they walked back into the hangar, Bill was being led into his office by the ranger. He tapped on the screen and talked to someone while unfastening the silvery flight suit. He hadn't closed the door, and his voice carried.

"Absolutely not. I was nowhere near the blimp. I was easily five miles away when it blew. I know because I had time to climb into a safe altitude before the shock wave hit me."

Samuel whispered to Rachael. "I'll meet you in a minute." He hurried over to Bill's office.

"No. It had its weapon systems removed long before I got ahold of the plane. Your ranger is here. I can give him a full inspection. There are no weapons of any kind on *The Dream*."

Samuel didn't recognize the face on the display, but he recognized the cut of the clothes and the lines on the face. This was someone in authority, someone questioning Bill.

"Sir." He was in range of the camera, and the person looked his way. "I have complete screen captures of the flight. It is just as Mr. Melear says. He was nowhere near the blimp when it exploded."

"Who is this?"

Bill gave Samuel a worn smile. "This is Samuel Bolls, of the San Diego Bolls screen group. He has been contracted to document this project. His cameras have been in and around every inch of the place. I've wanted the main flight on the twelfth presented in a real-time screen."

The man on the display nodded. "I've heard of that." He shifted his view. "Ranger Craddik, could you close the door now?"

Samuel took a step back and smiled when the door closed in his face. That was all he wanted to say. Bill could have probably held his own, but now they all knew he had the option to call up screen proof of what he was saying.

Rachael looked up from the edit terminal. "What was that all about?"

He shrugged. "Bill's plane was in the air when the blimp exploded. Some official was asking questions."

"Oh? Do you think he could get in trouble?"

"I don't see how. He didn't do anything."

Her face twisted. "Yeah, like we didn't do anything in San Diego."

...

Marcos and Matt checked at their door. Marcos said, "Hey, we're taking off a little early to celebrate. You're welcome to join us."

Samuel and Rachael were set up with facing edit terminals, working to put together the remaining tags, especially the one scheduled for the eleventh.

They shared a glance. He shrugged. "If we take the edit stations with us, we can set up at the motel later." She nodded. It might be fun.

They packed up and followed the other cars over to a well-known Midland restaurant. Rachael felt surprisingly timid, staying close to Samuel as they gathered around a large table. Everyone was there. Bill and the crew had been in a habit of Mexican food every Friday, back before the project started, but they'd been too busy lately. Chips and hot sauce were supplied and drinks ordered. Samuel claimed ignorance of the local brands, but Rachael just ordered the type chosen by Manny, who sat to her left.

The place was noisy, but not for this group. Every one of them were used to making themselves heard over metal grinders and spinning turbines. The waitress in a colorful traditional dress leaned close to her and said, "Are you new with this crew of louts?"

Rachael shook her head, "Taking pictures of their plane." She was really conscious of her plain outfit. It felt like all the women in the place were dressed better than she was.

Samuel leaned her way. "We're from Bolls. We're doing a documentary."

The waitress seemed impressed, but Rachael wasn't confident she'd ever heard of them.

She had enchiladas. Everyone else had their own favorites. The talk was mostly family and machinery.

"Hey, Manny, should I tell Charlotte how close you're sitting with 'Clark'?"

A couple of the guys had girlfriends, others had wives. From the ribbing, she gathered that Bill had recently lost the latest of a long string of girlfriends. He'd been quite popular with the girls back when he first cracked the sound barrier.

She was getting comfortable, finally, when a slightly overweight older man with an impressive mustache and a wide brimmed hat came out banging on a metal pan with a ladle.

"Hey, hey, hey, there. Listen up!"

The tables gradually quieted down. He pointed his ladle at Bill. "You all know Bill Melear and his crew of aircraft mechanics here. Well, what you don't know is that just ten minutes ago, King Thomas of Australia..." There was a loud chorus of boo's. "King Thomas threatened Greater Texas with disaster if Bill's latest airplane wasn't destroyed. Our great King Jess told him to shut up! Bill Melear is ours and he'll fly what he wants!"

The house shook with cheers. Chairs scraped on the wooden floors and people came over to shake Bill's hand. Smaller than the rest of them, Rachael was squeezed from all sides as the mass of bodies came over to wish them all well. It was chaos.

"You show 'em Bill!"

"Stupid genies, the lot of them. Not even people anymore."

"Show them what a Texan can do!"

There were many more comments, far too many of them uncomfortably tinged with people's growing hatred for the Australians.

Samuel captured her hand, and squeezed it gently until the crowd dwindled and they were allowed to finish their meals. The owner of the place in his broad hat told them the meal was on the house and how proud he was that they'd come to his establishment.

It was another hour before they went their own ways.

Samuel looked at her. "Did you survive?"

She chuckled. "Next time we eat at one of my places! But no, I enjoyed it."

He put his finger in his ear and wiggled it. "I think I'm still a little deaf. You didn't mind that Bill was the center of attention?"

"Not at all. Look at all he's done. I'm just pretty."

He nodded. "You are, at that."

Rachael felt warm and safe beside him. If they could just get back to that roof-top garden, she'd definitely keep her eyes closed.

"Where should we set up the edit stations?" *Next to my bed or yours?*

"Are you still up for a late night session?"

She nodded. "We still have a lot of things to get right."

He smiled and put his arm around her shoulder. "We do."

...

They chose his room and borrowed a chair from the manager. It was tight in the room, and Samuel had to stow his extra clothes and luggage in the closet.

Rachael tested out his mattress while he finished.

"Hey, quit bouncing on that. It's distracting."

She tilted her head. "You said I had to use my imagination if I were going to become a better screencrafter." She eyed him. "I'm using my imagination."

"So am I. Come over here and set up your station."

She looked disappointed, but sighed and slid off the bed. He pulled her close and kissed her once.

"No more, for now."

"Aww."

They were twenty minutes into smoothing the scene transitions in the next tag when there was a knock on the door.

Samuel frowned as he opened it up.

It was Ranger Craddik. "I'm sorry to bother you this evening." His eyes took in the displays, the cramped chairs and the still-made bed. "However, I have been given new orders, and it concerns Miss Nue."

A large figure stepped up beside the ranger. "Is there a problem?"

Samuel shook his head. "I don't believe so, Mr. Mason." To the ranger, he asked, "What are these new orders?"

Craddik looked uncomfortable, with the bodyguard standing behind him. "May I come inside?"

Samuel nodded, "Yes, of course, both of you. Come on it. Plenty of room for all." He had to back up to let them enter. He squeezed around to stand behind Rachael's chair.

When the door clicked shut, he asked, "Orders?"

Craddik leaned against the wall. There was no place to sit, other than the bed. "You have heard about the Australian ultimatum?"

"Only indirectly. We have been hard at work."

"King Thomas has taken the position that Bill Melear's new plane is a weapon, one that destroyed the blimp. He has threatened a shipping blockade against Texas if the plane flies again. Our king has firmly denied his request, and has indeed ordered the Rangers to insure that Australian agents have no opportunity to sabotage the plane again.

"Unfortunately, Miss Nue has been placed on the list of people restricted from the airfield."

"What?" she asked. "What did I do?"

He looked uncomfortable, but firm. "As I understand it, you were present at the Queen Helen when it was bombed..."

"I was gone by then!"

"... and you were there in the hangar when the Australian agents planted the bombs on the airplanes." He held up his hand when she was about to object again. "You were also in Australia for several months this year.

"While I personally don't believe these prove anything about your guilt or innocence, we are not making any such claims. We are not arresting you. The Rangers are just taking the precaution of putting a 'fence' around the airbase, and anyone the least bit suspicious will not be allowed inside until the flight of the twelfth is over."

Samuel said, "She is an important member of the documentation crew. I need her help to provide the real-time coverage that Bill Melear has requested for the flight."

Craddik shook his head. "The restrictions were made by my supervisors." He looked directly at Rachael. "Until further notice, you are not allowed within five miles of the airfield. If you wish to leave the area by rail, I can escort you to the train station until the train leaves."

She was a little numb. "I'm already closer than five miles."

He nodded. "Yes, you cannot stay here." He looked at Mason. "I assume you will have no problems finding other accommodations."

Samuel said, "I need her."

"There are a couple of days yet. Another cameraman can be obtained in time."

Craddik looked from face to face. "I have other issues to deal with tonight. Another blimp has crashed fifty miles from here. No explosion or fire this time, but there was no crew aboard either. It is likely that there are a number of real Australian agents in the area that I need to be tracking.

"Miss Nue, you have one hour to relocate."

Forget the Blimps

"Captain Dibbs?"

The man standing watch winced and gestured the engineer closer. He put his hand on the smaller man's shoulder. "Miles, you call me 'captain' one more time and I'll deck you. First names only, until we're safe. Got that?"

"Uh, yes, John."

"Now, what do you want?"

"Anna says she needs better clothes and hard shoes."

John Dibbs looked down at their air boots. He sighed. "She's right. If nothing else, these rocks will wear them out in a hurry. We all need Texas clothes."

They were waiting in a barn, shielded from the harsh sunlight. It was part of a long-deserted farm, near the rail line and an old major highway. The distant glint of city towers wavered from the heated soil. They would need to move into the city to find transportation to the coast, as well as food and water. But they couldn't walk the whole way in the baking sun. They'd travel at night.

Coorain looked happy in the heat. He'd shed his shirt, glorying in his black skin, and carried a couple of old mugs. "We found some water. There's an old hand-operated pump that didn't need too much effort to get working."

John took one and sipped. It was a little metallic, but he couldn't complain.

"How is the farmhouse?"

"Gutted. It burned a long time ago. I rummaged and found those mugs, but other than some knives and some very rusted farm equipment out back, there's nothing much here. It was a nice place, but that was pre-Star. Someone made repairs since then, then gave it up."

He looked at the barn, all metal construction, so it hadn't rotted, but it was still standing only by the grace of the winds and he wouldn't bet on it being there much longer.

"We can't stay here, and as soon as we reach the town, people will know we're outsiders."

Coorain chuckled, "Well, maybe they'll spot me as a Koori from Australia, but you white guys all look alike."

John shook his head. "No, we're all too pale to pass as Texas people. We've lived inside a blimp for so long that even at home, people can point to a fleet guy in a crowd."

"Then quit hiding in the barn and get some color on you."

"I'd turn red like a lobster." He tried to shake off his feeling of depression. He'd lost everything when he stepped out of the *Green Monster* and turned her loose to fly to her doom. He had no resources, and his people needed him.

Well, at least we're on land. So many blimps went down at sea.

...

Caleb stared at the waves, trying to remember how the platform was constructed. He would need take it apart and put it back together again—all the while making sure he didn't destroy the one thing that was keeping him alive.

It would have been better if it had turned upside down when we hit the water. But it hadn't, and it was impossible to make it happen now.

The whole structure was built of notched boards and ropes that fit in those notches, holding it all in place. To form a flat surface for the cattle's hooves, resting on the curved belly of the *Lance*, a framework of crossed beams was built that curved to fit, resting on six-foot wide planks like feet to bear the weight.

Ducking his head under water when the sun was up to provide light showed that many of those feet had ripped free, but the framework was mostly intact, acting like an anchor to keep the raft moving with the current, no faster.

The top surface decking was built from three by six foot sheets. He'd used one of those as his surfboard when he'd rescued the captain. Eight of them now formed the shelter in the middle of the raft.

There's no help for it. I'll have to build a new raft, gradually taking apart the old one. I wish I had a pencil.

It was one thing to imagine a new raft and another to design it.

He glanced over to where Captain Kelly spent her time sleeping. Nothing was rousing her from the depression she'd fallen into. He had to make progress so he could have something to show her when it was time to eat.

I'll need to figure out how to make a net, too.

He'd toyed with the idea of making some kind of fish hook out of the metal can, but it was all too flimsy. Any fish worth its weight in protein would bend it loose in an instant.

But the ligaments holding the raft together were hundreds of short lengths of twine. Taking apart unneeded sections would give him something that might be made into a net. Possibly.

Carefully, he walked to the shallow end of the raft, where many of the floorboards had been discarded back when they delivered the cattle. This part was just structural framework. Holding on tightly, he edged out waist deep and began picking apart the cord that held the end pieces lashed together.

Every move had to be done carefully.

He could not lose the knife. It was his only tool. Maybe he could loosen the cords with his teeth, but he couldn't open the food cans without it. He had to preserve the cord with the fewest cuts possible so it could be reused. And he had to hang on to the structural beam as it came loose so he wouldn't have to go swimming for it.

By late afternoon, he had moved four beams, one long one and three shorter pieces, and a spool of twine back to the shelter. Another day of this, and he could start laying out the new raft structure.

"Captain. Come look at what I've done."

She woke, and smiled. "Caleb. Are you still here?"

He laughed. "I'm not going anywhere. Sit up and come out into the sun. We're going to have yams for dinner."

The captain was doing a little better, now that he made sure she ate regularly and took her water ration. But she wasn't her old self.

She looked around. "Where are we?"

He'd been asked that several times now. "We're in the Pacific Ocean, drifting west with the North Equatorial Current."

Nodding, she sighed. "We should put up a sail."

"I'm working on it."

"Good boy." She smiled at the breeze. Sometimes, when she relaxed, she looked like her old self.

He began cutting into the can of yams. Everything had to be done carefully. No spillage. No cuts that could get infected.

"Caleb!"

"Yes, Captain?"

"I've got spots all over me!"

He paused with the yams. He tried to calm her down. "Yes, you've got spots. You've had them for a while now."

She frowned at him. "Are you okay? You should stay away from me! You might get infected."

He set aside the can. "No. Don't worry. See. I don't have any spots, and I've been with you for days now. I'm healthy."

"We have to be careful!"

He moved closer and against her will, he put his arms around her and held her gently until she settled down. After a few minutes, she relaxed.

"I wish I had a boy like you."

"Oh?"

She sniffed and nodded. "They told me, when I had the work done, that I couldn't have children."

"I didn't know that."

"It was okay. I had my *Lance*, and my boys."

"Was it the gene change that did it?"

"No. It was something else. Something I was born with, they told me. I wish I had known from the beginning. I wasted too many years wanting to be a mother."

"Well, I can be your boy. My mother died many years ago."

She held his hand for a bit.

"Where are we?"

...

Admiral Dale asked, "Are you sure? I can't go public with something so vague."

Dr. Tuck gestured to his display. "Some people get spots, a small percentage, and others don't. And thus far, my lab tissues are still immune. Even more disturbing is that the symptoms are showing up in the general population, not just fleet personnel. The most severe cases are blimp workers who were on infected blimps, but then again, the workers alongside them, with the same exposure levels, weren't affected.

"But non-fleet, non-Australian cases in Texas, Central Mississippi, Louisiana, the Caribbean, and Carolina are showing up on the Medical Exchange. They haven't yet made the connection between the blimps and their new disease, but it won't be long before they do."

Dale nodded. "Airborne spores, with the same pattern we saw with the blimps. It will soon be everywhere."

"Probably the same spore. It's designed to attack the blimps, but breathed in or ingested, the spores would likely attack any kind of tissue. I just don't know why it's replicating in non-blimp hosts. Not yet. I have a deep simulation running of the spores in a simulated human cell. I should know more in a few hours."

He nodded. "You know, people will blame us."

The doctor frowned, "Surely not. We were the ones attacked."

"A new disease, associated with blimps, while anti-Australian sentiment is at a world-wide high. Of course they will blame us."

The doctor shook his head. "That's your problem to solve. I can't worry about anything outside the lab, not now. Have you told the king?"

Dale frowned, "He's not taking my calls. I think he's written us off. We're not one of his useful weapons anymore."

...

Baron Jenner was comfortable talking to Lorraine. His elevation to Admiral of the European Navy was a trial post and he knew it. King George was keeping his distance, both politically and personally. If he turned out a hero, then the king would embrace him with open arms. But if this war was a disaster, then it was all on the new guy.

Jenner waved his hands, "Forget the blimps. Australia has no air force, not now."

"But how can you be sure?"

"Experience. I've been watching their every move for years. There is definitely some kind of disease attacking the numals, and from my observation reports, it's taking them all down. Within a month, there should be no blimps Australia could use to attack our ships."

"Surely, they could grow new ones?"

"Perhaps, but not quickly enough. Selected ships from ports close to Australia could be in place, outside Sydney harbor, before they could even realize it had happened. We could land an armed ground force and take Graythwaite Castle and force a submission from King Thomas before there was even a chance for a major siege.

"Thomas is so confident that he can bend the world to his will by moving his chess pieces by remote control that my observers have seen no build-up of local defenses. Outside of the blimp fleet and the royal court, the average Australian may not even know there's a war going on. Certainly, they're not seeing the same death and destruction that we're suffering."

Duke Lorraine looked over his charts. "This will certainly have to be a World Court action. Europa is too far away, and our harbors are so besieged that we can't put any of our ships into the armada."

"I agree, but it seems that Greater Texas is about to catch his anger next. That will give us some breathing room to clear our harbors. While we don't have a full idea of how many attack ships King Thomas can deploy, he hasn't been able to totally shut down Europa. I think it's significant that there hasn't been a single new harbor attacked since he started paying attention to Texas. He's re-deploying his forces."

Jenner flagged the list. "It's urgent we quietly get the armada nations to agree to this. We have police forces and the men you are training. We even have a few old deck guns. Once we have an agreement, we can begin flying Europa's contribution to the effort to the ports in Africa, Polynesia and China."

The duke frowned. "I wish we could do something smaller—a limited team to capture King Thomas."

Jenner shook his head. "And if they failed? Thomas would be that much bolder. We need a force that will shock the Australian populace into realizing how badly things have gotten off track. An armada of ships in Sydney harbor with deck guns rattling their windows will be much better. And if one attack on the castle fails, we will have people in place to mount an alternate attack.

"They are just about to wake up to the idea that their king has lost their blimps. We need to force all the anger onto him."

...

King Thomas played the new tag through the third time, shaking his head.

Do they really expect me to believe that this is simply a new airplane, and they're going for a high-altitude record. 'Going into space' on the twelfth?

The narrator's voice is lovely, but I think it's a diversion.

He went back to his maps. His people were already in place, most of them having moved up from the Caribbean and the South American zones over the past few days. The Greater Texas coastline had a lot fewer ports than Europa. He could pull a blitzkrieg on them—show the world what would happen when they disregarded his demands.

The Fleet

Samuel tapped the display. Rachael, in her full sparkle incarnation, appeared.

"Well, what did he say?"

He nodded, "Bill was open to the idea, but I'll have to get the tripod mount installed and integrated today. I think it will be straightforward."

"Great. Then I'll re-work the tag line. How about, 'On the twelfth, humanity is going back into space, with you in the copilot seat.'"

Samuel thought a minute. "Maybe 'with the whole world in the copilot seat'."

"Maybe. I'll do both of them and run them by you a little later today."

He wished he could reach through the display and touch her. "How are you holding up?"

She smiled a careless mask, "Poor me, stuck in a luxury suite in the biggest tower in the city, with great food on call—I think I'll survive." Her face dropped back to a frown. "I can see the airport quite well from here, but the windows don't open and they're all tinted. I am going to sweet-talk the manager into letting me set up a camera station on the roof. Can you bring a camera with the Teleview extender and a tripod when you shut down for the night?"

He liked the idea. Once the plane was off the ground, her vantage point would provide better views of the flight than his.

His insistence that she take one of the edit stations when she was ordered out of the motel had been a gesture of desperation on his part, but it was working well. They both had solid Net connection and were calling each other all the time. She was a bit of a pest the first couple of hours, as she climbed up the learning curve on the edit station like a mountain climber with a rock hammer. "How do you do a three-way merge?" "I need to drop just the background noise." "Can I put a blur effect on an overlay?"

Before, she had been content to watch over his shoulder and follow his instructions. Now she had to do everything herself, and she was making serious progress.

The idea of putting a remote control camera in the copilot seat had been hers, and he was jealous that he hadn't thought of it first. Net linkage at the peak of the flight might be difficult, but he could put enough buffer memory into the package so that the entire flight could be replayed once Bill returned.

He gave her a nod and walked off. She was obviously busy on her work as well.

Marcos walked by and when he glanced at the girl on the display, he paused in his tracks. She glanced up.

"Oh. Hi there, Marcos."

He nodded, "Hey, you clean up nice, 'Clark'."

She gave her off-display work a tap and then turned her full attention on him. "Oh, you knew it was all an act. This is the real me."

"So," he rubbed the side of his nose, unsure quite what to say. "Is is true the ranger kicked you out?"

She winced and nodded. "I'm too risky—an unsavory character and all."

Marcos shook his head. "Things are changing here, too. When I drove up this morning, there was a man with a uniform and a gun stopping all the cars. He checked my driver's license against names on a checklist before he let me in."

"Another ranger?"

"I don't know. Some kind of security. Now that Australia is threatening to attack, everything is getting all strange."

She sighed. "I had this summer all planned out. I was going to spend it all in San Diego becoming a famous screen personality. Then this war stuff happened. I thought humanity had outgrown it."

Marcos smiled. "Life never works out like you plan it. Take the good with the bad."

She smiled. "Oh, it hasn't been all bad."

Samuel called from across the way, "Hey, Marcos!"

"Gotta go."

She waved. "See you."

He walked over to where Samuel was struggling with his equipment cart. Somehow, it had gotten surrounded by power cables running to the plane.

"Need help?"

Samuel glared at the wheels. The cart rolled smoothly normally, but the small tires and fat cables didn't mix. "Yes! Help me lift this gently over the cable. I don't have time to unload it."

It was quick work for the two of them.

"Marcos?"

"Yeah?"

"Do you remember when she first showed up?"

"'Clark'? Yep."

"She called herself a pack mule."

Marcos chuckled. "I seem to recall you made her regret it."

Samuel nodded solemnly. "Well, I need another one."

"A pack mule?"

"Yes. Rachael is taking on a lot of the desk work, stuck off-site. That's great, but I still need someone to do grunt work. I need to say 'take this over there' and 'rewind this cable' and they'll do it without breaking anything.

"And I don't really have time to call my uncle in San Diego and have someone sent here. It's probably not a good idea to bring in another foreigner anyway, even if it would just be a Californian.

"Do you know someone? It's nothing technical, just lift-and-carry type stuff."

Marcos thought a moment. "Matt's boy Ed has been around the place a number of times. I'll pass the word."

"Thanks. The sooner the better."

...

John Dibbs, trying not to think of himself as captain anymore, walked into the train station as evening approached. His clothes had been deliberately ground into the dust to give them a tan color and to flag him as poor. His hair was scraggly to the same end. His poor air boots would never be usable on an airship again, stained from mud embedded with grit. They were giving him blisters as well.

But thanks to a kind stranger who had given him a lift into town, he was well ahead of schedule.

The rest of the crew were still back at the farm. At least Coorain was enjoying the experience. Claiming captain's prerogative, this scouting visit into town was just a test. He had to see how dangerous it was for stranded Australians and to attempt to scrounge up needed resources.

The train station was a big risk, but he needed cash. If he could just locate a public terminal... there!

He slid into a vacant seat in a compact little four-way bench, divided into relatively private booths where everyone sat back-to-back to face their displays.

All it took was a Net ID and he was into his personal account. In a moment, he had drained his Bank of Canberra account and converted all his Australian dollars into Net credits. He was hardly a rich man, but every bit would help. The rest of his crew would likely have to do the same before they reached safety.

He was about to log off when he noticed a message alert. He tapped it.

Message from Fleet Admiral Dale

John looked around. There didn't appear to be anyone looking his way, and his display was hidden from view. He slow-tapped. It was text-only.

This is a personal message to each and every member of the fleet:

Beginning just a few days ago, a carefully engineered biological weapon was released into the air, designed to destroy every blimp on the planet. You have probably seen the results—gray spots that compromised the skin of the blimps, causing them to lose hydrogen, crash and in some cases explode.

The evidence is very clear. We were attacked.

If we are at war, then we have already lost, for this infection appears unstoppable.

There are many questions: Who did this? Why were we attacked? Is this all? It appears that some people have been infected as well.

But for me, as leader of the fleet, the largest question has been: "Are we at war?"

We loved our blimps. All of us, or we wouldn't have been part of the fleet. But the blimps weren't the fleet. We are. This collection of merchants and engineers and administrators are all people who have become an organization knit together by nothing more than some rank and tradition, and an idea.

If that idea was just blimps, then it's done, we're disbanded.

If that idea was to make money, then poof, the gas has gone out of that idea.

But if the idea was to bring the world together, by trade, and by travel, and by exchange of ideas and by forging connections to people with different faces and different accents—then that idea is still strong, and the fleet is still alive in every one of you. We'll change our tools, we'll learn new skills, but we aren't done!

One thing that the fleet has never been is an armed force of a single nation. We've never carried weapons. A blimp is a very vulnerable target. As admiral, I have never ordered any of you to perform military operations in all my years here.

Citizenship of any nation has never been a condition to join the fleet. We have people from Australia, of course, but some of the first were from Polynesia and the American nations. Although, up until recently, the fleet was in a close relationship with the Australian court, we have a very real claim to be an international organization.

I have come to believe that although we were attacked, we are not at war with any nation. We are still bound by the idea that we can bring humanity together by our actions.

And we are an organization of people, not blimps. And to that end, I pledge all my resources to bring to safety all the members of the fleet.

It is up to you to decide if you wish to remain part of this international organization. It always has been thus.

For those of you who are stranded and who need help reaching safety, use this contact ID to request resources, mediation with the locals, transportation—whatever you need. I will do my best.

But know that, in no case are you required to act as military agents against any nation. You are the enemy of no one, because we are not at war.

Fleet Admiral Dale, Earl of Coonabarabran, Australia

John Dibbs—Captain John Dibbs—nodded. *I had thought that the whole world had gone insane.* He took a moment to memorize the admiral's contact ID and then he typed a quick summary of his condition, his location, and the status of his crew.

I'm still stuck in potentially hostile lands. We may not be at war with them, but the Texans don't know that. I don't think my plan has changed much.

But was a nice feeling to know that he might just have the option of walking up to a local policeman to ask for aid.

Across the walkway was an Exchange Station. He cleared his terminal, went over and converted Net credits to Texas dollars. He had some things to buy.

...

King Thomas snarled as he read the copy of the fleet message. One of the pilots, more loyal to his king than to his admiral, had forwarded him a copy. It had taken hours to get through his protective layers of administrators, but it stung no less.

"Well, he's an earl no longer. I'll get that pushed through quickly enough."

He leaned back in his chair. *Do I need anything from his organization?*

There were some laboratories and all the blimp breeding facilities. Which of those places were likely to be useless with this spore contamination? How much distraction would it be to send his personal guard to take over the fleet headquarters and install a new admiral?

Later, when I have him arrested. For now, my black organizations are all the forces I need.

He had to concentrate on the Texas campaign.

248

Nailed

"There's no doubt about it." Dr. Tuck shook his head. "And I'm one of the victims."

"You're augmented?"

He nodded. "Years ago. Simple thing, really. I have a little trigger. I say a chant in my head, and it adjusts my ability to concentrate. It's great for times like these when I have to stay on a project for days on end. But it means my genes have a little splice in them that connects the new code that adjusts my endocrine system."

He took a deep breath. "So now, when a spore lands on my skin, or I breathe one in, it'll dig into my cells and find that splice sequence. That's all it'll need to replicate itself. Probably the only reason I'm still alive is that I've been living in a clean room laboratory. But my luck won't last. It can't. Not unless I want to live in a bubble the rest of my life."

Admiral Dale sat in the seat across from him in Tuck's lab. He'd wondered why the doctor had insisted he put the protective gear back on when he showed up.

"Explain it to me, simply. I'm not a biologist, but really, what's this splice?"

Tuck gestured with his hands, "Oh, back a hundred years ago or so, when the basics of gene manipulation was worked out, there were many different techniques for changing gene sequences. I mean, we've been doing it for thousands of years by simple techniques like selective breeding. But the new technology found easier, faster ways."

He hesitated, trying to find the words. "Think about carpentry. There are a simple set of tools used, no matter what you build—hammer and saw, nails and screws, what have you. Back then, they invented the tool set for genetic engineering, and everyone standardized on the same set. The splice is a mechanism for inserting new DNA code segments into an existing chromosome. It's a non-coding sequence that latches on to well-known locations in the gene and cleanly inserts the new code.

"Many decades of use has proven how effective the technique is, so it's in everyone's 'toolbox'. It's the nail that holds gene modifications in place. All gene modifications.

"The spore designers coded a dozen targets in the blimp genome where their attacker could hook into the blimp's DNA and begin replicating. Eleven of those are fairly unique to blimps. One of them is the standard splice code."

Dale leaned forward, "So are the spores just one twelfth as effective on other life-forms?"

Tuck shook his head. "No. All it takes is one. The spore designers, by either accident or design, created a plague on every gene-modified organism. All numals. All augmented humans.

"They've destroyed all the nails on the planet. No augmented person on earth is safe."

...

Two floors down from the top at the Black Gold Tower, Samuel knocked on the door.

Rachael opened the door with a beaming face, and then jerked when she saw the two of them. "Uh, hello?"

Samuel smoothly nodded, "Good evening. Rachael, this is Ed James, my new pack mule. Ed, this is Rachael Nue, the most perfect girl you'll ever meet."

Ed was paralyzed. She was radiant and the thin golden gown caught the light of her room and made it appear she was clothed only in a cloud of light. Rachael smiled and Samuel felt weak just catching the edges of it.

"It's very nice to meet you, Ed." After a second or two of his tongue-tied silence, she moved a step forward and held out her hand.

He almost flubbed that one too, but he shook it.

Samuel watched for a moment then said, "Did you get approval for your roof-top camera position?"

She smiled, "Of course I did."

"Good. Where do you want the gear?"

"I'll show you."

Samuel turned, "Ed, go bring up the cart."

He nodded and hurriedly turned back toward the elevator.

Rachael grabbed Samuel's arm and pulled him into her room. "Why did you bring him?"

He pulled her close and kissed, with an urgency that told how much he'd missed her.

He mumbled, "Self defense."

She leaned her head to his chest. "Oh. Explain."

He looked around at the suite, larger than any room in any place he'd ever lived. Even without a bed visibly in view, there were plenty of places where they could spend some lingering moments.

"I knew what would happen if I came here alone. I'm not that strong. You've worn me down."

They sat down on a couch, moving together as one.

"Is that so bad?"

With the knowledge that Ed was hard at work, due back in minutes, he held her desperately. "I grew up in a little town. Hey, on O'ahu, even the cities were small towns. I know how it's supposed to work." He felt her quivering beneath his touch.

"How?" she mumbled, her hands playing with his buttons. "How is it supposed to work?"

It was hard to think. "Boy, girl." He sighed. "A guy meets a girl and spends some time with her. They express interest." He kissed the top of her hair. "And, eventually, he asks her."

"Asks her what?"

He cleared his throat. "He asks her to spend the rest of their lives screencrafting together."

She laughed, and the ripples against his chest knocked most thoughts right out of his head.

She asked, "Is that what they do in grass huts on the islands? Make screens?"

He chuckled. "You'd be surprised."

Far too quickly, there was a timid knock on the door.

He straightened up. She adjusted his collar and ran her fingers through his hair.

Samuel took her hand. "I'll be on the job through the flight, and for a few days after that. But I'm serious. If you're ever going to escape, that will be the time."

She was very quiet. "Bolls and Nue Productions?"

"Think about it."

They went to the door. Ed was there with the equipment cart.

Rachael led the way. She'd already located the service elevator that took them all the way to the roof.

Samuel held her hand as they walked. "When I found out that Ed had a license to drive, I figured he should know the way here, just in case we're both tied up behind the terminals and we need to move data sets or gear one way or the other."

She nodded thoughtfully, then whispered, "That's a good idea. I might need a strong man around the place while you're stuck at your display."

"Hey, watch it. It's Matt's kid."

They set up the tripod and locked the camera in a storage bin. Ed headed down with the cart.

He held her tight as they took advantage of the moment, alone in the dark. Below, the city's lights shimmered from the cooling summer heat.

"How much time?" She sounded lonely.

"Just a couple of minutes. I have to drive him home."

"I wore this dress for you. It probably tears easily."

"Hmm. I'll look forward to it."

Bottling up his feelings, his face was solemn on the painful ride down the elevator. If it weren't for the job...

On the ride back, Ed said, "Boy, she's something!"

He nodded and smiled. "Smart, beautiful, terribly rich, and very ruthless. You're sure to see her on the screens before too long."

...

"Hello, Ellie." The terminal lit up with her shopping buddy. In the background was the Dallas skyline Rachael remembered from her quick visit there.

"Rachael. Oh! I see the yellow dress got there in time." She paused, looking at her friend's expression. "Or did it?"

She sighed. "Oh, I don't know. Maybe it was too early."

"The fish got away?"

"Didn't even nibble. Oh, I'm not sure. It's not working out like I planned."

Ellie looked carefully at the image. "I don't see anyone in the background. Are you alone tonight?"

"Unfortunately. You?"

Ellie shrugged. "No one I can't put off until tomorrow. Do you want to pop up a romantic comedy and we can make snide remarks at it?"

Rachael shook her head. "I've still got some final detail work for the screen we're releasing tomorrow. I just had reserved an hour or so for... something else, and that didn't happen."

"This is your screencrafter we're talking about?"

"Yes."

"And you haven't tumbled him yet?"

"No. I think... I think he's an all-or-nothing kind of guy."

"Umm, well not to be anything but complimentary here, but maybe he just doesn't realize you're too big to swallow whole. A small town guy just can't understand the kind of life you lead."

"That's the thing, Ellie. I think maybe he does."

...

The Duke of Lorraine's call woke Jenner, but his people had orders to put him through any time of the day or night.

Lorraine frowned as Admiral of the Court Jenner rubbed his eyes and straightened his robe. "When are you going to come back to Europa? Negotiations to release the private guards of ancestral lines is tough enough when I can't introduce the new admiral."

"It would be a waste of time and effort. I need to be closer to armada operations, not farther away. I had been thinking of relocating to Hawaii. Take an airplane, maybe. I can't afford to be away from a strong Net connection for the length of time it would take a liner to get there."

"I suppose." Lorraine shrugged. "But that's not really why I called. What do you know about the man Dale, Admiral of the Blimp Fleet?"

Jenner tilted his head up, staring at nothing in his darkened room while he put a face on the man. "Earl of something unpronounceable in the Australian court. First and only admiral appointed when the Blimp Operations Consortium brought the three major companies under one umbrella. Chummy with King Thomas. An able administrator, I've heard, but not on the fast track for a government post."

"Well, things have changed. There's been a falling out, I gather. And the Earldom of Coonabarabran has been declared forfeit, so it seems that it's more than just a tiff."

Jenner nodded. "Probably Thomas needed someone to blame for the collapse of the blimps. He recognizes that his famed 'fleet' is over and done with."

"Perhaps. But Admiral Dale doesn't seem to think so."

"Oh?"

Lorraine referred to a piece of paper in his hand. "Berlin received an interesting message from Dale, under his own authority as 'Admiral of the Fleet'. He makes the claim that his fleet is an international organization, and that their blimps were attacked and destroyed by a targeted biological spore."

Jenner was instantly fully alert, but he kept his breathing even and made no move. Lorraine wasn't even looking at him as he kept reading.

"It says here that he has given direct orders to all members of his fleet to cooperate with the authorities in the places where they are stranded, and that the fleet is at war with no one."

"That makes sense. He's powerless, and he's just trying to keep his people from being targets. Without the blimps, that fleet of his has no power and is nothing on the international stage. He's distancing himself from King Thomas and Australia's actions."

Lorraine nodded. "There's more. He says here, 'While my scientists have proven that the spore was specifically designed to attack the blimps, there is a defect in the design that makes it a danger to people and other life forms. To avoid public panic, this information has been kept close, but contact this Net ID for complete details. The matter is urgent.'"

Jenner muttered, "Other life forms? What does he mean, I wonder?"

Lorraine shrugged. "That's what I don't know. That's why I called you, to get a feel for the man. Is this a legitimate danger that we should know about? Or is this a sham, just an effort to bolster his claim to be the leader of an international organization?"

Jenner's mind was churning. He had to find out what Admiral Dale knew.

"Yes, we need to follow up. Get the information and send it to me, no matter what it's worth. He's not asking to be paid for it, is he? But if the spores are fatal to other numals, then I would very much like to know that!"

When Lorraine clicked off, Jenner called his people in Bremerhaven and ordered them to collect spores from any downed blimps that they could locate and see if they had any effect on the acidic algae attacking his shipyards.

Wow

When the touring-carriage style car pulled up at the tumbled-down farm outside of Midland, nothing stirred. The car paused and then drove carefully over to the barn, avoiding anything in the dirt ruts that might cause trouble for the tires.

The engine stopped and Captain Dibbs stepped out. His people appeared out of the shadows.

"Hey John, I couldn't see through the tinted glass. How did it go?"

He smiled and reached into the car. "Help me bring this stuff inside the barn."

Anna asked, "What's that on your head?"

He smiled under his Stetson, "It's what all the good Texicans are wearing."

Coorain ducked his head in. "Hoo. Air conditioning. Are you sure we don't want to all climb in here?"

"For now, the barn."

He'd brought food, bottled water, clothes, and two handsets.

"John, are you rich or something?"

"I'll tell you in a minute." Once they were in the shade and Coorain passed out the water bottles, Dibbs passed around the handsets.

"Open your personal account and read the message from the admiral, then hand it to someone else."

It took a few minutes. Paul apologized as he had to read messages from his wife and send back a terse reply letting her know he was alive.

Dibbs then got their attention. "I've spent a little time checking the news. King Thomas is on the verge of attacking Texas. People around here are very edgy. I was lucky the shop owner where I bought clothes was just too bored to pay much attention to the news. That explosion we saw two days ago in the distance was the *Kiwi*, and it was so close to town that it shattered windows and put the local police on the lookout for any Aussie spies."

"That's us," Miles muttered solemnly.

Anna said, "Not really. Didn't the admiral say we're not at war?"

Coorain wrinkled his forehead. "Maybe. As fleet, we're noncombatants, but as Aussies, what are we?"

Dibbs shook his head. "All this is lawyer logic. Here's the breakdown as I see it: The admiral says as fleet, we're friendly. King Thomas gave me, Captain John Dibbs, an order to go look at Midland. I failed in that order. The *Green Monster* didn't make it that far. None of you got that order—you were just the crew doing your jobs. None of you took hostile action against the Texas people, and unless the king calls your personal accounts, which he probably doesn't even know, you won't receive any orders to be hostile in the future. As for me, my blimp is dead, so I'm not going to even check the ship's ID until we're all home again."

Miles said, "That's all great, but the Texans don't know this, and won't be in a mood to stop and have a lawyerly debate with us. They'll point their guns, and if we twitch, they'll shoot."

Coorain asked, "What about the admiral? He said nice words, but can we trust him to help, like he said?"

Dibbs nodded. "See the car, and the supplies? That's his money. When I checked the news, there was flap in the Australian Exchange. The ASX index took a big dip when Dale liquidated his holdings. He's sold out to build cash to rescue stranded fleet members.

"There was another story that says King Thomas revoked his title. He's not an earl anymore, just the admiral."

Anna said, "That's good enough for me. He's gambling on us. I'm gambling on him."

Paul reached into the sacks and pulled out another Stetson and tried it on. "What now?"

Dibbs said, "If war is heating up here, we need to leave, within minutes. The only question is the direction."

Coorain said, "I thought we were headed toward the coast, to catch a ship."

"That's where King Thomas will attack, if it's anything like what he's done in Europa."

"That's what I thought. Louisiana?"

"What about north?" asked Miles the engineer. He rarely talked, so they all turned to look. He shrugged. "The farther from the coastline, the less twitchy people will be. I hear there is a highway open to Olympia now. This conflict blew up from name-calling to a shooting war in just weeks. Maybe it will be over by the time we drive that far."

Dibbs nodded, "It has its points. It would be difficult to get a ship berth under the current conditions in any case. We now have handsets, so we can monitor the news.

"Coorain, you're navigator, find us a route north that steers clear of Midland."

...

"This is Rachael Nue, reporting from Midland, Greater Texas."

She smiled at the camera with all the confidence a perfect new outfit could bring. The crisp khaki outfit, all big pockets and shiny buttons, went well with the skyline of Midland behind her. According to the mirror, she looked every bit the professional on-the-scene reporter.

With a sweeping gesture, she turned to look at the panorama. Obscured by her hand, she tapped the control that panned the remote control tripod mount to a pre-set position.

"The long-time center of the Greater Texas petroleum industry, this desert oasis has taken an abrupt position, center stage, in the world drama. Beginning two days ago, the landscape echoed with the explosion of a conflict escalating toward war." She'd edit the captures they'd taken of the explosion and the shock wave into place later.

"But the events to unfold in just a few hours may soon eclipse all the fears and rumors of war." The camera zoomed in on the airport below, showing something quite new for the place—a crowd gathering outside Bill Melear's aircraft company.

She clicked the camera off and hurried inside to edit the intro into some other scenes she'd already collected.

Samuel had called early this morning as their long tag had entered the Public Queue and people were waking up to the historic possibilities due to happen "on the twelfth". People were remembering the time when Bill had rattled the public imagination when his plane cracked the sound barrier. This was a man who had delivered before. *He* was the one behind this mysterious event.

Add to that the peculiar twist that came from the King Thomas' ultimatum. Greater Texas was standing up to him, and whether Bill Melear was successful or not, this was likely a triggering event in another round of this strange war.

"Are you *sure* you can pull this off on your own?" Samuel had asked Rachael, a strange intensity in his eyes. "I've got a solid request for a fifteen-minute follow-up, to alternate in the Queue with today's tag. This isn't another tag, it's a fully-paid, subscribed news screen. And I'm tied up getting the copilot camera working properly. Can you do it?"

She'd said yes, and it was all hers. She'd sketched out the dialog and raided the documentary captures for bits and pieces.

The idea was all her design. People already knew the political ramifications of what was about to happen, they just needed to understand what all the fuss was about. Why was this event tomorrow going to be important?

It took longer than she'd hoped. There were pre-Star historical images of rockets and more recent images of Bill and his previous record-breaking airplane. She timed out the succession of images and put her most professional voice over it all, telling the tale.

She hesitated, looking at the metadata. With her very first news screen as a template, she copied most of the items over. But this time, it was all hers. *Should I call Samuel about the licensing?*

Her fingers shook over the keys. Then taking a deep breath, she put her ID in all the places where Samuel's were in the first one and credited him for some of the camera work. *He said to do it all myself. This is what he meant. I guess.*

...

Samuel heard someone walking up the metal steps behind him. He was draped halfway into the copilot cockpit, adjusting the cut-down camera tripod. Bill had warned him that there would be strong forces during the flight and that if it wasn't securely bolted in place, it could be disastrous.

"Um. Mr. Bolls?"

"Yes, Ed."

"You said to tell you when Rachael's screen came up in the Queue. Well, it did."

He couldn't stop what he was doing, and there was no one else to take over. Bill was encased in his flight simulator, training up until the last minute. Marcos and the others all had their own jobs to do. When he was done, Marcos would check his work, but if there were problems, his orders were to rip it out. There was no time for half-measures.

"Did you watch it?"

"Ah. Yes."

"How was it?"

"Well... She was pretty."

Samuel had time for a smile, nearly balanced on his head, tightening a bolt. "How was she dressed?"

"Oh, I dunno. Business-y. Lots of buttons."

"How about the story?"

"Oh, that was great. Spaceflight. Wow. I didn't know my dad was working on anything like that!"

Good enough, then. It got a 'Wow'.

...

"Wow."

Dibbs was driving, following a minor road just south of Brownfield. Anna was looking at a handset, supposedly checking the news.

"What is it?"

"There's this news report about the new airplane in Midland—the thing that King Thomas wants stopped. But that's not what I saw. There's a little segment showing the explosion of the *Kiwi*, only they didn't know its name. John, it *detonated*. This was no crash and burn. It must have been over instantly for the crew."

Miles, in the third row of seats said, "It was the ballonet. Had to be. Ours were nearly stressed to the max with all the hydrogen loss. I knew that if one of them blew, that it would be all over. Anything could set it off, once the hydrogen bag had a healthy load of oxygen added to it."

Dibbs nodded. "Well, it's not our problem any more. But I'll pass the word, in case they start work designing a new generation of blimps."

Anna muttered, "If they ever do."

He didn't say anything more. Not his problem. But he remembered Captain Bourke chatting with him. Another one gone for sure. He almost wished he were at war with someone—the monster who designed the spots.

...

No. No. No. Jenner read through the biological analysis of the spores again. The Australian biologist who had deconstructed the attack agent was right on track. His careful paragraphs echoed the enthusiastic reports he'd gotten from his anonymous workers who had created it.

They too, on his insistence, had run tests on human tissue, making certain there could be no jumping across species barriers to cause a human plague.

Did they use the same standardized human lab tissue this Dr. Tuck used?

They understood the danger. He had made sure they understood the danger. How could this error have slipped through the design and testing?

Oh, for a time machine to reach back and fix it!

But the designers were gone as if they had never existed. That was part of the conditions of their transaction. Designing a disease, even if just a disease for numals, was solidly on the black side of ethics.

They should never have let this happen!

But regrets and fantasy weren't helpful. He had to face the new information, and to make the best choices available.

On the bright side, the spores should wipe out the algae and kelp. Likely most of the weapons King Thomas had amassed were biological. That was the way his mind worked.

Isn't he augmented as well? Cultivated insomnia, or something like that.

Let him die with his weapons!

But he wasn't the only one at risk.

Hurriedly, he tapped a code.

Lorraine appeared, looking annoyed. "Yes?"

"Are you alone?"

"Yes, what is it?"

"I've done my analysis of the fleet data as you requested. And I have to ask, is any member of the royal family genetically augmented?"

Space

"I was hoping you'd come by tonight," she pouted.

Samuel turned his display so that it wouldn't be visible from outside the door to his office, "I can see. And I appreciate your outfit, but I'm stuck here in the hangar. We all are, even Ed."

"Oh." She reached for a robe and covered the exotic lace. "I hope he didn't see."

"It's just me here in our office, but he's in and out. And for what it's worth, I would have come by if I could. It's really a lock-down. Food is being delivered. Cots and bedding have arrived."

"They're serious about it."

"You bet. The Texas king, Jess Fuller, put his reputation on the line standing up to the Australians. Nobody here is going to let him down."

She smiled. "You would have come by without a chaperone?"

He nodded. "I said I was weak. Even when I saw your face, I wasn't ready to give you up."

"My face?"

"Yes, 'Bolls and Nue Productions'?"

"Oh, that." She sighed. "You think I'm a lost cause."

"Maybe 'Bolls and Nue' is the lost cause. As it stands, we're going to end up in tears, and I'm not sure you can cry, so I guess they'll be mine."

...

Dawn was cool on the top of Black Gold Tower, so she was bundled up in a coat, hoping it wouldn't crease her on-camera outfit beneath.

"Samuel, take a look at this."

He had her camera images lined up on his display. She had his.

On the telephoto, zoomed all the way up, she had focussed on a outsized news truck with the whole side of it covered in a large display. People who had come to see the event in person were clustered around the image.

"I'd like to lead off the event with this—to give the locals a thrill at being here live."

"Sounds good. Bill is on a roll. He got all of three hours of sleep last night and he's up and dressed in his silver suit."

A few minutes later, the sun brought a hint of warmth. She hoped it would be enough to keep her teeth from chattering. Excitement alone was keeping her breathing fast. It was about time.

The news truck had a clock counting down to the real-time report and it clicked three, two, one. Rachael dropped her coat, picked up her hand control and began.

"It's early here in Midland, Greater Texas, and the crowds have already been in place for hours." She switched the camera's zoom so she was in the frame. "And I'm not sure, but I may be able to hear them cheering.

"Samuel."

His camera took over the feed. "This is Samuel Bolls, live at the aircraft design and testing facilities of world-famous Bill Melear, the designer and pilot who, just seven years ago, cracked the sound barrier for the first time since the Star."

They alternated, depending on which camera angle was needed next. They had roughed out the first thirty minutes before the plane took off. They wanted enough time to catch the people who had forgotten when the event started. Neighbors and relatives were calling each other, asking if they were watching, too.

Bill waved, giving no speech this time since he would be talking in the cockpit, and climbed in.

The remote-controlled camera caught the awkwardness of getting into place and fastening down the seals.

"Microphone check. This is Bill Melear."

"We hear you fine," replied Marcos from the control tower. "No clouds in range."

"That's good."

Samuel narrated to the real-time feed in a low voice. "No clouds means there can be no hidden blimps in the area, which was a shock to everyone during the early test flight."

Bill spoke to his automated copilot camera. "You might want to face forward. You don't want to miss this."

Samuel at the controls aimed the view forward, out the cockpit windows.

The engines began screaming and the plane seemed to jump forward. The airstrip was all straight lines off to the vanishing point. And then the ground dropped away.

They had several camera angles—Rachael on the roof, a remote on the platform they had used before, and Samuel's second angle on the ground among the crew, and of course, the copilot view.

Rachael was ready with the telephoto and caught the shock-wave off the plane as it passed through the sound barrier. Samuel coached the audience to listen for the sonic boom, and Rachael was able to pick up crowd cheers as the group on the ground had their teeth rattled.

...

At the entrance to Galveston Bay, a mound of water erupted off Port Bolivar. Sirens sounded and a dozen small boats jumped from their moorings, directed by the coastal defense airplane flying overhead.

Galveston operations came rattling over speakers. "Wake signature detected rounding Pelican Island, turning toward Trinity Bay. 'Ware depth charges."

Sabine Pass operations reported machine-gun fire at wakes in the water near Texaco Island.

Observation plane five, off the entrance to Matagorda Bay reported three merchant ships on fire.

A string of mines across the channel at Port Aransas erupted almost at once.

All up and down the Greater Texas coastline, sirens were sounding and emergency craft were heading to their designated positions. The attack had happened on schedule, and they were ready. There were survivors to rescue and positions to secure. The training video showing the dolphin-like wakes in the water had proved their worth.

A Galveston Harbor rescue boat snared a body—a strange looking creature, like a man with fins.

...

Bill Melear's calm voice sounded from millions of terminal displays. "You can see the curve of the earth." His gloved hand pointed. "We're still hundreds of miles inland, but you can see the blue of the ocean off that way.

"Notice how the blue sky has compacted down into a thin layer. The higher we get, the blacker the sky will be."

Samuel wanted to ask questions, but this was Bill's show, and he hesitated to interrupt.

There was a string of numbers on one display—telemetry from *The Dream*. Samuel whispered to the audience. "One of the pre-Star traditions is that space begins above sixty-two miles altitude. He has climbed beyond that."

The narration to the feed didn't go up to the plane, but Bill tapped his instruments. "It looks like I just passed seventy-five miles." Samuel steered the camera to get a better look at him. "According to my calculations, from this point on, I'll need to steer using air-jets, because there's no air for the control flaps on the wings. I'm truly in space, and I'm glad you are all here with me to enjoy the moment.

"Reaching space was the first goal of this flight." He chuckled. "But we're not done yet!"

He let go of his yoke and tapped on a control pad. "Now that I don't have air to worry about, let's go higher." He adjusted the aim of the plane and everything within the cockpit, camera included, sagged a bit. Samuel compensated.

"With apologies to Doctors Nance and Bate, I've decided to call their beams 'tractor' and 'pressor'. Right now, I'm pushing against the Earth with a pressor beam, and we're accelerating much faster than I could while in the atmosphere. I want to reach an altitude of one hundred and fifty miles for my next goal."

Marcos came over the private tower channel. "Rachael, Samuel, Bill told me that the next phase uses the detachable pods. You might get ready."

Rachael sent Samuel an image of the plane with the pods circled. "Marcos warned me to be ready for this. They weren't there on the first flight."

He was about to search his captures for good images when several popped up on their private channel. She even had a short script talking about the way the pre-Star military plane on which *The Dream* was based had used the pods to carry weapons.

"If you're prepared, go for it."

She put her face in a small window in the static image and then shifted it to the real-time feed.

"Bill Melear has more surprises for us, and I've just been told that the second goal will be using these two pods carried beneath the wings of the plane." She continued with more scenes and the history. She timed it well, ending just as the plane reached the 150-mile mark.

"Here we are," said Bill, "at an altitude used by many of the space satellites in the pre-Star era. It seems that you can place an object in a nearly permanent path around the Earth if they're moving fast enough. I'm now going to launch two of them."

He tapped his controls and shifted the position of the plane. Since both the plane and the pod were falling upward at the same velocity with no air, it seemed as if the pod drifted weightlessly in front of the plane.

"Take a good look. This is the first orbiting satellite of the current era."

The elongated egg-shaped pod cracked open, showing two wings. "This is *SpaceNetRelay-1*. Just as people used the flying Net relays on the blimps, this relay will provide superior Net connection over a wide circle of the Earth. It will come and go in just minutes, but as I add more of them over time, many places on the Earth which were limited to slow, short-wave bandwidth will be able to send and receive higher speed data.

"Of course, if I just left it there, it would soon crash back to the Earth, so I have to give it a push, up to eighteen thousand miles per hour. Watch closely. Here goes." He tapped a button and it appeared as if the satellite vanished almost instantly.

"I've got two pods. So let's do *SpaceNetRelay-2*. Not quite as historic, but necessary nonetheless." He repeated the steps.

Marcos fed them a document, detailing the orbits, and how to use the relays. But they barely had time to glance at it.

Bill sounded happy, very happy. "Ah, now its time for my third and final goal—other than landing safely, of course.

"Many people, including my own crew, asked me why this flight had to happen on the twelfth. Why couldn't it be delayed a few days?

"Well, take a look out the window, just above the horizon of the earth and see that red dot just above the haze of the atmosphere. That is the planet Mars."

Samuel frantically adjusted the camera, zooming in and tweaking the brightness and contrast. Yes, there was a red dot there, but he wasn't able to make it appear any larger.

Bill must have been watching his antics. "Got it? Okay. Mars is behind us in its orbit around the sun. It's moving away from us.

"Now hang on, I'm going to flip the plane end over end. Don't get space-sick." He chuckled.

As the image steadied, the curve of the Moon was climbing above the horizon.

"As you can see, in exactly the opposite direction—the Moon. I'm now sending a narrow-focused double-ended tractor beam, one side to hit the Moon in a couple of seconds, and the other side to hit Mars, in about ten minutes. It will take twenty minutes for the link to establish. Once both are in the same tractor beam, it'll be like a rope lassoed around the retreating Mars, which I can use to metaphorically spin up my generators.

"Now, one of two things will happen then. If I'm wrong, then I'm going to explode in a big ball of energy. If I'm right, then a great surge of energy is going to flow into my storage cells.

"I started this flight with my batteries only twenty-percent charged. I've used most of that to get here. If I planned things right, I'll land with five times that much. That's enough for five more flights, or if I sell it, enough to supply all the electrical power to run Greater Texas for several days."

Samuel finally understood some of the numbers coming from the plane's telemetry. He selected the ones showing how long until the beam would be established, annotated it and overlaid it on the real-time feed.

Bill sighed. "There's not much to do but wait, and I'm glad you're all with me at this moment, because to be honest, I'm a little frightened.

"Let's see if I can roll the plane and get a better view of the earth while we wait, okay?"

He tapped the controls and soon the earth was hovering like a second sky overhead. Samuel's screencrafter instincts said to avoid static images and dead air, silence, like the plague. Bill was content to wait in silence, but he had to do something.

He steered the camera, while narrating. He clicked the switch that fed his voice up to Bill's headset as well.

"This is Samuel Bolls, and I must say, my nerves are on edge as we wait for the beam to arrive. But Bill, this is one glorious view, and one I never imagined I'd be able to see in my lifetime. Thank you for letting me, us, be here with you."

"You're welcome. I've been dreaming of being up here most of my life. I've seen the edge of space in some of my earlier test flights, but this is something entirely different. Take a look over there. You can see the Rocky Mountains, where that line of clouds bunches up."

Samuel steered the camera and zoomed in for a closer view. "I guess you could predict the weather pretty accurately from here."

"And they did, before the Star."

They chatted like that with the clock ticking away. Bill would point out some feature on the earth, and sometimes Samuel would ask about something.

Samuel was watching the countdown timer as it ticked away relentlessly.

"Um Bill, it's getting close."

"You're right. I've got the whole process on computer control, because my fingers are just not fast enough to hit the button on time."

The counter hit zero and Bill gasped. "I could feel that—the edges of the charging beam. And... it's done. The beams are quenched. Hey guys, I'm alive! And with a very valuable load of energy."

Samuel could tell something was different. The image outside the window was drifting to the side.

"So Samuel, and all my other copilots, we're in the new Space Age. Everything has changed. It's real. It's doable. It's a benefit for all of humanity, and it's profitable.

"The Space Age is here to stay.

"But I guess it's time to go home." Bill muttered, "Now where did I misplace Texas?"

Fenced In

Blimp Fleet HQ in Brisbane overlooked the harbor from a slight rise, just walking distance from the water, but no one looked outdoors anymore. For years, the heart of the operations had been in the theater-like room where everyone's work station faced the big world display on the wall. Slightly darkened, lit by displays and instruments, it had been a constant hum of activity, where people in the light gray uniforms of the fleet staff were kept busy with the activity of the world.

Until today.

An armed force of six men in the strong green favored by the Royal Guard of King Thomas entered and stalked the nearly vacant corridors until they reached the operations room.

An elderly man in gray stood as they entered. "May I help you?"

"We have come for Lawrence Dale, former Earl of Coonabarabran."

He nodded. "My apologies, but the admiral is not currently here."

"Where is he?" asked the stern Captain of the Guard.

"Currently? I'm not sure. He's with a rescue operation. I know that much. Why don't you check his Net ID?"

The captain looked around the large room. There were five people distributed around perhaps three dozen work stations. The big world map was dark. "Where is everyone?"

"The fleet is reorganizing. Our current task is to rescue stranded blimp crews. When we lost the royal patronage, the admiral decided to expand our operations from this one single location. Most of what we are doing now can be handled across the Net."

The guards were at a standstill. The king's order had been explicit. Dale was to be brought to him in chains. The word of the admiral's private communications with the other royal houses had come to his attention. He was to be displayed to the world as a traitor.

"Perhaps if you don't believe me, you could search the place? Here, let me pull up a map. Or, have you tried his house?"

...

King Thomas sealed his soundproofed doors and let out a scream of rage.

Nothing was going right. The plane had launched, and it had presented itself to the world as a peaceful operation—although he could see it was still a weapon in disguise.

His attack on Texas had only scored minimal damage, and nearly a third of his mermen were killed. Not only had the attack been rebuffed, their use as surprise attack agents was compromised.

"And now Dale has turned against me, consorting with my enemies. He'll die for that."

He tapped at his display. There were nearly a dozen rejected messages from Dale, dating back to when the blimps fell out of the sky.

On impulse, he called the number.

The screen lit up, attempted a visual connection, but bandwidth was insufficient. "Hello?"

"Dale!"

"Your Majesty. I was hoping we'd be able to talk again."

"Where are you?"

"Hmm. It appears I am approaching Antananarivo, Madagascar."

Bandwidth improved and the image came up. Dale was sitting in a comfortable chair. The image out the airplane window showed him still high above the terrain. Someone in a gray uniform was walking past, just slightly out of the frame.

"I recently acquired a plane to help in my rescue operations. There are two blimp crews on Madagascar, and I'm attempting to get them home."

"I want you here, now!"

Dale looked sad. "Yes, I imagine you do. However, with the greatest respect to the crown, lives are at stake in my current task. I'm sure you understand. I will return to Sydney as soon as I am able.

"And I'm sorry to say that you should get that rash on your arm looked after as soon as possible."

The image went dark. King Thomas looked at his arm where he'd been absently scratching. There was a cluster of gray spots on his skin.

...

Admiral Dale stared at his darkened terminal all through the descent to the airport.

Lieutenant Glynde put her hand on his shoulder. "Sir, we have landed."

He nodded. "I'm afraid I must make a phone call."

"Privately?"

A nod.

"I'll take care of the arrangements. I'll have everyone out in a minute."

Soon, the rush of boxes being moved and hushed voices moving away stopped, and he realized he was alone.

He opened his list of contacts and found one he had not used in a number of years. A royal seal appeared on the screen, followed by a familiar face.

"Dale!" The princess looked shocked to see him.

"Greetings, Lady Catherine. Are you alone?"

She looked at him in silence for a moment. "Yes. I'm in my quarters. No one is around. I've heard the news."

"About the earldom, or the arrest order?"

She nodded. "I hadn't heard about the arrest, but I don't suppose I'm surprised. Father judges betrayal harshly."

"I wish I could say it wasn't true, but I did act in the interests of the fleet, rather than the crown."

"Well, don't expect a good word from me. It wouldn't do any good. He's practically locked himself into his study day and night, staring at his displays and grumbling about world politics."

"Catherine, how are you holding up?"

She sagged slightly at the concern in his voice. "There's a lot of stress around here. A lot of secrets. You shouldn't have been surprised I was alone. I think he's keeping me restricted to my chambers for my own safety. His actions aren't popular."

Dale nodded, imagining the place. "Is Mary still ruling the dining room?"

She smiled and nodded. "I've missed your visits."

He shook his head. "It was just one of your father's ideas that didn't work out. I was, and still am, too old for you."

"Well, no one else has passed his tests either, and I'm starting to fade."

"I differ. Thirty-two is quite young for a royal princess."

She shuddered. "I hate it when people remember my age."

He was suddenly solemn again. "I'm afraid you will be feeling even older soon."

"What? What do you mean?"

"Your father is... ill."

"Oh, no. I mean he is erratic, and this war stuff has caused him to be angry about things..."

"No. I'm sorry, Catherine. It is not my position to judge the sovereign's mental state. He is physically ill. I suspect he will die within days, a couple of weeks, perhaps. Take a look at this. It is the document that triggered my arrest order."

He sent her the medical information from Dr. Tuck.

In the display, her face was drained, and her lips compressed as she read page after page.

After a long time, she asked, "And Father has these... spots?"

Dale nodded. "We talked just minutes before I called you. I saw the spots on his left arm, just above the elbow.

"Unless a miracle happens and a cure is created, the king will succumb. Even before that, I am sorry to say that the World Court may take action. Fleet members have mentioned ships being prepared for some secret action. We know that Baron Jenner has been elevated to the leadership of the European Navy, and we know that he can be vindictive. Rumor says that Jenner took your father's attacks on merchant ships as a personal attack on him."

"What can I do?"

He paused a moment, "Catherine, I have to ask. Have you ever had any genetic augmentation?"

She shook her head, eyes bright. "No. Father was proud of his engineered insomnia, but I... didn't like the way he acted, sometimes. I never had anything done."

Dale let out a breath he had been holding. "Okay, then you are probably safe from the disease. It might be a good time to take a holiday, somewhere remote, somewhere an invading force might not find you."

She sat upright, her face firm. "I can't leave my father. Not in his condition."

"I didn't think you would."

Her mind was in a whirl. Then, she focused on his eyes. "Your advice?"

"Either share your concerns and urge him to act..."

She gave a sad little laugh.

"...or act in his behalf."

Thirty-two years growing up in her father's household brought suspicion instantly to her eyes. But in seconds, it had faded. "Act how?"

Dale shook his head. "If he were my father..."

...

Ed James plopped down in the next chair. "When are they going to let us go free?"

Samuel looked up from his edit station, where he'd been folding in events from the real-time stream into his documentary. "I'd like to be out of here, as well."

Down in a little window on his display, Rachael gave him a wink.

Across the break room, Larry nodded. "I need to go home, too."

Samuel sighed, "I'll go check with Marcos. He seems to have better connections." He closed his session and walked over to Bill's office.

Bill waved him in. "How're the screens coming?"

"Good. Good. Nothing will match the viewership of the real-time event, but we'll have the first documentary ready within a few days."

Bill nodded. "That's great, but I've already accomplished what I wanted. The rest is gravy. You'll turn a profit on the Net with this?"

Samuel smiled, remembering the big list numbers. "We already have. But the guys were wondering when the Rangers were going to let us leave."

"There's a call coming. After that, I suppose."

"A call?"

"Yes, it's... Here it is."

Bill tapped his terminal and sat up straight.

Samuel wasn't a Texan, but he recognized the voice. King Jess was calling in his congratulations. He stood still and quiet as a mouse. Bill was beaming at all the compliments.

"And you know, Bill, that Texas is happy to claim you as a native son. We need our heroes desperately, especially with the dark times coming."

"Dark times?"

The king sighed. "I know you've been busy, and you deserve all the adulation you're going to receive, but I'm afraid the world is going to be distracted soon enough. There's a plague coming—a horrific, deadly plague. The World Court is already in talks to find ways of dealing with it, but war was bad enough. Now we're looking at plague, famine and death."

Bill shook his head, "I know I've been out of it, but this is the first I've heard of this."

"We're keeping it quiet, trying to curb panic. You've heard of the spots—the blimp disease? Well, it seems it'll attack anything with a genetic modification; crops, cattle, and of course all the people who've had work done. There is no cure. I thank God my family happens to be clear. Some houses will be wiped out.

"Keep a lid on it please, until we announce it officially. But you can see why we're going to need our heroes."

Samuel was pale. He slipped away silently. He grabbed his edit station and packed all the datastores in his bag. He found a quiet corner and made a call.

"Tad? Yes, Tad this is Samuel." He listened impatiently to his Hawaiian friend's compliments on the spaceflight event.

"Tad, listen carefully. Has Clarissa shown any gray spots on her skin?"

Close Examination

Admiral Jenner stood on the bridge works, feeling the sea breeze, stiff and bracing as his flagship put Tonga in the distance. It was good to be back at sea. With a military emergency to fund the upgrades, he had a forest of radio antennae to insure adequate Net bandwidth. The airplane flight across the Pacific to get him here had been memorable, but there was nothing like cutting through the waves at top speed.

Curtis, the captain of the *Tangaroa*, handed him a clipboard—in the salt air, quite a bit of the paperwork and documentation was handled like this, on paper. He glanced over the numbers.

Sydney in ninety hours. By then, we'll have three times the ships with us. Separate convoys were enroute, and juggling their speed and position had been a chore. They had to maximize their impact on the local population, if they were to end this quickly.

He initialed the required lines and handed it back. Military operations weren't his preferred style. Sitting behind his displays, moving pieces across the world—that was where he should be. And where he would return once this was completed.

Back in Europa, a mulch of blimp skin was proving a panacea in those ports inflicted with kelp. The algae cleanup was taking a little longer, but with resources coming available as the kelp died out, he had hopes the stigma of Bremerhaven would be lifted soon enough.

In fact, the only thing that annoyed him was the stiff military suit he wore. It itched. He surreptitiously slipped his fingers up his left sleeve and scratched.

He glanced down and frowned. There was a small darkened circle on the back of his hand.

No. It can't be.

His mind went into high gear, racing through decades of things medical.

Oh, no.

He excused himself and went to his cabin. He sealed the door, sat at his terminal and pulled archives from several years back.

It was the Beautiful People protection project. That's where he acquired the gene mod. It was a simple drug, taken for several days. It was the same one he had sold to businessmen and leaders around the world. He'd never looked that closely into the details of the drug. He'd funded it. Everyone was happy. It wasn't up to him to sweat over every little detail. Why was he plagued by all these incompetent assistants?

But one overlooked sentence would kill him. It would kill them all.

He clenched his teeth and stared at a map of Sydney harbor he'd put up on the wall.

"But not before I've seen you burn!"

...

Samuel knocked. Rachael was in her khaki outfit as she let him in.

"So, you're free. You should have called. I'd have been better dressed."

He set his bag down and pulled her to the couch.

She opened her mouth to be kissed, instead he gripped both her hands by the fingers, and said, "Marry me."

"Oh. What?" She collected herself and brought a smile to her face. "So that wasn't a business partnership you were talking about?"

He tried to smile. "You know it wasn't. Marry me, tonight. We can pull up the form, code in our personal ID codes and file it with Texas Legal Archive. We could be married in a few minutes."

She pulled her fingers loose. "Whoa there. This is a little fast, even for me. Give a girl a moment to think."

He said nothing, but moved close, stared at her face, and then kissed. They broke a minute later and he began holding her left arm, kissing it every few inches as he worked up to her sleeve. Barely had he finished when he switched to the other arm, giving it the same close attention.

He paused a moment and then unfastened her top collar button.

"What's going on here?" she asked.

He whispered, "If I had called, how would you have been dressed when you opened the door?" He unfastened the next button and folded the collar back on both sides, and then reached for the next shiny button.

"Well, the lace shift never got its full appreciation, but that's not the question. What's going on with you?"

"Can't a guy try to get a girl undressed?"

She batted his hand away and grabbed his chin, forcing him to stare her in the eyes. "This isn't you."

"Yes, it is." He reached up for a button, but she shook away.

"You're hiding something. Tell me. Tell me now, or get out."

He dipped his head and closed his eyes. "I want to be married to you, as soon as possible."

"And you thought having sex would seal the deal?"

He shook his head. "No. I'm not that stupid." He sighed. "I overheard something."

His refusal to look her in the eyes was frightening. She pulled him closer, chest to chest, where he didn't have to look at her.

Quietly, she asked, "What is it?"

His arms clasped behind her back, he told the story of the king's call to Bill. He tried to repeat it all.

"And then I couldn't listen anymore. I called a friend of mine, back in Hawaii. His daughter is four. She had some work done to fix a birth defect. I called him... and asked if Clarissa had any gray spots on her skin."

A whimper escaped as he took another breath. "Tad had noticed them. She'd been itchy. He thought it was just a rash! And... and I told my friend his daughter was going to die!"

He choked up and shook in her arms. She rocked him back and forth. The pieces fit, almost.

"And you think I might have spots?"

He nodded, still locked close to her.

She pushed him back, to stare him in the eyes. "Well, I don't. No rash, no spots, and I don't itch anywhere. I'm okay.

"I have an excellent immune system. Even more so, after they boosted it in Australia. Daddy never wanted to worry about me catching anything by hanging out with the wrong kind of boys." Her eyes twinkled. "So you don't have to worry."

"I worry. I will worry. And I want you to marry me."

"Why?" She tried to look past his eyes and see what was inside him.

"I want to take care of you." He blinked under her searching gaze. "And I know they won't let me any other way."

"Who is 'they'?"

"I want to check for spots."

"You don't believe me?"

"No. The spots organism attacks gene altered organisms, from numals to plants to animals. You're the most augmented person I know. You can't be immune."

"Who is 'they'?"

He was stubbornly silent.

She gave him a smile, with just a hint of worry in her eyes. "A clinical search for spots?"

His jaw was clenched as he nodded.

"I'll let you, but you have to keep talking. Answer all my questions, okay?"

He sighed. "Okay."

She lifted his hand to her button. "Then go. Who are 'they'?"

He swallowed and unfastened a button.

"King Jess said something about the World Court finding ways to deal with the plague, and I know he wasn't talking about finding a cure." It was distracting as he exposed her skin.

"You see, I grew up on Oahu, part of the Hawaiian islands, and learned a lot about the place's distinctive history. Back before the Star, way back, during a global conflict they called World War Two, Hawaii was a critical location in the war between Japan and the American states. Hawaii was owned by America, but a big fraction of the population was made up of Japanese immigrants."

Clinical. Clinical. He pulled the blouse free and set it aside.

She had to prompt him. "What about the Japanese?"

He leaned closer to examine her skin, starting at her collarbone.

"The Americans couldn't trust the Japanese. They took the leaders and put them in camps, away from everyone else. No one knew if they were even still alive. The Japanese residents started hiding all their cultural items and began dressing and acting like the Americans, just to keep from being taken away and maybe killed."

She wiggled when he touched her. "Well, that's horrible, but what does it have to do with us?"

He turned her around to examine her back. "If the World Court wants to protect the main population from the plague, they will have to quarantine the people who are afflicted. They'll have to, just to avoid riots and lynchings. Frightened people, who don't understand the medical details, will want to do anything they can to protect themselves.

"And the scale of this is massive. Just imagine how many people today have some kind of genetic tweak. There are dozens of routine medical procedures done all over the world. We aren't just talking about people who went to Australia for extensive processing. Everyone will know someone who has spots. And if the symptoms of spots are the same as for blimps, then it will be a horrible, mutilating death."

She shivered, and it wasn't just from his finger on her spine.

"Find anything yet?"

"No. Now... could you do the skirt. I just can't..."

She took pity on him, put her blouse back on and then shed everything else.

He was down on his knees, checking her legs, when he continued. "I just think the way it will play out is this: The World Court or the individual governments will announce free, but compulsory medical care for the people with spots. To handle the scope of the problem, people will have to go to camps, or special hospitals. Maybe, just maybe, family will be allowed to accompany them.

"Then as the cases advance, and people die, the camps will be sealed off from the public—to protect the general population from the horrors of the disease."

He shook his head. "But for the people inside, it will be a prison, maybe with real care, maybe not. It will be a place to die, surrounded by others suffering from the same disease."

"But I don't have spots, do I?"

He shook his head. "It won't matter. They will check all the records. They will ask all the doctors. Privacy protections will be shredded for the public good. All augmented people will go there, and if they haven't been infected yet, then surrounded by the others producing the spores, they will soon be. Think about how much anti-genie sentiment there really is in this world. It will be easy to calm the population down by interning the 'different' people."

His fingers probed around her hips, then he sighed. "Sit down. I need to check the soles of your feet." She propped her legs up on an ottoman. He searched even between her toes.

"Well?" she asked breathlessly.

"No spots, yet."

"I told you. I'm the healthiest person you'll ever meet. I'll outlive everybody."

He plopped down beside her and gave a big sigh, as if he'd held his breath during the whole examination. "You could live inside a sealed building."

She laughed. "Not likely." She draped one bare leg over him and asked, "Do I get to examine you now?"

"I've never been anywhere near a gene doctor. We're off the subject. Marry me."

Rachael leaned close, and his hand settled on her leg higher than it had managed before.

She whispered, "There's more to marrying than just filing a legal document."

"What do you want? A white dress, a church?"

"No, that's not what I'm talking about."

"Tell me. Is it love? I love you."

She shivered, and it surprised her. What she had been about to say caught in her chest.

He was looking at her, waiting.

She looked away. "Did you ever make a promise that you had to keep, but it turned your stomach?"

"Never anything that big, no." He shifted a little closer.

Her eyes were wide and she held him tightly. What was happening to her?

"My family is different."

"Umm. Probably. You're rich. You need me to sign a pre-nuptial agreement to protect the family's cash. I'll do it. No problem."

She sighed. "That's one part. What do you know about my family?"

"Umm. Nue Electronics. Live in Carolina. Horribly rich. Oh, there was one thing. That snoopy policeman in San Diego said you're part of some other family. I forget the name. German sounding."

"Rhineberg. It's one of the royal families of Europa. Daddy is like twelfth in line to the throne, but only if he drops Nue and re-takes Rhineberg. He was something of a rebel when he was young and started his company. But when he got older, he couldn't bear to break the connection entirely.

"Daddy made me promise that if I ever married, there's a stack of legal documents that has to be signed. The pre-nup is half the stack. The royal college owns the other half. Basically, they get the right to approve. They'll check your family back to the Star, or further, if they can. If you don't measure up, then the marriage is annulled—or I have to give up all right and title to the Rhineberg lineage."

He nodded. "It sounds like your risk, not mine. I have no objection."

She started to object—he was too flippant! She'd known of other people in her circle of acquaintances that had casually signed the pre-nuptial agreements, and then the institutional distrust inherent in the idea grew and soured their relationships.

But what if Samuel is right? I might not have long to live.

He waited while she thought. She glanced down and saw him toying with one of her shirt buttons.

Am I crazy?

She grabbed his fingers. "Come on, let's do this thing before I change my mind."

Closing In

"Marry me."

Anna shook her head. "Now, Coorain, I told you, you're ninth on my list, and there's no way to check with all the people in front of you, so you'll just have to wait."

Dibbs took a side look at her in the seat beside him. The *Green Monster's* healer had been playing this game with the male members of the crew since Brisbane, and seemed pretty confident she could keep juggling all their attentions. He suspected she had no intention of selecting any of them. On the gentle side of forty, and taking her profession seriously, he suspected she would have been content to sail the skies up into her seventies.

But things were different now. Her profession had been ripped out from under her, and they were all packed elbow to elbow in a car with barely any time available to get out and stretch their legs.

Anna spent most of her time on the handset, monitoring the news as they drove north. But she came alive when they had to deal with the locals. She often was the one to go into the stores and make purchases.

Their story had matured as they made changes over time. A fueling center attendant had asked about them and when she told him she was a large animal veterinarian, the clerk nodded and said, "...rodeo people."

So that's what they had become. Rodeo performers, a vet, and a clown, heading north to some event.

"John?" she asked, "What do you think about the spaceflight?"

He shrugged. "I watched the playback last night. The view was great, but it looked uncomfortable. I prefer to fly from an easy chair, giving orders and letting all the other people pull the levers."

Paul, sitting behind him, muttered, "We all knew that."

Miles, to the right of Paul, was staring at his handset. "There's a new message from the admiral."

Anna tapped her display. "Same here. 'There is an opportunity for extraction if you can arrive in Calgary in two days. Please update your status.'"

"Calgary, that's northeast, very much inland. It sounds like he has access to an airplane. Coorain?"

"On it. Somebody hand me a terminal."

...

Lorraine called at about two in the morning and Jenner was still awake, but he didn't turn on the lights.

"Sorry, I keep forgetting you're on the other side of the world. How goes the armada?"

"Five ships arrived today, but to keep the group together, we're having to drop our speed a couple of knots."

"Good, good." The duke was oblivious to finer points of sailing.

Jenner asked, "What prompts this call?"

"Well, since the king regards you as the expert on all things related to the blimps, he asked me to get your feel for this Admiral Dale and his people."

"I thought we already discussed this. He's powerless."

"Right. We know this, but is he valuable as a pawn? Currently, the man is flying in an airplane around the world, collecting stranded blimp crews and ferrying them to safe havens. Several nations are co-operating with his efforts. Getting the Australians out of their hair is seen as a win for both sides. He is even in discussions with us about the people that were arrested when their blimp went down at Lake Annecy."

The duke frowned, "It would be possible to take this Australian admiral hostage with minimum risk to us. In your judgement, would his possession be of any use to us in the conflict with King Thomas?"

Jenner toyed with the pieces in his mind. The former earl was an irritant to Thomas. But would that be of any importance at all when the armada moved into Sydney Harbor?

He shook his head. "Play the high road. 'In spite of Australia's criminal actions, the king is happy to extend humanitarian aid, et cetera, et cetera.' The blimp fleet has no blimps, his people have no useful skills anymore. Having them around just complicates the spots mess."

"The king will be happy to hear it. The spots cases are growing in number and there's no hiding it anymore. Some of the advanced cases are really rather horrible. It's not a pleasant way for anyone to die. We'll be announcing the quarantine later today."

...

Caleb woke with the dawn light. He scanned the horizon for rain clouds. Their drinking water was nearly gone. Perhaps he could use some of the boards to build a catching basin to divert rain and dew into the crate. There were erratic showers sometimes, leaving few splashes, but every drop counted. His net was almost done. He'd try it out after he checked on the captain.

He crawled over to the shelter and there was blood smeared on the boards nearby. He checked inside. She was gone.

The the dark red stains were regular, as if she had crawled while bleeding. The streaks were dried, and they led to the edge of the water.

She left me, in the night.

He didn't know she had that much strength—to crawl that far.

He stood up and yelled, "Captain! Captain!" There was not even a gull's cry in answer.

He went to the tether rope and checked the new raft, a catamaran-like structure with two large bundles of boards for floatation and an elevated platform riding on top.

I was going to move her over there today. We talked about it.

Or rather he talked about it. She rambled. The disease had destroyed her mind faster than the rest of her. It had been hard to make her eat and to make her drink. She didn't want to take his share, she said.

Suddenly, the new raft looked bigger than it needed to be. He pulled the line closer and stepped over. With the slight extra height, he put his hand above his eyes and peered at the water, scanning carefully in all directions. Nothing.

I'm alone. His eyes blurred, but as dehydrated as he was, tears couldn't fall.

...

Morning had come a few hours earlier in Midland.

"Hey," she poked him. "We overslept."

A morning overcast left him confused as to the time. "Ah. I guess it's a good thing that this is the tallest building in town."

She grinned as he held the blanket up to his chest. The roof-top garden bench had been wide enough for the both of them, just barely.

"Body modest? You don't have anything to be ashamed of."

"Well, I'm not an exhibitionist, like someone I know."

"Hey, it was your idea to search for spots by flashlight."

He smiled, "Yes, that's it. That's the reason."

She turned from side to side. "See any?"

He leaned back. "No. Not a one. But we'd better get some clothes on before someone comes up here."

"In a minute."

When they came up for air, Samuel frowned, "Come on, we can finish this down in your room. I have a low tolerance for embarrassment."

"Oh, I'm sure Ben and Ira have the entrances secured." She reached for her robe. They had come up well past midnight, a few hours after all the paperwork had been safely tucked in the legal archive and both had confessed that they had dreamed about that first night on the roof-top. With the corridors deserted, they threw on a few things and used her code to the service elevator to relive the experience, only with a different ending.

He grumbled as he slipped into his pants and put his robe over that. "I'm surprised that your guards haven't broken down the door and rescued you from my devious plan."

He grabbed up the blanket and pillows and they padded barefoot over to the elevator. "Do you think they told your father?"

She chuckled. "Dad probably told them. He has lexical crawlers running on most of the world's legal archives, checking on new postings that mention family or his company or things like that. He knows we're married."

The elevator dinged at their floor. When they rounded the corner, two men standing at her door looked up with bemused expressions.

One was Ranger Craddik. "Now what have you been up to?"

Samuel raised his nose, "We're on our honeymoon. It's no business of yours what we've been up to."

"Honeymoon?" His smile lasted a moment, then dropped. "Ah, this is Dr. George Smith. We have some business with Miss...Mrs?"

"She's still Rachael Nue. Professional name."

Rachael had unlocked the door and wordlessly moved inside. Samuel paused at the door. "Please wait. Either here or down in the lobby. We will be with you before too long."

He pulled the door shut behind him.

Rachael looked frightened. "They're here, so soon."

He nodded, "You see why I was so pushy last night." He glanced back. "They aren't banging on the door, so it's not an arrest warrant."

"Time enough for a shower?" she asked.

"Right behind you."

Twenty minutes later, cleaned up and dressed, Samuel invited them in.

Craddik was irritated. "We have other people to meet today. We waited as a courtesy."

"How many?" asked Samuel.

The doctor looked disturbed. "If we can begin with the examination."

Samuel shook his head. "You're here to look for the spots disease, aren't you?"

"Well, yes."

"She shows no spots at this time. I examined her myself just minutes ago. Nor do I have any spots."

Craddik said, "You're not on the list."

"But I should be."

"What?"

"You have a list of everyone with genetic alteration, is that not correct?"

The doctor was flustered that they weren't staying on the script. He looked at the ranger.

"Say what you're going to say."

Samuel glanced at Rachael. "My wife and I are aware that the government is beginning a response to a severe outbreak of the spots plague that originally appeared in the blimps. We are unwilling to be separated. I want you to know that on the voyage from Hawaii to San Diego, I received an undocumented treatment that likely added me to the list of the genetically altered.

"We will cooperate with the government, but we insist on being treated as a pair. We go together."

Rachael looked puzzled.

Smith asked, "What was the nature of this treatment?"

"I don't know the specifics. It was given to me by Baron Jenner. It supposedly protected me from artificial pheromones. My research after that event suggested it might have been achieved by a genetic process."

Rachael put her hand on her waist. "Well, I'm insulted."

He grinned. "Hey, it was self-protection. How do you suspect I kept myself pure before our wedding night?"

"Humpf!"

Smith was tapping through something on his handset. "There is a note here about a process sold by Jenner." He turned to Craddik. "I suppose he should be added to the list."

Samuel smiled.

"It's not something to be happy about. This is a very serious disease," the doctor warned. "We're here to notify you that you need to go to a hospital in Big Springs specifically set up for cases of spots."

"Like I said, neither of us show symptoms."

Craddik pulled out a sheet of paper and handed it to Rachael. "By order of the Crown, all genetically-altered persons in Greater Texas must appear at their designated care facilities either when spots appear or within three days of this notice. Should transportation be required, it will be provided."

Samuel asked, "Not that we're thinking of running, but some people will. As a reporter, I'm interested. What are your plans for them?"

The ranger didn't look happy. "If you don't show up in three days, we'll come looking for you. But it's not just Texas. There's nowhere to run, and from what I hear, you can't outrun the disease." He nodded to the both of them. "I'm sorry."

"And how many?"

Craddik shrugged. "My list has several hundred names. And that's just part of Midland. We suspect there's even more."

When they left, Rachael rushed up and held him. "It's just like you said—concentration camps. And you're at risk too, why didn't you tell me!"

He shrugged. "It was a bluff. Jenner gave me a pill that took the shine off your first impression, that's all. I didn't get the full life-time immunity package. I'm here to take care of you, not the other way around. But I doubt they'll bother to check. The current medical system is just about to be overloaded, if it isn't already."

They held each other, neither wanting to let go.

"Three days, eh? I don't want to show up early."

There was a knock on the door. It was Ben Mason. He nodded to Samuel, but spoke to Rachael. "Your father needs you to call him."

Her handset had been left to vibrate by itself all night long beside the bed. There were several messages queued up.

"Rachael! Thank God! I've been trying to reach you. You have to get back to Carolina immediately. I'm sending the plane."

"Hello, Daddy. I'm married."

"Yes, I know that! You can bring him too, if you want. But it's urgent you get here quickly. Carolina—the whole world—is arresting augments."

"I know, the Texas people were just here."

"Oh, God."

"Sir. This is Samuel Bolls." He moved into the frame. "I need to know, are you augmented?"

The strong-featured man with a touch of gray hair, but clearly Rachael's father, frowned, then nodded. "Math visualization."

"Then they're coming for you as well?"

"Yes, but I have connections. I'm sealing off the South Wing. They'll let me stay there."

"Sir, have you begun to show spots?"

The man froze, sweat visibly on his forehead. Samuel couldn't see any visible signs, but he whispered. "Yes. A few."

Samuel sighed. "Sir, you know this is a fatal disease?"

"Yes, but I have doctors. I'll have the best care."

Samuel put his arm around Rachael. "Sir, there is no cure, and it's very aggressive. I've heard two weeks is the expected lifespan, once spots appear. Please make what succession plans you need to make, and make sure the people you select are not augmented."

He had been shaken when the call started. Now he looked even older. "Rachael?"

She blinked away tears. "I don't have symptoms yet. I don't know what I'm going to do."

Samuel reached for the handset. "We'll call you back." He tapped it off.

She bawled into his arms. There was nothing to say.

They sat on the couch, until she settled down and wiped her face.

"So," she cleared her throat. "Do I go to Big Springs, or hide in the Carolina House?" She looked at him. "What do you think?"

He shook his head. "There's no good solution. If your father wasn't augmented, and if I had confidence that the house could be sealed off to keep spores out... But no, I'm sure you've been exposed already. Your immune system is helping, like you said, but how long can that last?"

She looked down at the carpet. "I grew up in that house. It can be very depressing. I can't say I look forward to dying there."

"It would be more luxurious than a hospital—if..." He shook his head.

"If what?"

"One of the reasons they're bringing people to quarantine camps is to protect them from frightened crowds. A private estate might be more vulnerable."

"Frightened people," she sighed. "Inside and out." She looked across the room at Samuel's bag as an idea took hold. "Do you think they'll let us bring our cameras?"

"Why?"

She took a breath and rubbed her nose. "Remember what you said before we interviewed Bill's crew? Something about little people deserve to have their stories told."

He smiled. "I'm sure I didn't call them 'little people'."

She poked him in the ribs. "You know what I mean. Ordinary people have their stories, too."

She looked out the window. "I'm never going to be a screen star, acting in comedies and dramas. I'll never be the stand-out world class personality I wanted to be. My only mark on history is the bits I helped report of Bill's spaceflight."

Her face was running in tears. "I think I want to tell the stories of the people around us, at the camp. Can we do that?"

He nodded. "That's a great idea. We'll make it happen."

Press the Button

Jason Bolls appeared on Samuel's display.

"Hello, Uncle."

He smiled, but he looked very tired. "Just checking on you. Finishing up with Bill's documentary?"

"As much as I can. I'm sure you've heard about the quarantines?"

"Unfortunately, yes. I've never seen the World Court move together like this. It's frightening."

Samuel nodded. "Um. Jason, I'd like you to meet my wife."

Jason raised his eyebrows as she moved into view. "Rachael Nue? Or is it Bolls? Either way, welcome to the family. I wish it could have been in happier times."

She nodded, with a determined look. "One way or another, we'll make it happy."

Samuel said nothing about the slight quiver in her voice.

Jason turned his head to his nephew. "I have something for you. A package of codes." The document appeared on his handset. "You might need them before too long."

Samuel looked looked puzzled, then, "Oh! Jenner's treatment. You've got it too. I'm sorry, I didn't think."

Jason tilted his head, "No use screaming about it. Half of my friends are going to the San Diego camp as well. Maybe some genius in some lab will make a breakthrough in time. But I've already got my spots."

He cleared his throat. "I've taken care of Bolls House. It will keep running, in case you want to come back. You can call here for anything you need—except legal advice. Ruel will be going with me to the camp."

Samuel was having trouble talking. "Uncle Jason. I'll be going with Rachael to the Big Springs hospital."

"You don't have it, do you?"

"No, but they think I do. It's okay. I planned it that way."

"Okay. Take care of yourself. I really enjoyed the work you did for Bill. I had hoped we could have worked together. A family thing, you know?"

"I know. Me too."

...

War intruded, just as they returned from the most elaborate meal that Samuel had ever eaten. The Black Gold Tower restaurant was grateful for Rachael's special order. More than half of their clientele had left town, and the rest weren't in the mood for a fancy meal.

As they returned to the room, Ben was standing guard by the door.

"Is there any trouble?" Samuel asked.

He nodded to them. "Due to the international news, I thought it would be wise to take extra precautions."

Rachael darted inside to check the feed. Samuel lingered.

"You do know we're leaving for Big Spring tomorrow morning?"

"Yes, sir. Ira and I would be honored to drive you. The train is reporting overcrowded conditions."

"Hmm. I guess that would be wise. Thank you."

"Sir, I'd like to say that we appreciate what you have done for Miss Rachael."

He smiled. "I sometimes wonder just how much you actually know."

Ben looked inside quickly. "We have been known to bug the place—but not the bedroom, sir."

Samuel shook his head in amazement.

"What will you be doing, once we're interned?"

"The plan is to go back east to defend Carolina House. However, we will be on call, if needed."

Rachael called from inside, "Samuel, come see this."

...

King Jess was gesturing toward a large static image of a merman being hauled out of the water.

"It has become increasingly clear that genetic manipulation has reached a point where it threatens not only world peace, but risks all life on the planet.

"The spots plague wasn't a freak of nature. It was a weapon of war with a simple design error. While it was unlikely that Australia designed the plague that wiped out their own blimps, it is a harsh fact of our world that anyone with enough Net Credits and the right request can have their own custom doomsday weapon created for them.

"We live in a world where bio-engineers can and will create stomach-turning monstrosities like this warrior merman. They can act without respect for ethics or morality, all behind the mask of Net anonymity. If there were a way to track down the offenders, I'd support it, but we must at the very least insure that nothing like the spots plague or these weapons of war can ever be created again.

"To that end, all nations of the world, save Australia, have agreed to strictly license all the tools of genetic manipulations, and to put a tight lock on it. The world's police authorities will use every available avenue to put a stop to this genetic disaster before even worse can happen."

Rachael tapped her controls and saw similar feeds coming from nearly every head of state.

"They're doing it. They're shutting down genetic technology." She sighed. "I just wish it had happened a *little* earlier."

...

"You're a little late." King Thomas talked to himself, as he watched the circus on multiple displays, looking for any difference in the positions of the major governments. Europa, East America, Greater Texas, California, Northern China, Quebec and South America had scripts, when accounting for language and the personalities of the leaders, that all seemed to come from the same hand.

"It's like the kids ordering their parents around. Without Australia, your licenses are null and void."

Eighty percent of new genetic development probably came from his domain, and ninety-five percent of the production of numals and custom crops.

This is a declaration of war. A public relations stunt to prepare the world for an invasion.

Which meant that the forces were already on their way—probably close at hand.

My coastal radar station hasn't reported anything, and Sydney is the obvious target.

He sat down in front of his terminal and called his research station, tethered under the surface just above the Taupo Tablemount nearly three hundred miles to the east. All that was detectable from a ship or a plane was a wide radio receiver just below the surface, and then only if you knew what you were looking for.

A bald-headed man with a particularly wide skull bowed. "Your Majesty, I am blessed by your call."

"Greetings Mano. I need to know what is happening on the surface. Are there ships? Could you ask Oomuoaho for me?"

The cetacean language specialist frowned. "She has been feeling unwell. There are strange spots that have appeared on her hide." His eyes frowned as he looked closely at his ruler. There was a little fear in his eyes, but his tongue was still.

Thomas scratched absently at his arm. "Yet, I still need to know what she can tell me."

Mano bowed and went to a special portal where he could dunk his head underwater and talk to the numal whale that lived in the area. King Thomas could hear nothing of the exchange—it was beyond the range of normal human hearing—but signal traces could be seen on special displays on the wall.

Shortly Mano reported what he had been told. The details of the ships, their sizes and speeds and their location and direction took a few moments to copy down.

Mano closed with "May health be with you." It was a bit unusual, but Thomas had what he needed.

Transcribed to a map plot, it showed three groups of ships, most mid-range cargo vessels probably, converging at a point just outside his radar range.

They want to appear overwhelming when they move on Sydney.

But he had their number. Another call reached the handler of a mermen squad stationed just offshore. When the ships moved in range, his warriors of the sea would be quietly waiting for them with a large cache of magnetic mines to attach to their hulls.

Thomas had learned his lesson in the Texas attack. His enemies were watching for the wakes of his fast-swimming mermen. But they could move slowly, if necessary.

I'll mine all the ships and when they approach the harbor, just when they think they have their victory in sight—it will be the last thing they see.

And he'd make sure all the world was watching. Everyone needed to know that his homeland was off-limits.

...

Captain Curtis called the admiral's number. Jenner replied, voice only. "What do you want?"

"The armada has been assembled. Would you care to review the ships or make an announcement?"

"No. Proceed to Sydney Harbor as planned."

The call went black.

Curtis signaled to the bridge crew. The command flashed to all the ships, and giant diesel turbines spun up to full speed.

The other vessels began reporting in, taking their positions in the formation. Curtis tapped his pen absently against his clipboard. He nodded to his XO and went to his quarters to report their status to Europa.

...

Emmanuel Busby's elderly face seemed drained as he hurried down the corridor of Graythwaite Castle. He looked up and came to an abrupt halt when Princess Catherine stepped out of her room directly in his path.

"You've seen Father?"

He nodded.

"How did he look?"

He clasped his hands together and kept his eyes downcast. "I... I think he's looked better."

"Speak up, man! Father has been locked in his study for days now. Now comes this order to prepare for a global announcement. He called for you to bathe and dress him. So you're the only one who has seen him. You know I have the right to inquire. So tell me."

Emmanuel shook his head. "He has the spots. They're all over him—but he doesn't seem to notice! The bathwater was dingy with the spores! And they say the disease is fatal! But, I couldn't say anything. He doesn't listen."

Catherine looked pale, but there was no time to indulge her own panic.

"Emmanuel Busby, for the sake of the Crown, I ask that you help me protect my father."

He gasped, but then nodded. Only then did he see two other men waiting in her room.

...

Captain Curtis brought up the Public Queue on his bridge terminal. King Thomas was due to make an announcement. The time was uncomfortably close to the moment when the armada would approach the North Head entrance to the bay. Their radar signals had been sweeping them regularly for some time now.

Could the Australians have gun emplacements there? It was logical, but spies had not reported any modern armaments. And gun technology takes time to develop. Their own deck guns were built fifty years before, right before the World Court was established and the idea of real shooting wars became remote.

None of the lookouts had seen the mermen's wake trails, but that was suspicious. This was the heart of Australian power. Surely they would be here, if anywhere?

He shook his head in thought. Jenner's command was to push all the way into the bay and begin shelling Graythwaite Castle with barely a warning.

Curtis felt in his bones that Jenner's bold attack wouldn't work. With the mermen almost certainly in the water, he felt that moving into such tight quarters left them vulnerable. That was tugboat water, not a place to turn and maneuver.

The display lit up with the Royal Seal of Australia. Curtis braced himself for the worst.

The image resolved to show a woman in a military-cut gown, crowned and seated on an ornate chair. She wasn't smiling. A banner at the bottom of the frame identified her as Princess Catherine.

"Greetings to the world, and especially to the invading force approaching Sydney Harbor. I have important news to report.

"My father, King Thomas of Australia, has fallen ill and is unable to perform the duties of his position. As heir, it has become my sad duty to take up the reins and to protect the domain as well as I am able."

She pulled up a small hand terminal and glanced at it. Her eyes then stared at the camera.

"To the armed fleet fast approaching Sydney. You are ordered to stop and hold your position. While I am reluctant to destroy you all in one instant, as was my father's plan, I am also resolved to prevent the massive death and destruction that would ensue should any of your soldiers be so ill-advised as to step on Australian soil without my permission.

"I have here in my hand the button that will detonate all the mines that have been previously attached to your ships. Come another mile closer, and I will choose to protect Australian lives at the expense of yours."

Curtis called out. "Signal the armada. All stop."

Their own engines began winding down.

There was a call on his handset. He held it to his ear as Jenner raved.

"Don't stop! Proceed immediately to Graythwaite Castle and shell it!"

Curtis blanked the call and yelled out. "Divers in the water to check for mines. Sharpshooters at the ready. Be alert for mermen."

He made another call to the ship's physician. "By advice of Berlin, I have been tasked with the duty to relieve Admiral Jenner of his post, should he show signs of erratic behavior. Please inspect the admiral for signs of spots, and notify me immediately. He may need to be confined."

...

Princess Catherine set down her hand terminal and nodded to the cameramen who had set up the patch into the castle feed so quickly.

The invaders have stopped, and we have an appointment to talk calmly. The bluff worked.

When the anesthetic gas had cleared enough to enable her to enter her father's study, the maze of displays and scribbled notes to himself had been a nightmare to try to understand. She shook her head to dismiss the memory of his screams of rage and frustration when the power had been cut to his control center, leaving him in the dark.

But when the power was restored, all were blank. What command channels he had established or what codes he used were his alone, stuck in his head. He had scribbled a timeline that he'd intended to use for his announcement, and it clearly stated that he would press the button and destroy them all, but that button had vanished when the power went out.

But her Father had a progressive case of the spots. The doctor gave him only a couple of days. She ordered that he be kept sedated. There was no time for goodbyes, and she had no stomach for his anger.

And she would be too busy. The spots epidemic had been kept from her ears when she was only a pampered pet of the house, but Australia had the highest incidence of augmentation of any people in the world, and altered crops were the rule. People were dying in the streets and famine was coming. She just might need the aid of those people on the invading ships.

Inside the Camp

Bolls and Nue Productions: *Inside the Camp*: **Episode 3.**
Big Spring Camp population: 897. Camps in Greater Texas: 33.

Rachael smiled to the camera. "Greetings to everyone, both inside camps and outside in the free world. In this episode, we want to interview a man who has made our entrance into this little society so much easier than it could have been."

Samuel moved around to sit beside her on the bed. "You said 'free world' there, and I know you were just joking, but from the inside, it certainly feels like it. This hospital is essentially a sprawling five-story complex that had been built pre-Star and most recently had been a care center for the elderly. They've packed four times as many beds in here as the place was designed to handle. There is little privacy. Still, it smells like a place that had been shut down for decades and then swept and splashed with antiseptic."

Rachael chuckled. "Hey, it's not so bad. I'm the one with spots, you're supposed to be cheering me up."

He looked at her fondly, "So you admit you have spots."

"Well... one or two. I'm still healthier than you are. I'm going to beat this."

He smiled. "Well, around here, one of the ways we have to keep our spirits up is to appreciate the wonderful people we have met here. Reverend Wilson, could you come join us?"

Samuel got up and repositioned the handset camera while the gray-haired man came and sat down facing Rachael.

"Reverend Wilson," she asked, "you were here our very first day, when we had to cross that line of shouting people with signs, saying all those hateful things. It was your smiling face and handshake that kept me from breaking down right there. When did you arrive?"

He chuckled, "Oh, I was here the first day. I live in Big Springs and knew that some of the people from my church were going to be here with me, and I had to be in place to make them feel welcome."

"Did anyone welcome you when you arrived?"

He shook his head. "Just the doctors, checking my symptoms and assigning a bed, like everyone else. Right then, I knew that people were going to need a friendly face more than anything else when they arrived."

Rachael gestured toward the window. "The hospital is in a wooded area with only two main entrances, and both of those have been blocked off with guards and gates. In spite of that, some people carrying signs made it into the area, letting us know they hate us, and that we are all doomed for our sins. What was the 'sin' that put you in here with us?"

"Don't mind them, they're just frightened. It's easy to make mistakes when you're afraid. But as for my genetic modification, it was a memory augmentation."

"Memorizing all those Bible verses?"

"Well, yes, but that wasn't what pushed me to spend the money. My church had seven hundred souls, and I needed help memorizing all their faces and names, and who their children were, and how they did at their baseball games. The augmentation made me a better helper and a closer friend. Even now, I can't regret it."

Samuel, who was not in the camera's view, said, "I guess your congregation is now close to nine hundred."

He shook his head. "Well now, I can't claim all of you, but I have a place to serve." He sighed, "Yesterday, I had to officiate at the cremations of nine."

Samuel added, "That's something we haven't mentioned in previous episodes. No one gets shipped home to be buried with family. It may make sense in this quarantine situation, but it *is* harsh."

The preacher said, "I wanted to compliment the two of you for signing up to be helpers. The staff is very overloaded. Without volunteers, many would be helpless here."

Rachael smiled, "Oh, we're young and active. I'm afraid the worst thing that could happen to me is to be bored."

She reached out and they shook hands. "Thank you so much for taking time to talk to our watchers."

Samuel said, "Next up. Ruth Lamar, owner of the local Lamar Bakeries."

...

King Jess gestured from his podium to the flyover image of huge gray-tinged fields, shown from miles high.

"As this capture shows, made by our local Texas spaceman, Bill Melear, huge expanses of our croplands have been burned gray by the spots. This year's crop has been destroyed by a disaster worse than the wildfires of '28. All seeds that were purchased from Australia and some of our local strains are now just a note in the history books. We will never see them again."

He tapped the podium. "We will be hungry this year. Corn, wheat, milo, and cattle—all have been devastated by the spots. Nor can we buy our way out, selling oil for food, because this isn't just a local crop failure—it's world wide. We put all our eggs in one basket, and they got spots."

He grinned his famous, wide Texas smile and said, "Now you farmers out there, you're our key to the future. I want every one of you to inventory your seeds, even that Mason jar of granddad's favorite blue-tip variety. As soon as the weather is right, we'll need you do bring all your experience and all your intuition to burn the gray and plant the good stuff. Resist any calls to eat the seed corn and insure our future!"

...

Bolls and Nue Productions: *Inside the Camp*: **Episode 7.**
Big Spring Camp population: 1053. Camps in Greater Texas: 33.
Samuel held Rachael's hand. "Before we start today's interviews, I'd like to comment on the conditions here in the camp. We have remarked that the doctors who made their brief rounds before, have now stopped coming. So it was notable when three men came around and talked with some of us.

"You know, there is always a rumor of some miracle cure that circulates around. Surely, it goes, if some scientist could invent the spots, then some other genius could invent a cure. I'm certainly praying for one.

"So when they came our way, my heart started hammering away. But it was much more mundane. They had run out of beds. Since we were a married couple, we were asked to double up."

Rachael giggled, "We didn't have the heart to tell them that we already had. But we had to move Samuel's bags over to my storage space, and it's rather crowded."

Samuel sighed, "We were told that it wouldn't be for long. The death rate is climbing. Soon, more will be leaving by way of the furnace room, but for now, previously un-diagnosed spots victims are still arriving. It seems that genetic alteration had crept into many more medical treatments than anyone knew. Quite a few peoples found themselves classed as 'genies' when they had no idea that they had been altered."

Rachael beckoned off screen, while Samuel went to adjust the camera. "For our first interview, Hank Weber has graciously offered to be on our show. He was one of the people outside the camp, angry at those who had altered themselves. He has come to confess a change of heart."

Hank came to sit in the camera's view, but he had trouble meeting Rachael's eyes.

"Sorry." He cleared his throat. "I realize I was wrong."

...

Admiral Dale sprinted over to the terminal. "Dale here," he answered the call.

"Admiral, they came for me."

"What? Dr. Tuck, explain. Who came for you?"

The doctor looked severely shaken. He was talking on a handset while moving, and the background was nothing but blurs.

"It was a mob. Someone remembered that there was a lab in the Fleet Head Quarters building. Once the queen announced that Australia would abide by the World Court ruling on licensing all genetic research, it seemed like a wave of madness swept the place. Even people who had done genetic work themselves grabbed pitchforks and torches and joined the mobs."

"Doctor, calm down. Pitchforks?"

He was in no mood to calm down. "Admiral, they broke into my lab with sledgehammers! They smashed all my samples, shattered all my equipment. Look, look!" He held his bloody left hand in front of the camera. "They broke my hand with a sledgehammer.

"But that's not the worst of it. Admiral, I was on the verge of a breakthrough."

"The spots disease?"

"Yes, the spots! I had a template for a blocker. It was a non-viable organelle that could be turned loose in the bloodstream. There was a perfect copy of the DNA that attracts the spores. Any spore that found the organelle first would latch onto it but wouldn't be able to generate any more spores. Flood a victim's blood with a dose of these and the pace of the disease would slow down. I hadn't reached a testing phase, so I don't know if it would just slow it down or reach a cleansing state. Any augmented person would have to take some kind of maintenance dose for as long as there are spores in the air, but at least there would be hope."

"There *was* hope, I mean. All my data has been lost."

"The design is still in your head. I'll forward this to the central clearinghouse in Berlin. Doctor?" Dale paused. "Tuck, where are you?"

"I'm out in the street, running for my life!" he yelled angrily. "I'm breathing the spores and I can almost feel them boring through my cells as we speak. They took a sledgehammer to all my samples, too. I must have breathed a massive dose before I got out of there."

"Find a safe place. I'll get fleet personnel to pick you up, and I'll have a plane waiting for you. Berlin has designated the University Hospital of Geneva as the only authorized genetics research facility for the present time. They have a full compliment of analysis and assembler gear. You need to be there. With luck, you'll get to experience your organelles yourself."

...

Bolls and Nue Productions: *Inside the Camp*: **Episode 11.**
Big Spring Camp population: 603. Camps in Greater Texas: 31.

"I'm sorry," Rachael sniffed. "I just got word that my father, Lawrence Nue of Nue Electronics, has died from spots." She tried to smile. "It just goes to show that the best medical care money can buy is not enough."

Samuel took her hand. He said, "Those of you who have been watching our interview show might have suspected that I've been trying to hide a little anger." He forced a smile for a half-second. "Today is a little harder than most to keep from screaming. Rachael might not have been able to receive the news about her father, because this morning, right before dawn, a crew of five armed men in gas masks came through the camp and confiscated every handset they could find.

"I know they were trying to silence our show, because they spent more than thirty minutes ripping our bags, our clothes, and even our mattress apart, looking for handsets. They found three.

"Let me show you how they left our area."

He scanned the little dorm-like area with five beds placed in a room that was probably designed for one. Fabric and boxes were scattered all over the place. The mattress, as he said, was ripped open and wads of stuffing strewn about.

He moved the camera close to his face. "We're still in the Queue. We *will* still be in the Queue. Because I knew this day would come. Someone's feelings were hurt by this reporting and decided to stop it.

"Yes, I had a spare handset. I have several. And no, it won't do any good to come looking for them. I have been here so long it seems like forever, and like a good little volunteer worker, I have had access to every room, every storage chute, every piece of equipment here. A bomb could flatten this place, and I'd still have a handset to capture another episode.

"This one will be slightly longer than normal, because the confiscated handsets have cut off communication between the dying here and their families back home. Since we have been here, about five hundred people have died, including some very good friends, like Reverend Wilson, whom we highlighted on a previous show. Since the only way we can be sure that their families are properly notified of their deaths is to tell you, we will begin a new feature where we list the names of those who have died. We will list one hundred a day until we catch up."

He aimed the camera back at Rachael, who put on a brave smile. "I'll now turn the show back to my wife, who is a lot stronger and wiser than I am about all this."

She gave him a nod, coughed, and then said, "One more thing. Some of you may have tried to contact us and hit our privacy filters. We're not trying to be rude, we just didn't want to deal with someone ordering us to stop doing the *Inside the Camp* show."

Samuel grumbled, "If someone wants us to stop, he'll have to walk into this place and tell us that himself."

Rachael smiled. "And now our first interview today is Mary Gibbs, of Odessa. Mary, what got you into this situation?"

She was very wide-eyed and a little timid at being in front of the camera. "Oh, well it was a little thing. I had liver cancer. They came up with a new cure and it worked." She gave a little laugh. "Who knew that the cure was worse than the disease?"

...

Late that night, huddled together under a blanket, Samuel worked by flashlight, applying lotion to the sores on her back.

"You know," he said, "we don't need this tent. We've got the room to ourselves now. A few goons with guns convinced Jake and Nancy to relocate to another room."

She relaxed with her head on her crossed arms. "I like it like this. There's still no privacy here, other than what we make for ourselves. And since I can't see the depressing beds all next to each other, I can pretend we're all by ourselves, on a romantic beach, in a *cough* camping tent."

He sighed, "That would be nice. We could still do it, you know. Ben and Ira sent their new codes. Give them twenty-four hours, and they can land a helicopter on the roof and have us out of here and in the wind."

"Hmm." She purred. "That sounds nice. But I still have interviews to do."

"On the job until it kills you?"

She swung back with an elbow and lightly connected. "You're no different."

"Two of a kind." He rubbed in places where there were no sores.

"When are you going to begin the real therapy for tonight? As you said, we have the room to ourselves."

He hesitated. "I don't know. I'm really angry right now. Angry with the world. I don't know if I should."

She twisted and squirmed until they were face to face. The flashlight gave their expressions sharp shadows. "You can't hurt me. You couldn't even imagine how. And you'll need to do something, or you'll explode. So let's get started."

A few minutes later, sounds echoing down the corridor lent a few smiles to people who desperately needed them.

Confessions

Caleb heard the cry of a gull and scanned the horizon. He could see nothing, although he had imagined land so many times that he had lost confidence in his own eyes.

Day followed day, and only the length of his whiskers seemed to change.

Still, the cry had seemed to come from the north, so it was as good a reason as any to adjust his course.

His sailboat was a joke, of course. A raft turned into a catamaran with a sail made of boards. He'd made some fixed rudders that at least kept the boat pointed downwind, pushed by the trades. His net trailed behind him, and every so often, a particularly clumsy fish would snag itself and provide something to gnaw on. He had about decided that eating the scales just wasn't worth it, although with enough chewing, he downed almost everything else. He was glad there was no way to weigh himself. From the size of his arms and legs, he was dwindling fast.

Rains came often enough to keep his food crate sloshing with drinkable water. He monitored how hydrated he was by how bright his urine was.

He tugged on the starboard sail and tilted the angle that the it spilled wind. *There, a little bit more northward.*

Nothing else to do for the day, he huddled down under the shelter, eyes closed, smelling the scent his long-departed captain on the old seat cushions.

...

Bolls and Nue Productions: *Inside the Camp*: **Episode 13.**
Big Spring Camp population: 298. Camps in Greater Texas: 18.

"We're on the downhill run," Rachael reported with as good spirits as she could manage, but she couldn't manage a smile. "I'm making this episode all by myself because Samuel is on double duty, carting bodies down to the incinerator."

She frowned. "This is where my husband would state, as calmly as he could manage, just how far downhill we have come. So I guess that's my job."

She thought a second and then faced directly into the camera. "People with spots die in about two weeks after the first appearance on the skin. I'm about twelve days in, but I have a very robust immune system that makes me a special case.

"The camps have been set up for about that long as well, so all the people who were infected early have died. In a calm and humane world, there would have been doctors here the whole time, giving palliative care and boosting our spirits. That was never the case. What doctors were here, were just to confirm our symptoms on the first day. For a week after that, there were two doctors down in the morgue, checking on how people died. Then there were none.

"When the late-blooming cases stopped coming, the doctors all left. The doors are locked and guards walk the grounds outside. I've watched them. They don't look our direction. Maybe it's because they care more about the demonstrators. But maybe because they don't want to look at us anymore."

She held out her arms, showing the spots. "These were washed just thirty minutes ago, but they darken progressively. During our first few episodes, I used what little makeup I had to hide the spots on my face. I am vain, I admit it. They hurt, and the pain grows a little worse every day."

Rachael paused. "Let me interview myself, if you don't mind.

"My name is Rachael Nue, and I was a very rich little girl. As most little girls go, I was reasonably pretty, and I had the idea that I wanted everyone to love me. As I progressed through school, I came to the realization that either I would have to be very nice to everyone, or else I would have to become famous, a screen personality. Being kind was too hard, so with Daddy's money, and his blessing, I went off to Australia to have some work done.

"Being a screen personality takes more than just good looks—I knew that. For everyone with beauty and talent, there are dozens, maybe hundreds that look just as good, and have just as much talent. I knew I had to hit San Diego like a bombshell. I got the full Beautiful People package.

"In case you haven't heard of it, the BP augmentation makes you beautiful in every way it can. Hair, eyes, skin, nails, posture, the sound of your voice, even the scent you give off.

"If anyone committed a sin by being augmented, it was me. I was taking every advantage, committing every cheat to gain the edge I would need to become someone people would see in a screen and immediately love.

"I had just finished my augmentations and took passage on the Queen Helen for San Diego. There, I would meet anyone and everyone who could give me an entrance into the screencrafting world.

"Then luck took all my plans and scrambled them. I met a new screencrafter, skilled but unknown, hardly worth my time—but he had a famous uncle, so I pursued him. I wasn't after a lover, just a connection, a tool to reach more important people.

"And then, he talked to me. He was trying to edge his way into the screencrafting industry, just like me. We could really talk about things that mattered to the both of us. It was so refreshing. I think I developed a little crush on him.

"When I suddenly had to leave San Diego because of the rising tide of anti-genie sentiment, he was on the same train, and he began teaching me skills that I could really use. I was grateful, and also hungry for the kind of things I could learn, if he would teach me more."

She shrugged. "His project was Bill Melear's spaceflight, although neither of us knew the importance of it at the time. I cheated and connived and forced him to use me as his assistant. He put up with it, and things clicked. We were of like minds and our skills meshed, and although he kept me at arms length, we were happy together."

She took a deep breath, "So, you would ask me, 'Rachael, how come you are here together, married, in this house of death, waiting for time to run out?'"

Her voice dropped to a whisper. "Because he was kind to me. He did the thing that had always been too hard for me. He dropped his whole life to take care of me while I was dying. And you know, I don't care about the whole world loving me anymore. His love is enough, and worth all the pain."

...

A genius with a trained staff and top-rate equipment can work faster than a genius alone. And Dr. Tuck would have been in heaven if that genius had been him. But he didn't speak German, and the Geneva doctors' English was only rudimentary. The face mask he had to wear only made communications that much worse.

All over the world, tainted crops were being burned in a crude attempt to reduce the spore concentration in the atmosphere. On a case by case basis, burning acres of wheat and corn did more that any other remediation. But it wasn't that clean and simple. Dead herds of cattle had to be bulldozed into pits and treated with lye. Even the genie camps were being considered for quick and flammable cleansing, once their patients all stopped moving, of course.

Such measures were being demanded by the general population, once ordinary people started suffering from the effects of the spores. They didn't get spots, but breathing spores made people cough and brought back the specter of lung cancer. Skin contact caused a rash. And everyone heard the tale that the spots disease was just a simple design error in the spores. What other effects might have gone undiscovered?

The rare infected individual like Dr. Tuck, who had not been sent to a camp was a walking dead man, avoided as a plague vector. They needed him in the meetings. He'd been down this path before and knew the pitfalls, but it was not his work. He feared he wouldn't even be considered a possible lab rat.

...

Bolls and Nue Productions: *Inside the Camp*: **Episode 15.**
Big Spring Camp population: 15. Camps in Greater Texas: 5.
"Samuel! Your gloves."

He hovered over the bed, the final resting place of John Dover. "We ran out yesterday. And they didn't do much good anyway. The spores were designed to cut through blimp skin, and latex only holds them back a little."

"Well wrap your hands in something. You can't afford too much exposure or you'll be crippled. You'll not be able to help any of them if your hands are all bloody."

Frustrated, he followed her orders, stripping a pillowcase and bundling it around his hand. She held the camera as she sat in the wheel chair.

"Unfortunately," she spoke to the watchers, "no one is strong enough to be interviewed today. I, myself, can't walk long enough to make these rounds with Samuel, but we decided to do what we could."

Samuel was slipping one of the body bags around Mr. Dover. "Here's something." He pulled a folded letter from the body's hands and gave it to Rachael.

She brought it in front of the camera.

"It's a letter, addressed in unsteady hands. I think it says, 'To Barbara' but I'm not sure.

"Samuel, what do we do with it? I... I'm not sure I should read it on a public show. It may be private."

He paused from his work, fastening the seal on the bag. He looked exhausted. "Pause the feed. Our viewers will understand. Take a static image of the letter and if we get a message from Barbara, then we'll send it to her. But we'll leave the letter by his bedside."

"Oh. Please bear with us. We'll return in a moment."

...

Bolls and Nue Productions: *Inside the Camp*: **Episode 16.**
Big Spring Camp population: 14. Camps in Greater Texas: 5.

Rachael looked tired, but she smiled from the wheelchair. "This is a continuation of episode 15, the same day, so if you are viewing an archive, don't be confused."

She aimed the camera at Samuel. "Today we interview Samuel Bolls."

A coughing fit made her pause, and his concerned image bounced around for a moment.

"Sorry about that. Samuel, let's make things clear for the watchers. Do you have spots?"

He shook his head. "No. I was never genetically augmented."

"So why are you here?"

"I suspected that they would be reluctant to allow anyone into the camp who was not afflicted. The size of the plague was going to put stress on the ability of the government to care for the people in the camps. So I was sure they wouldn't just allow family members in because they wanted to.

"So, I lied."

He explained his bluff, and Rachael coaxed an admission that he did it for her. "I didn't want you to go through this alone."

She cleared her throat and said softly, "You said you'd cooperate with anything I asked in this interview."

He looked at her suspiciously. "What is it this time?"

"Hold out your hands. I want our viewers to see them."

"Are you sure? I mean..."

"Do it."

He sighed and spread his hands out before the camera. She zoomed in close, showing the open wounds and the seeping blood. All of his skin looked like it had been scraped raw and only partially scabbed over.

"Doesn't it hurt?"

He dabbed at the sores with a sheet. "Yes, but I have to keep going."

"What are you doing?"

"I'm preparing the dead. I'm putting them in their body bags and filling out the names and times of death. Up until yesterday, when the crematorium's gas stopped flowing, I was moving them down to the morgue area. Now, I'm just leaving them in their beds."

Rachael was breathing hard, but she pulled herself back together. "Why is this important?"

He paused. "It just is. If we are just animals to be disposed of, they might just burn the place down. People dispose of their kind with dignity. If I had thought to learn the words from Reverend Wilson, I would say them, but I was too caught up in my own life to think of that. I'm just doing what I can."

Rachael swallowed. "Thank you, Samuel, for all of us."

She turned the camera back to her face. "I suppose that's all for this episode."

"No, Rachael, it's not."

"What?"

"I made you come along on the rounds today because there's something you should see."

"Oh?"

He stood up and wheeled her over to the corridor and stopped before a window. He held her arm as she stood.

Out across the yard, where a fence had been set up to keep people out, a large white banner was spread across a ten-foot span.

In large black lettering, it said, "WE LOVE YOU RACHAEL."

"Oh my."

Samuel took the camera from her limp hands and scanned the view and panned over to see her face, streaming with tears.

Outlive Them All

Caleb could see something. The birds had been appearing in ever greater numbers, and he steered the best he could to follow them.

It might not be enough. There was definitely something off the starboard bow, and no matter how much he changed the sails, he could never steer directly toward it. *I might sail on past.*

But it could be his imagination, or maybe just a mid-ocean nesting ground for birds. Or maybe a school of fish that had attracted scavengers.

If there were just a decent mountain he could see. But this wasn't anything tall. If it was land, then it was all low, nearly at sea level. If there were trees, then it was still too far away to make them out.

I could stay on the raft, or else swim for it.

But if he swam, then that was it. The raft would sail on without him. He'd given no thought on how to anchor it.

But the Pacific Ocean was empty in these parts. He'd sailed over it for days without seeing land of any kind. On a blimp, with his friends, it had been one thing. Alone on the ocean, it was quite another.

If I wait too long, I'll have to swim against the current and the wind.

But he still wasn't positive it was real.

He watched it for another ten minutes. *Awful real looking for an illusion.*

The clutter on the raft all called to him—the water collector, the spool of twine, the shelter. He needed them all to stay alive, but he couldn't swim with all that stuff.

Feeling his window of opportunity shrinking by the second, he snatched up the twine and wrapped cord around his waist a dozen times, cut it with the knife and used a couple more feet to secure the knife into the makeshift belt. He snatched up the seat cushions and jumped into the water.

...

The two huddled under their blanket, not for privacy any longer, because by Samuel's last check, no one else was left in the camp. Beneath their tent was their private island.

Rachael's voice was giving out. She coughed, then whispered, "If this hadn't happened, and a child had come into my life, she wouldn't have had my enhancements."

"Oh, I thought they were built into your genes."

"It is, but for an extra charge, my ovum were protected from the change."

"It costs extra? Why?"

"Because selfish parents, like I would have been, didn't like the idea of their kids having that much power."

He carefully nestled closer, conscious that touching her now was painful. "I think you would have been a good mother. You've grown wiser every day. A child would have brought out the best in you."

She coughed, and he was careful to move back another inch.

"Samuel," she asked after a moment, "When you marry again, could you name a daughter after me?"

...

Dr. Tuck looked out through his hazard suit. No one would get close enough to face him otherwise.

Dr. Hoffman shook his head, "No. We cannot produce the blocking agent in enough quantity to run the tests, and we cannot wait."

"You know that you are condemning me to death."

The older man nodded. "And if I had a choice, I would act differently. There is only enough for one person, and it can't be you. We will bring another assembler on line as quickly as possible, but nearly all of the necessary equipment in the world has been destroyed. The mobs have been most ruthless."

Tuck sighed. "Yes, I know."

"Your only hope, and for my sake I hope you never repeat this, is if Prince Karl dies quickly."

...

Caleb stood atop the lone rock on the island, a single outcropping that rose just a couple of dozen feet above the atoll. It had taken him a while to recover from the swim, and even longer to climb the puny excuse for a mountain.

But from this high point, he could see the whole island. It was mostly barren, maybe a couple of miles across. The center lagoon was drinkable, barely, probably collected rainwater, but contaminated with a trace of salt and guano from all the birds nesting here. There were a few palms, and he prayed for coconuts.

Off on the shoals, he could see the skeleton of a long-decayed sailing ship.

Likewise, resting in the shallows of the lagoon were the bones of a blimp. The skin had all rotted away, but there were plainly the engines and to the side was what was probably the command deck.

But in spite of watching for nearly two hours as he rested, there was no motion on the island other than the shifting flocks of birds.

If the blimp came down here, where is the crew?

...

Bolls and Nue Productions: *Inside the Camp*: **Episode 19.**
Big Spring Camp population: 2. Camps in Greater Texas: 1.

Samuel spoke softly, looking off to the side of the frame. "I've got the air in here so saturated with steam that our viewers couldn't see anything anyway."

Rachael's voice was barely a croak, "I don't want anyone to see me naked."

"They won't. I have the camera pointed at me. But you need to be soaking. Your skin is cracking. And you did want this one last episode, didn't you?"

She paused, and then she muttered, "Yes."

"Well then, we'll begin," he said. "Thank you, all the watchers whom we've never seen. This show has been a way to keep our spirits up, and you've helped."

She coughed, and his frown deepened. Barely, understandable, she whispered, "I love you all. You made... Samuel? Did you cut the lights?"

"No, you just closed your eyes. Are you okay?"

"Fine. Outlive 'em all."

"Rachael?"

He moved out of the frame to check on her. There was a splash, and the camera plopped into the tub. There was a swirl of gray water, and then the signal stopped.

...

"I'm going to get in so much trouble for this!" Oscar whispered into his handset, his voice muffled by the dust mask he had strapped over his face. There was barely any light to see what was going on.

"Shut up," said Jed, "they've shut off the power to the camp, but there are still guards walking the grounds. I don't want to be arrested for this."

"Then why did you come?"

"My wife made me. She's a basket case ever since Rachael died."

"Are you sure she's dead?"

"It's been three days since the show stopped. Quiet, here's the fence."

Oscar captured the snips of the wire-cutters by the light of the moon. They squeezed through, and hurriedly made their way to a ground floor window, partially hidden by a bush. Jed pulled out a glass cutter and cut a hole large enough to reach the latch inside.

"This place smells."

"Then don't breathe. A thousand people just died here and the body bags are packed up somewhere near, there's no help for it."

"Do you have the map?"

A small flashlight showed the paper, drawn out by Jed's wife Linda. She had watched every episode and traced out those scenes where Samuel walked his rounds.

"There's a stairwell down this way. The elevators will be out."

"Are you sure the spores won't get us?"

"Keep your gloves on and try not to touch anything."

They worked their way up to the third floor, and reached the room where Samuel and Rachael had lived. They had several target rooms marked on the map, places where Linda thought they might find him.

She had been right the first time.

Samuel sat quietly beside Rachael's tightly-wrapped body, draped out on their bed. He had been sitting silently in the dark. His shiny eyes blinked as if the little flashlight had been a thousand times as bright. He put up a hand to block it, and it was wrapped in a bundle of white, just like the other one.

His voice croaked, but then got stronger. "Who are you?"

"We're here to get you out."

"Why?"

Jed said, "They've burned several of the camps already. Nobody was sure whether you were still alive or not. Thousands of people have petitioned the Crown to stop the order to burn this one—people who watched your show. But the smart money is on the burn order. We had to save you."

"I'm... I'm not sure. Maybe I should stay." He looked back at his wife's shape on the bed.

Jed's voice was patient and low. He said, "We've watched all the episodes. What would Rachael tell you to do?"

Oscar nodded. "And if we can get you out, people will listen to you. You may be the only one who can stop them burning this place."

Samuel reached over with his wrapped hand and stroked her head. "Okay."

Epilog

Although September had come and it was still quite warm, Samuel could feel winter's approach in his bones. Living and breathing in the spores had left permanent scars, both on the surface and inside as well. He chilled easily.

The Bremer had taken the drive well, and it had been like a cruise on the ocean, traveling the mostly-deserted highway. Taking the train to Midland would have been unbearable.

The intercom lit. Samuel pressed the button with a gray kid-gloved finger. "Yes, Mr. Tate?"

The chauffeur had looked disturbed when he had first mentioned the drive all the way from San Diego, but he had loosened up over the miles.

"We are approaching the airfield."

Bill Melear had offered to fly him out, and maybe someday he'd take him up on it, but the opportunity to go where he wanted, at whatever pace seemed appropriate, was just what he needed after weeks in the hospital and a hectic speaking schedule.

Out the window, the hangars and landscape were all the same, including that black skyscraper on the horizon. But there were more people working here than before, and they all seemed to be walking about in a hurry. Mr. Tate pulled into a parking spot.

Bill was there to greet him. Samuel took his hand, but he had no strength to match the airman's grip. Bill was dressed just as casually as he had before he became a spaceman. Samuel felt overdressed, but after all the speaking engagements, the suit was comfortable now.

"I'm glad you could come. I have so much to share with you. Come on, I want you to meet someone."

They went inside. A vigorous-looking middle-aged man in a light gray suit stood up as they entered Bill's office.

"Fleet Admiral Dale, I'd like you to meet Samuel Bolls."

Samuel shook the man's hand. "I've heard of you. You ran the blimp fleet, and helped fight the spots."

Dale nodded. "I just wish we had been able to find a cure in time."

Samuel could only nod.

Bill gestured, "Have a seat, both of you." He eyed the two of them with a calculating eye.

"Samuel, Admiral Dale has become a working partner. Most of those people out there are his blimp fleet people."

Dale interrupted, "Just 'fleet', now. When King Thomas's War collapsed, I was left with a large, dedicated workforce, and no task big enough for them. Rescuing our own took some time, but that's mostly done. Many have moved on to find new jobs, but there is a loyal core that still have the intelligence and skills to take on a new endeavor."

Bill nodded, "And I had just started a new technology, with great potential, and only a handful of men—not enough to see it through. We were the perfect match." He eyed Dale with a grin, "Besides, the admiral here needs vessels for his fleet." Samuel had noticed several planes in various stages of construction.

Dale looked out the door at the busy workers. "This is the place for us. It's a dream not too different from where my people started. They are fliers at heart, with the organizational skills to make something great for mankind."

"And my dream has been moving out into space. You know that," said Bill.

Dale asked, "Mr. Bolls, we would like you to join us."

Samuel had been leaning forward, gloved hands clasped together, listening to their grand plans.

"Why me? My money?"

Dale shook his head, "No. It's more than that."

Bill chuckled, "You weren't stupid before, and I see you're still sharp. Yes, we need money, but we could advertise around and scare up the funding we need in no time at all. We'd form our little enterprise and soon, we'd be one big money-grubbing company."

Dale agreed. "We need you, 'the conscience of the world' they call you. We want to be a great force for good, for all of humanity."

Samuel shook his head. "That was my wife. The interviews were her idea."

Dale said quietly, "And I'm glad she did it—the both of you. You put the face of humanity on the 'genies' that had all been herded into camps to die. Everyone could see themselves in the people you introduced. Their motives were our motives. One little change in my life and I would have been in there with you during the Die-off.

"And you put it all together. Your wife could see it in you. You have the heart to build our dream."

Samuel frowned. "What is it exactly that you hope to accomplish?"

Bill leaned back in his chair and stared up at the ceiling. "Back when North America was being explored by the Europeans in the 1700s, a company was established to go explore and trade in the northern reaches, far in advance of normal colonization. This Hudson's Bay Company administered a huge expanse of land and was the *de facto* government of the area. It made huge fortunes and built its own legends.

"I think we're going to need something like that as we move into space. These royal courts won't be able to administer all of space as a bunch of little colonies. There'll be orbits to assign, asteroids to mine, and even patches of the Moon and Mars to control. We can't even imagine what it will be like. But there will need to be someone in place that everyone can look to when problems happen."

The admiral added, "I took a leap of faith, back when the blimps crashed, and declared the fleet an international organization. Amazingly, the World Court is letting me get away with it. Bill's space planes will be shuttling people and moving cargo from one nation to the next, and this new fleet needs to be even-handed.

"King Jess would love to claim it all for Texas, and that would set up the same kind of situation that knocked King Thomas off his rails.

"But if you were the third prop on our structure, then with your Polynesian history, and your vast fortunes in California and Carolina, added to Bill's Texas and my Australia, widens our international standing."

Samuel smiled. "You have quite a dream here."

Bill nodded. "Samuel. You had a lot of fire when you came here to help me the first time. What is your dream now?"

Samuel chuckled sadly. He held up his gloved hands. "These are some of the most expensive gloves available, and I need them." He wiggled his fingers. "These are useless. All I've got are masses of scar tissue where I used to have skilled hands. I can't work a camera. I can't use an edit station. I *need* a driver, because I can't handle a car myself.

"I'll never be a reporter again. I'll never be the kind of hands-on screencrafter that I dreamed of being. The best I can do is advise other, more capable people.

"And as far as my wealth, it's still far away. Most of the major fortunes in this world are changing hands, clogging up the probate courts with disputed wills and royal endowments. Uncle Jason put me in administrative charge of his fortune before he died, but it's not really mine yet. The Nue fortune is even farther away, and the Rhinebergs may dispute it."

Dale nodded. "As we said before, we need you for your conscience, not just—"

He looked startled and reached into his pocket. He scooted over to one of Bill's terminals and tapped some codes. "Sorry, but I *have* to take this. It's a stranded fleet code."

A voice-only call came over the terminal's speaker.

"Hello? Is anyone there?"

"This is Admiral Dale. It's wonderful to hear from you. Who are you, and where are you calling from?"

"Um. I'm Caleb Race, of the *Lance*. I don't know how long this call will last."

"Give me your location, so we can come get you."

"It's an atoll in the Pacific, there's markings in French on a stone, but I don't know the location."

"I know the *Lance*. You went down close to Salvador, right?"

"Yes, and I drifted west for ages on a raft I built from our cargo deck."

"Probably Clipperton Island. Is there the remains of a blimp there? We rescued the crew of the *Green Gene* from that atoll."

"Yes! I salvaged its Net relay but there was no electricity. I moved a generator from an old weather station wind vane to power it. I managed to get it into diagnostic mode, but there was no signal—except two days ago,

Net connection appeared from nowhere long enough for me to check my account and found your message waiting for me, sir. But the signal faded. It was only there less than five minutes and I'm afraid this one will fade too."

"A float plane will be headed your way within twelve hours. Hang on! The fleet is still alive and we need good men like you."

Barely had the words gotten out, when the call dropped.

Bill and Samuel listened to the whole exchange as the admiral made calls to an air station in Mexico and set the rescue operation in motion.

He looked up. "Thanks Bill, for the satellite relays. They saved the day this time."

Samuel tilted his head in thought. "I'd like to meet this man and get the whole story." His heart pounded, and for a brief instant, he thought he detected her scent. He marveled at his old instincts showing their presence after so long. He'd thought they were dead. *What would she want me to do?* It didn't take much to imagine.

"Bill, Admiral Dale, I think I *will* join you."

The End

The Story Isn't Over
Follow both branches of this Saga

On Earth

Or Off

More Soon

More Soon

Small Towns, Big Ideas

A collection of science fiction tales where highschool-aged adventurers take that extra step into the unknown

www.ingramcontent.com/pod-product-compliance
Lightning Source LLC
Chambersburg PA
CBHW072053020726
47501CB00003B/569